SQUAD

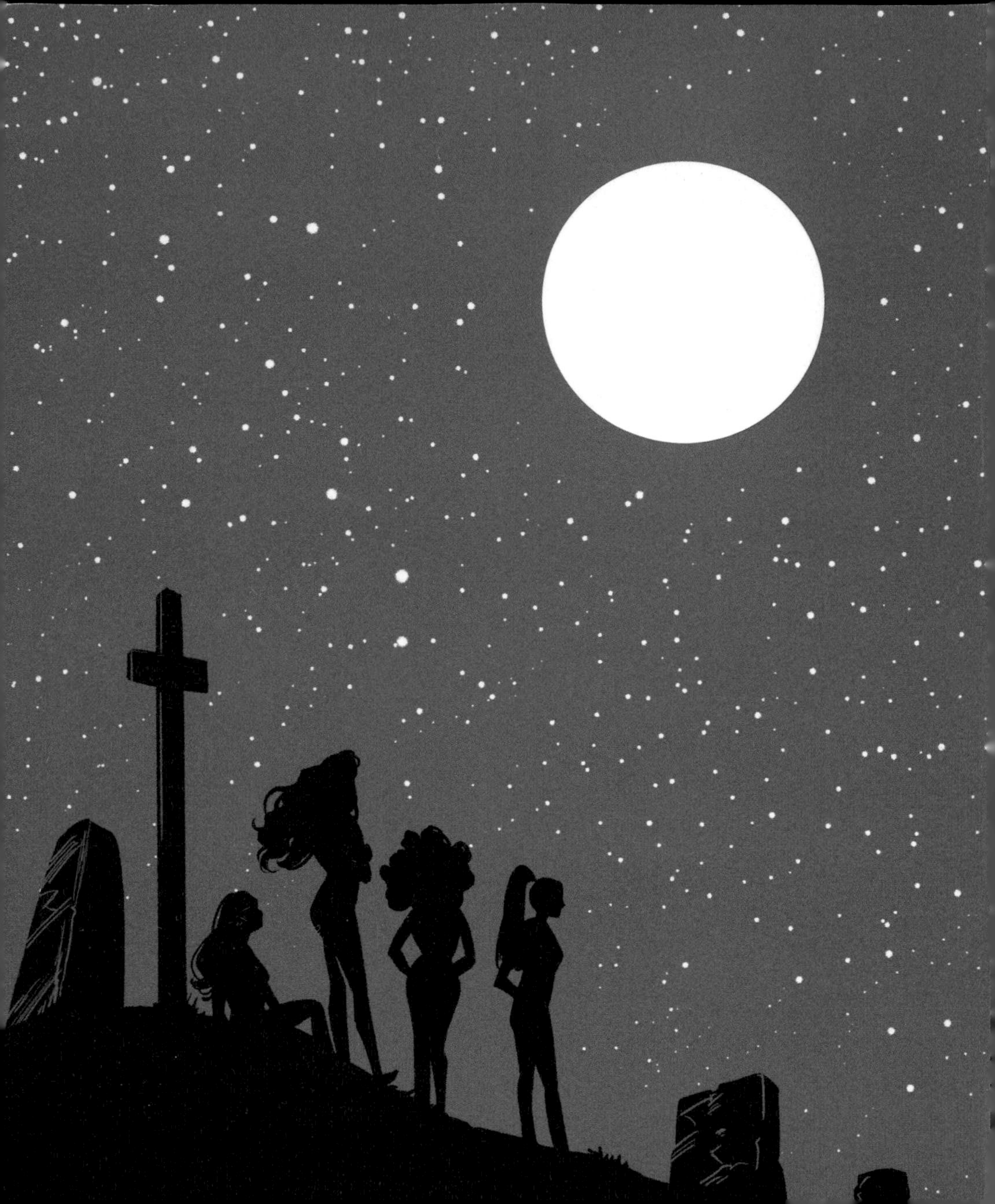

MAGGIE TOKUDA-HALL
LISA STERLE

SQUAD

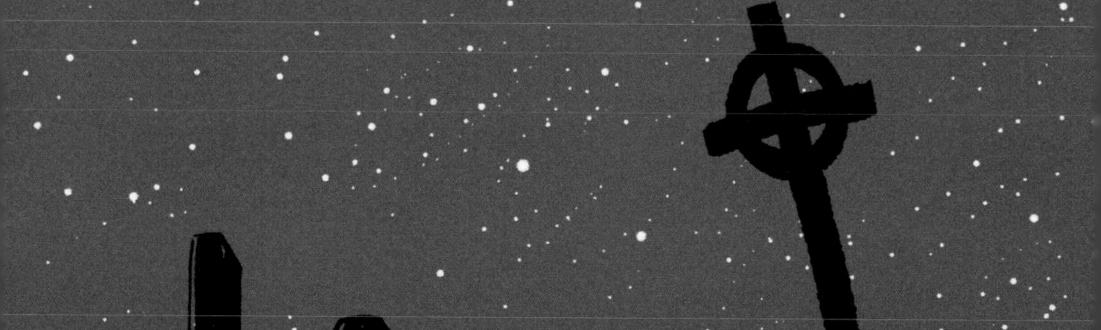

Greenwillow Books
Imprints of HarperCollinsPublishers
HARPER alley

Printed in Spain. For information address HarperCollins Children's Books, a division of HarperCollins Publishers, 195 Broadway, New York, NY 10007.
www.harperalley.com

Library of Congress Cataloging-in-Publication Data

Names: Tokuda-Hall, Maggie, author. | Sterle, Lisa, illustrator.
Title: Squad / by Maggie Tokuda-Hall ; illustrated by Lisa Sterle.
Description: First edition. | New York, NY : Greenwillow Books, an imprint of HarperCollins Publishers, [2021] | Audience: Ages 14 up. | Audience: Grades 10-12. |
Summary: "Becca moves to an upscale Silicon Valley suburb and is surprised when she develops a bond with girls who belong to the popular clique—and even more surprised when she learns their secrets"— Provided by publisher.
Identifiers: LCCN 2021015865 | ISBN 9780062943149 (paperback) | ISBN 9780062943156 (hardcover) | ISBN 9780062943163 (ebook)
Subjects: LCSH: Graphic novels. | CYAC: Graphic novels. | Werewolves—Fiction. | Shapeshifting—Fiction. | Popularity—Fiction. | High schools—Fiction. | Schools—Fiction. | Lesbians—Fiction. | Racially mixed people—Fiction.
Classification: LCC PZ7.7.T637 Sq 2021 | DDC 741.5/973—dc23
LC record available at https://lccn.loc.gov/2021015865

21 22 23 24 25 EP 10 9 8 7 6 5 4 3 2 1
First Edition

Greenwillow Books
Imprints of HarperCollins*Publishers*
HARPER alley

To BH: I remember
To BL: I'll never forget
—M. T. H.

To my mom, who has been my unwavering support
and biggest fan for as long as I can remember
—L. S.

CHAPTER ONE

WELCOME TO PIEDMONT

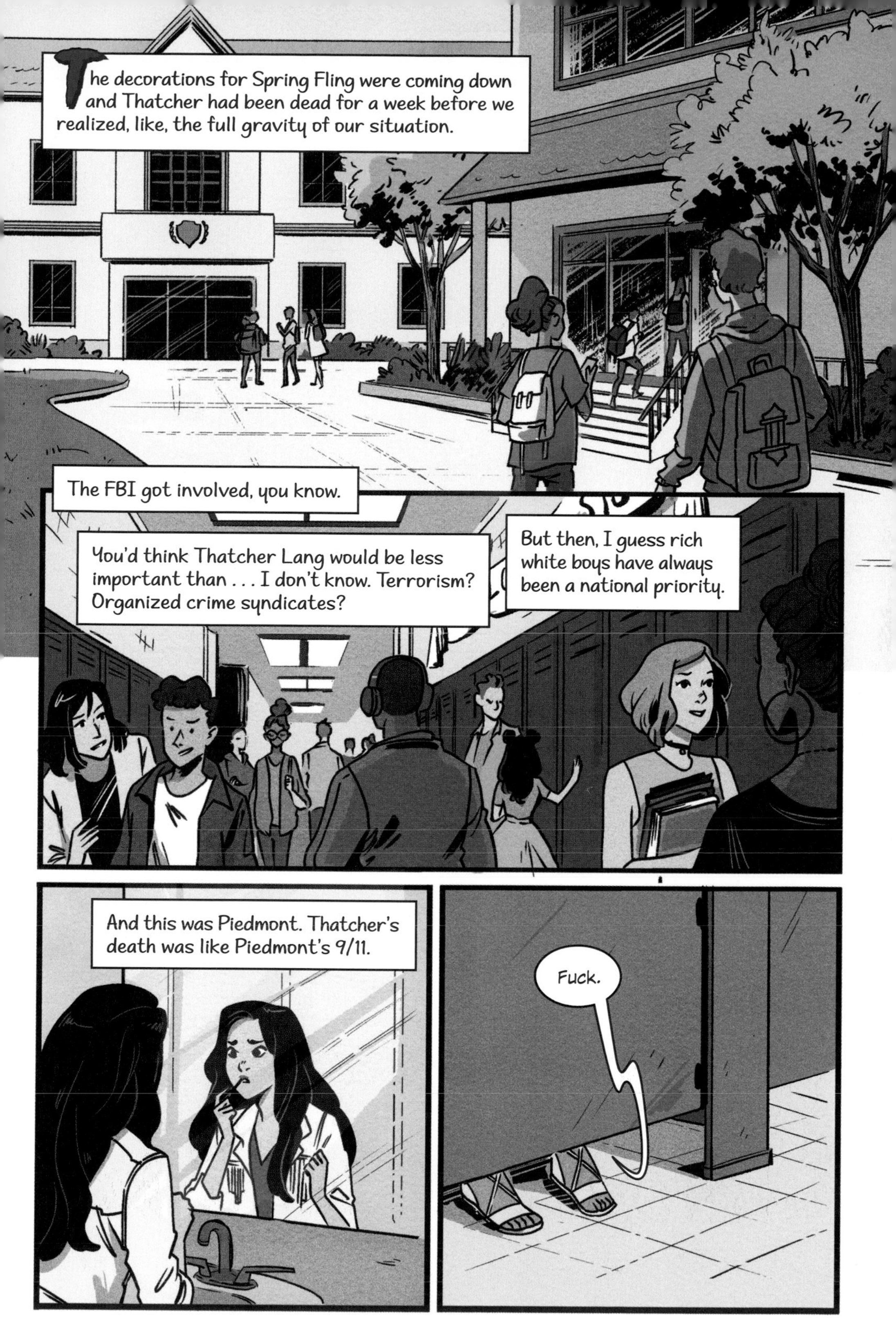
The decorations for Spring Fling were coming down and Thatcher had been dead for a week before we realized, like, the full gravity of our situation.
The FBI got involved, you know.
You'd think Thatcher Lang would be less important than . . . I don't know. Terrorism? Organized crime syndicates?
But then, I guess rich white boys have always been a national priority.
And this was Piedmont. Thatcher's death was like Piedmont's 9/11.
Fuck.

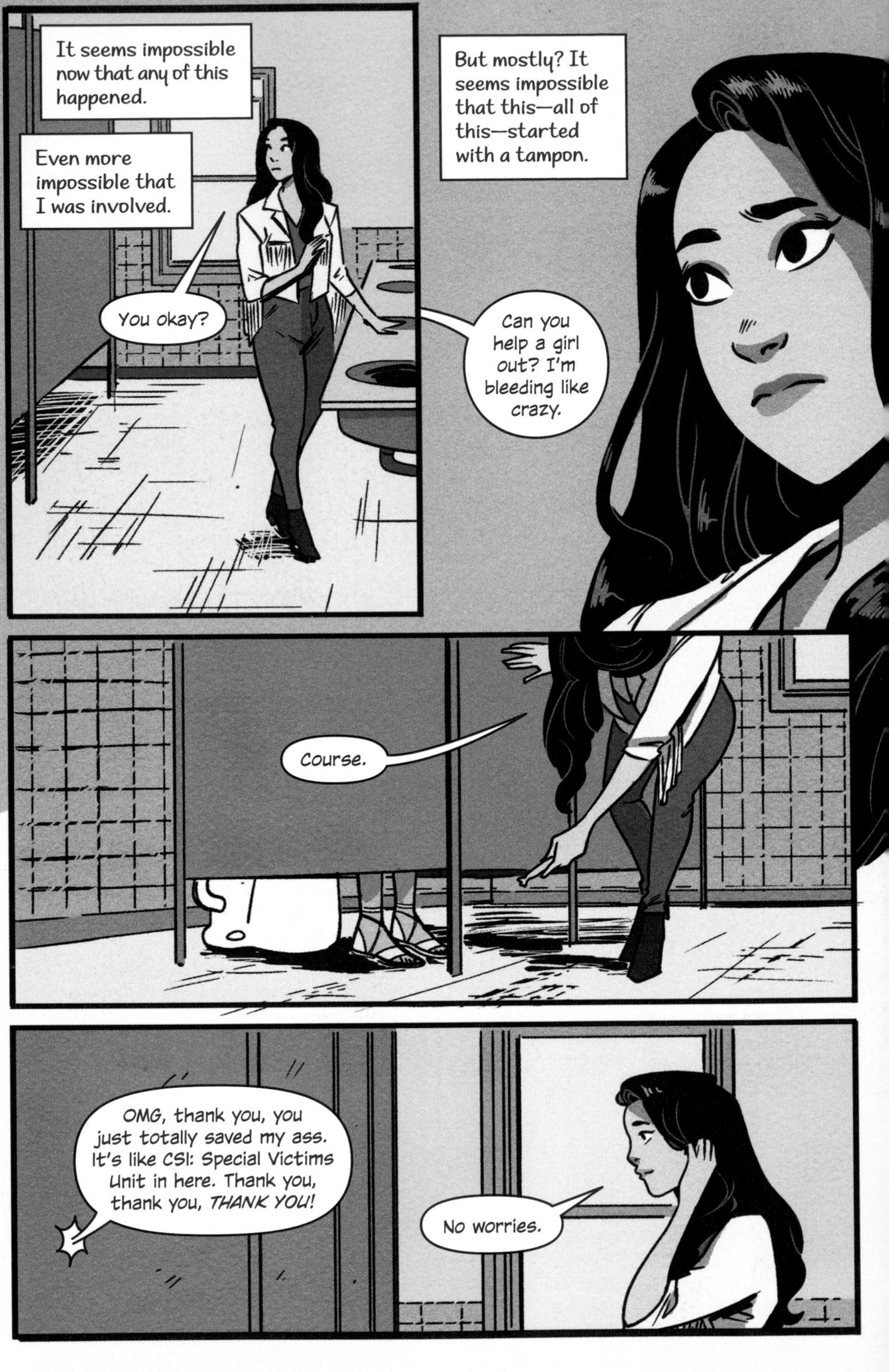
It seems impossible now that any of this happened.
Even more impossible that I was involved.
You okay?
But mostly? It seems impossible that this—all of this—started with a tampon.
Can you help a girl out? I'm bleeding like crazy.
Course.
OMG, thank you, you just totally saved my ass. It's like CSI: Special Victims Unit in here. Thank you, thank you, *THANK YOU!*
No worries.

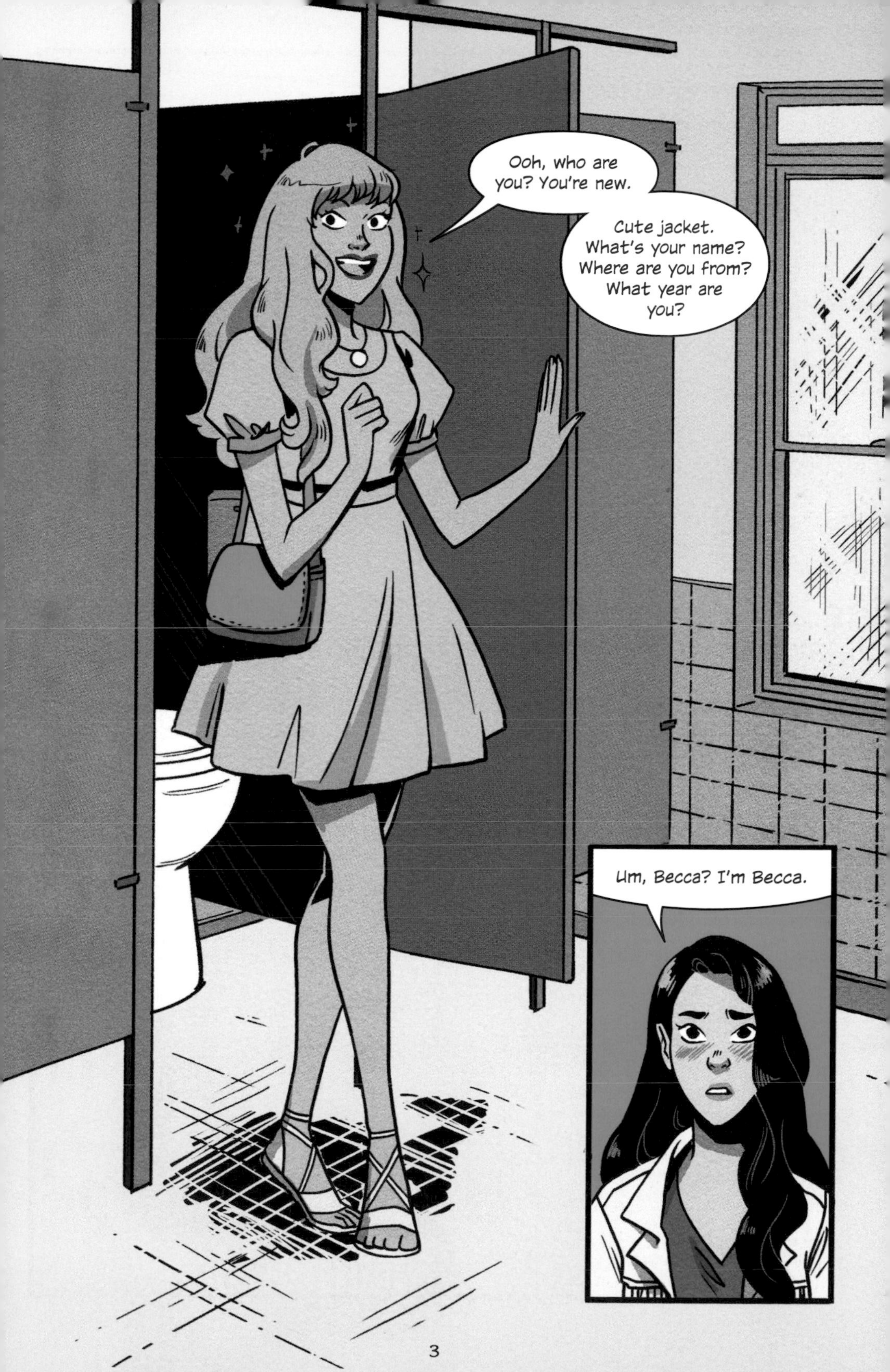
Ooh, who are you? You're new.
Cute jacket. What's your name? Where are you from? What year are you?
Um, Becca? I'm Becca.

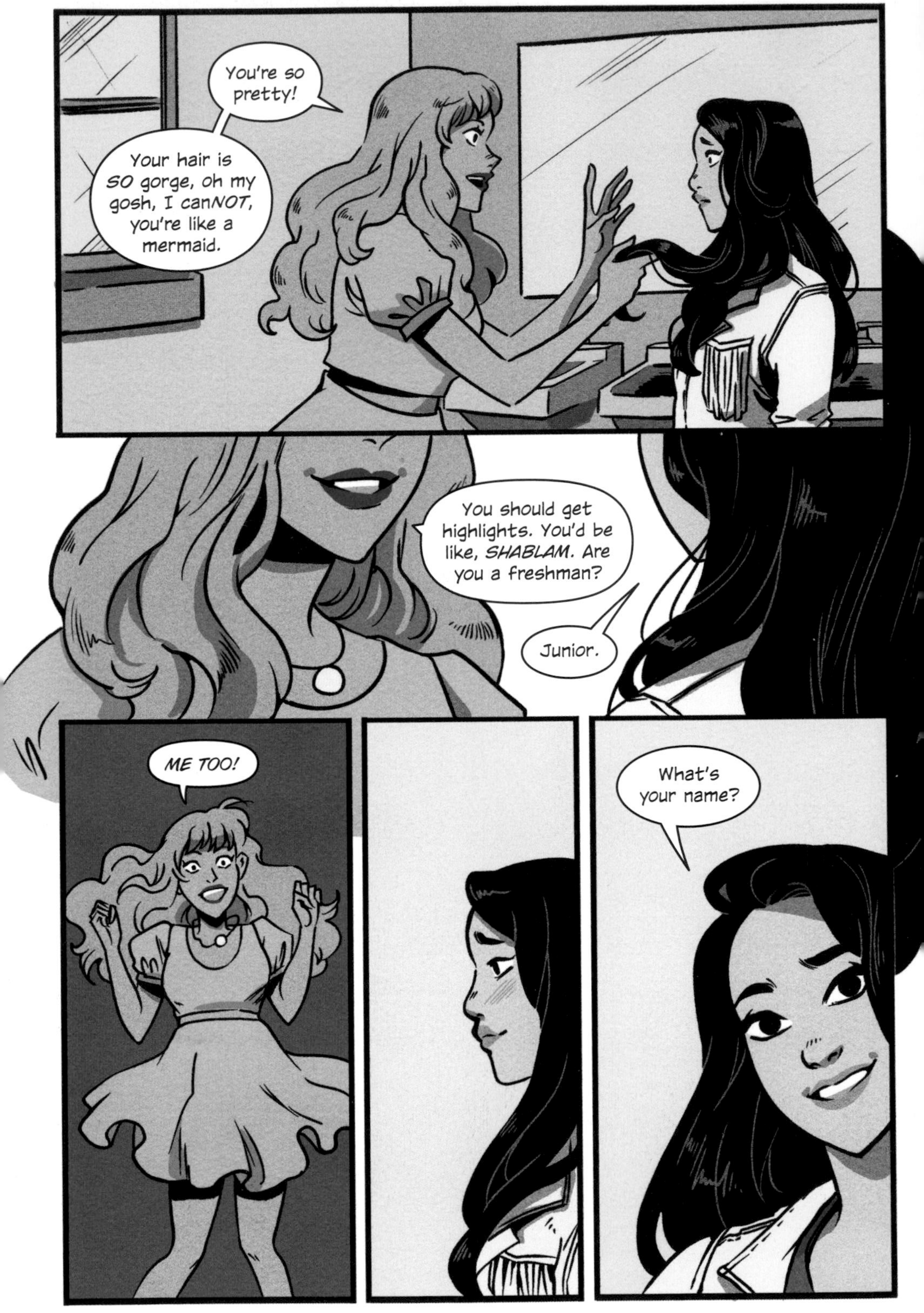
You're so pretty!
Your hair is SO gorge, oh my gosh, I canNOT, you're like a mermaid.
You should get highlights. You'd be like, SHABLAM. Are you a freshman?
Junior.
ME TOO!
What's your name?

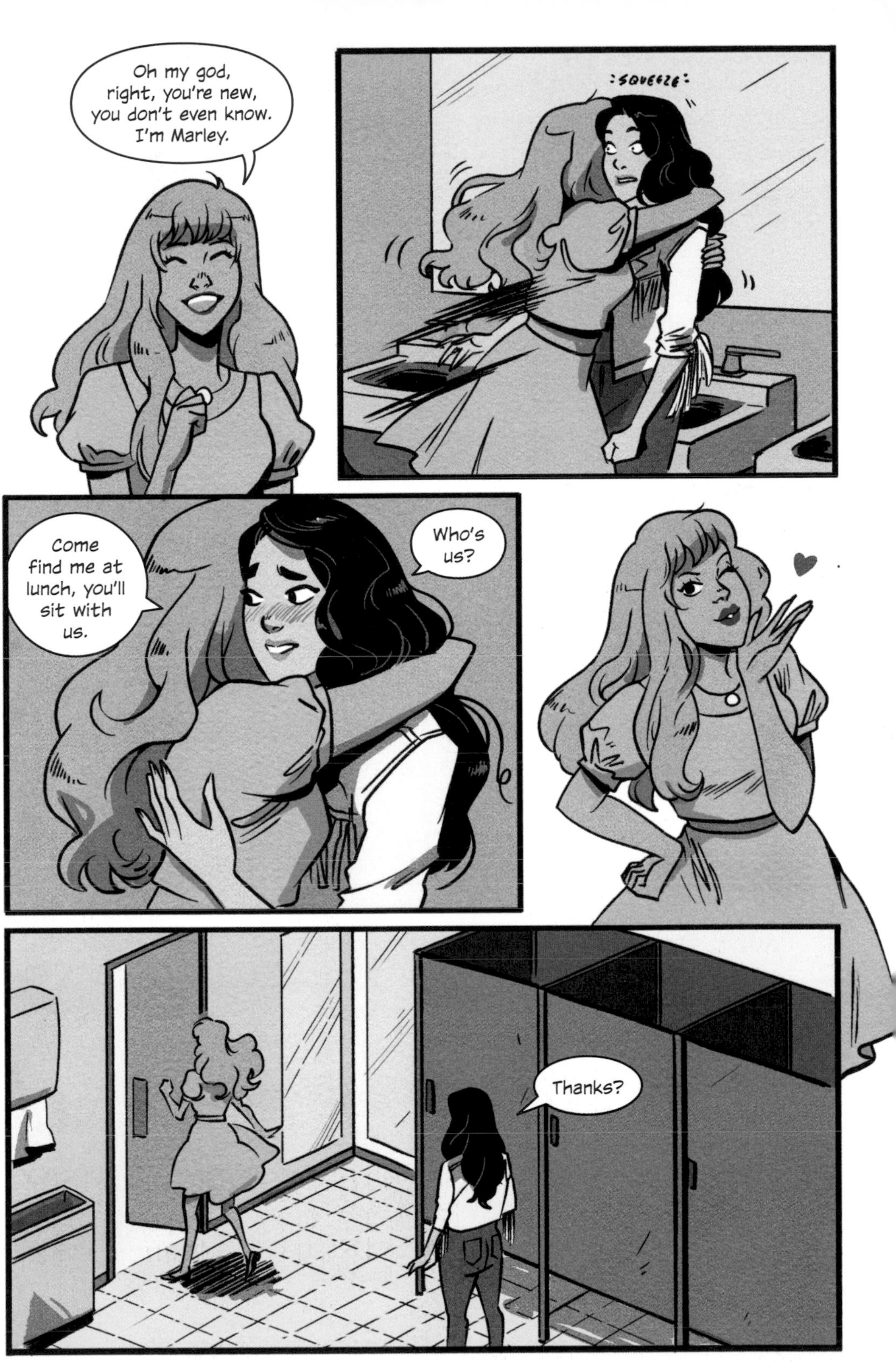
Oh my god, right, you're new, you don't even know. I'm Marley.
:SQUEEZE:
Come find me at lunch, you'll sit with us.
Who's us?
Thanks?

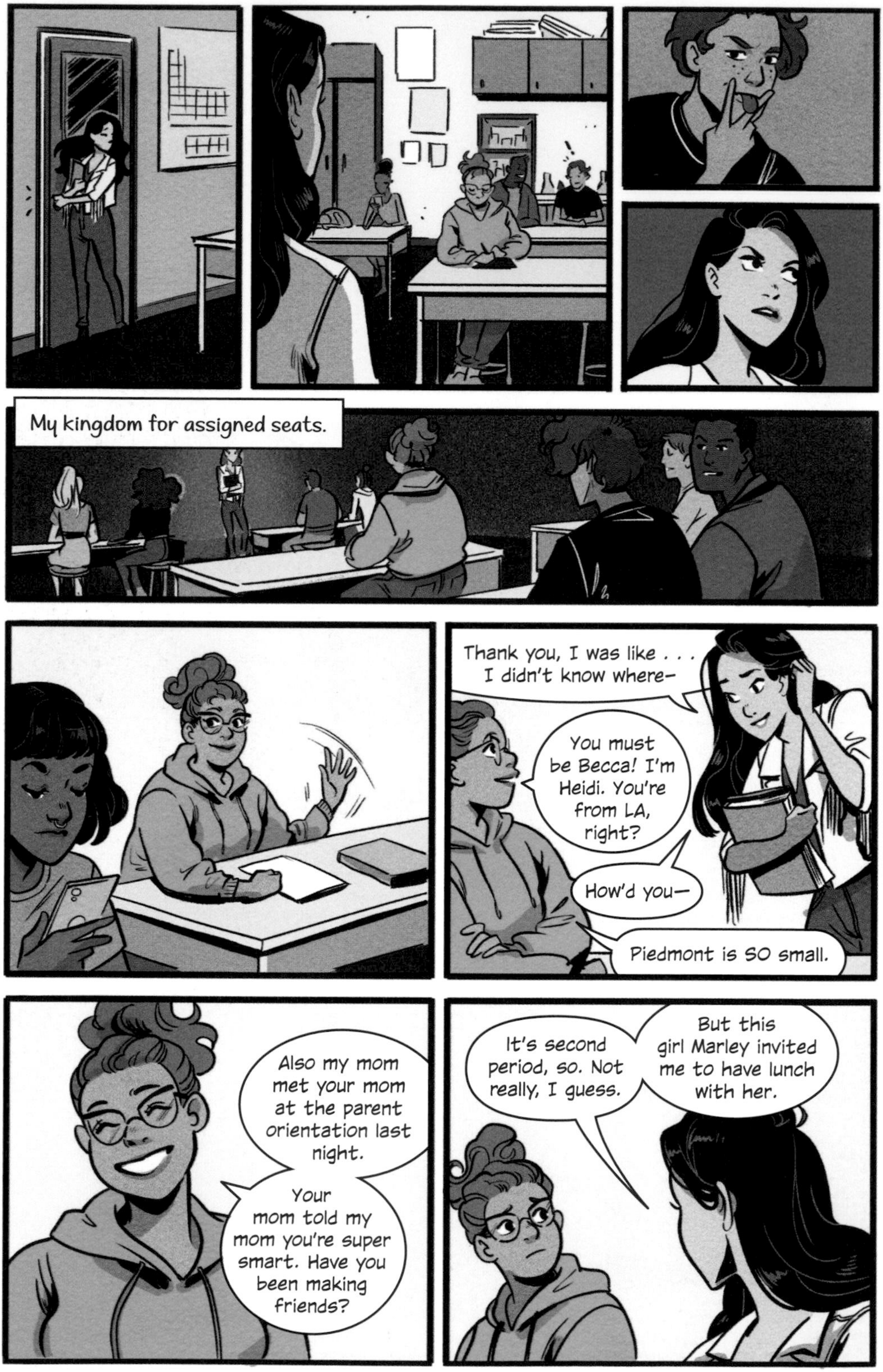

My kingdom for assigned seats.
Thank you, I was like . . . I didn't know where–
You must be Becca! I'm Heidi. You're from LA, right?
How'd you—
Piedmont is SO small.
Also my mom met your mom at the parent orientation last night.
Your mom told my mom you're super smart. Have you been making friends?
It's second period, so. Not really, I guess.
But this girl Marley invited me to have lunch with her.

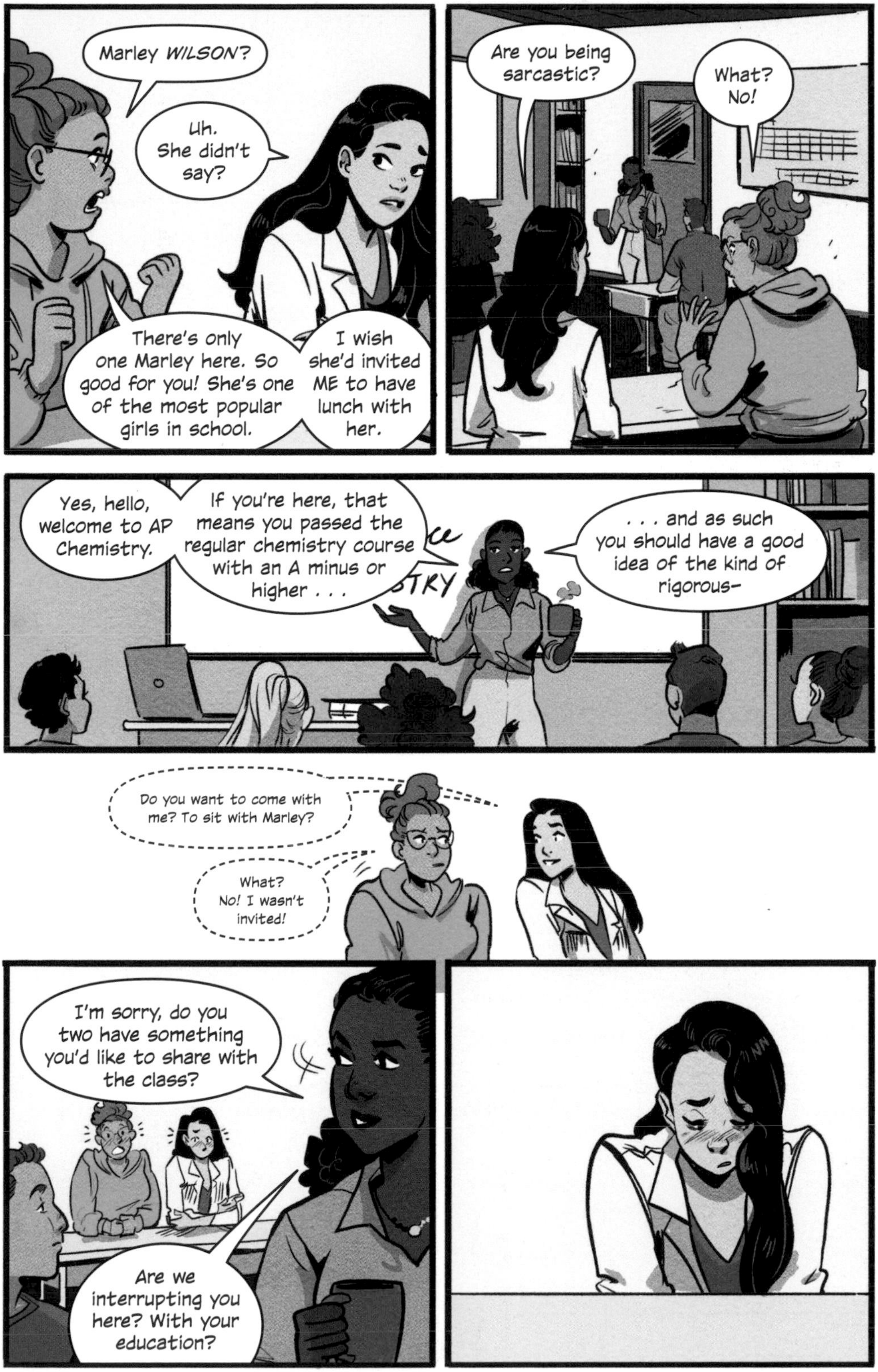
Marley WILSON?
Uh. She didn't say?
There's only one Marley here. So good for you! She's one of the most popular girls in school.
I wish she'd invited ME to have lunch with her.
Are you being sarcastic?
What? No!
Yes, hello, welcome to AP Chemistry.
If you're here, that means you passed the regular chemistry course with an A minus or higher . . .
. . . and as such you should have a good idea of the kind of rigorous–
Do you want to come with me? To sit with Marley?
What? No! I wasn't invited!
I'm sorry, do you two have something you'd like to share with the class?
Are we interrupting you here? With your education?

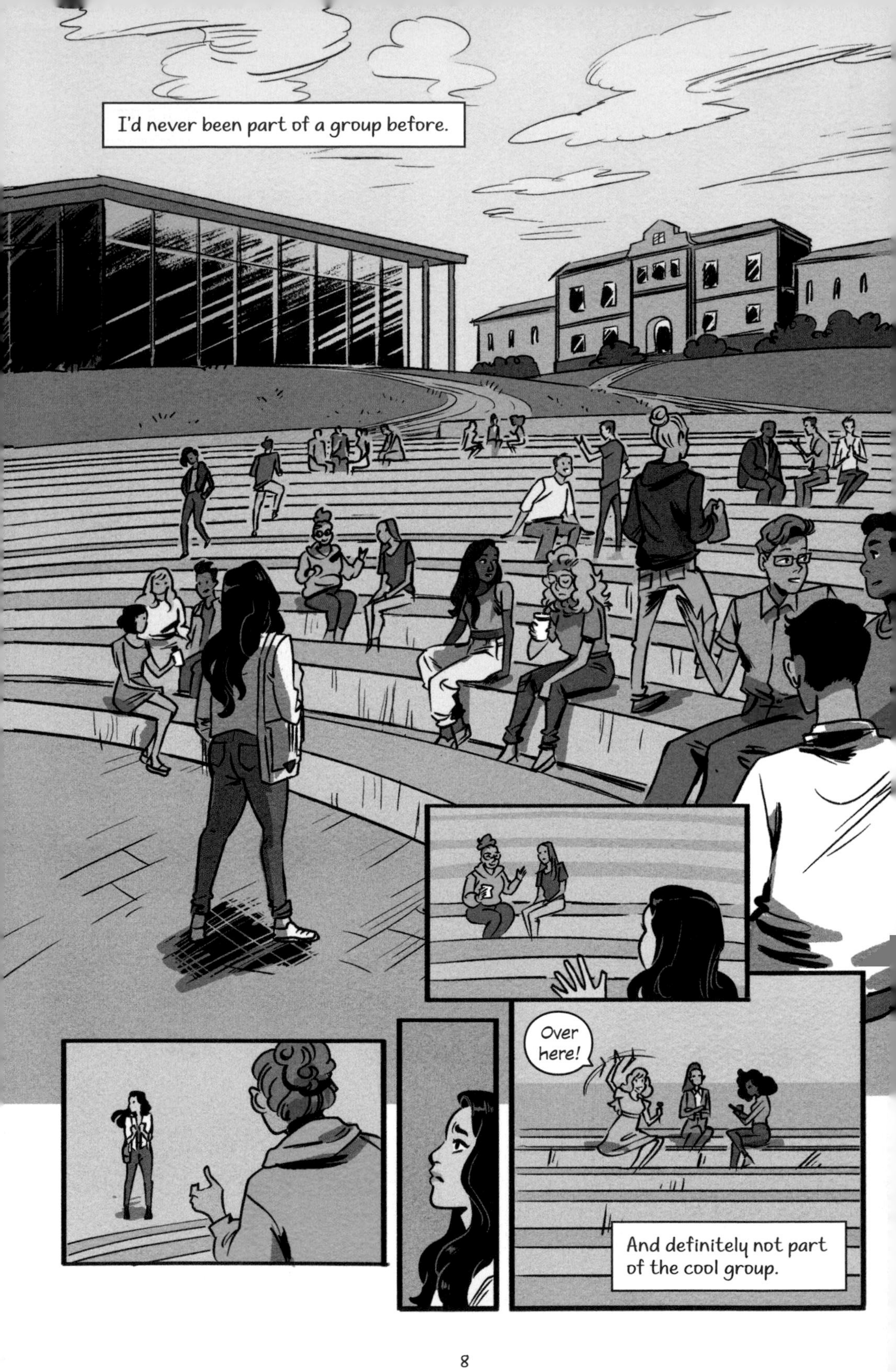
I'd never been part of a group before.
Over here!
And definitely not part of the cool group.

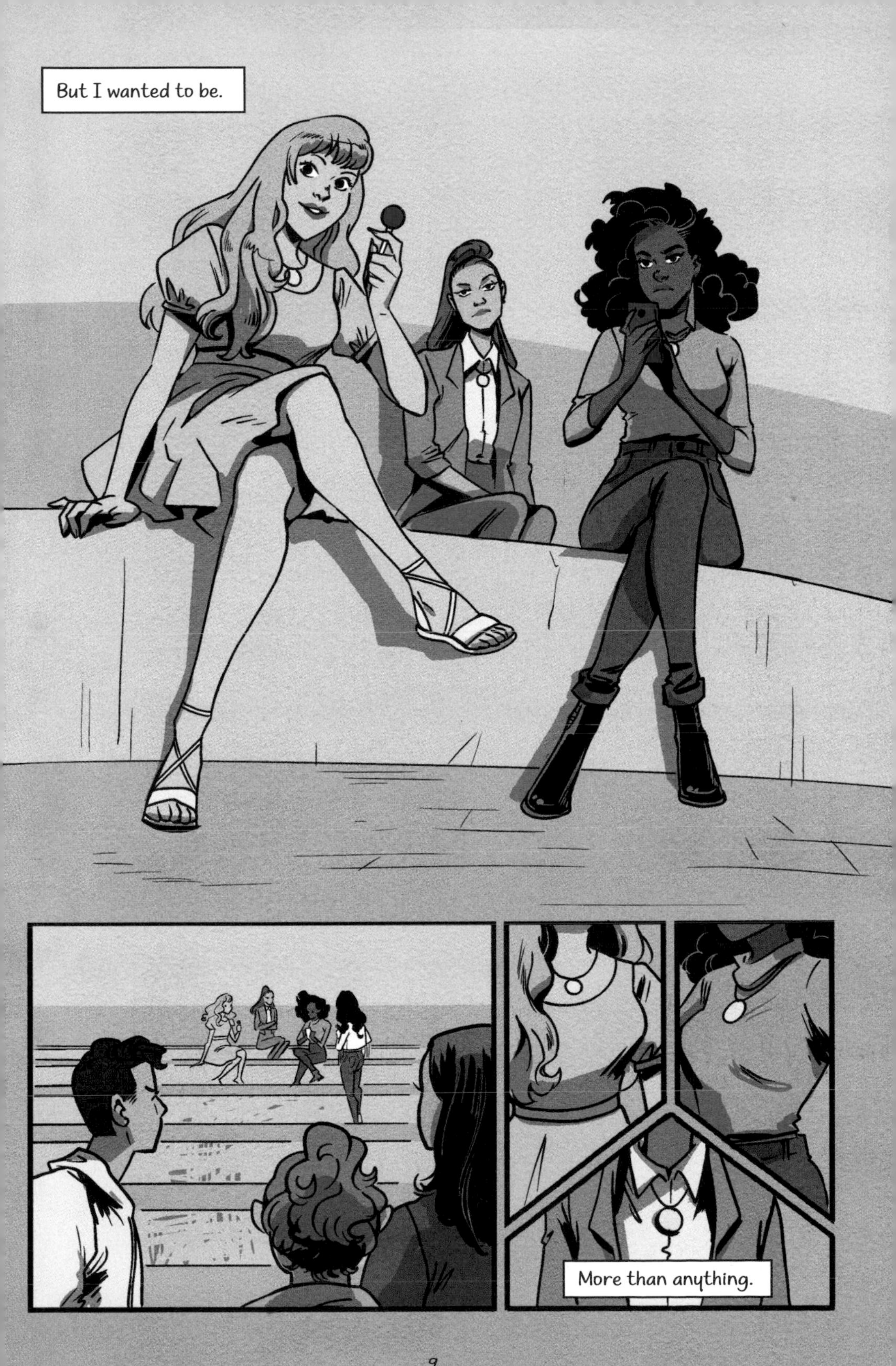
But I wanted to be.
More than anything.

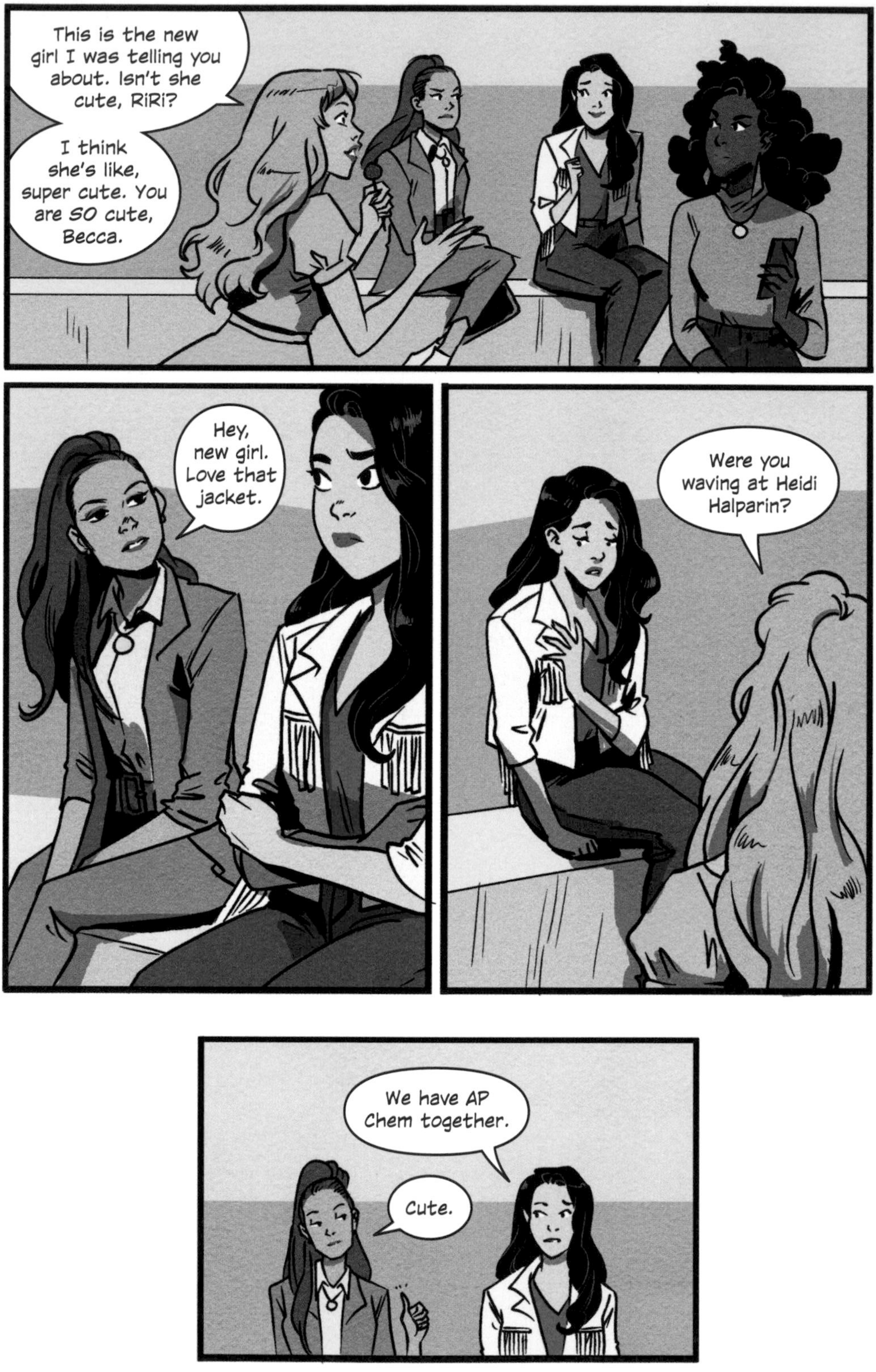
This is the new girl I was telling you about. Isn't she cute, RiRi?
I think she's like, super cute. You are SO cute, Becca.
Hey, new girl. Love that jacket.
Were you waving at Heidi Halparin?
We have AP Chem together.
Cute.
...

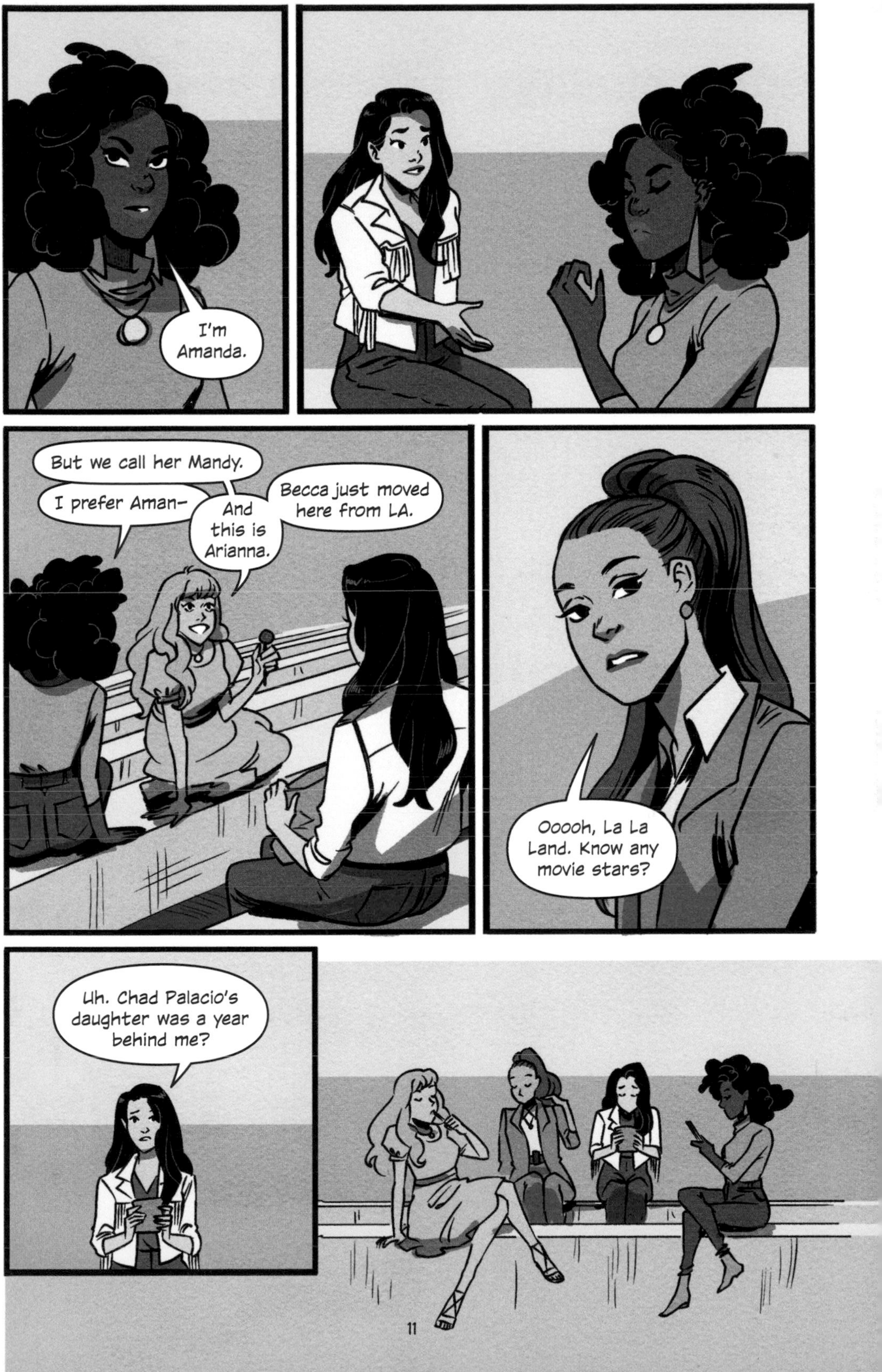
I'm Amanda.
But we call her Mandy.
I prefer Aman–
And this is Arianna.
Becca just moved here from LA.
Ooooh, La La Land. Know any movie stars?
Uh. Chad Palacio's daughter was a year behind me?

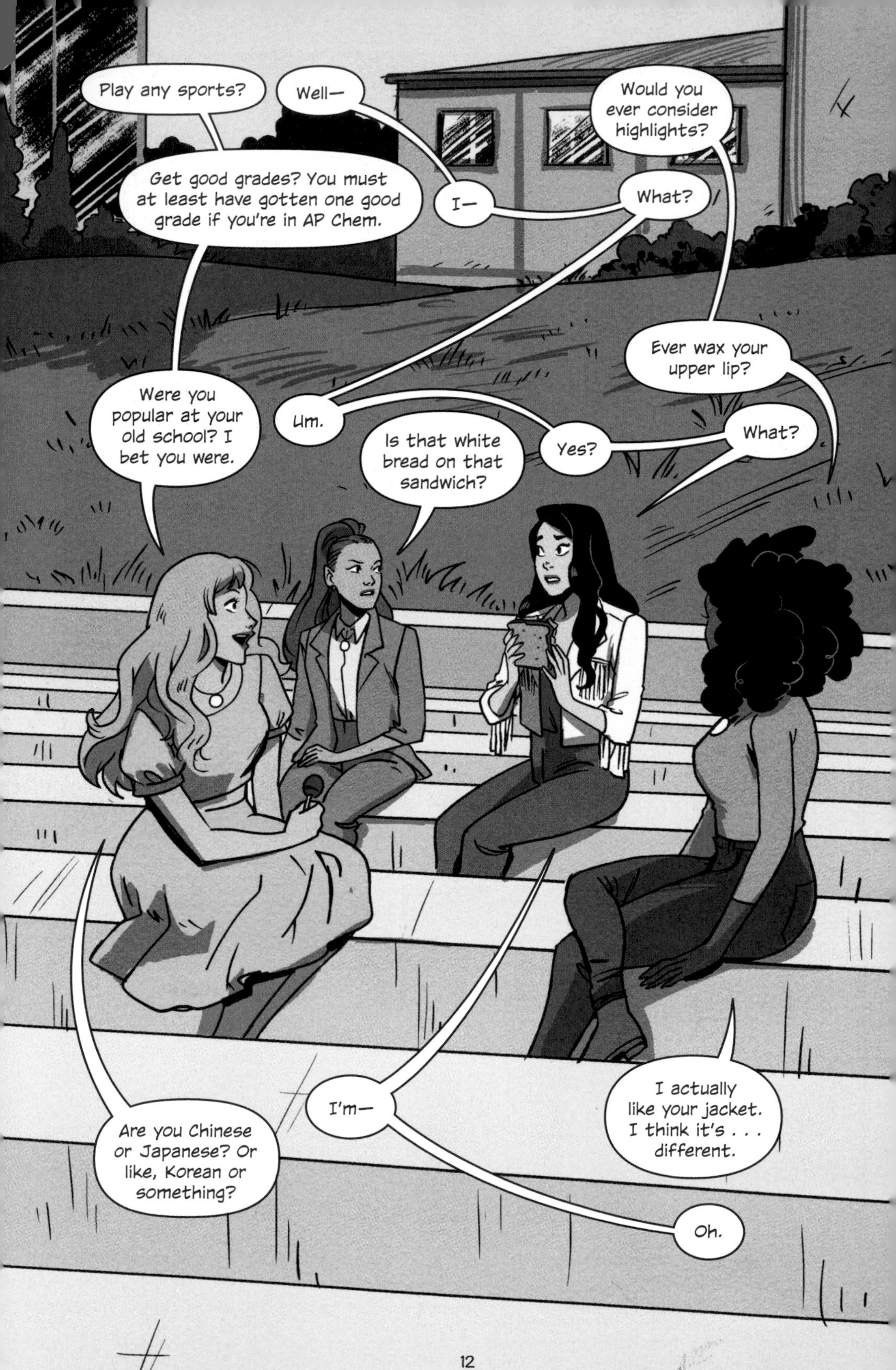

Play any sports?
Get good grades? You must at least have gotten one good grade if you're in AP Chem.
Were you popular at your old school? I bet you were.
Well—
I—
What?
Would you ever consider highlights?
Ever wax your upper lip?
Um.
Is that white bread on that sandwich?
Yes?
What?
Are you Chinese or Japanese? Or like, Korean or something?
I'm—
I actually like your jacket. I think it's . . . different.
Oh.

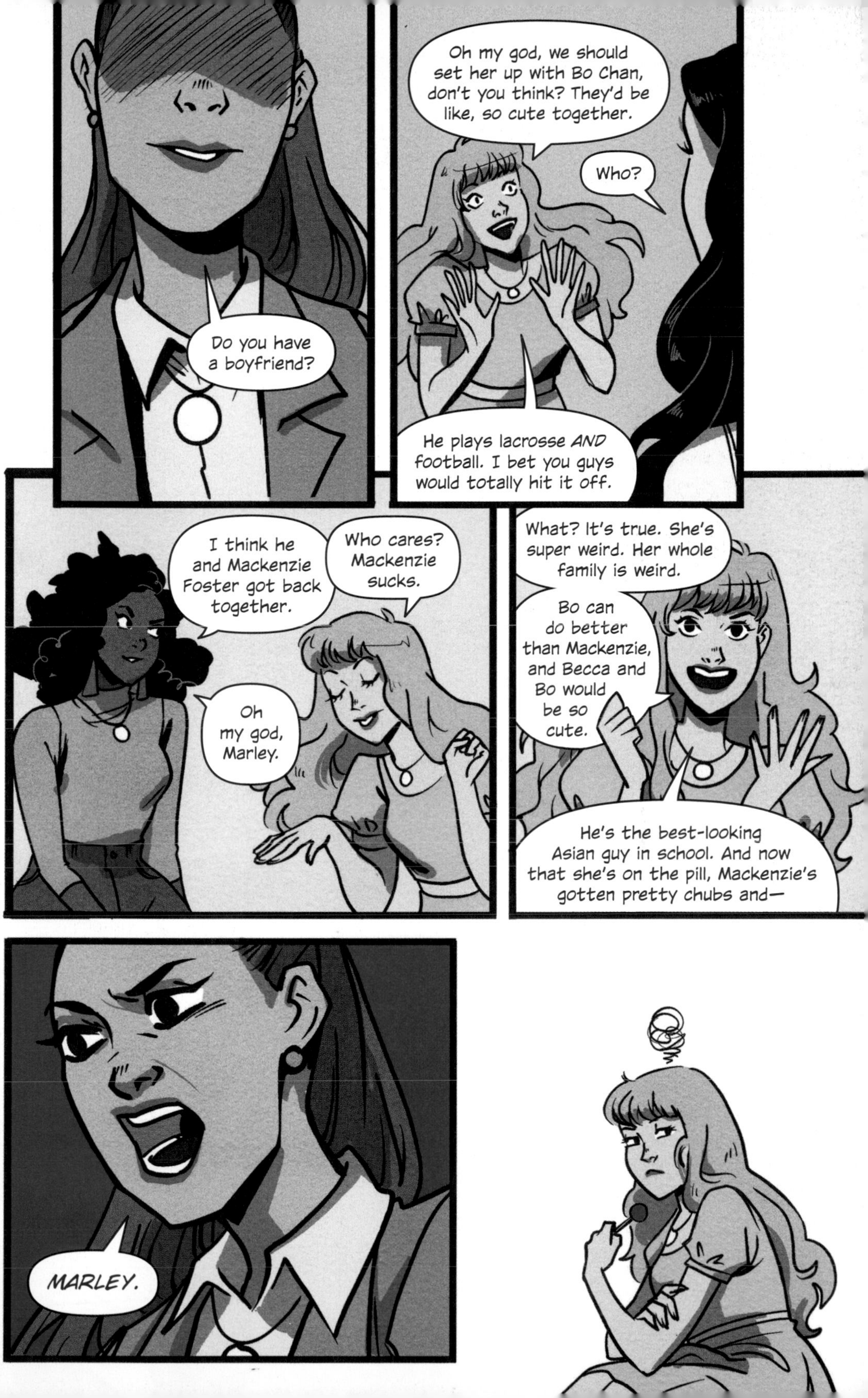
Do you have a boyfriend?
Oh my god, we should set her up with Bo Chan, don't you think? They'd be like, so cute together.
Who?
He plays lacrosse *AND* football. I bet you guys would totally hit it off.
I think he and Mackenzie Foster got back together.
Who cares? Mackenzie sucks.
Oh my god, Marley.
What? It's true. She's super weird. Her whole family is weird.
Bo can do better than Mackenzie, and Becca and Bo would be so cute.
He's the best-looking Asian guy in school. And now that she's on the pill, Mackenzie's gotten pretty chubs and—
MARLEY.

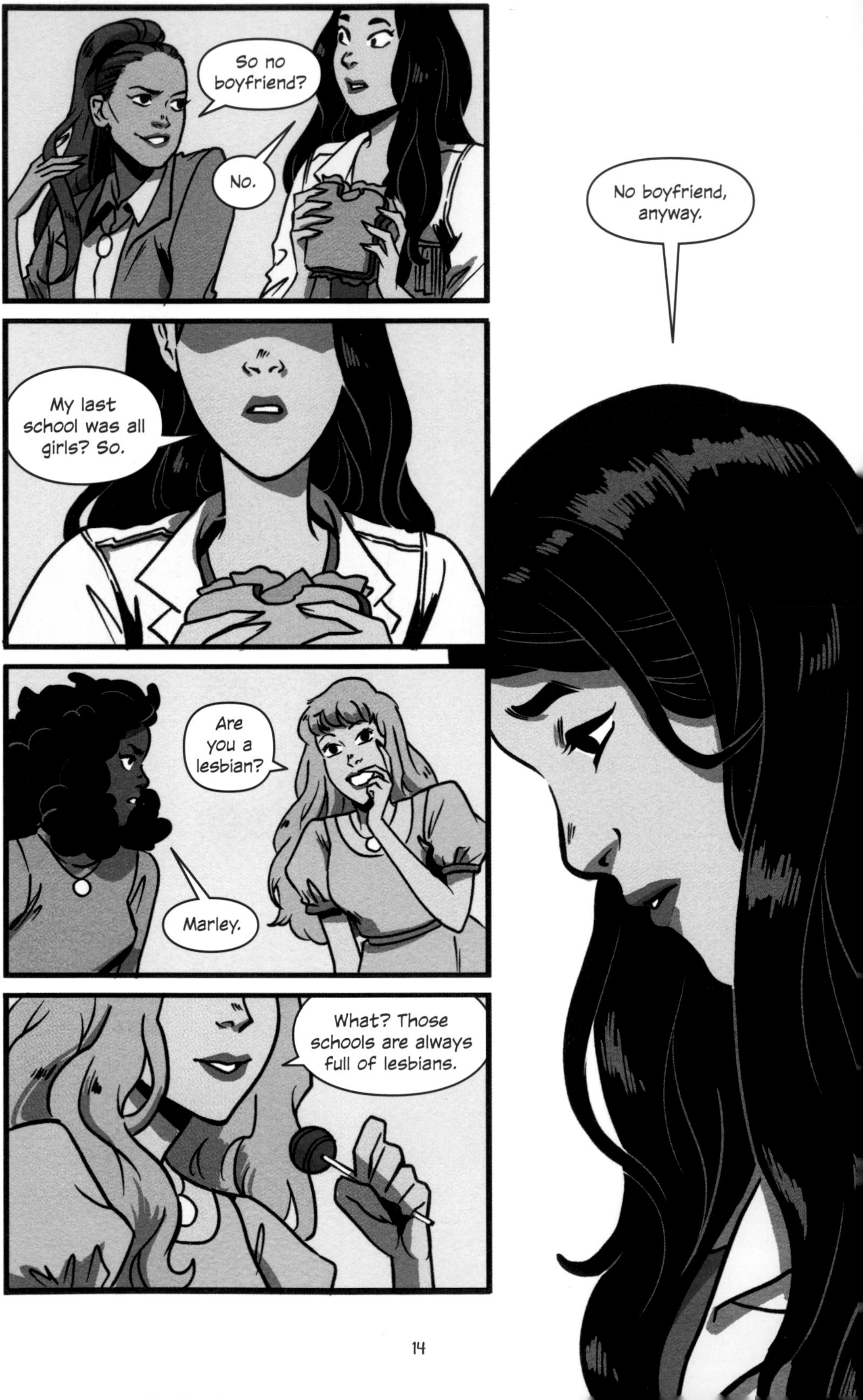
So no boyfriend?
No.
No boyfriend, anyway.
My last school was all girls? So.
Are you a lesbian?
Marley.
What? Those schools are always full of lesbians.

Uh, no thanks.
HA
HA
HA
HA
HA
HA

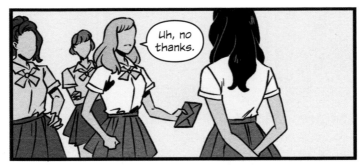

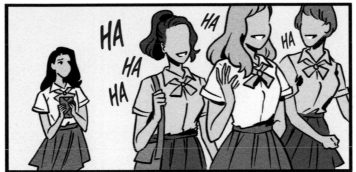

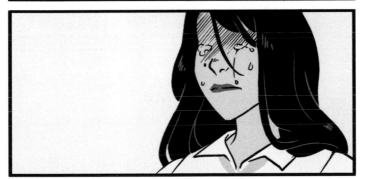

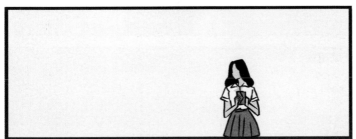

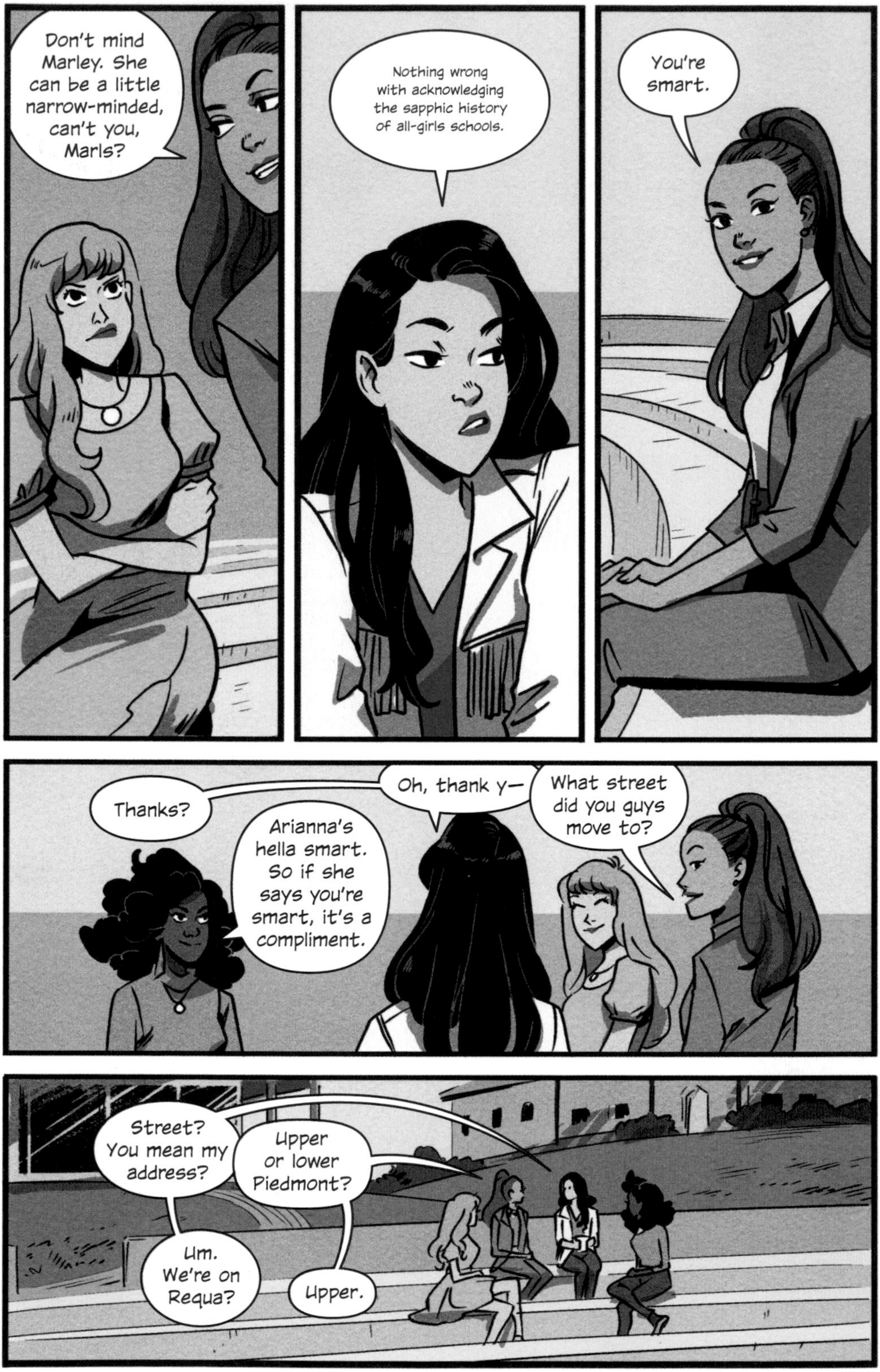
Don't mind Marley. She can be a little narrow-minded, can't you, Marls?
Nothing wrong with acknowledging the sapphic history of all-girls schools.
You're smart.
Thanks?
Oh, thank y—
Arianna's hella smart. So if she says you're smart, it's a compliment.
What street did you guys move to?
Street? You mean my address?
Upper or lower Piedmont?
Um. We're on Requa?
Upper.

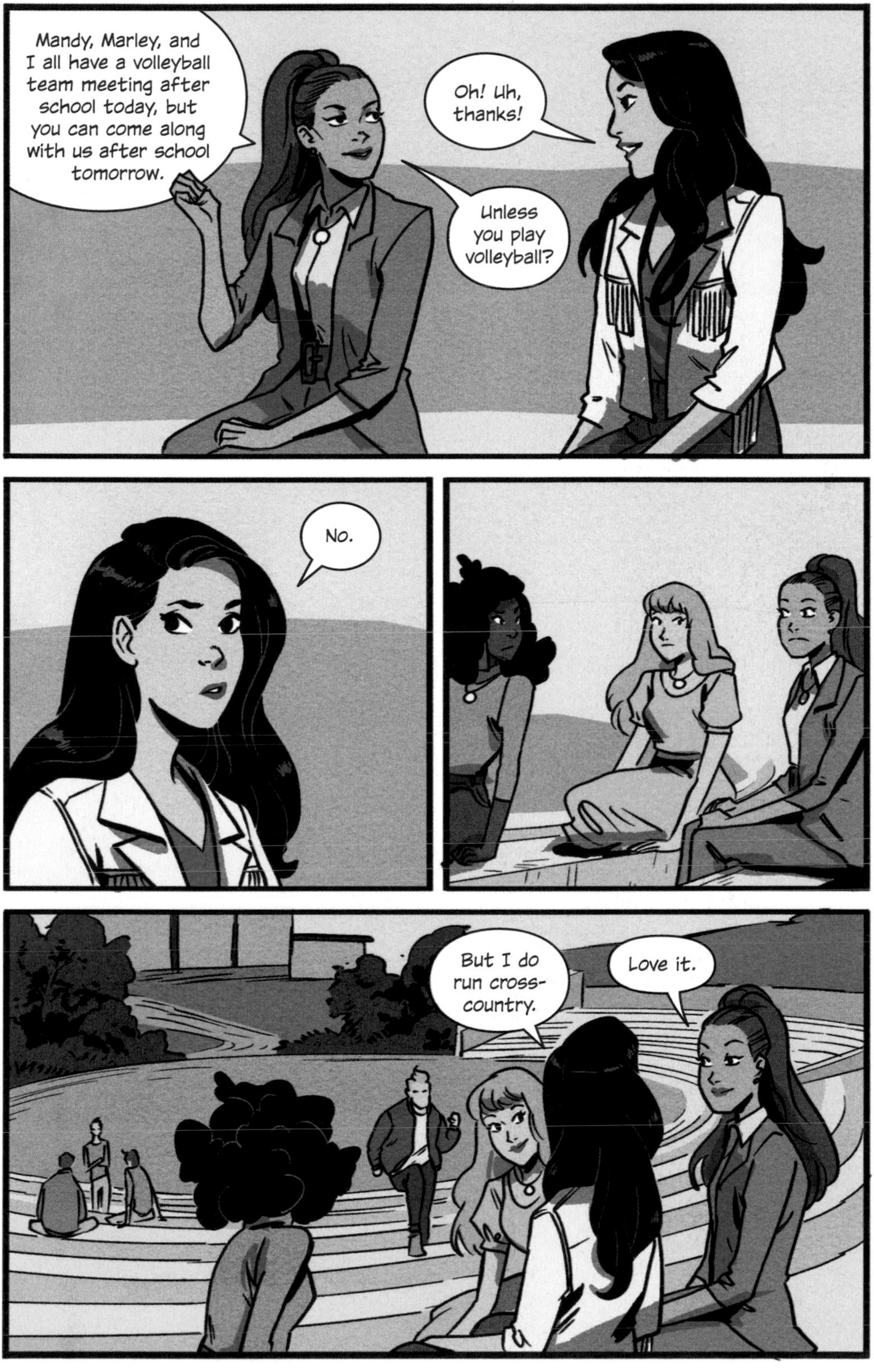

Mandy, Marley, and I all have a volleyball team meeting after school today, but you can come along with us after school tomorrow.
Oh! Uh, thanks!
Unless you play volleyball?
No.
But I do run cross-country.
Love it.

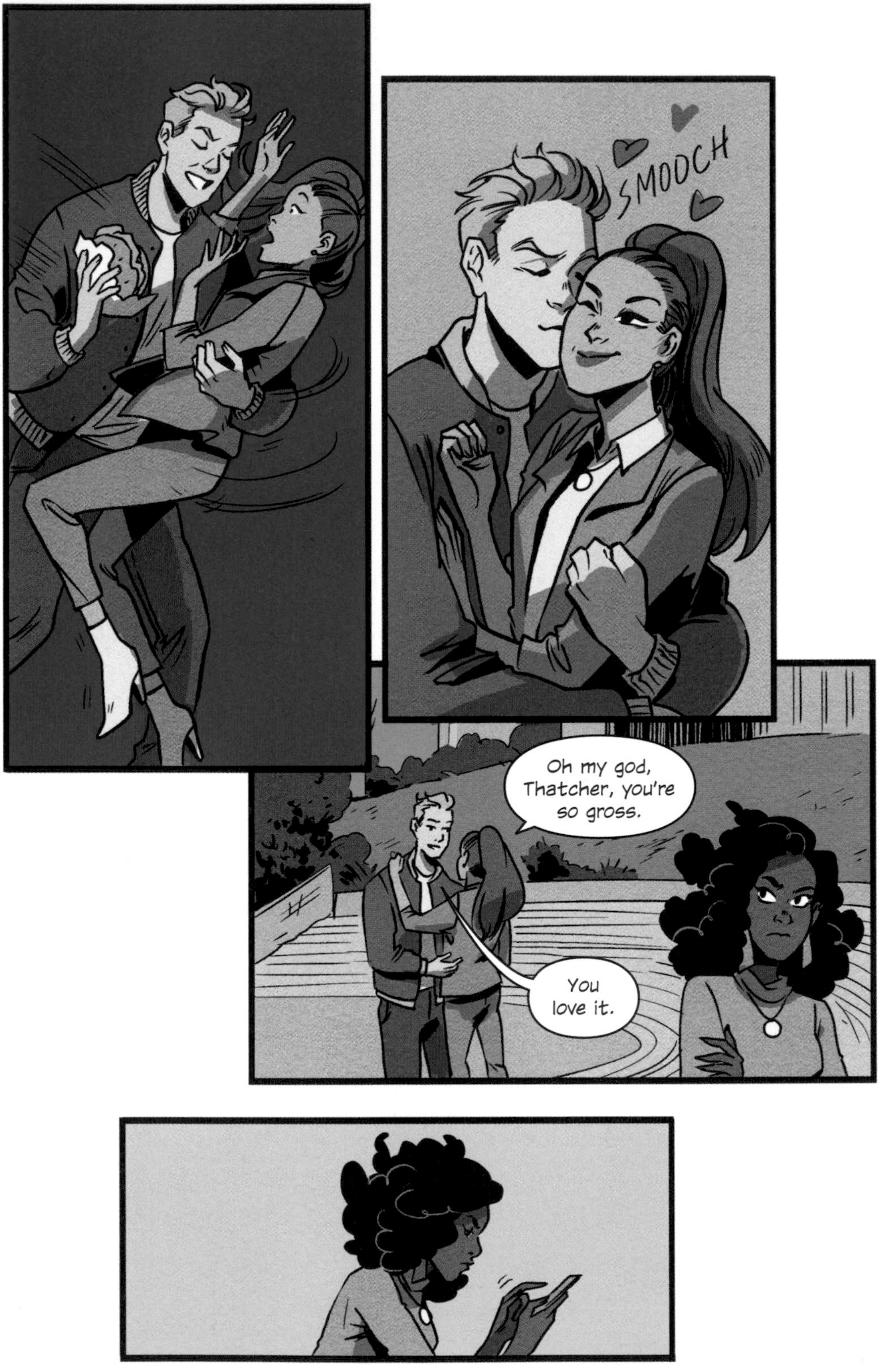
SMOOCH
Oh my god, Thatcher, you're so gross.
You love it.

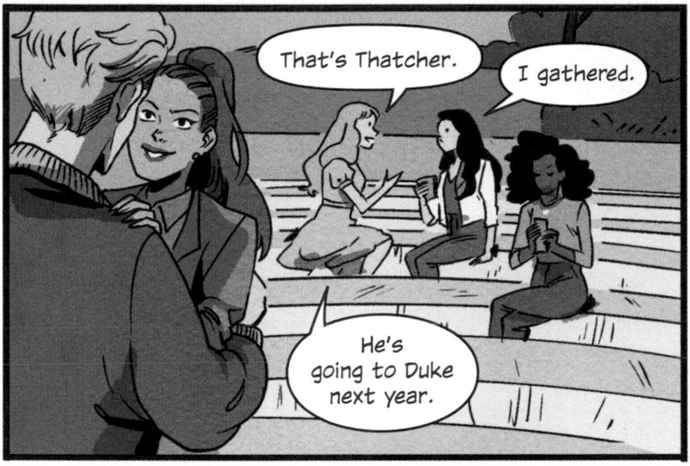
That's Thatcher.
I gathered.
He's going to Duke next year.

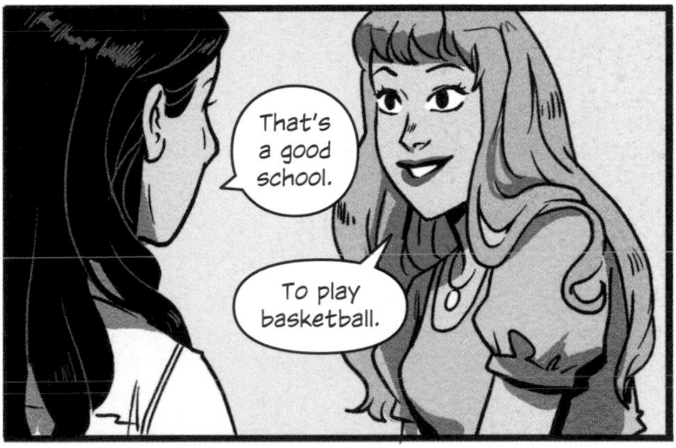
That's a good school.
To play basketball.

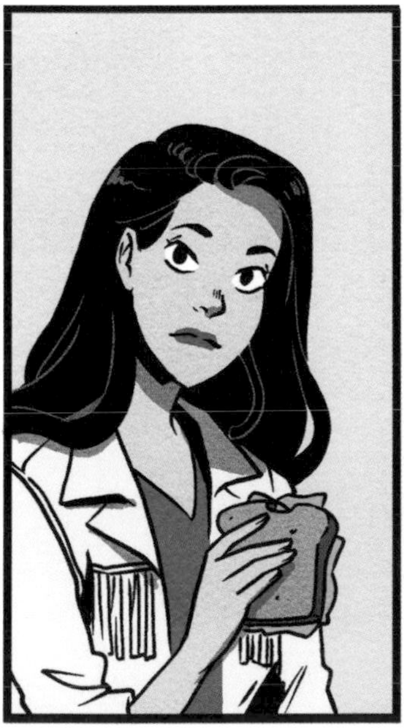

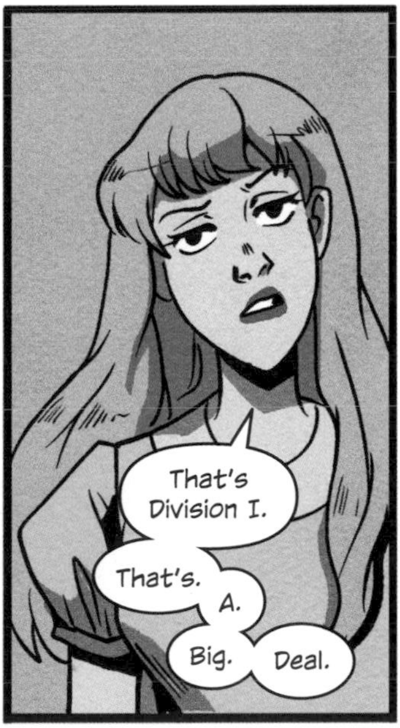
That's Division I.
That's.
A.
Big.
Deal.

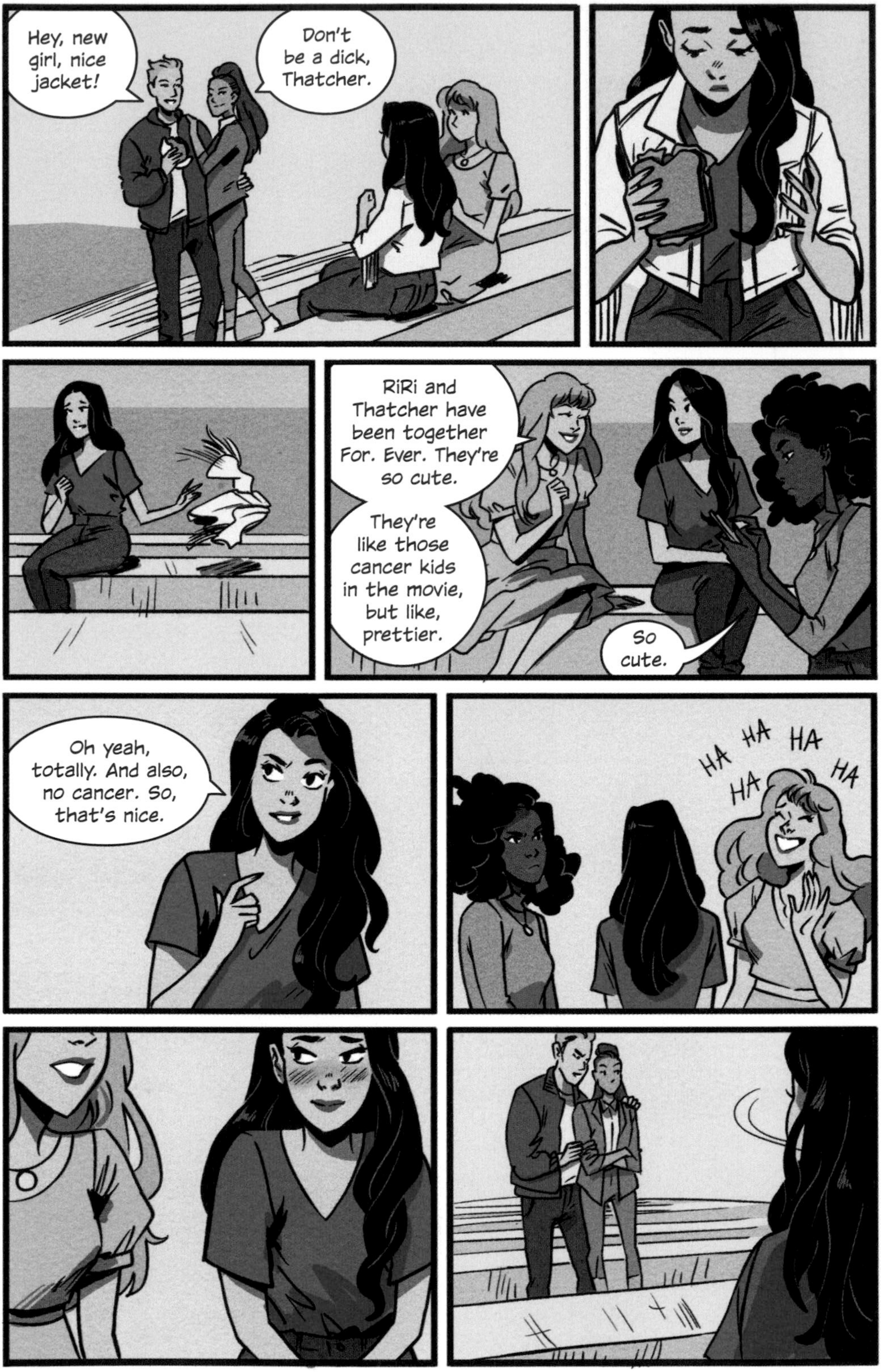
Hey, new girl, nice jacket!
Don't be a dick, Thatcher.
RiRi and Thatcher have been together For. Ever. They're so cute.
They're like those cancer kids in the movie, but like, prettier.
So cute.
Oh yeah, totally. And also, no cancer. So, that's nice.
HA HA HA HA HA

RIIIINNNNNG!
Shoot.

You'll get used to it.

Get used to?
We don't eat lunch.

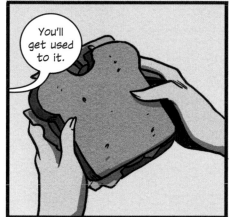

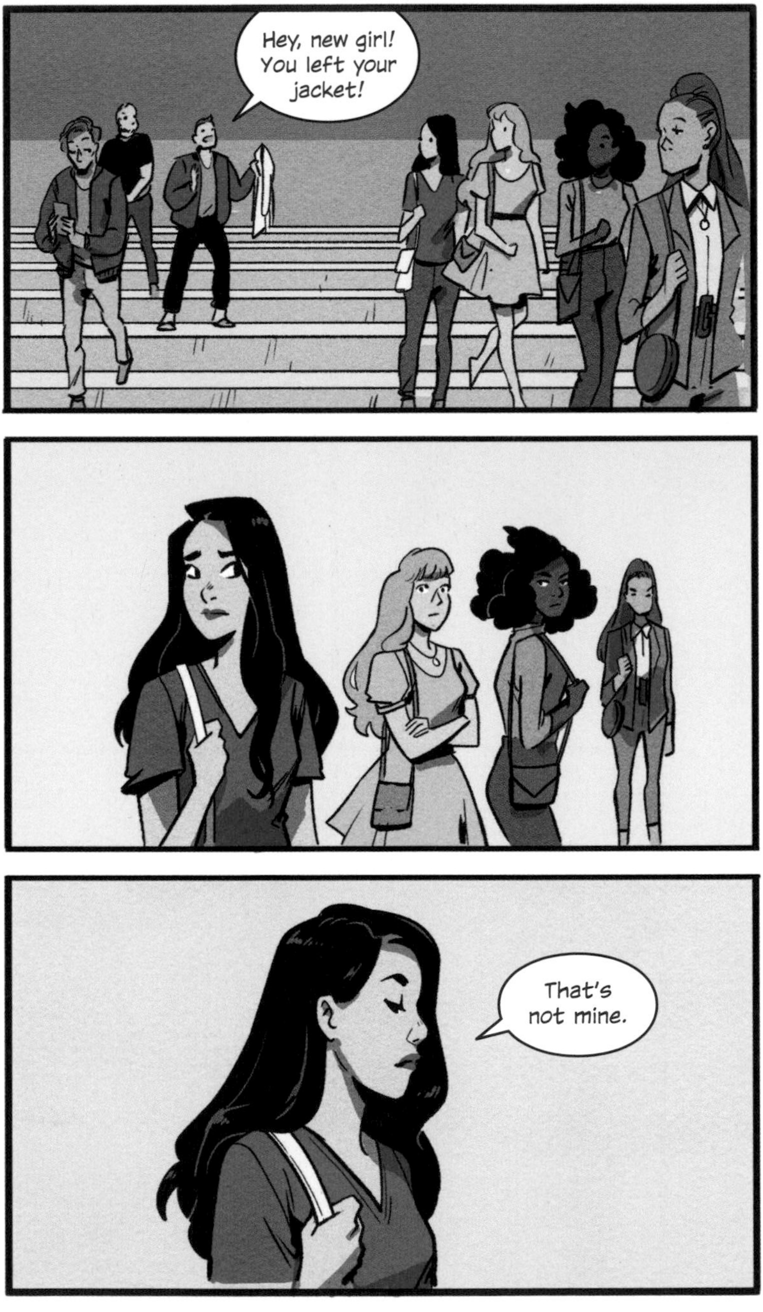
Hey, new girl! You left your jacket!
That's not mine.

CHAPTER TWO

SQUAD GOALS

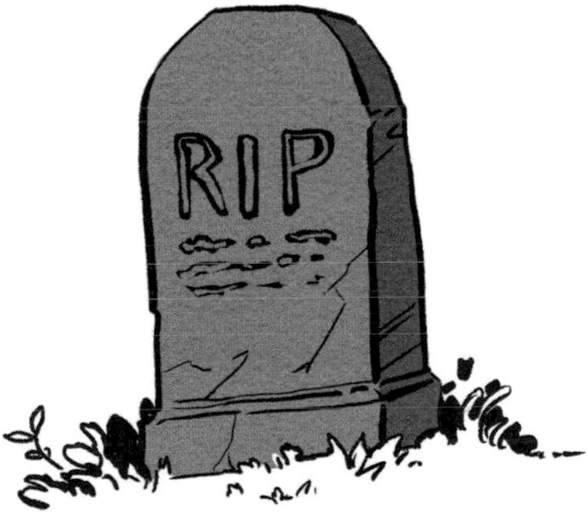
RIP

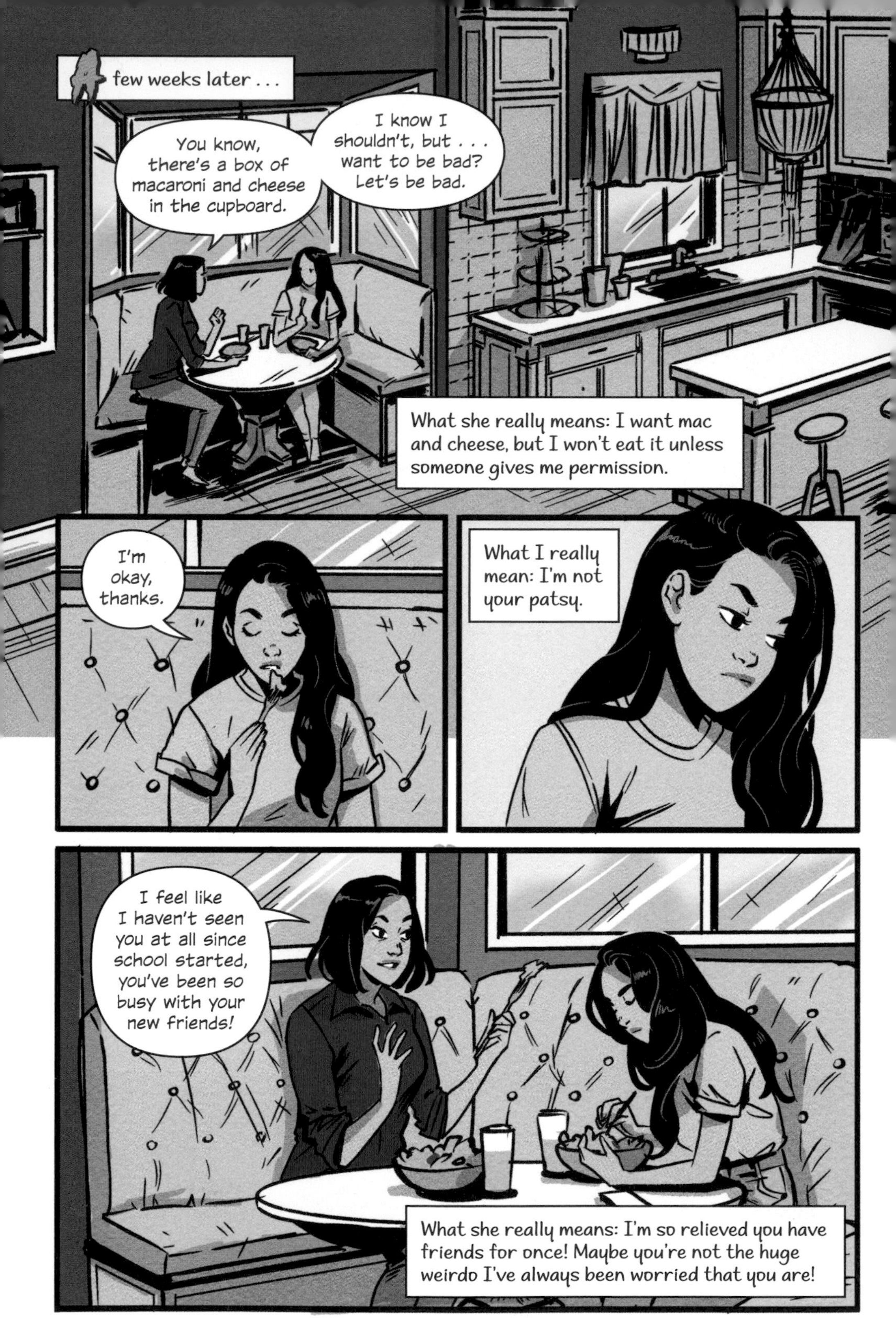
A few weeks later . . .
You know, there's a box of macaroni and cheese in the cupboard.
I know I shouldn't, but . . . want to be bad? Let's be bad.
What she really means: I want mac and cheese, but I won't eat it unless someone gives me permission.
I'm okay, thanks.
What I really mean: I'm not your patsy.
I feel like I haven't seen you at all since school started, you've been so busy with your new friends!
What she really means: I'm so relieved you have friends for once! Maybe you're not the huge weirdo I've always been worried that you are!

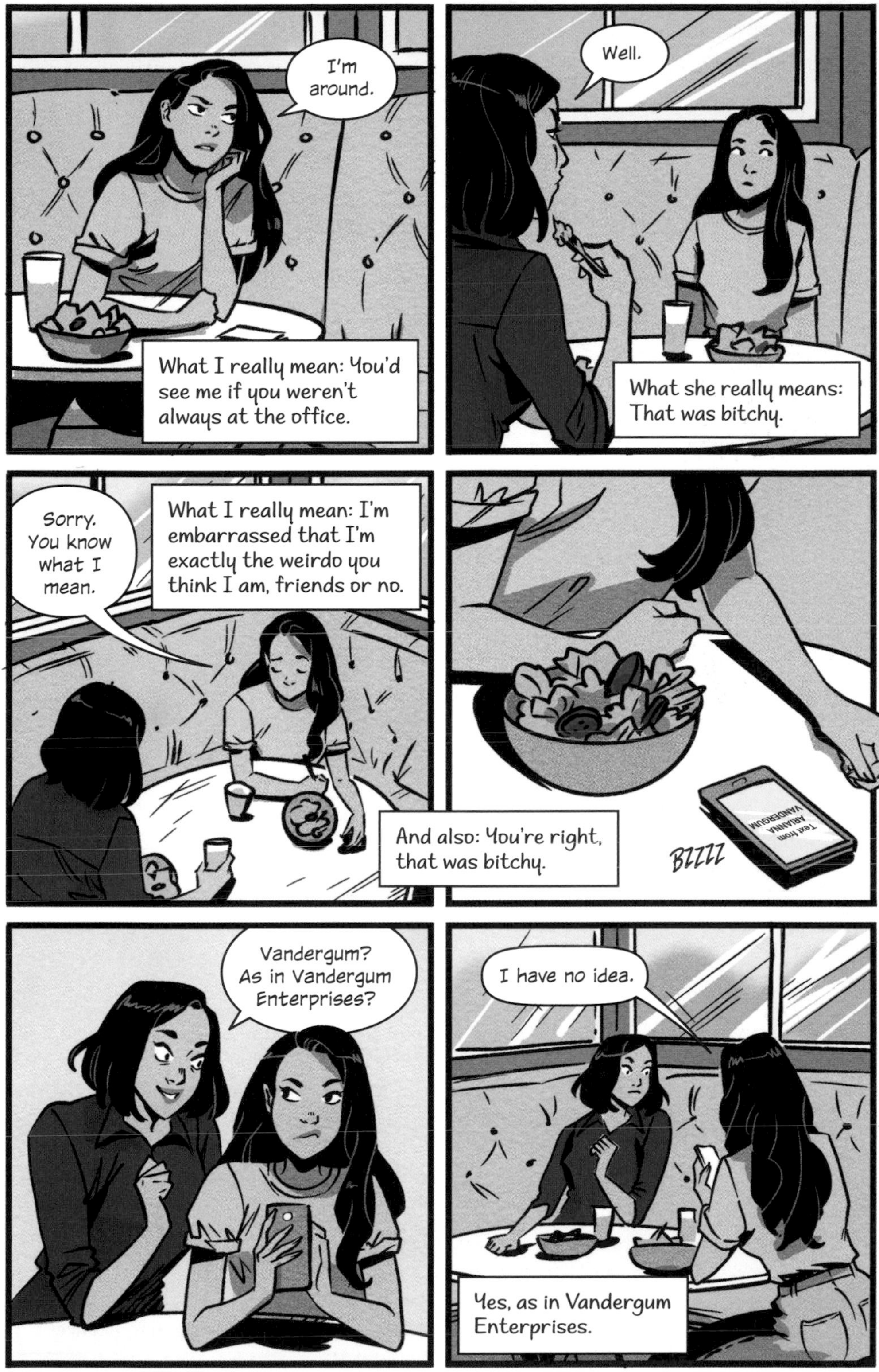

I'm around.
What I really mean: You'd see me if you weren't always at the office.
Well.
What she really means: That was bitchy.
Sorry. You know what I mean.
What I really mean: I'm embarrassed that I'm exactly the weirdo you think I am, friends or no.
And also: You're right, that was bitchy.
Text from ARIANNA VANDERGUM
BZZZZ
Vandergum? As in Vandergum Enterprises?
I have no idea.
Yes, as in Vandergum Enterprises.

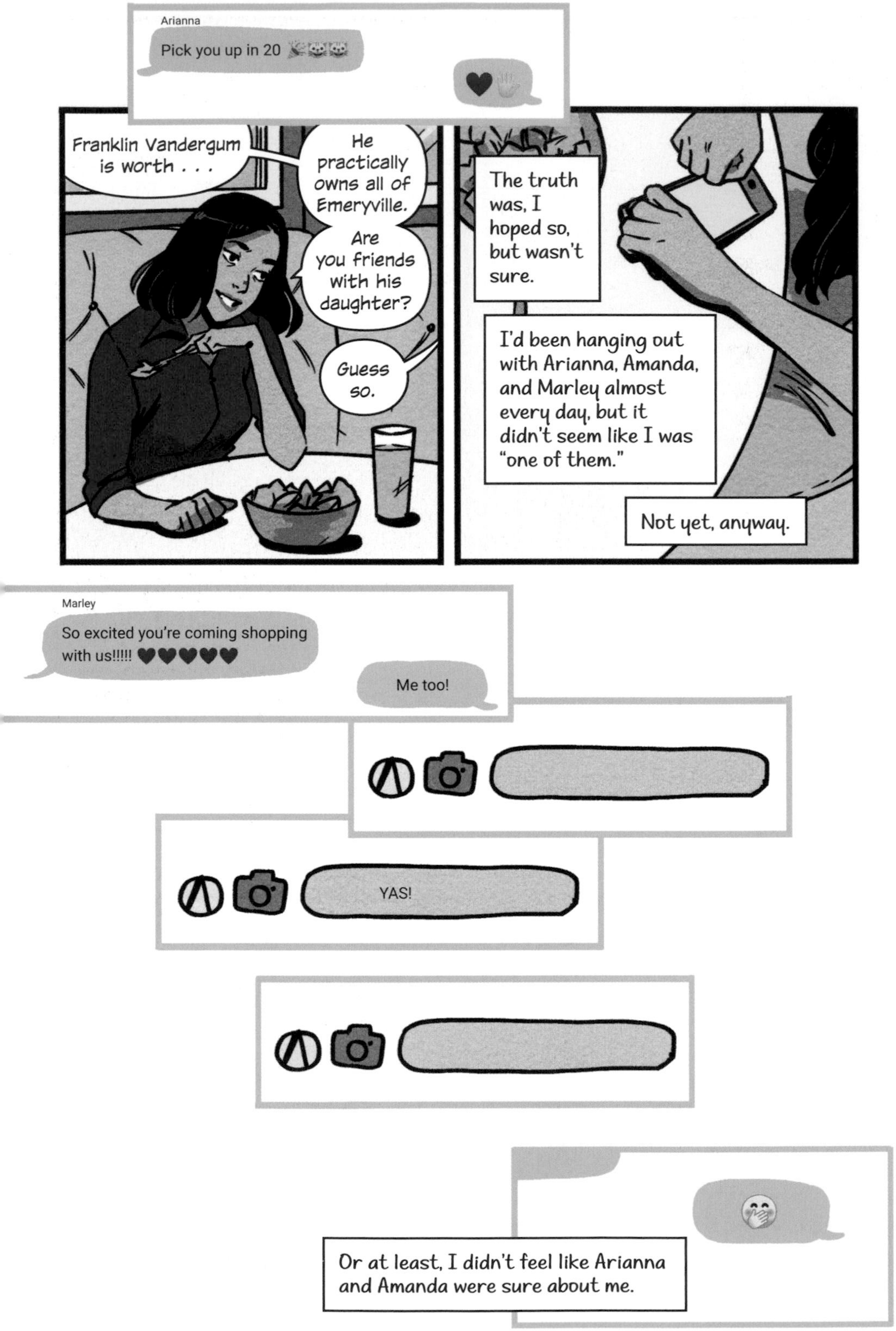
Arianna
Pick you up in 20
Franklin Vandergum is worth . . .
He practically owns all of Emeryville.
Are you friends with his daughter?
Guess so.
The truth was, I hoped so, but wasn't sure.
I'd been hanging out with Arianna, Amanda, and Marley almost every day, but it didn't seem like I was "one of them."
Not yet, anyway.
Marley
So excited you're coming shopping with us!!!!!
Me too!
YAS!
Or at least, I didn't feel like Arianna and Amanda were sure about me.

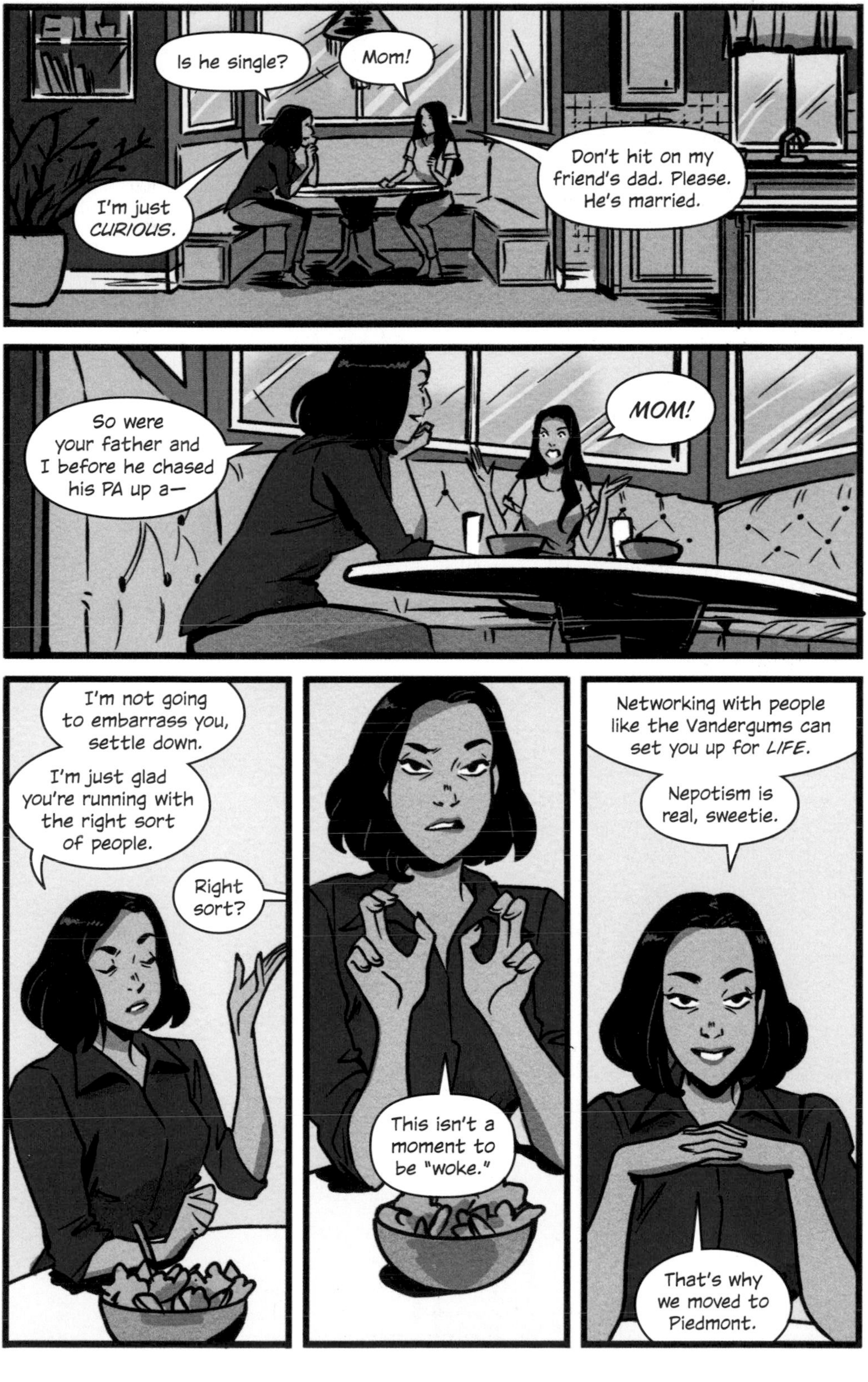
Is he single?
Mom!
I'm just CURIOUS.
Don't hit on my friend's dad. Please. He's married.
So were your father and I before he chased his PA up a—
MOM!
I'm not going to embarrass you, settle down.
I'm just glad you're running with the right sort of people.
Right sort?
This isn't a moment to be "woke."
Networking with people like the Vandergums can set you up for LIFE.
Nepotism is real, sweetie.
That's why we moved to Piedmont.

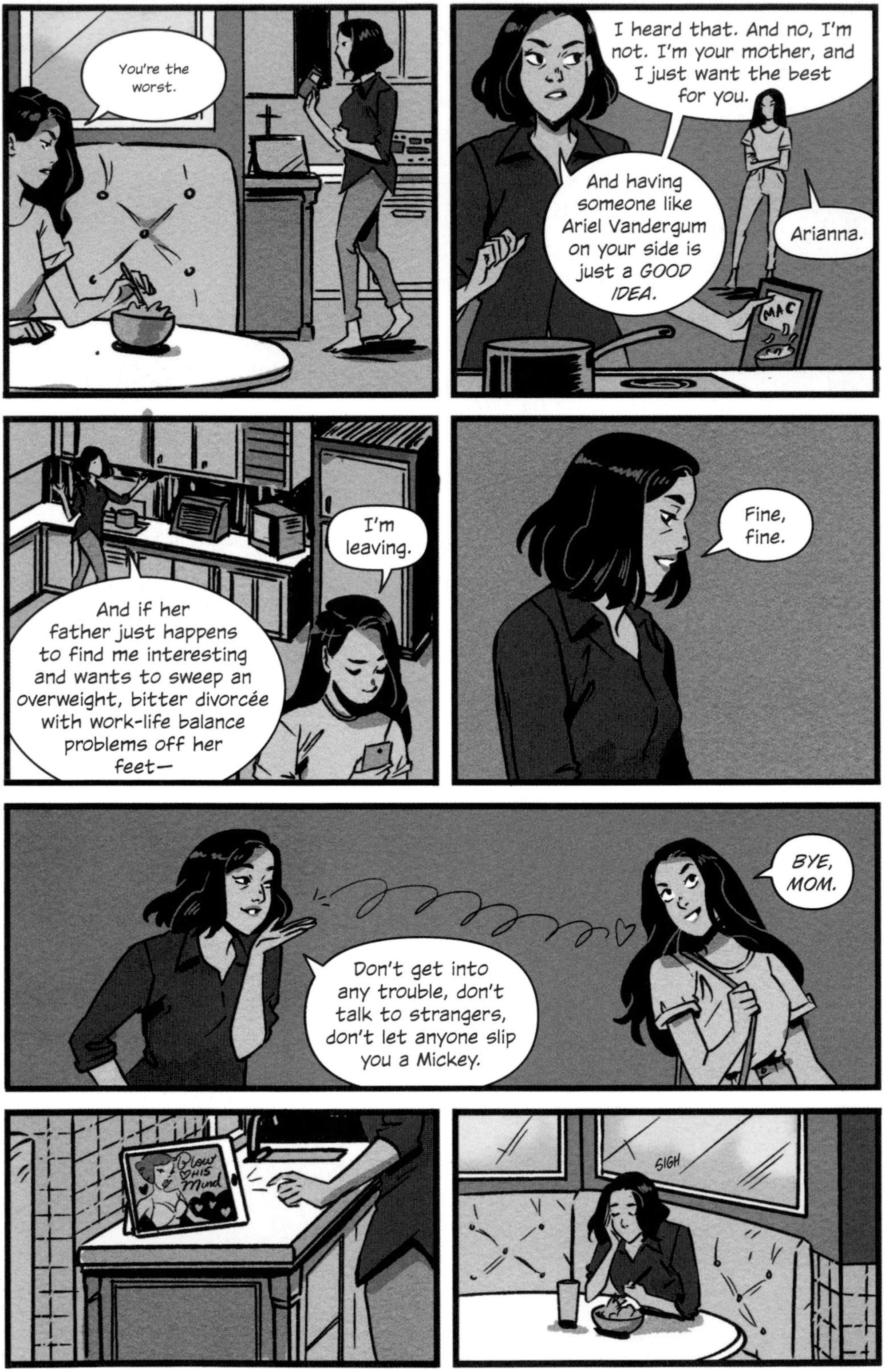
You're the worst.
I heard that. And no, I'm not. I'm your mother, and I just want the best for you.
And having someone like Ariel Vandergum on your side is just a *GOOD IDEA*.
Arianna.
MAC
I'm leaving.
And if her father just happens to find me interesting and wants to sweep an overweight, bitter divorcée with work-life balance problems off her feet—
Fine, fine.
BYE, MOM.
Don't get into any trouble, don't talk to strangers, don't let anyone slip you a Mickey.
Blow HIS Mind
SIGH

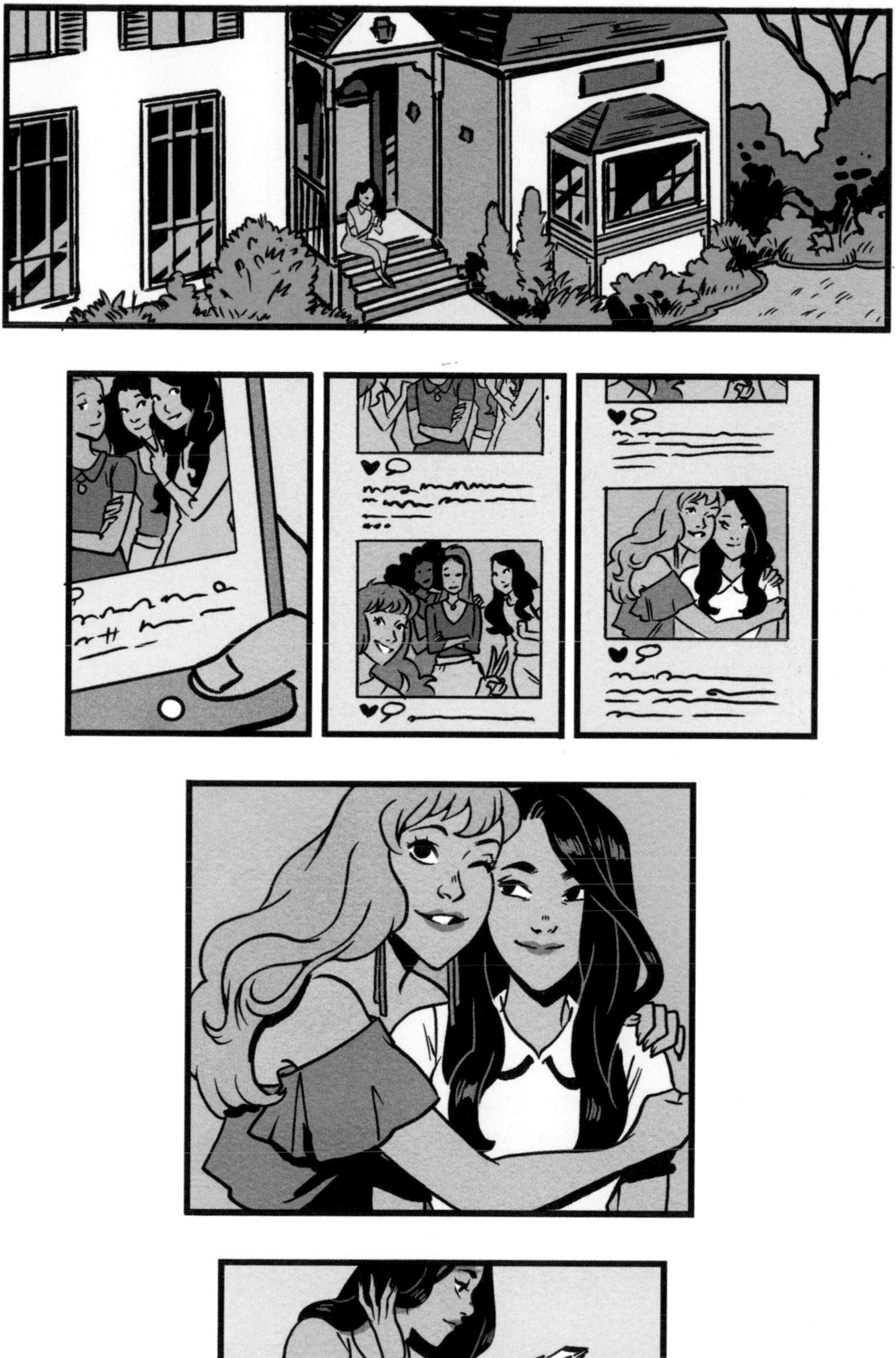

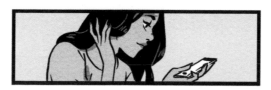

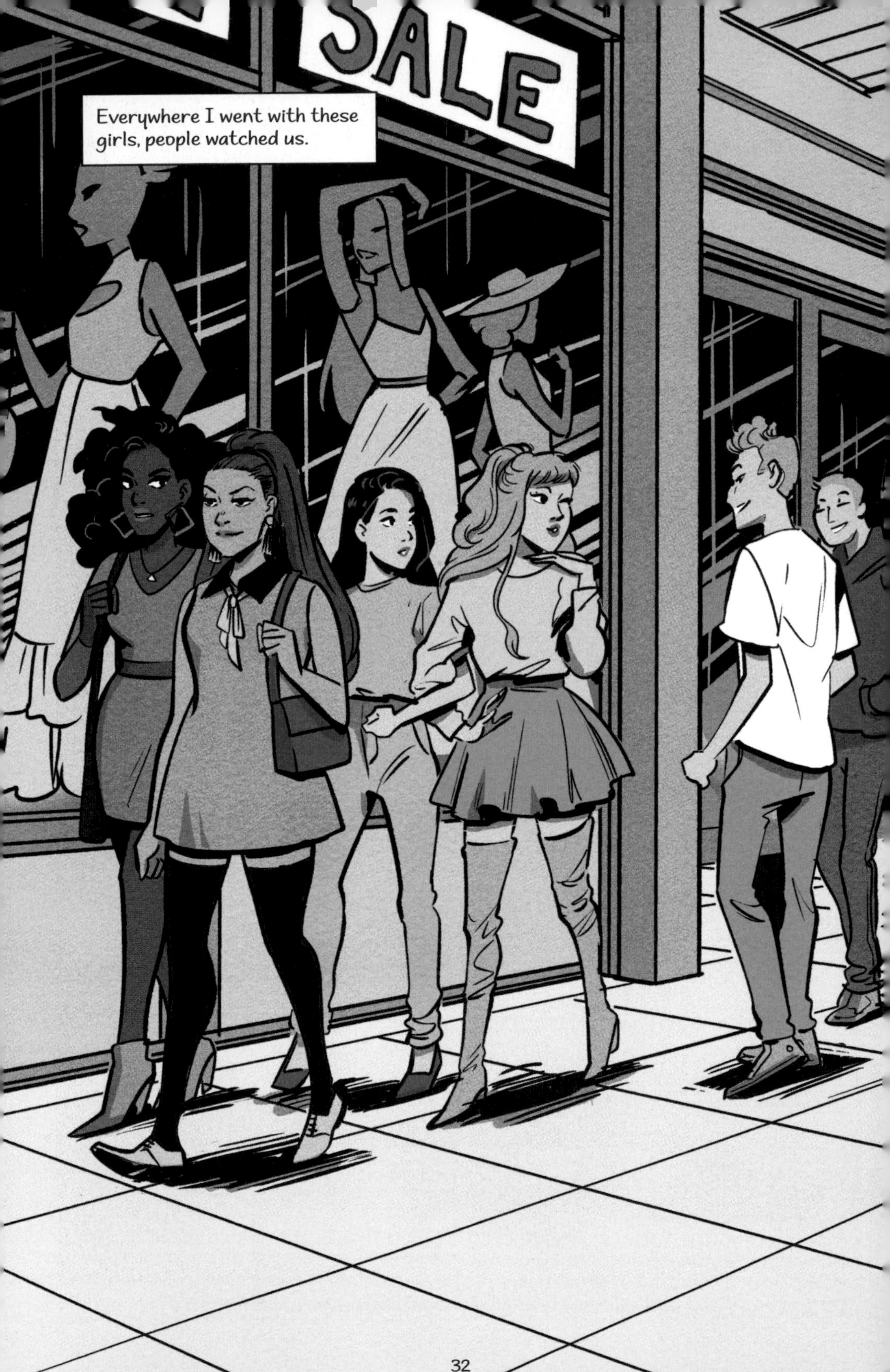
SALE
Everywhere I went with these girls, people watched us.

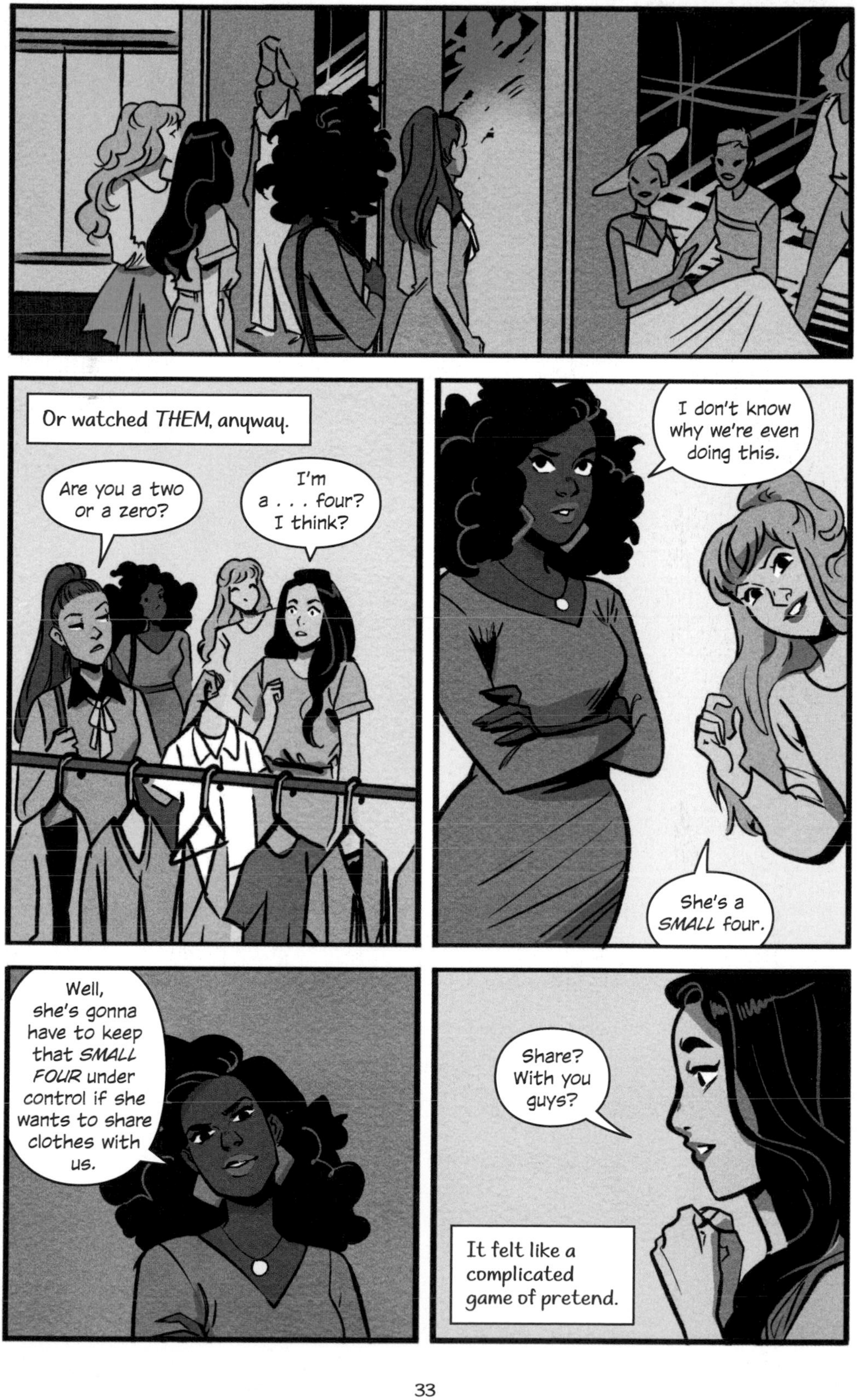
Or watched THEM, anyway.
Are you a two or a zero?
I'm a . . . four? I think?
I don't know why we're even doing this.
She's a SMALL four.
Well, she's gonna have to keep that SMALL FOUR under control if she wants to share clothes with us.
Share? With you guys?
It felt like a complicated game of pretend.

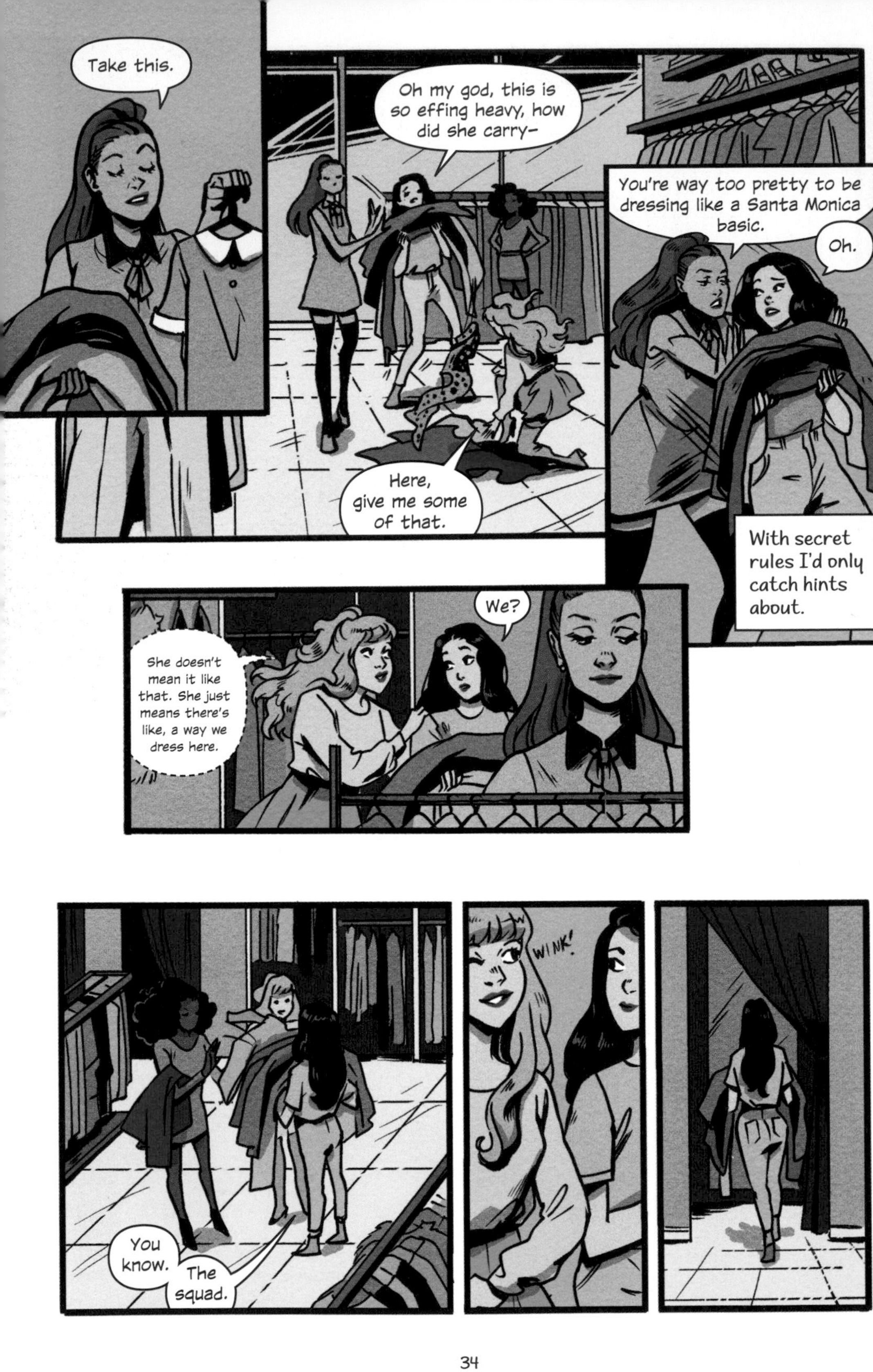

Take this.
Oh my god, this is so effing heavy, how did she carry–
Here, give me some of that.
You're way too pretty to be dressing like a Santa Monica basic.
Oh.
With secret rules I'd only catch hints about.
We?
She doesn't mean it like that. She just means there's like, a way we dress here.
You know.
The squad.
WINK!

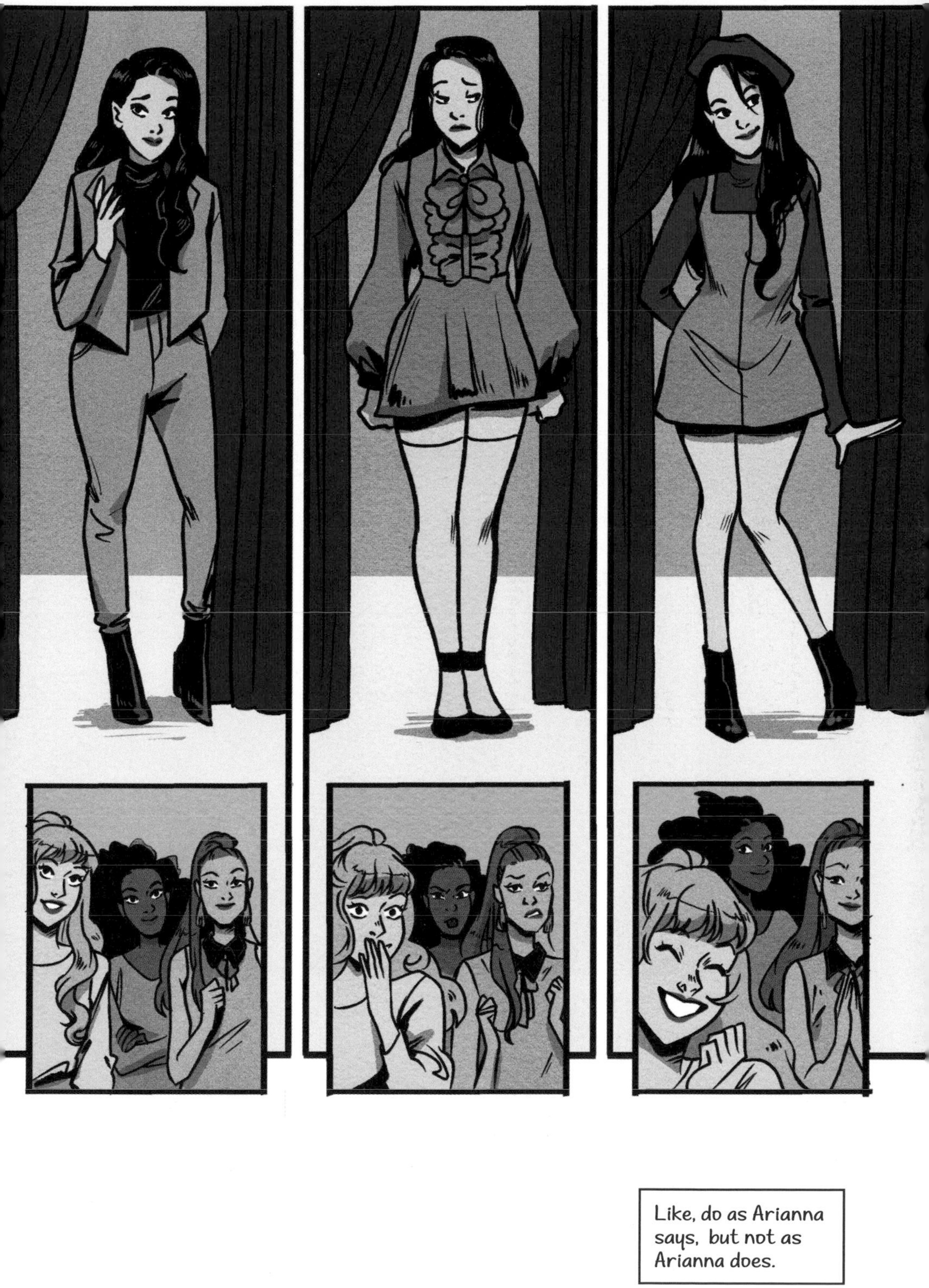
Like, do as Arianna says, but not as Arianna does.

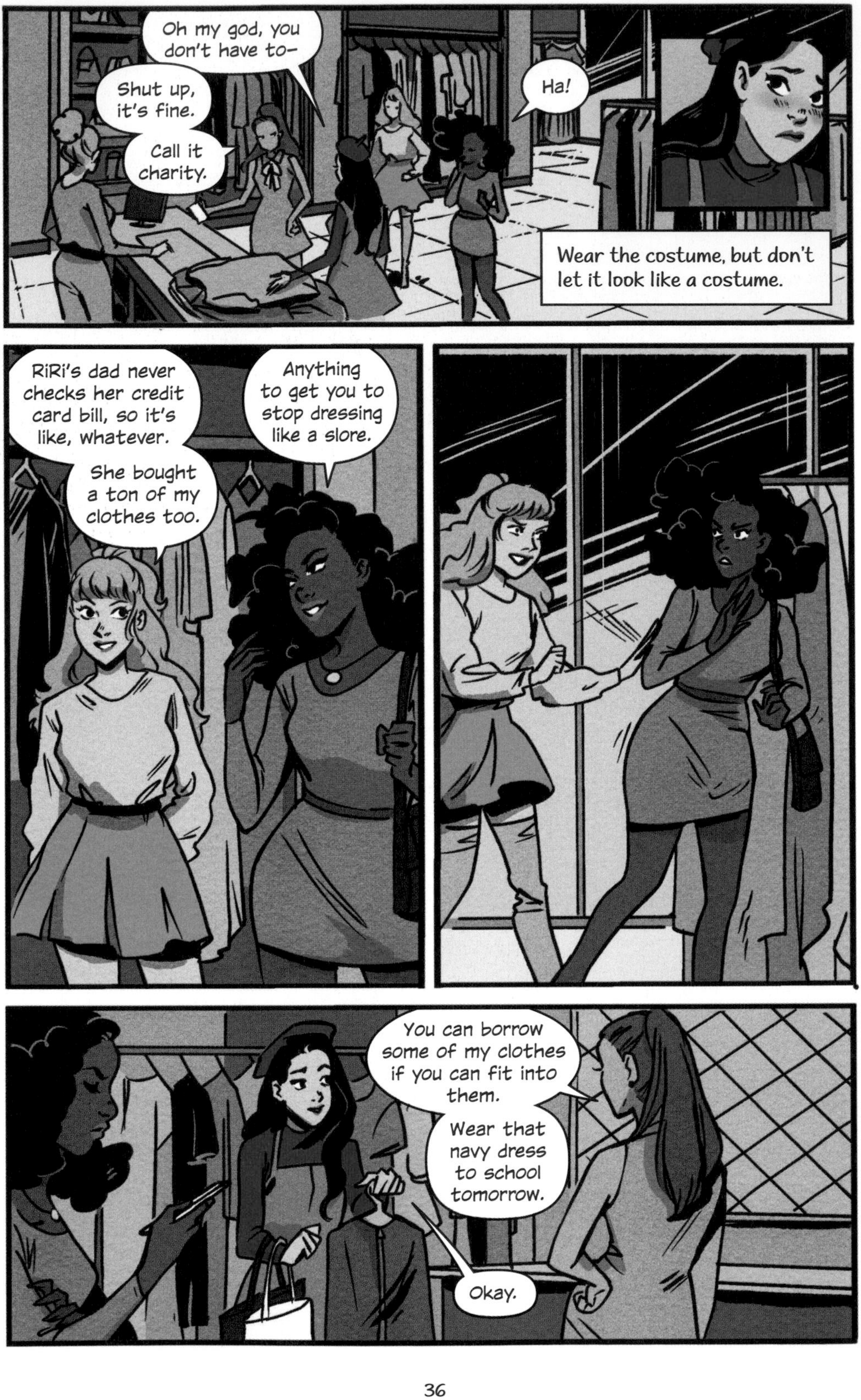
Oh my god, you don't have to–
Shut up, it's fine.
Call it charity.
Ha!
Wear the costume, but don't let it look like a costume.
RiRi's dad never checks her credit card bill, so it's like, whatever.
She bought a ton of my clothes too.
Anything to get you to stop dressing like a slore.
You can borrow some of my clothes if you can fit into them.
Wear that navy dress to school tomorrow.
Okay.

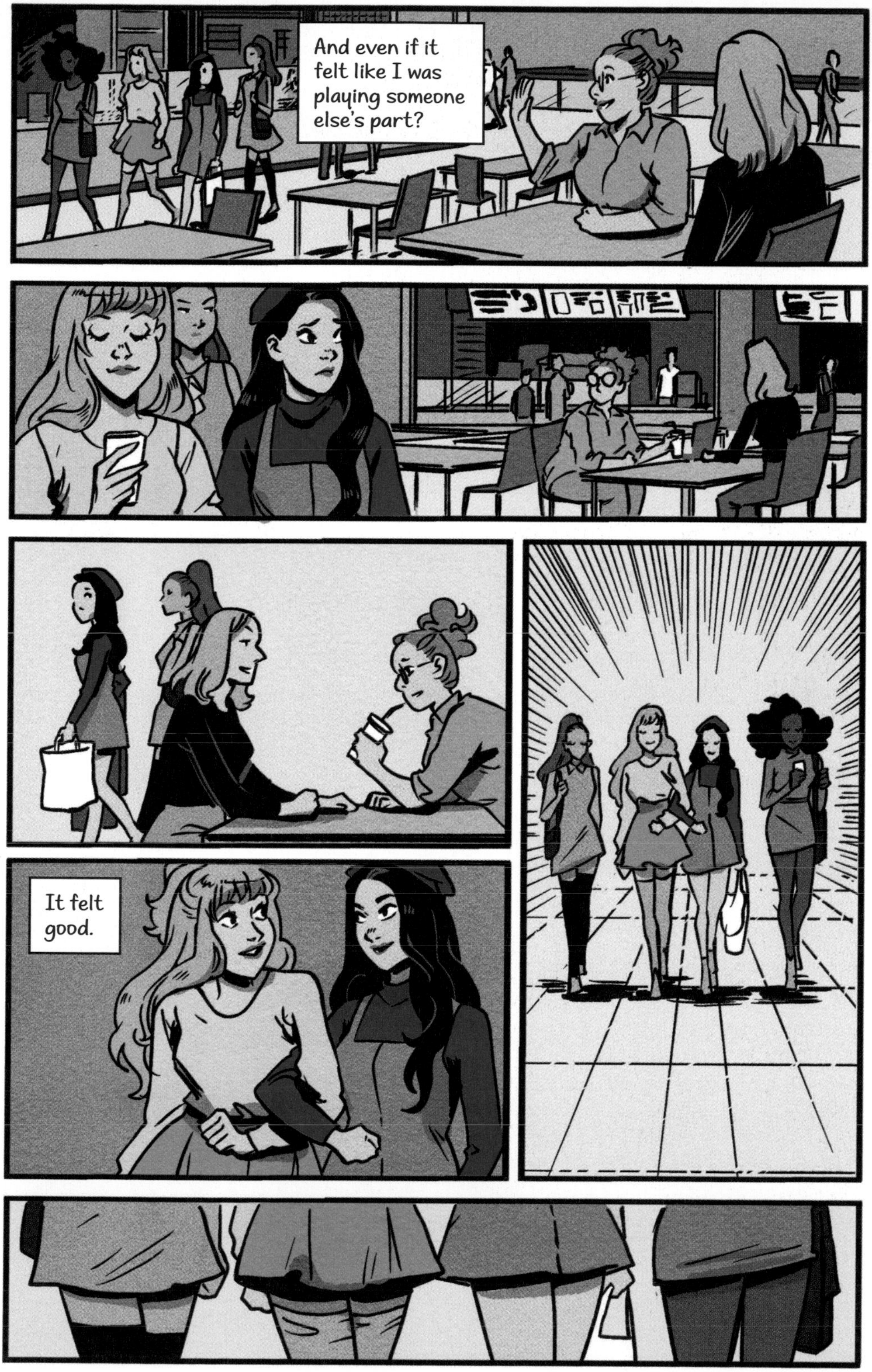
And even if it felt like I was playing someone else's part?
It felt good.

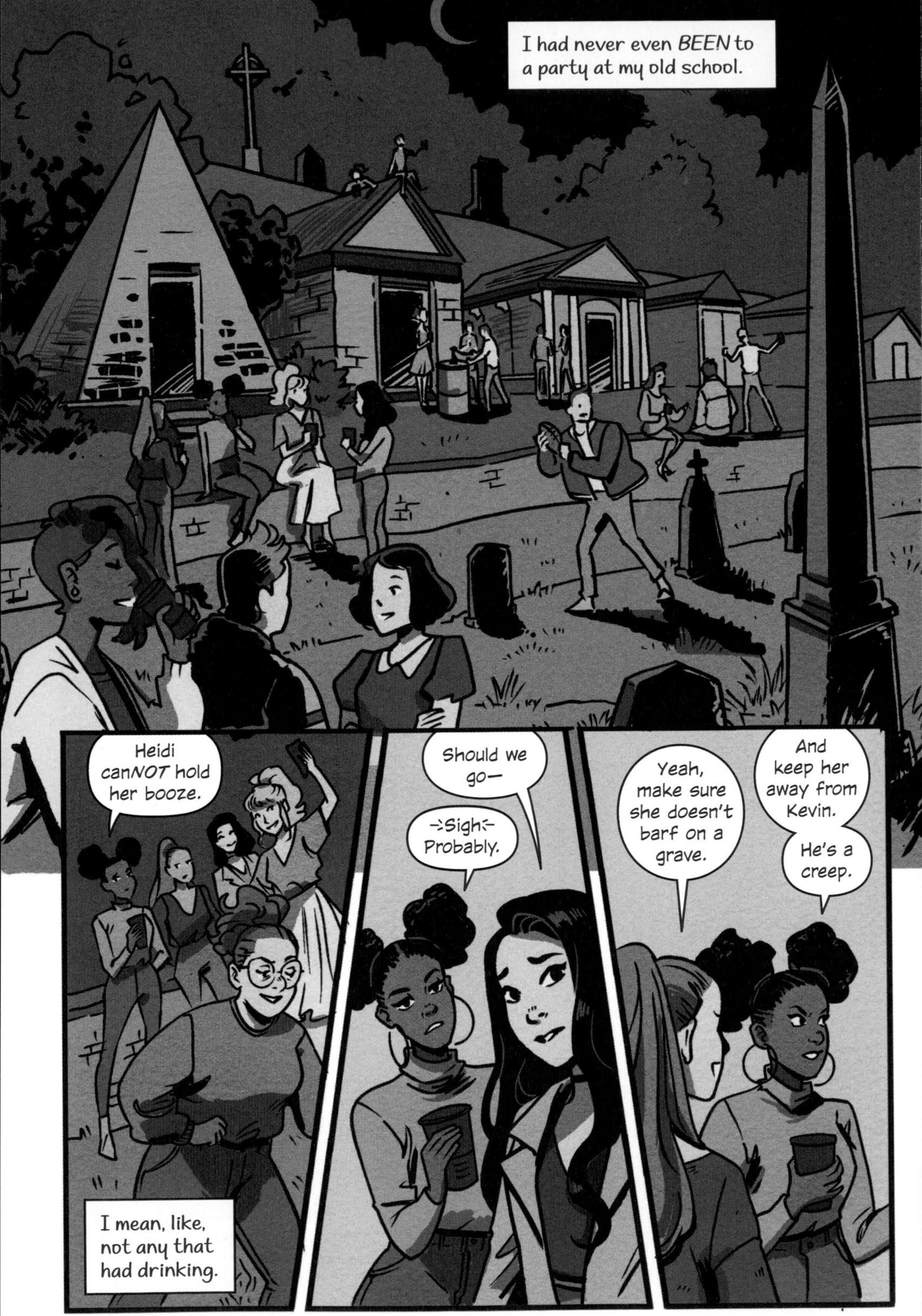

I had never even BEEN to a party at my old school.
Heidi canNOT hold her booze.
I mean, like, not any that had drinking.
Should we go—
-Sigh- Probably.
Yeah, make sure she doesn't barf on a grave.
And keep her away from Kevin.
He's a creep.

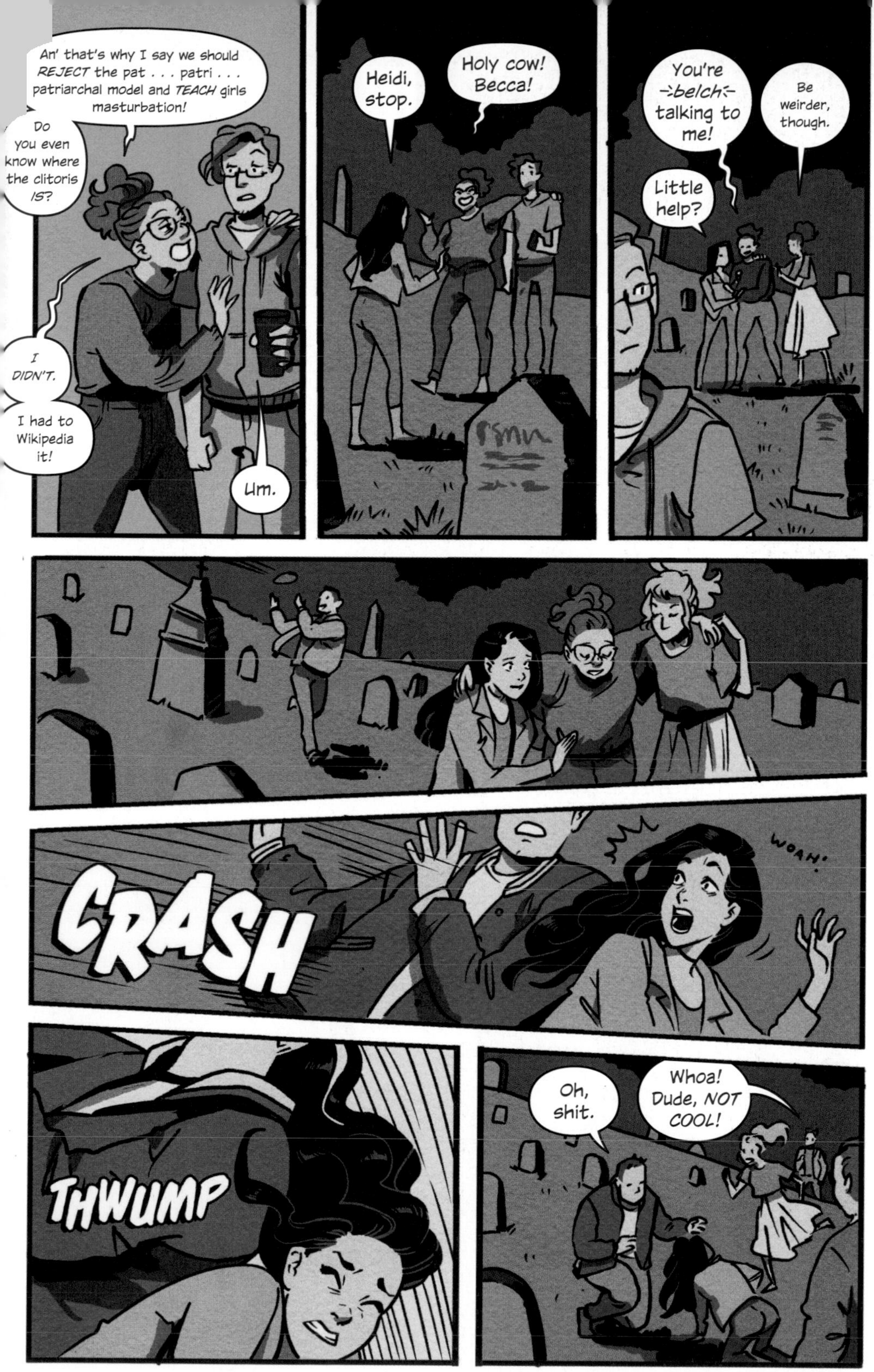
An' that's why I say we should REJECT the pat . . . patri . . . patriarchal model and TEACH girls masturbation!
Do you even know where the clitoris IS?
I DIDN'T.
I had to Wikipedia it!
Um.
Heidi, stop.
Holy cow! Becca!
You're ~belch~ talking to me!
Be weirder, though.
Little help?
WOAH!
CRASH
THWUMP
Oh, shit.
Whoa! Dude, NOT COOL!

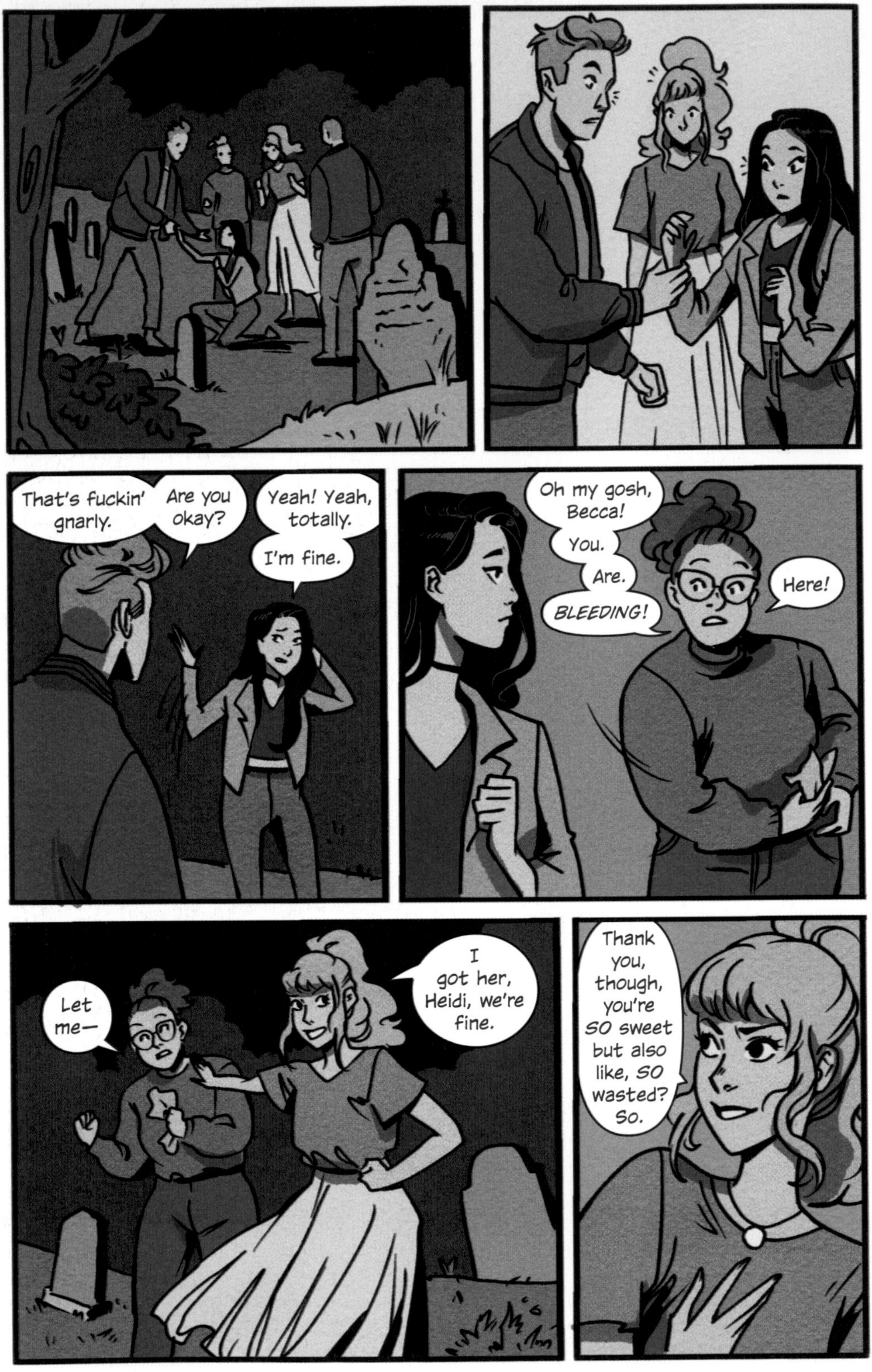
That's fuckin' gnarly.
Are you okay?
Yeah! Yeah, totally.
I'm fine.
Oh my gosh, Becca!
You.
Are.
BLEEDING!
Here!
Let me—
I got her, Heidi, we're fine.
Thank you, though, you're SO sweet but also like, SO wasted? So.

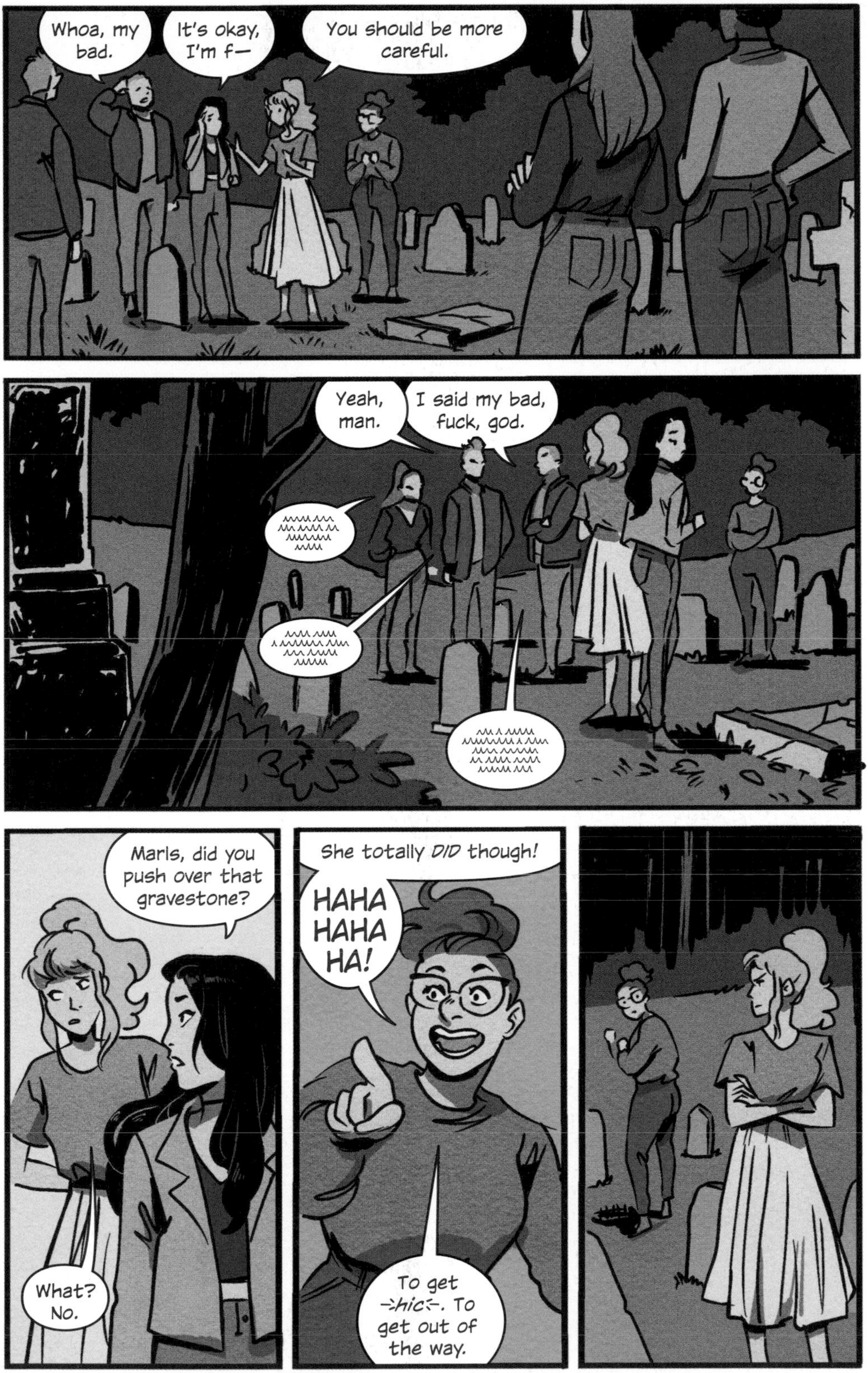
Whoa, my bad.
It's okay, I'm f—
You should be more careful.
Yeah, man.
I said my bad, fuck, god.
Marls, did you push over that gravestone?
What? No.
She totally DID though!
HAHA HAHA HA!
To get -hic-. To get out of the way.

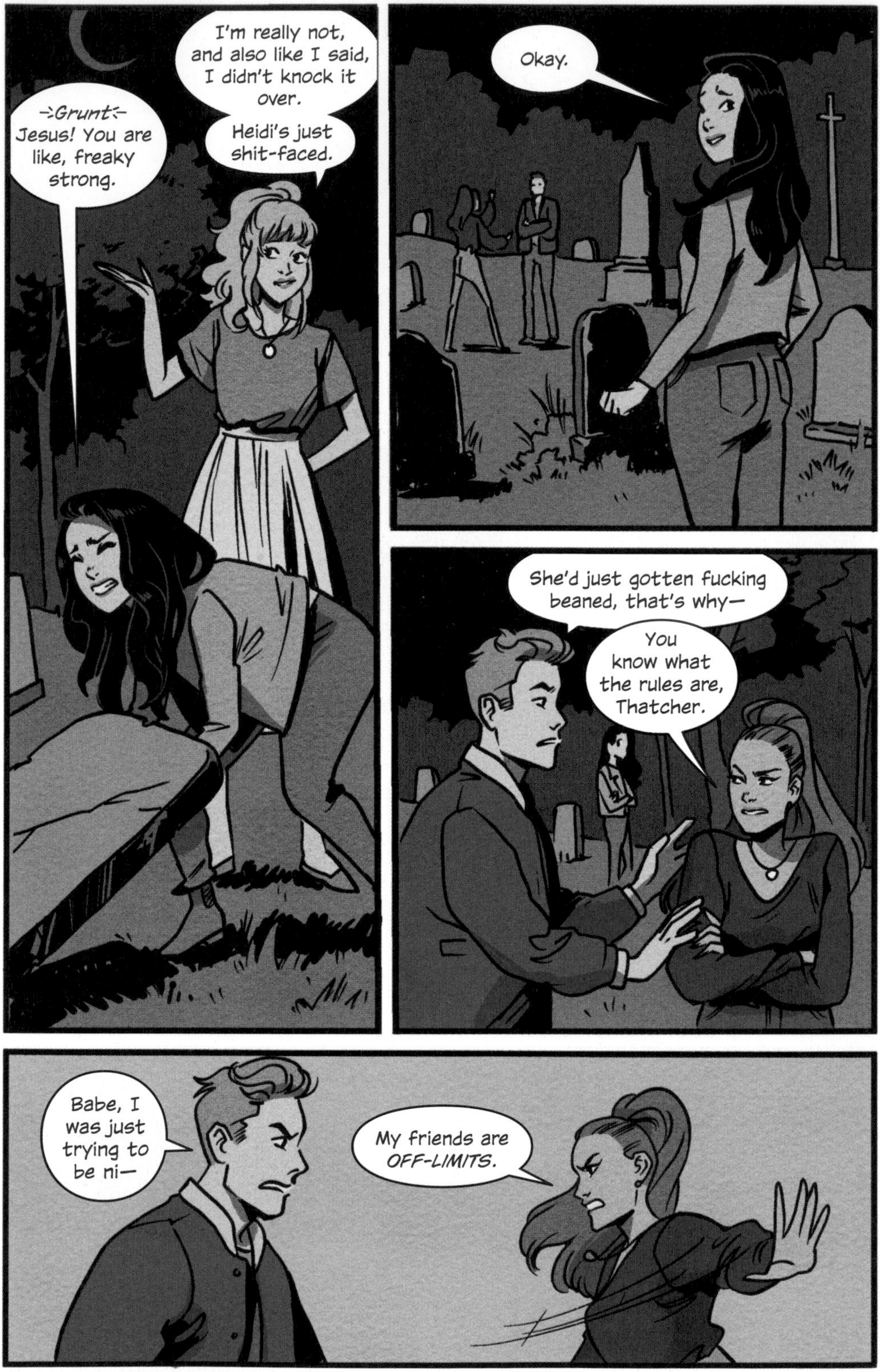
-Grunt-
Jesus! You are like, freaky strong.
I'm really not, and also like I said, I didn't knock it over.
Heidi's just shit-faced.
Okay.
She'd just gotten fucking beaned, that's why—
You know what the rules are, Thatcher.
Babe, I was just trying to be ni—
My friends are OFF-LIMITS.

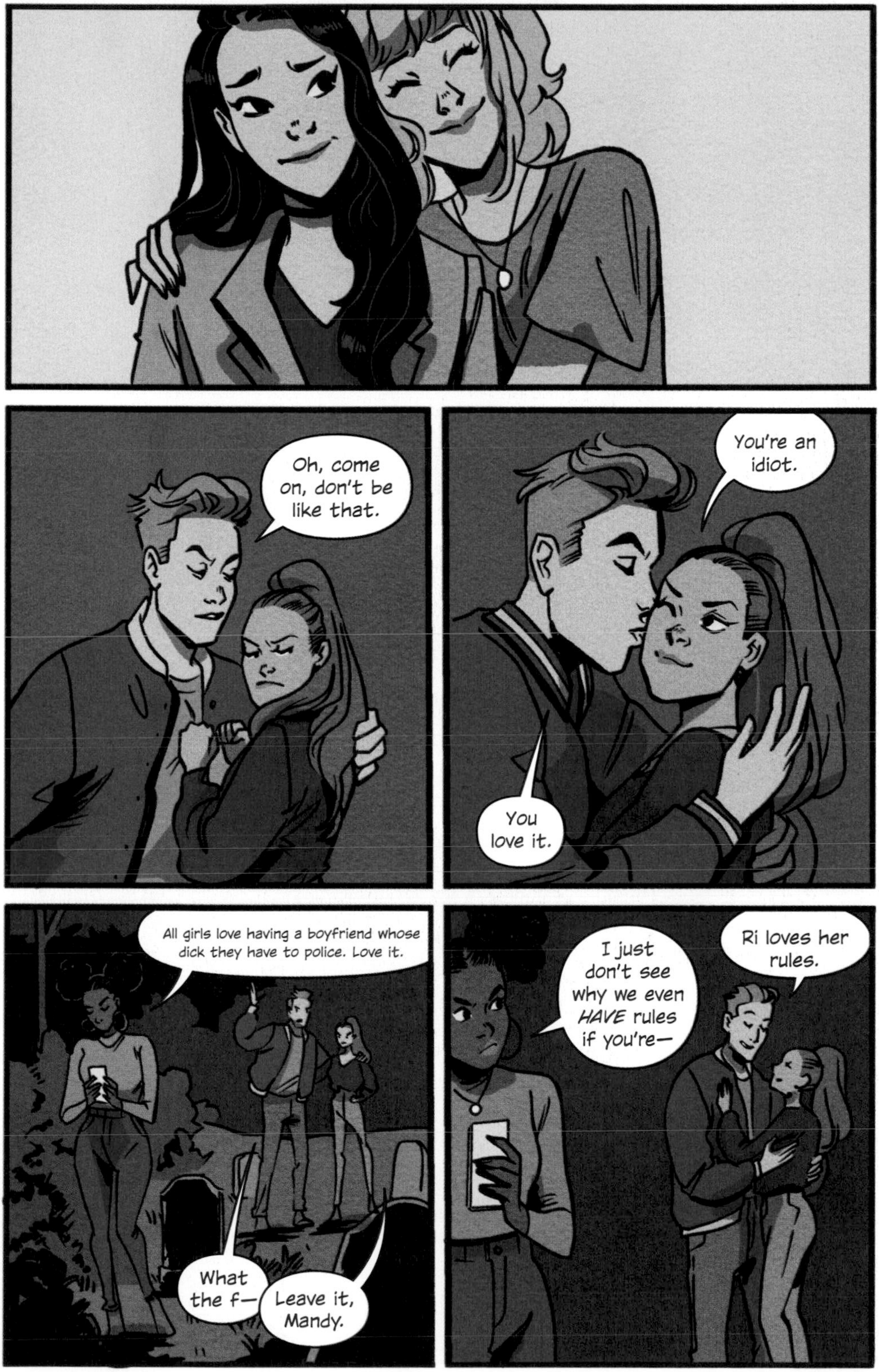
Oh, come on, don't be like that.
You're an idiot.
You love it.
All girls love having a boyfriend whose dick they have to police. Love it.
What the f—
Leave it, Mandy.
I just don't see why we even *HAVE* rules if you're—
Ri loves her rules.

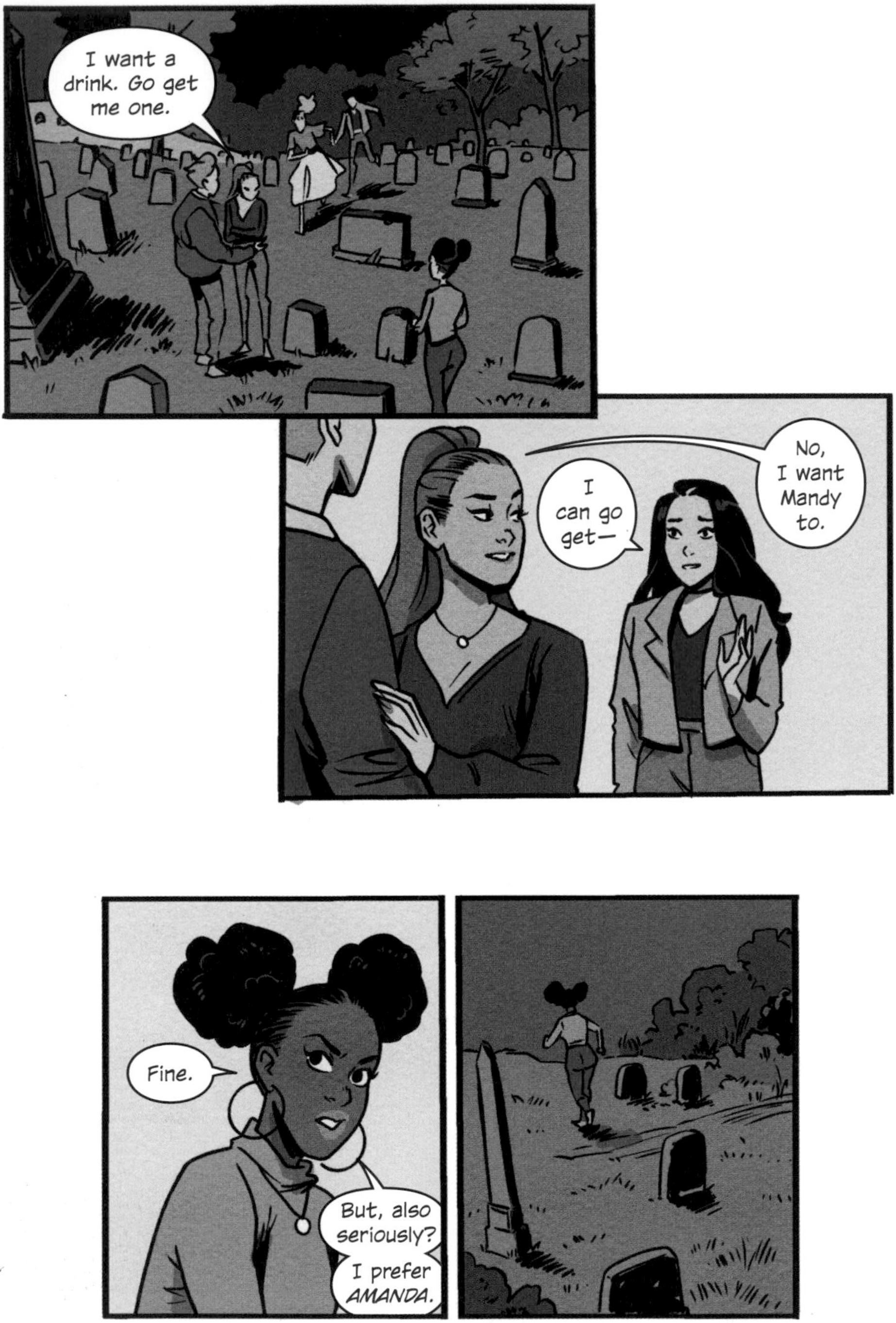
I want a drink. Go get me one.
I can go get—
No, I want Mandy to.
Fine.
But, also seriously?
I prefer *AMANDA*.

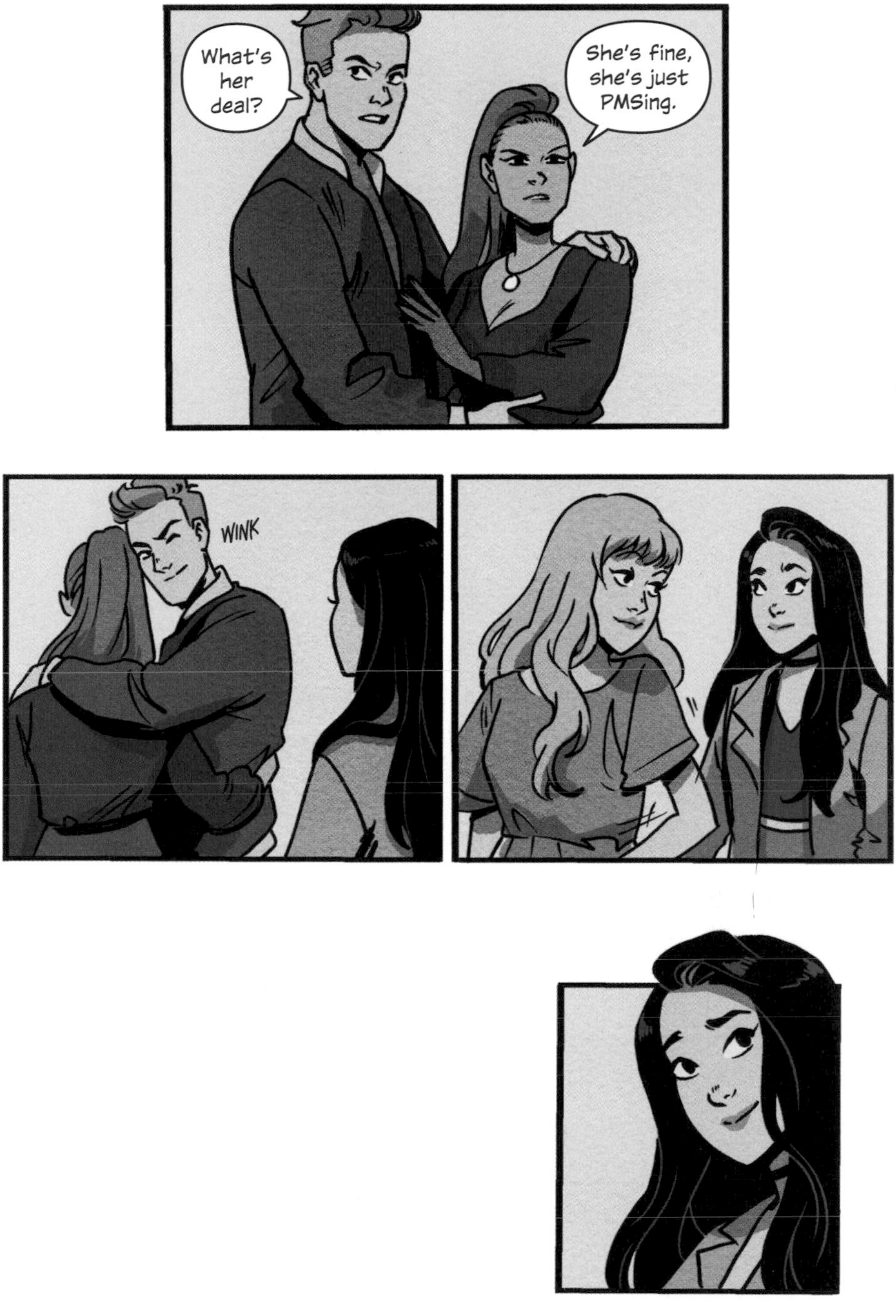
What's her deal?
She's fine, she's just PMSing.
WINK

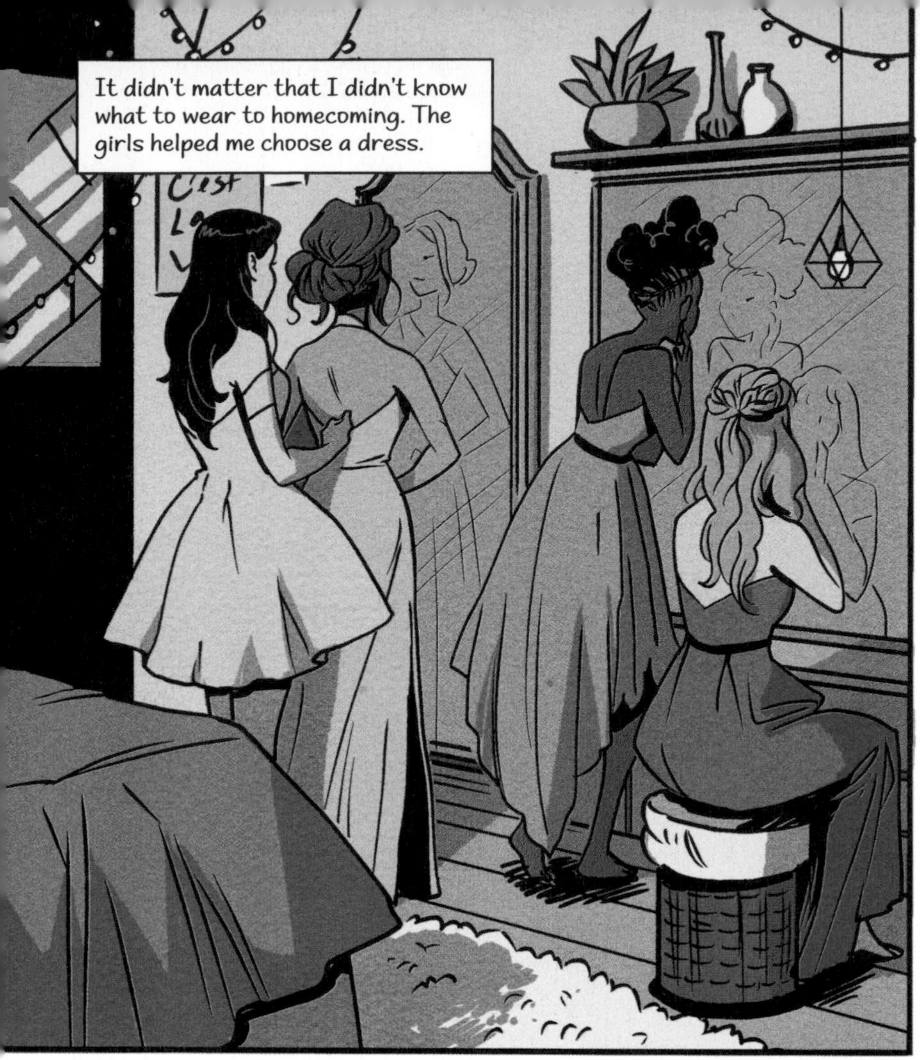
It didn't matter that I didn't know what to wear to homecoming. The girls helped me choose a dress.

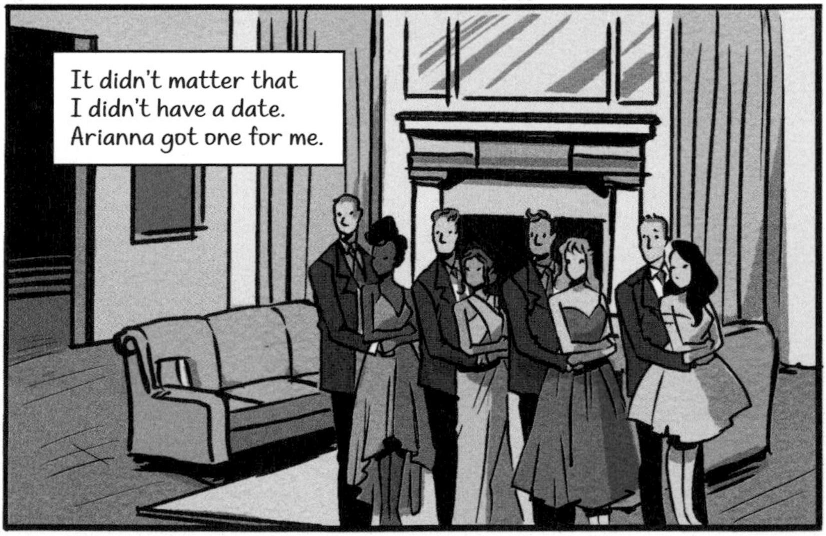
It didn't matter that I didn't have a date. Arianna got one for me.

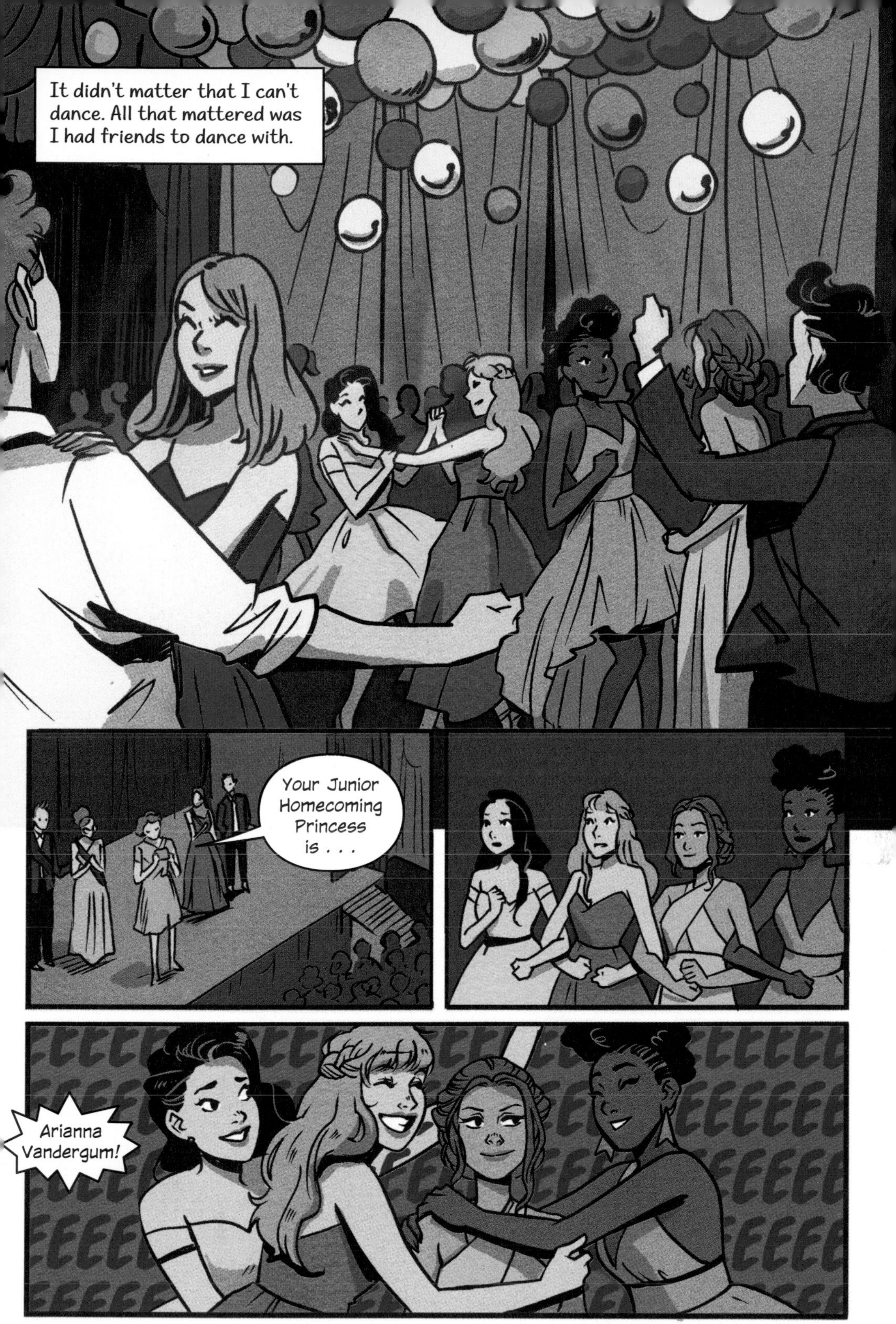

It didn't matter that I can't dance. All that mattered was I had friends to dance with.
Your Junior Homecoming Princess is . . .
Arianna Vandergum!

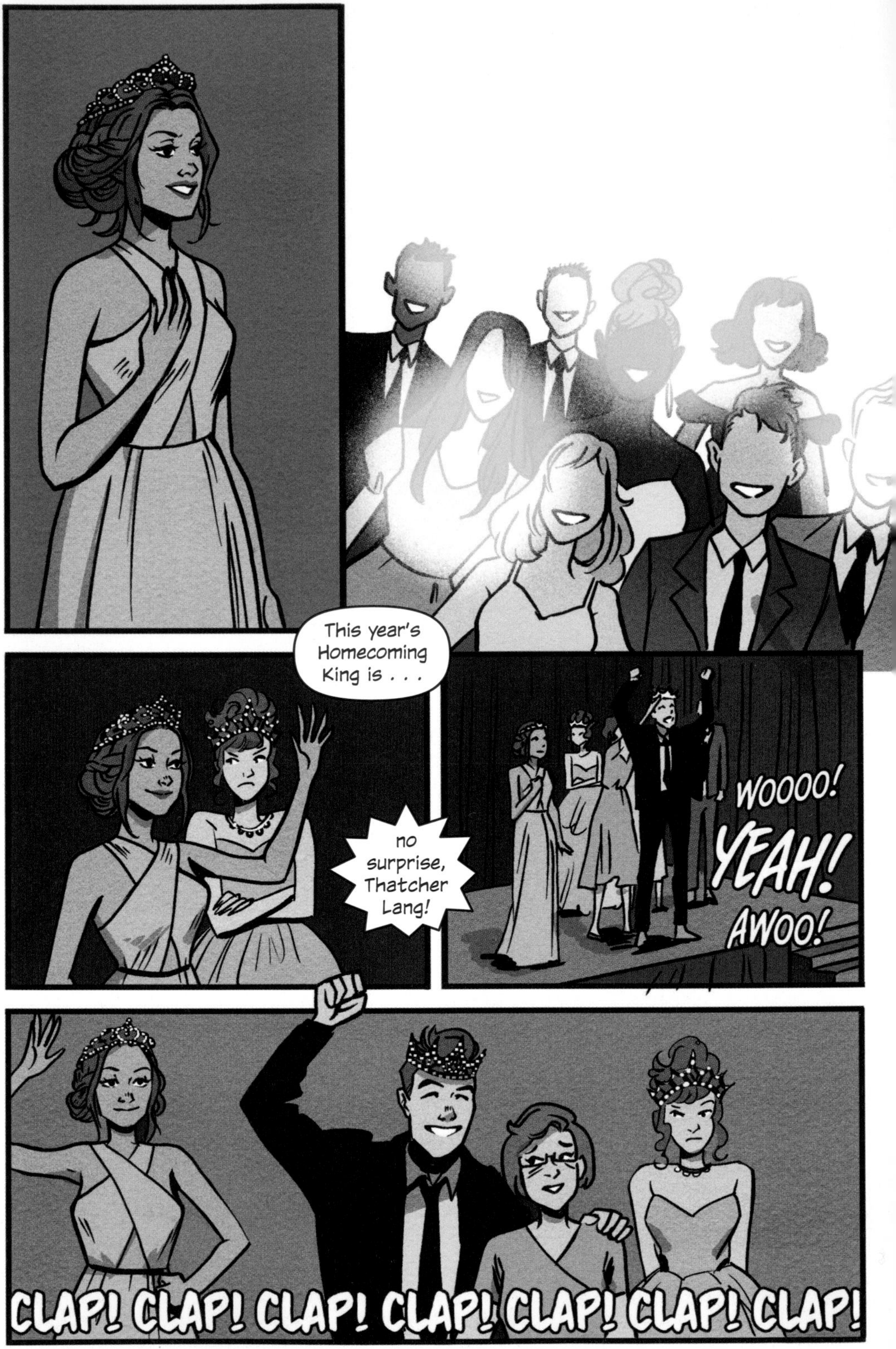
This year's Homecoming King is . . .
no surprise, Thatcher Lang!
WOOOO!
YEAH!
AWOO!
CLAP! CLAP! CLAP! CLAP! CLAP! CLAP! CLAP!

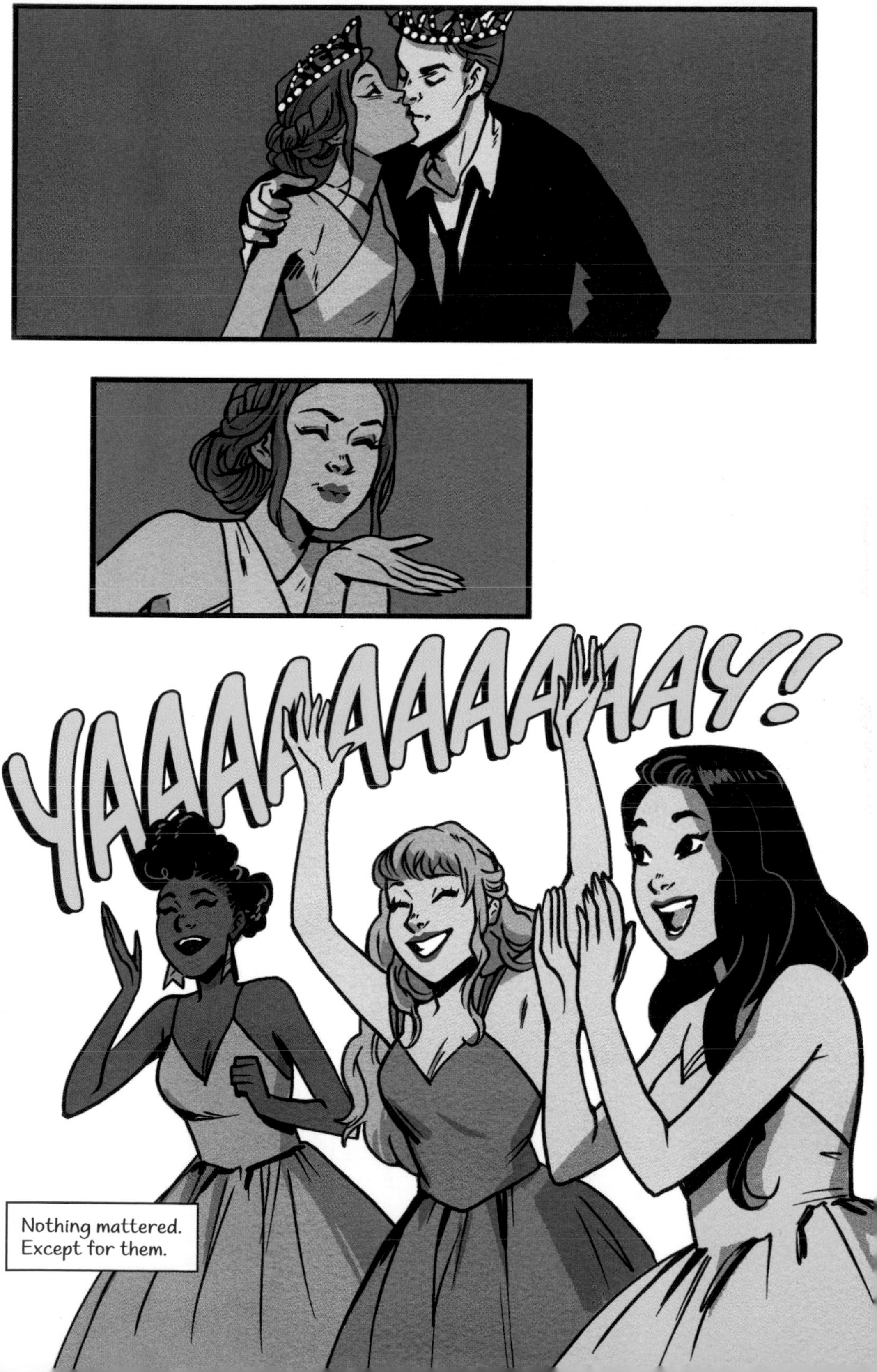
YAAAAAAAAAAAY!
Nothing mattered. Except for them.

CHAPTER THREE

SCREAM BLOODY MURDER

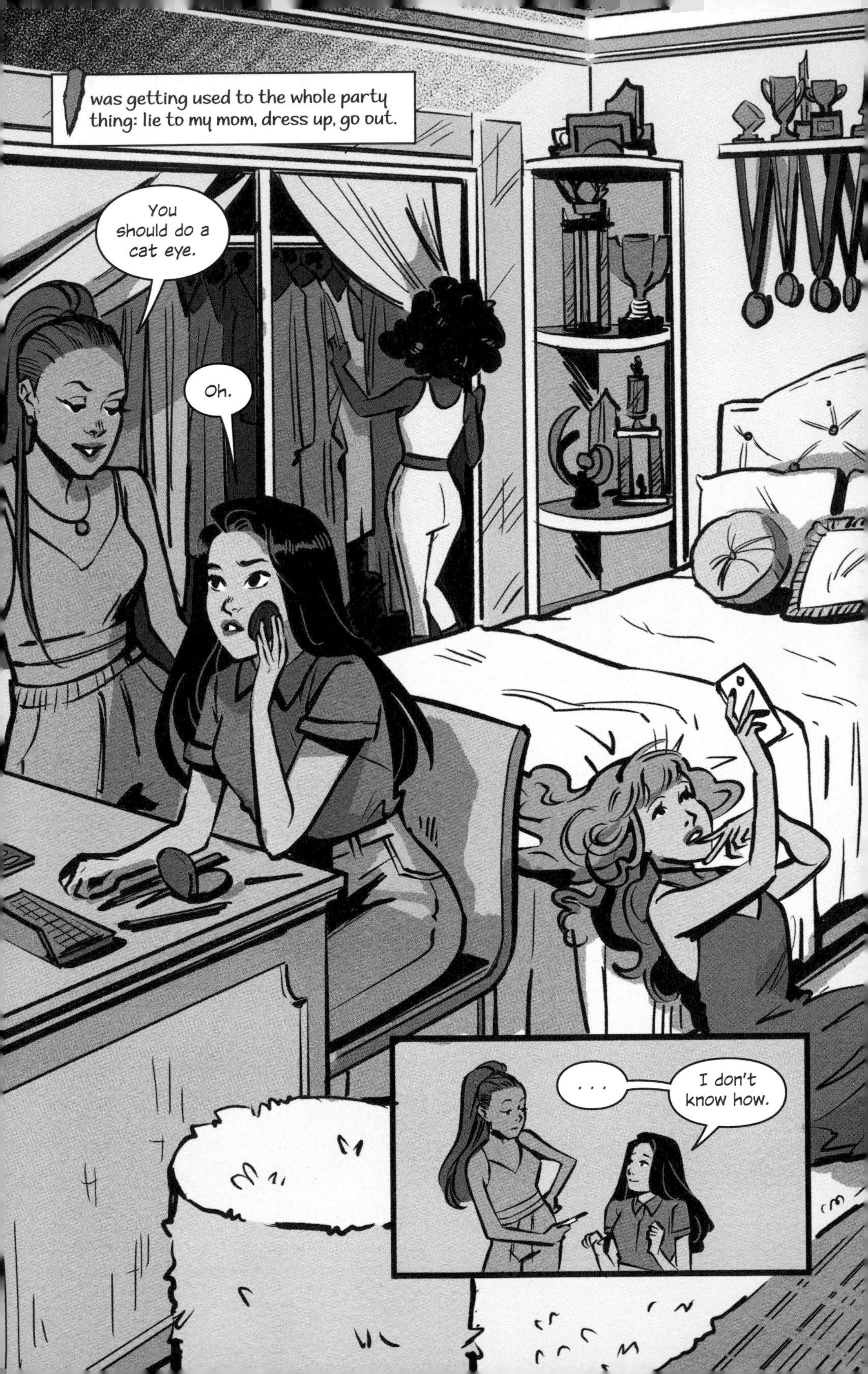
was getting used to the whole party thing: lie to my mom, dress up, go out.
You should do a cat eye.
Oh.
. . .
I don't know how.

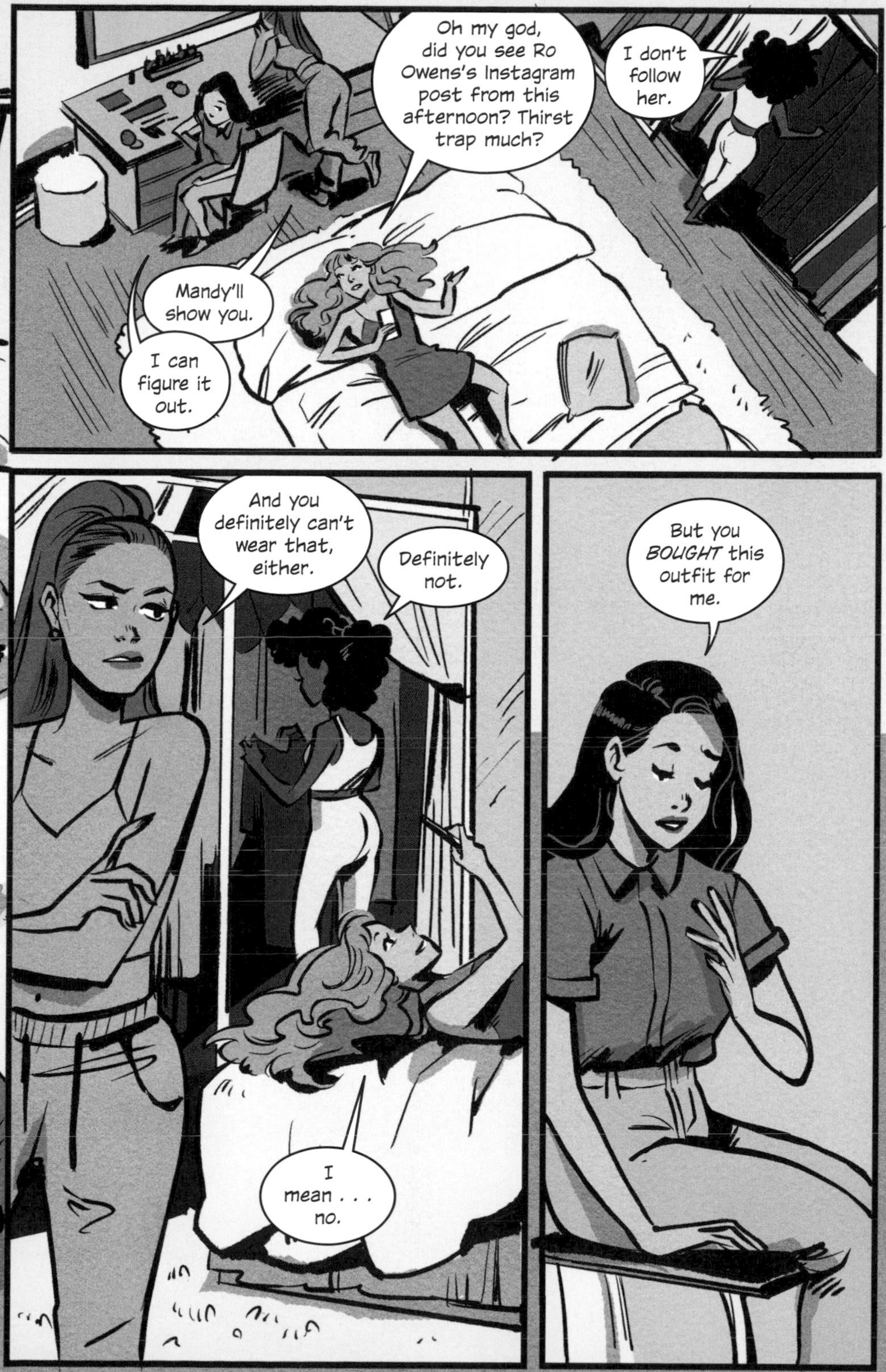
Oh my god, did you see Ro Owens's Instagram post from this afternoon? Thirst trap much?
I don't follow her.
Mandy'll show you.
I can figure it out.
And you definitely can't wear that, either.
Definitely not.
I mean . . . no.
But you *BOUGHT* this outfit for me.

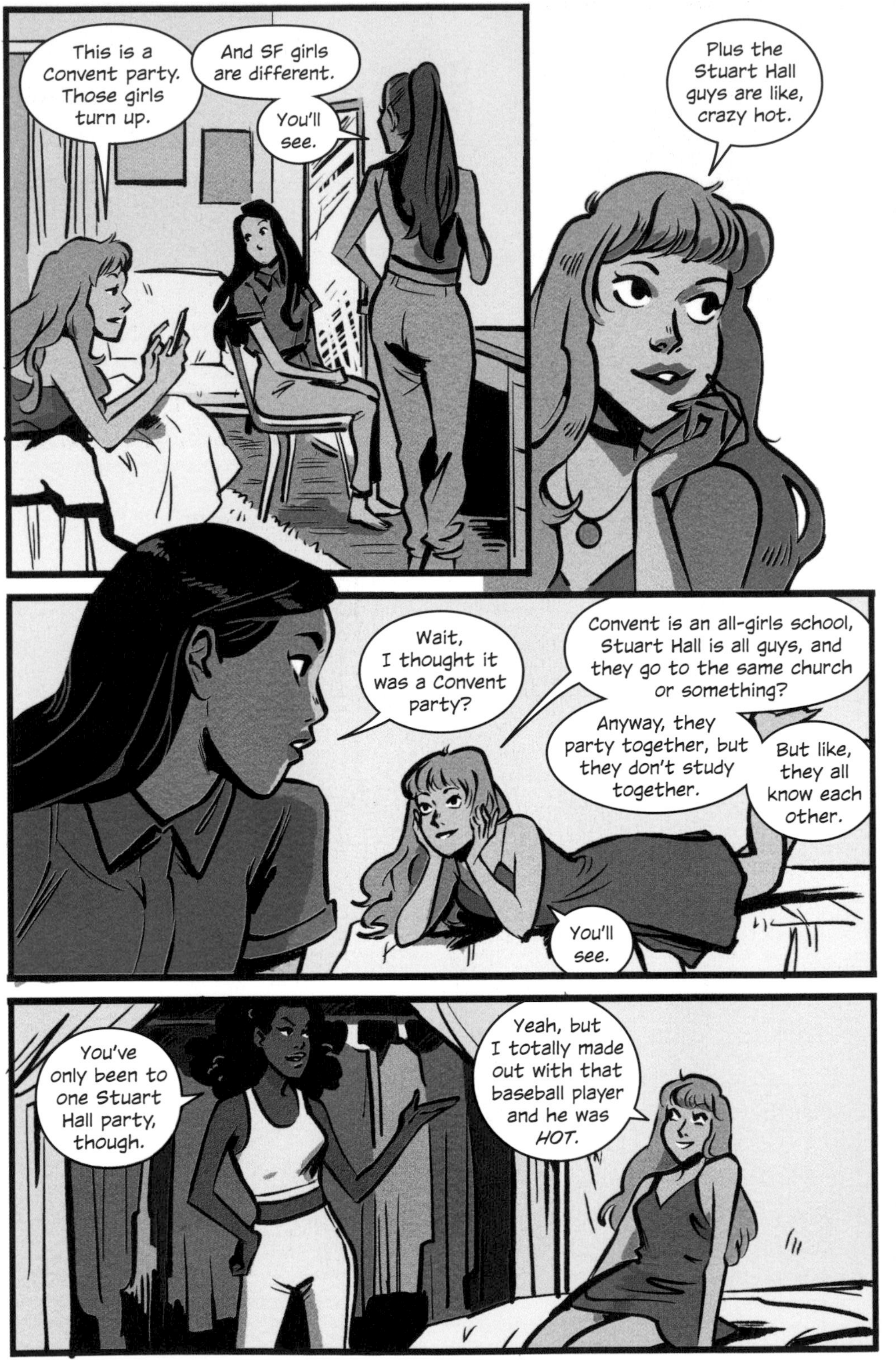

This is a Convent party. Those girls turn up.
And SF girls are different.
You'll see.
Plus the Stuart Hall guys are like, crazy hot.
Wait, I thought it was a Convent party?
Convent is an all-girls school, Stuart Hall is all guys, and they go to the same church or something?
Anyway, they party together, but they don't study together.
But like, they all know each other.
You'll see.
You've only been to one Stuart Hall party, though.
Yeah, but I totally made out with that baseball player and he was *HOT*.

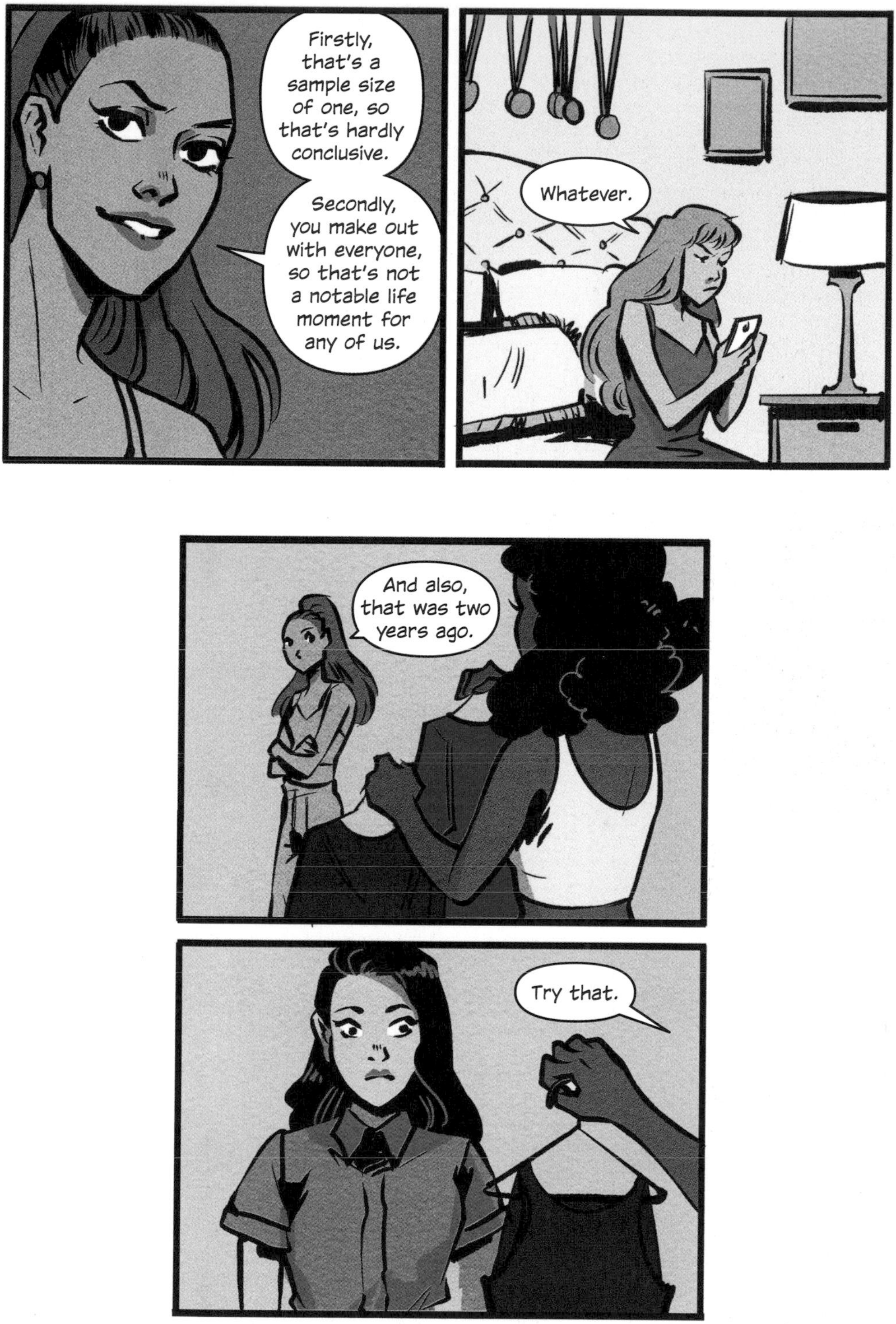
Firstly, that's a sample size of one, so that's hardly conclusive.
Secondly, you make out with everyone, so that's not a notable life moment for any of us.
Whatever.
And also, that was two years ago.
Try that.

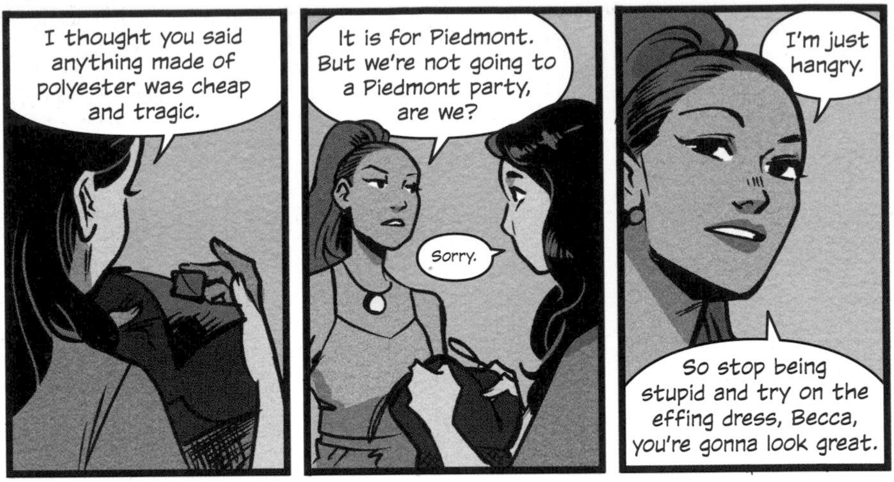
I thought you said anything made of polyester was cheap and tragic.
It is for Piedmont. But we're not going to a Piedmont party, are we?
Sorry.
I'm just hangry.
So stop being stupid and try on the effing dress, Becca, you're gonna look great.

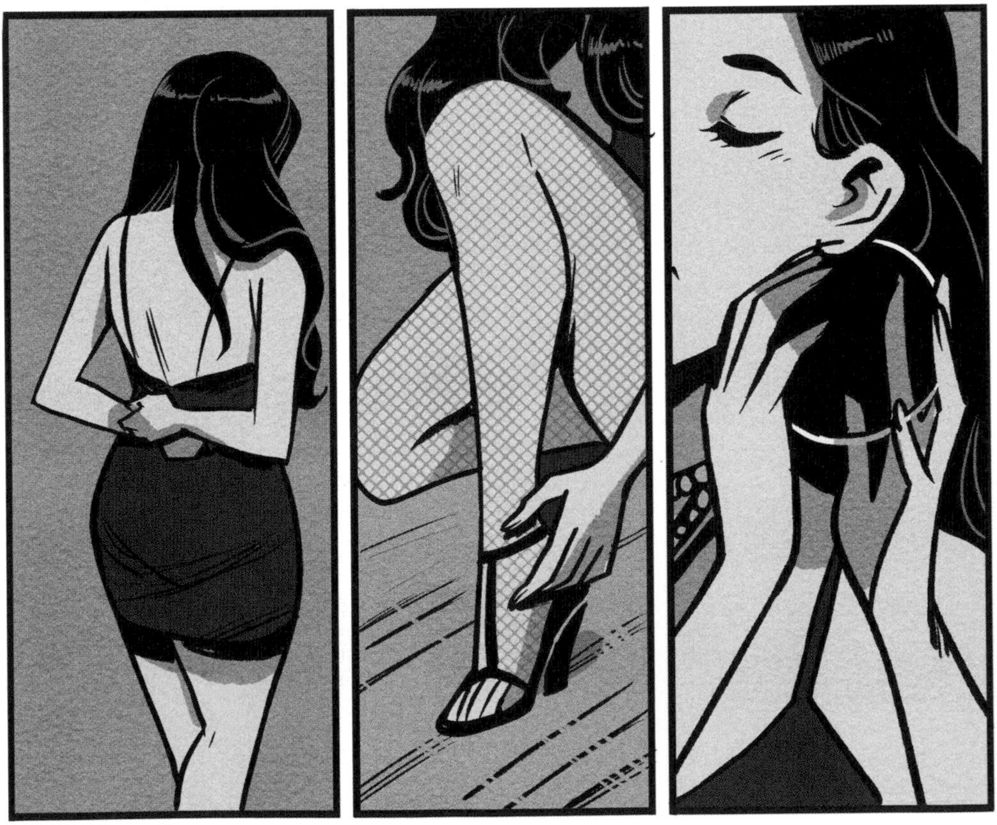

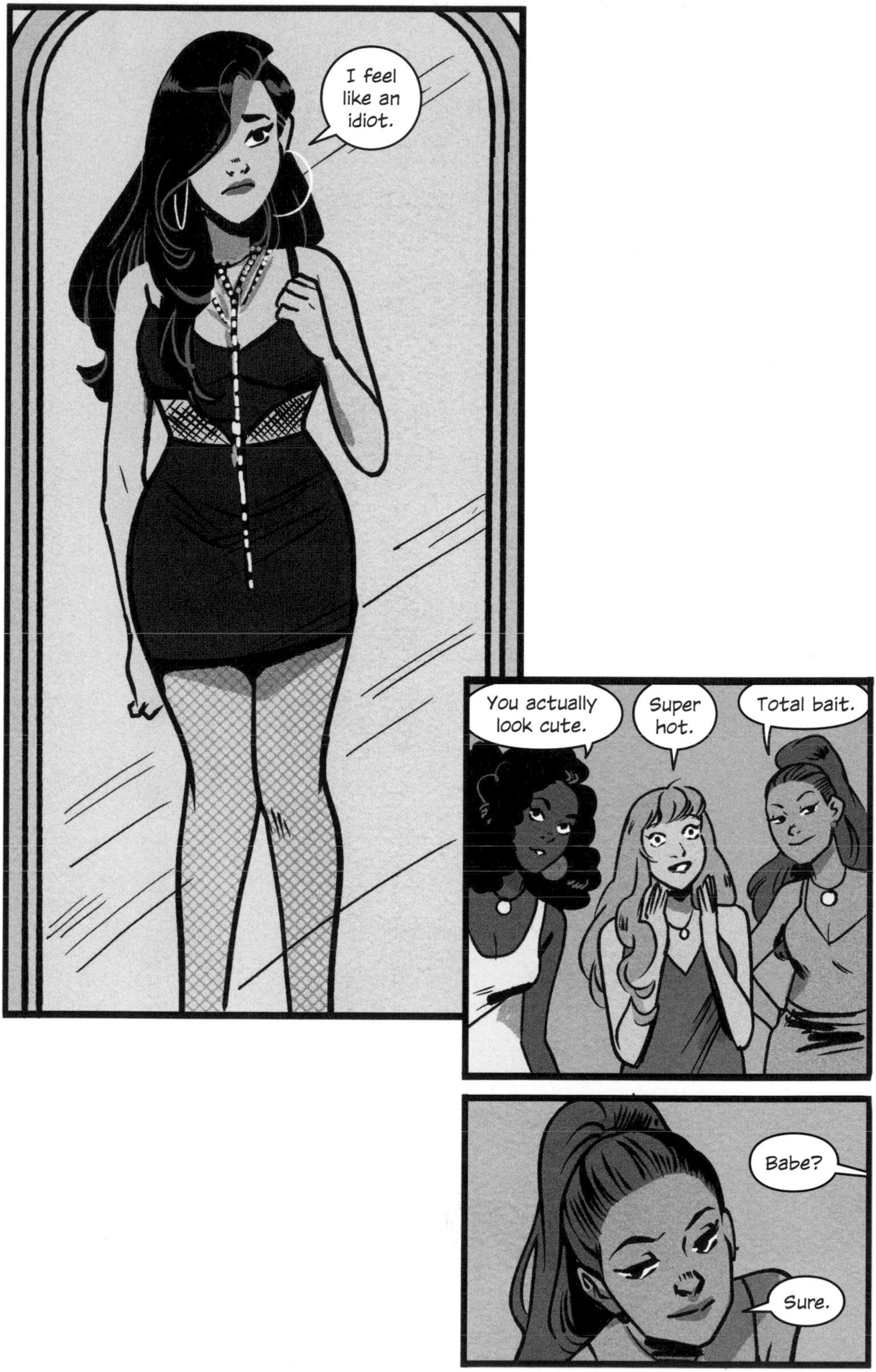
I feel like an idiot.
You actually look cute.
Super hot.
Total bait.
Babe?
Sure.

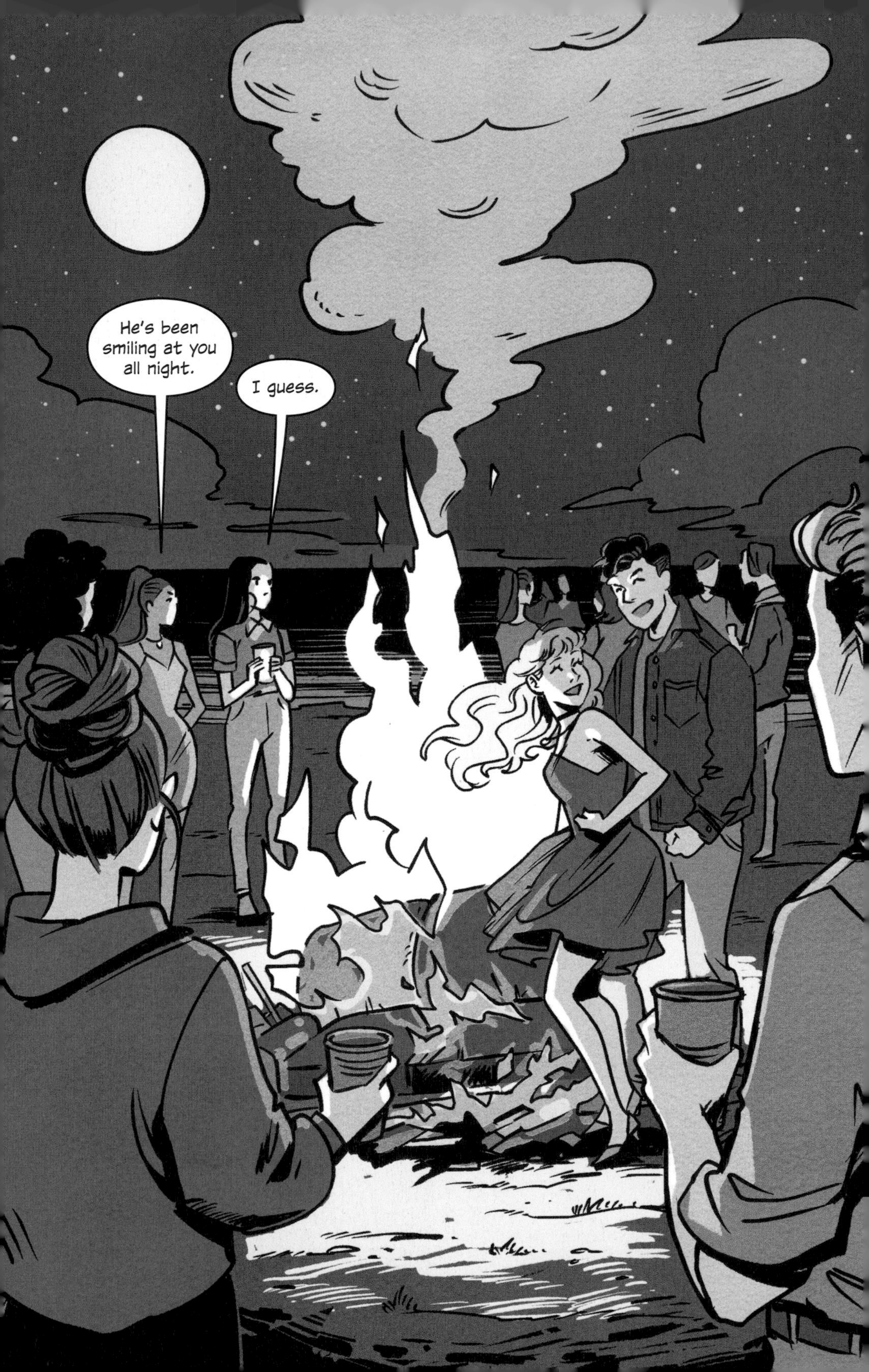
He's been smiling at you all night.
I guess.

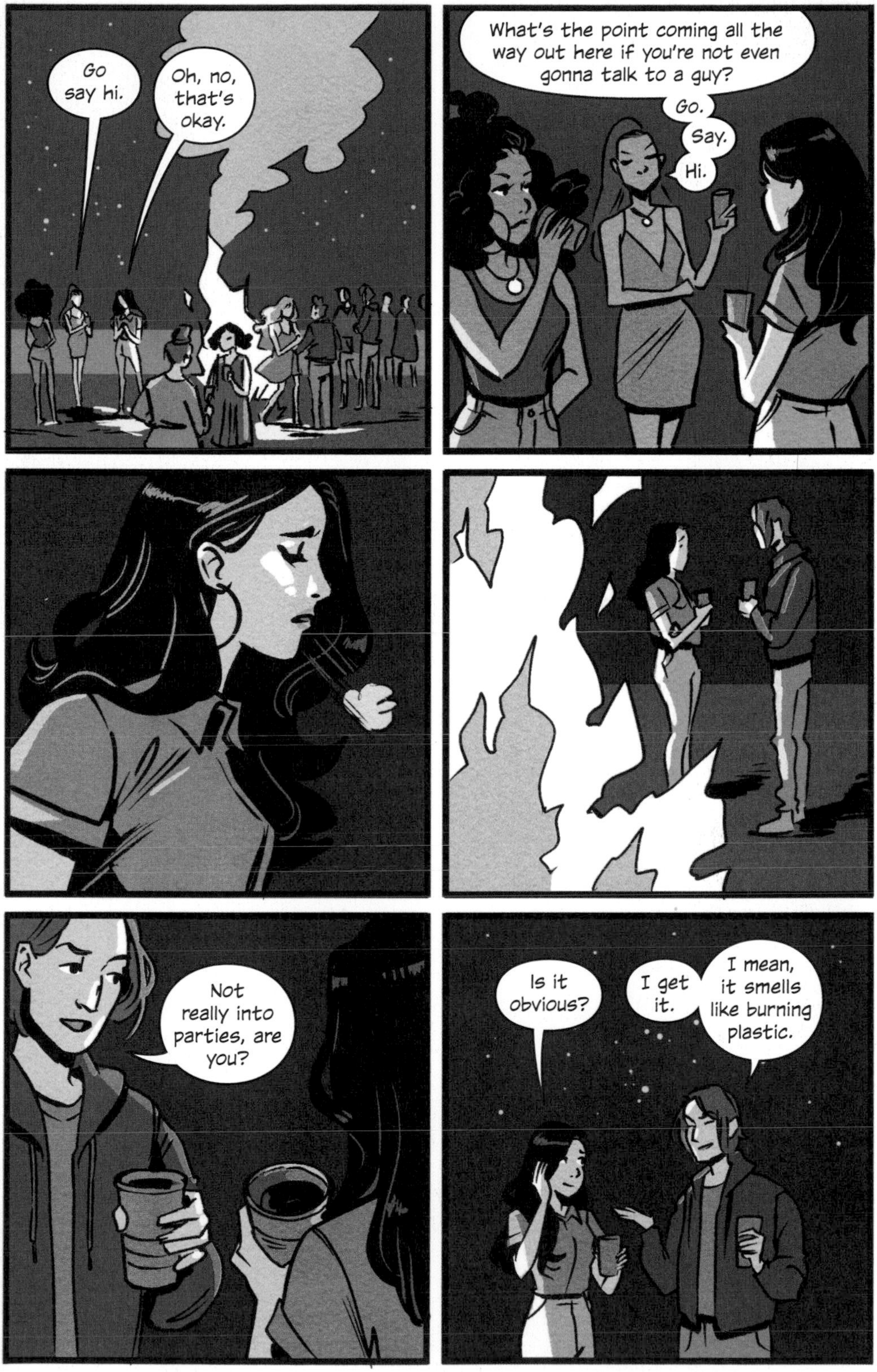
Go say hi.
Oh, no, that's okay.
What's the point coming all the way out here if you're not even gonna talk to a guy?
Go.
Say.
Hi.
Not really into parties, are you?
Is it obvious?
I get it.
I mean, it smells like burning plastic.

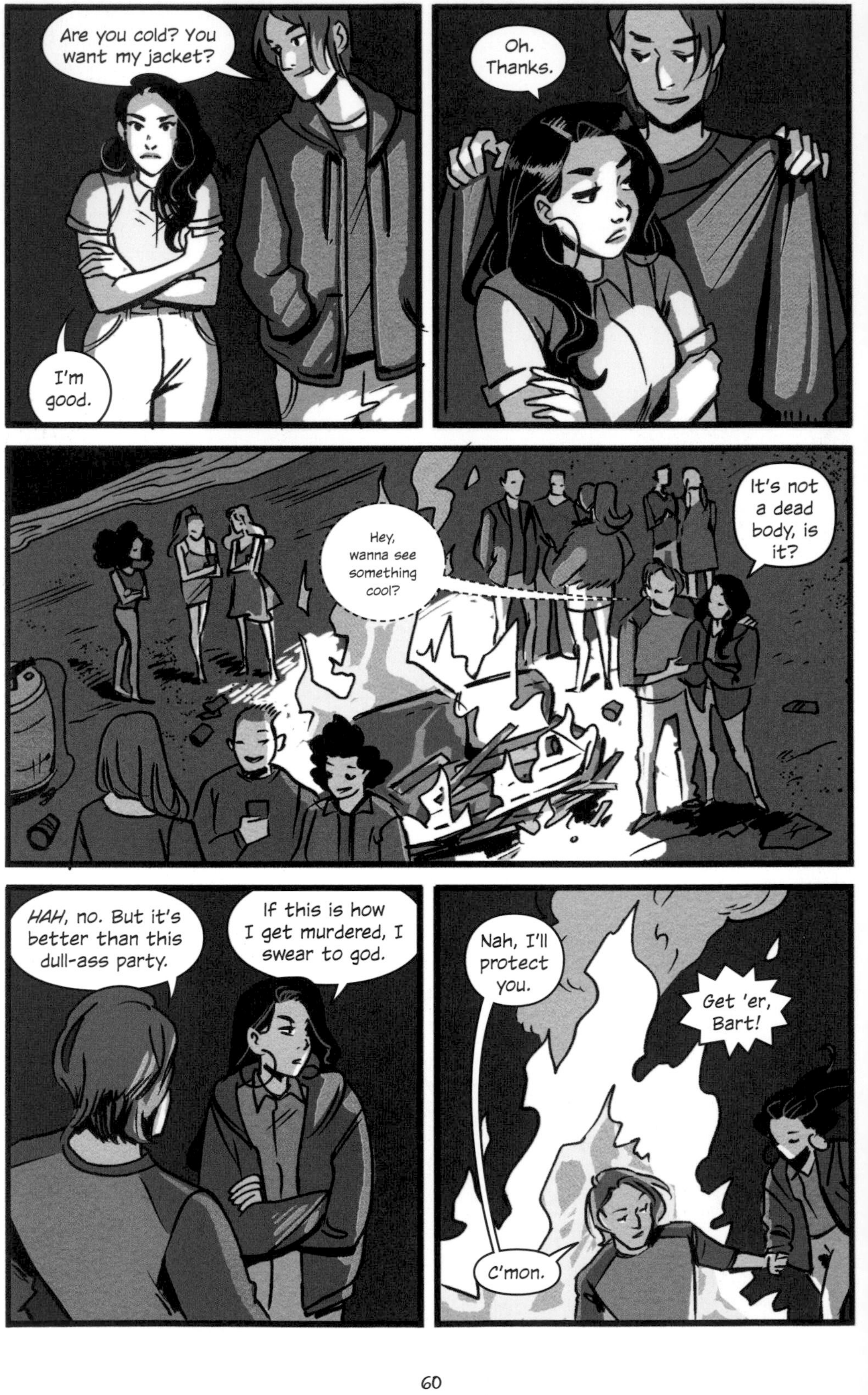
Are you cold? You want my jacket?
I'm good.
Oh. Thanks.
Hey, wanna see something cool?
It's not a dead body, is it?
HAH, no. But it's better than this dull-ass party.
If this is how I get murdered, I swear to god.
Nah, I'll protect you.
C'mon.
Get 'er, Bart!

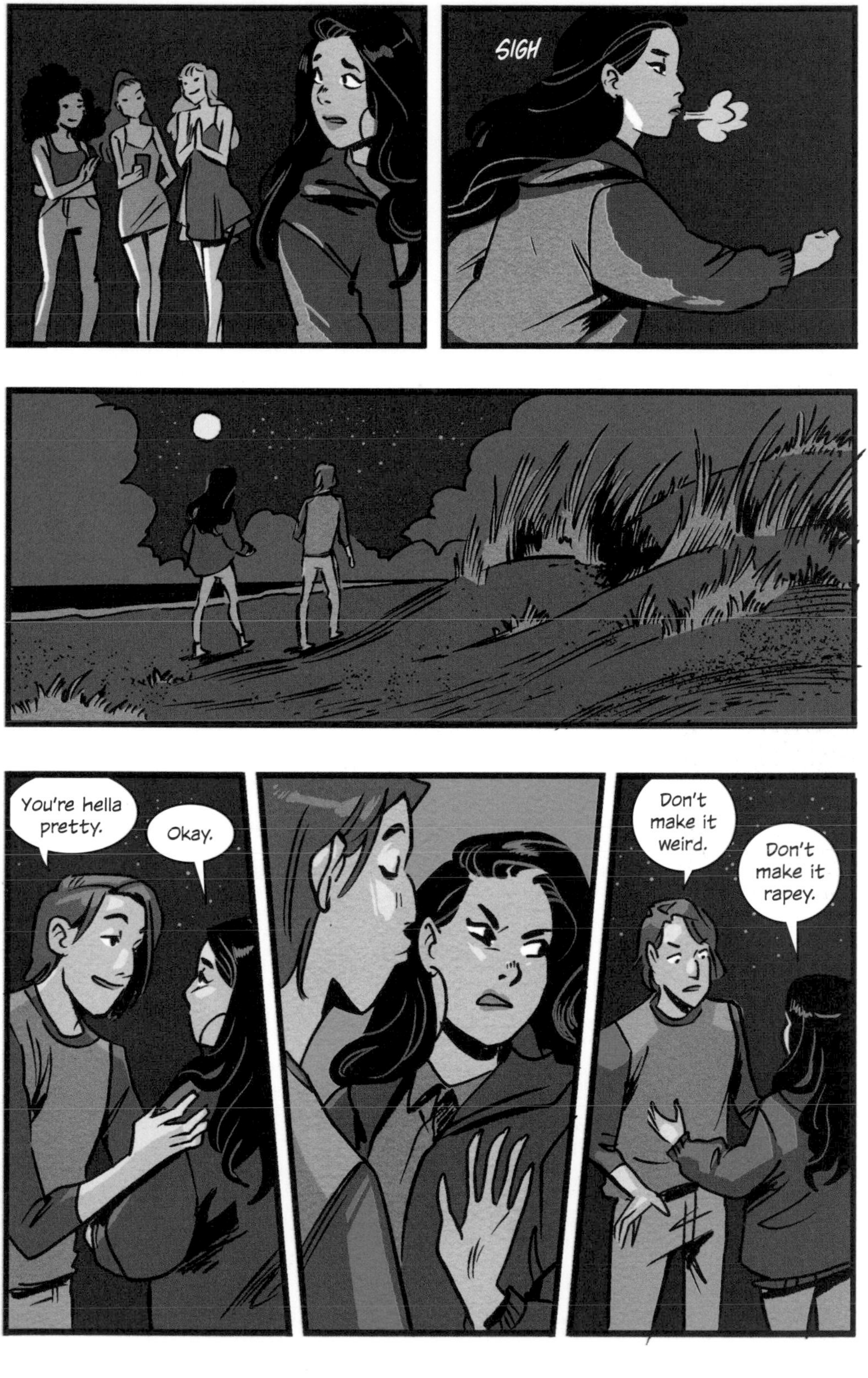
SIGH
You're hella pretty.
Okay.
Don't make it weird.
Don't make it rapey.

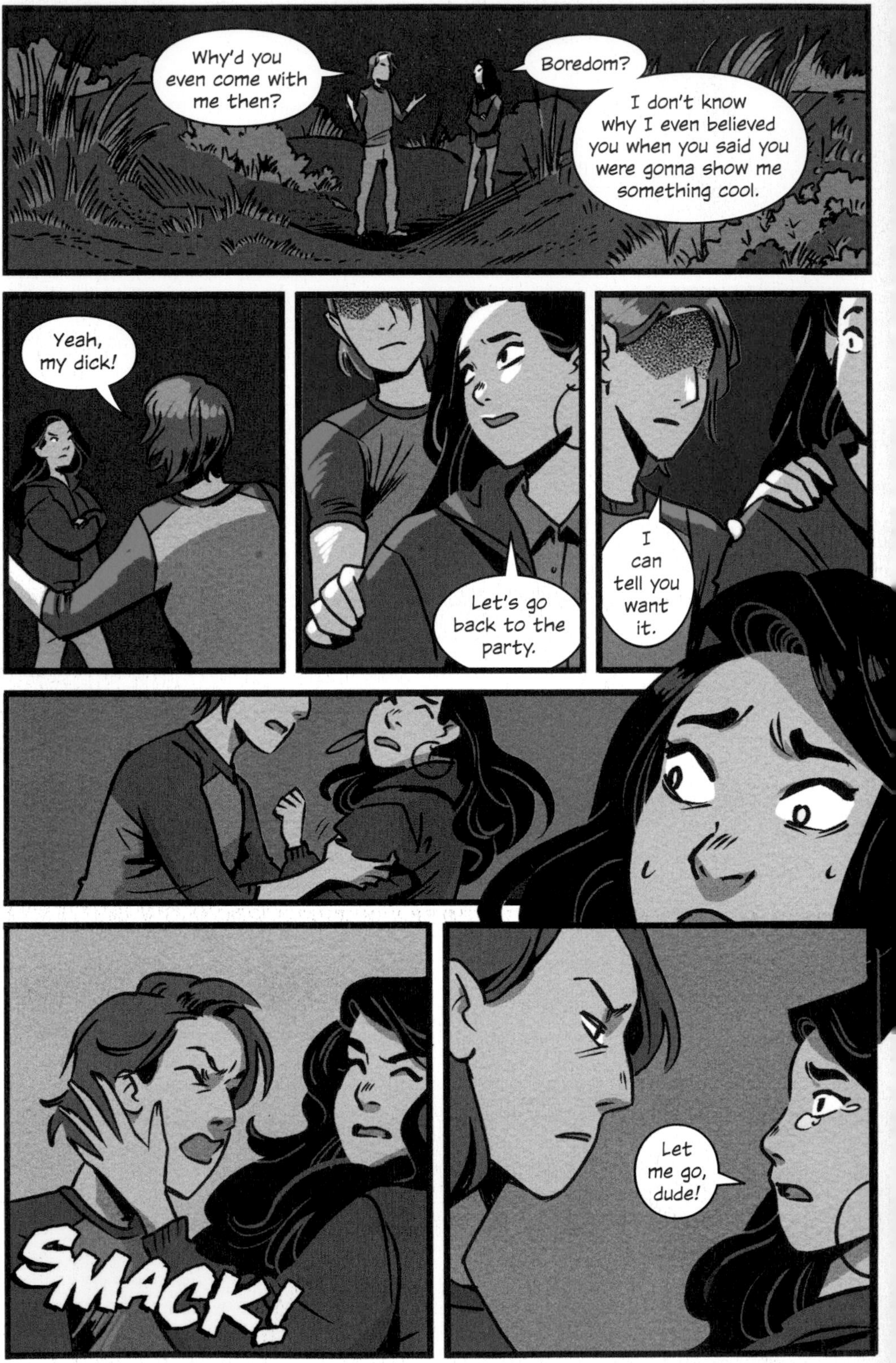
Why'd you even come with me then?
Boredom?
I don't know why I even believed you when you said you were gonna show me something cool.
Yeah, my dick!
Let's go back to the party.
I can tell you want it.
SMACK!
Let me go, dude!

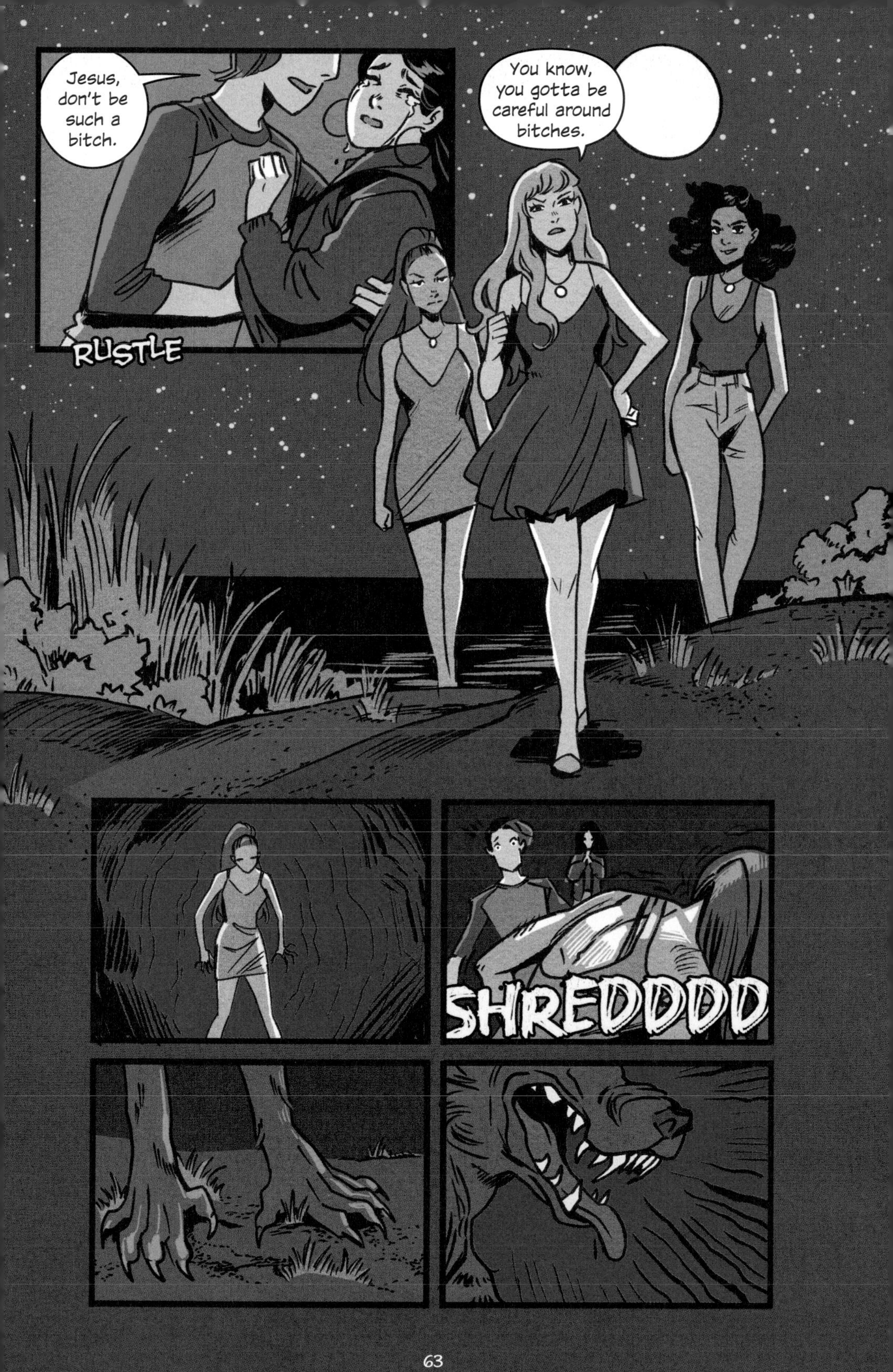
Jesus, don't be such a bitch.
RUSTLE
You know, you gotta be careful around bitches.
SHREDDDD

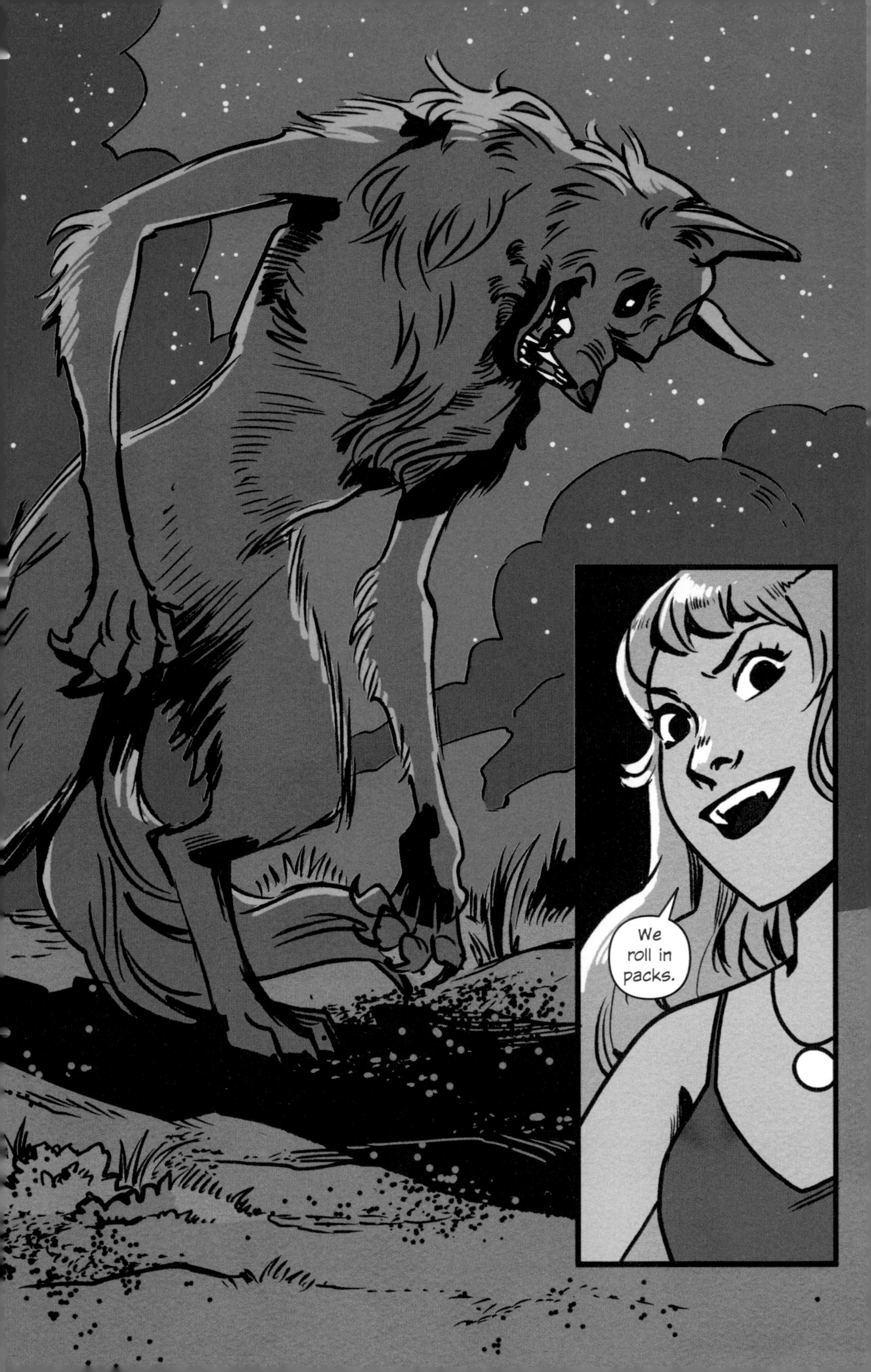
We roll in packs.

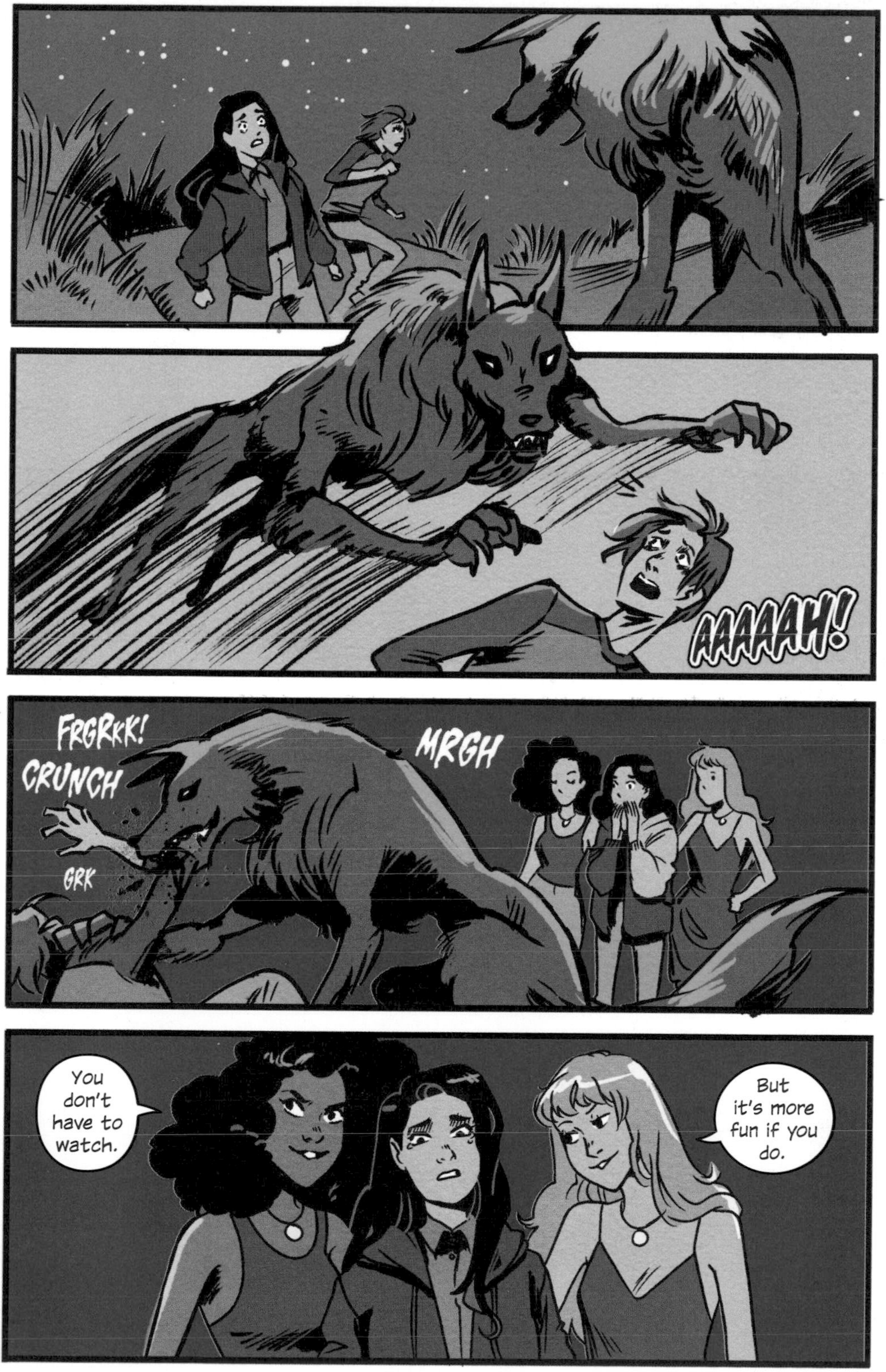

AAAAAH!
FRGRKK!
CRUNCH
MRGH
GRK
You don't have to watch.
But it's more fun if you do.

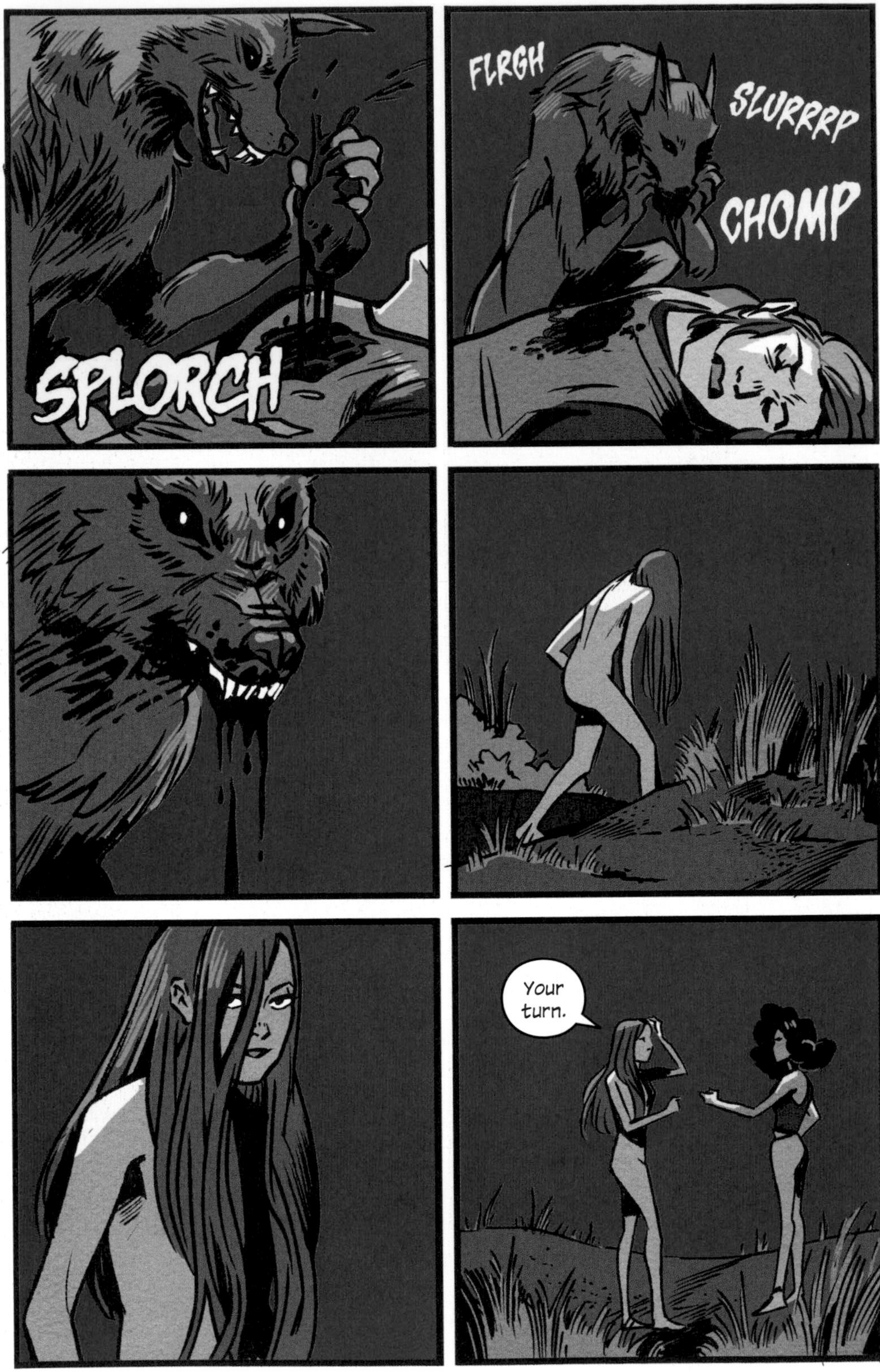
SPLORCH
FLRGH
SLURRRP
CHOMP
Your turn.

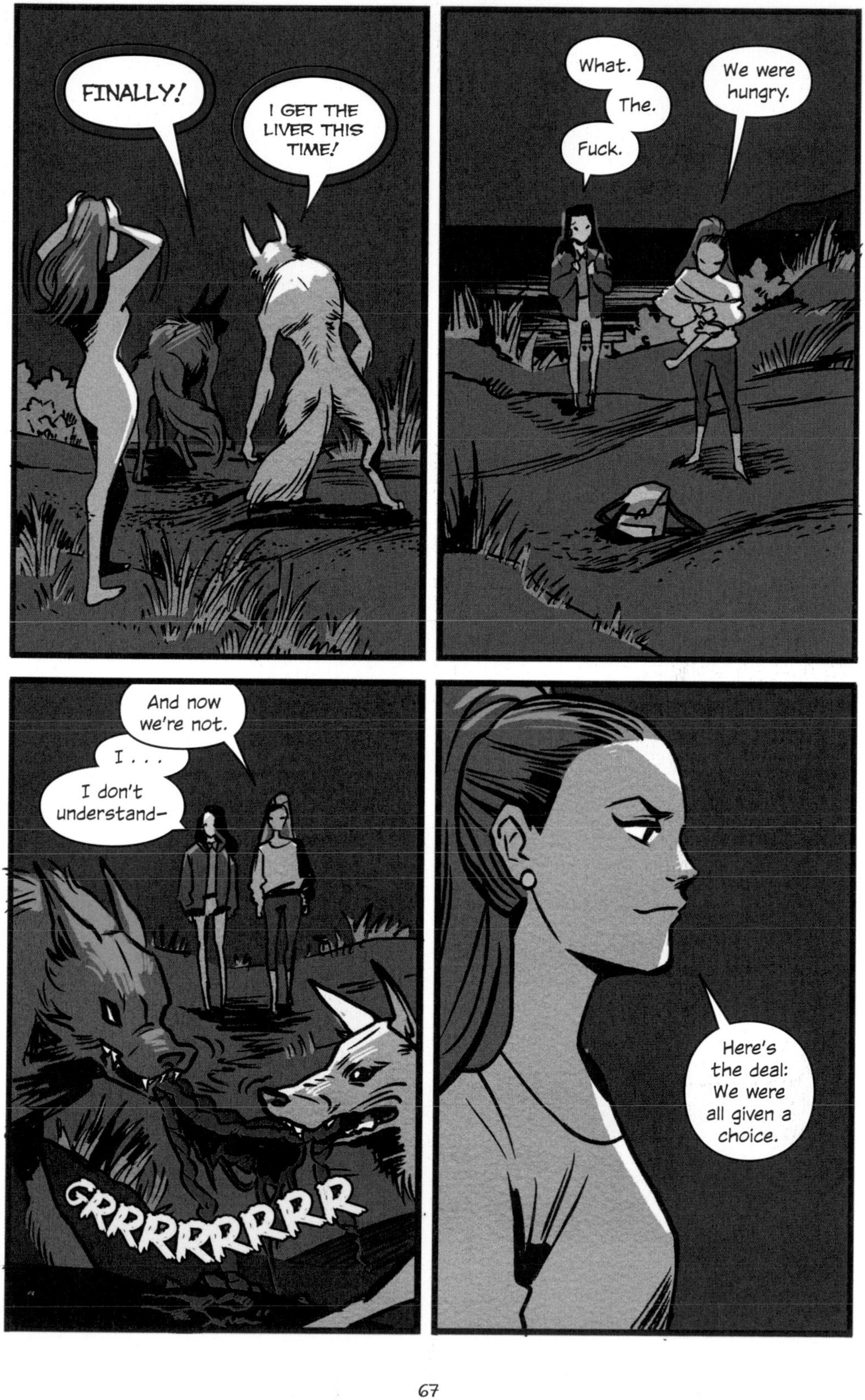

FINALLY!
I GET THE LIVER THIS TIME!
What.
The.
Fuck.
We were hungry.
And now we're not.
I . . .
I don't understand-
GRRRRRRRR
Here's the deal: We were all given a choice.

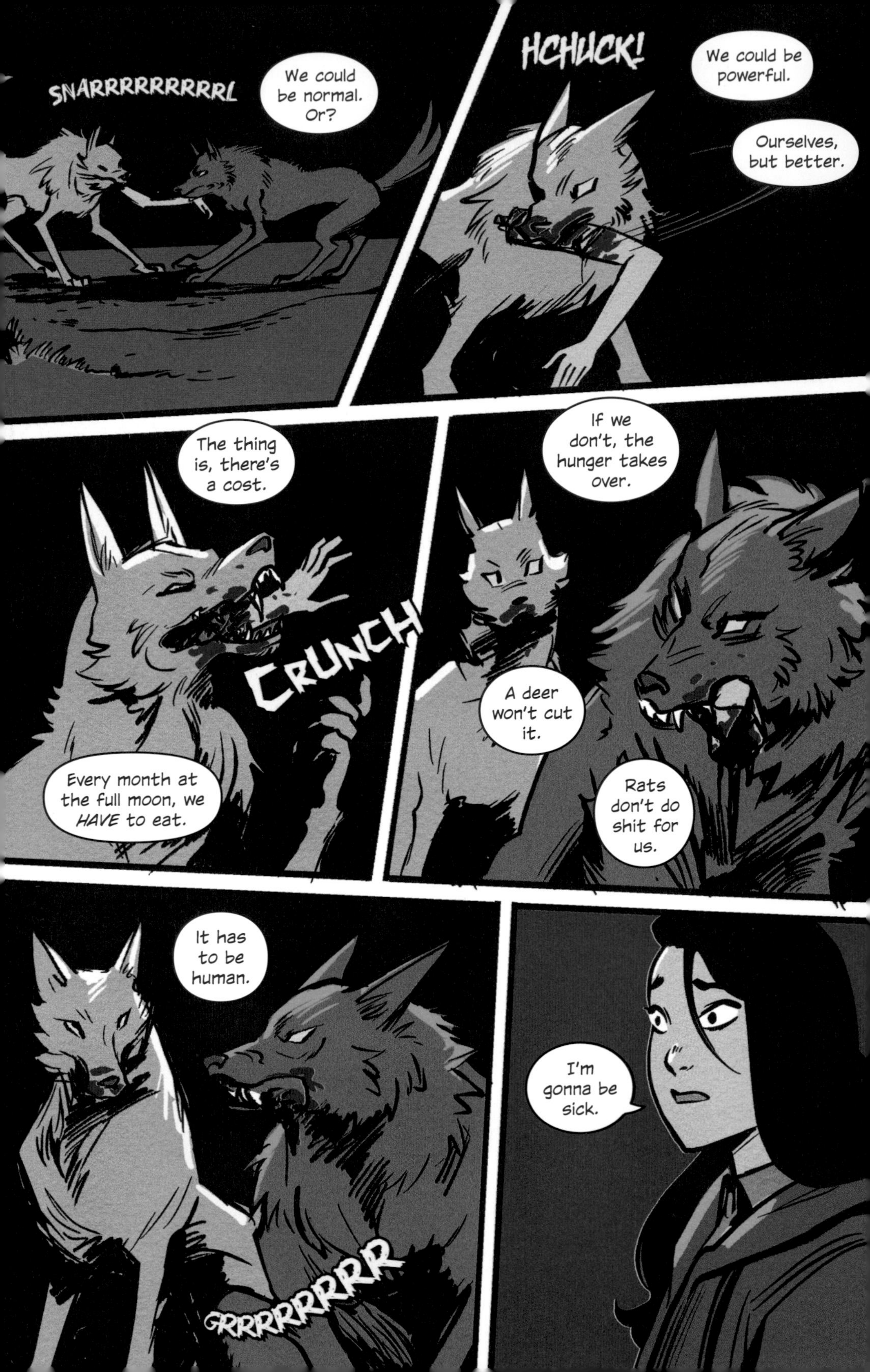
SNARRRRRRRRRL
We could be normal. Or?
HCHUCK!
We could be powerful.
Ourselves, but better.
The thing is, there's a cost.
CRUNCH
Every month at the full moon, we *HAVE* to eat.
If we don't, the hunger takes over.
A deer won't cut it.
Rats don't do shit for us.
It has to be human.
GRRRRRRRRR
I'm gonna be sick.

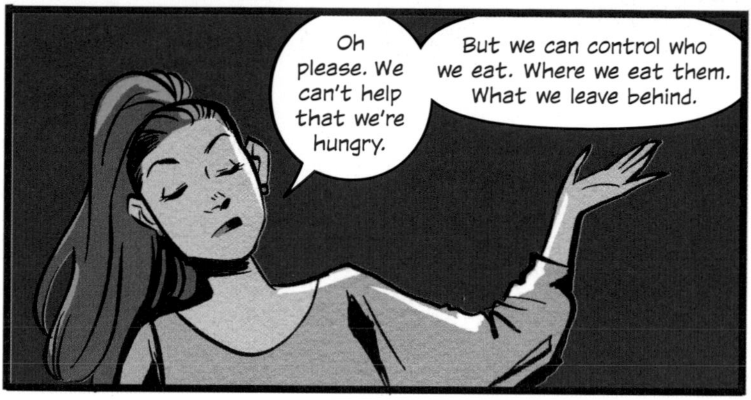
Oh please. We can't help that we're hungry.
But we can control who we eat. Where we eat them. What we leave behind.

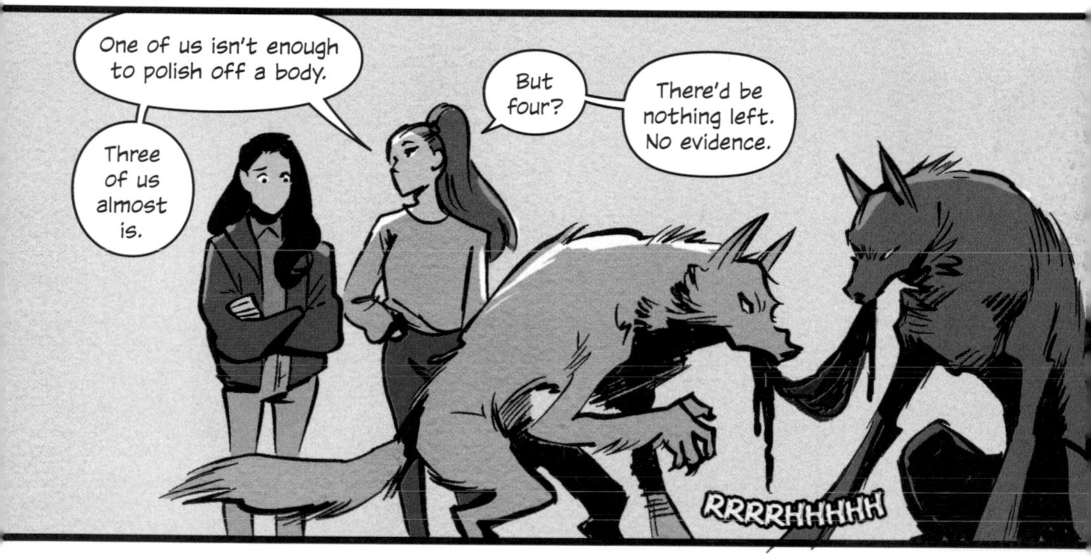
One of us isn't enough to polish off a body.
Three of us almost is.
But four?
There'd be nothing left. No evidence.
RRRRHHHHH

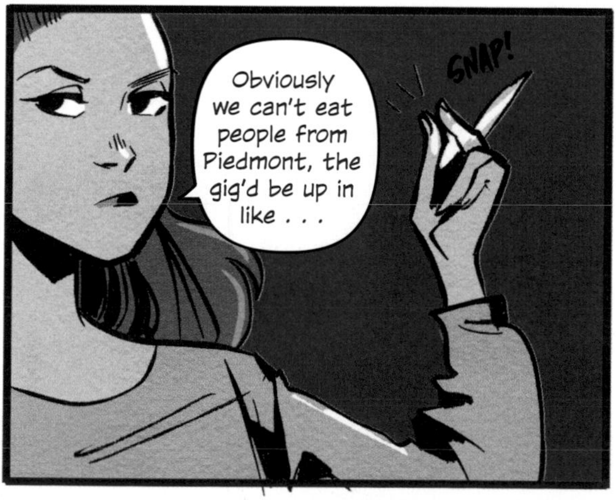
Obviously we can't eat people from Piedmont, the gig'd be up in like . . .
SNAP!

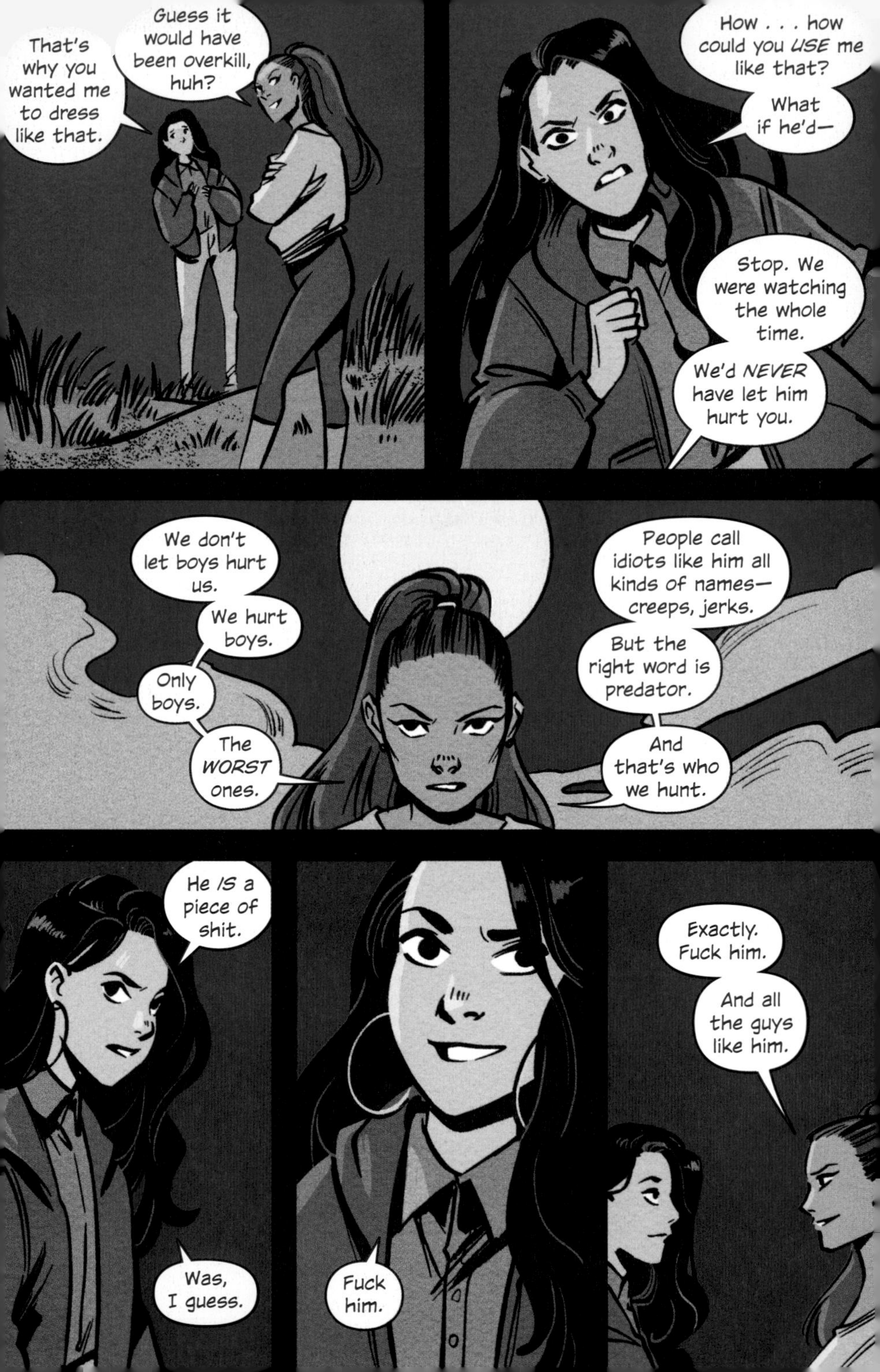
That's why you wanted me to dress like that.
Guess it would have been overkill, huh?
How . . . how could you USE me like that?
What if he'd—
Stop. We were watching the whole time.
We'd NEVER have let him hurt you.
We don't let boys hurt us.
We hurt boys.
Only boys.
The WORST ones.
People call idiots like him all kinds of names—creeps, jerks.
But the right word is predator.
And that's who we hunt.
He IS a piece of shit.
Was, I guess.
Fuck him.
Exactly. Fuck him.
And all the guys like him.

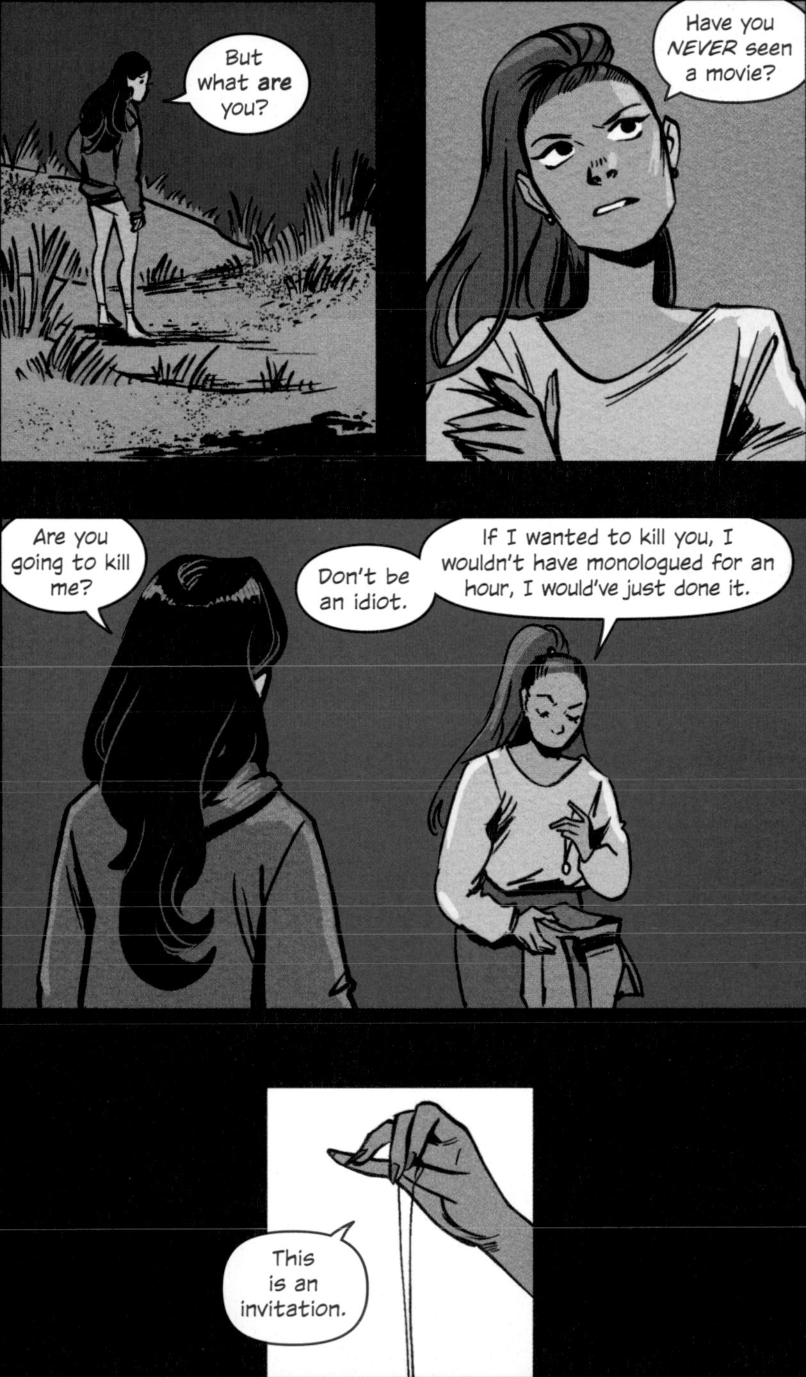
But what are you?
Have you NEVER seen a movie?
Are you going to kill me?
Don't be an idiot.
If I wanted to kill you, I wouldn't have monologued for an hour, I would've just done it.
This is an invitation.

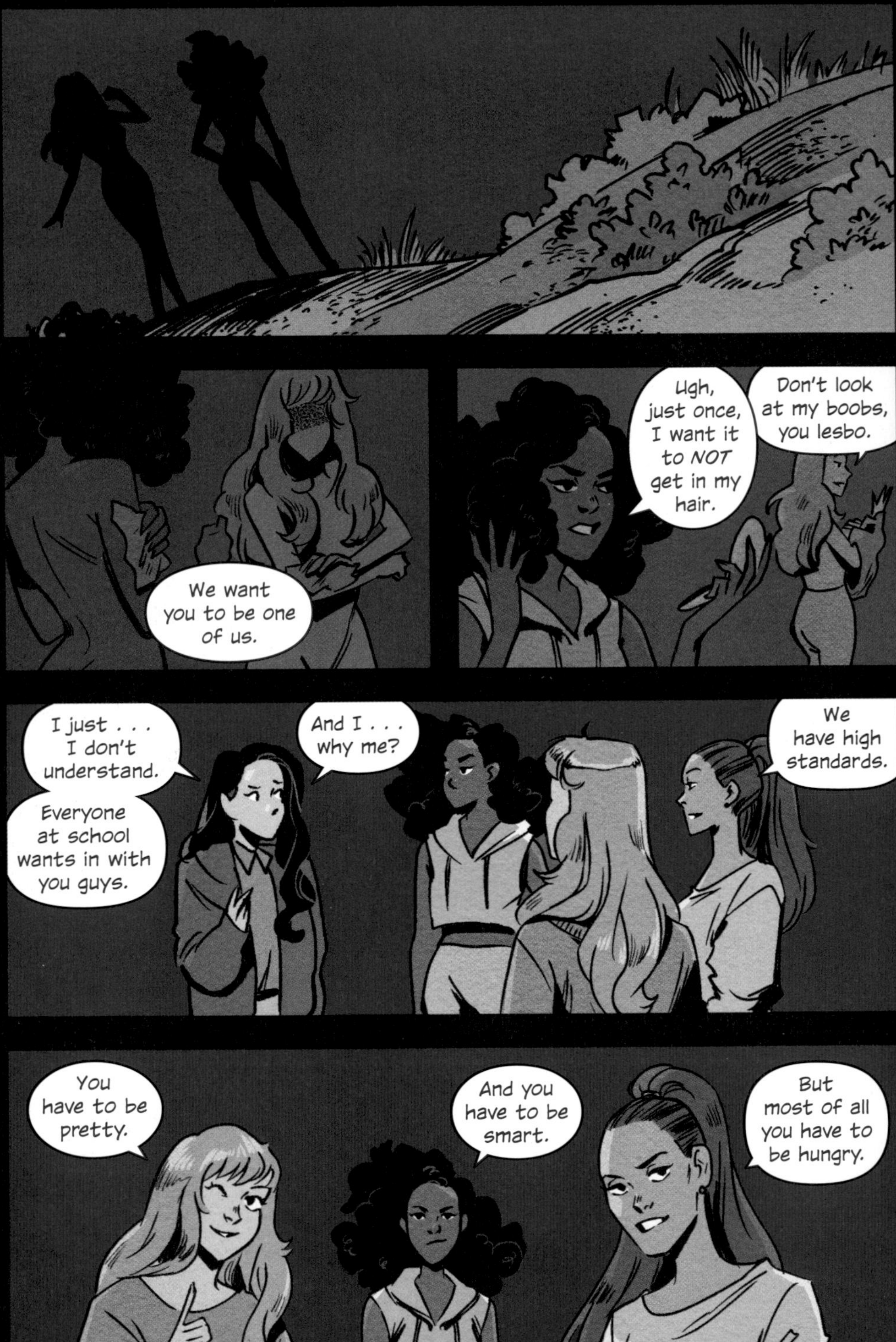
We want you to be one of us.
Ugh, just once, I want it to *NOT* get in my hair.
Don't look at my boobs, you lesbo.
I just . . . I don't understand.
Everyone at school wants in with you guys.
And I . . . why me?
We have high standards.
You have to be pretty.
And you have to be smart.
But most of all you have to be hungry.

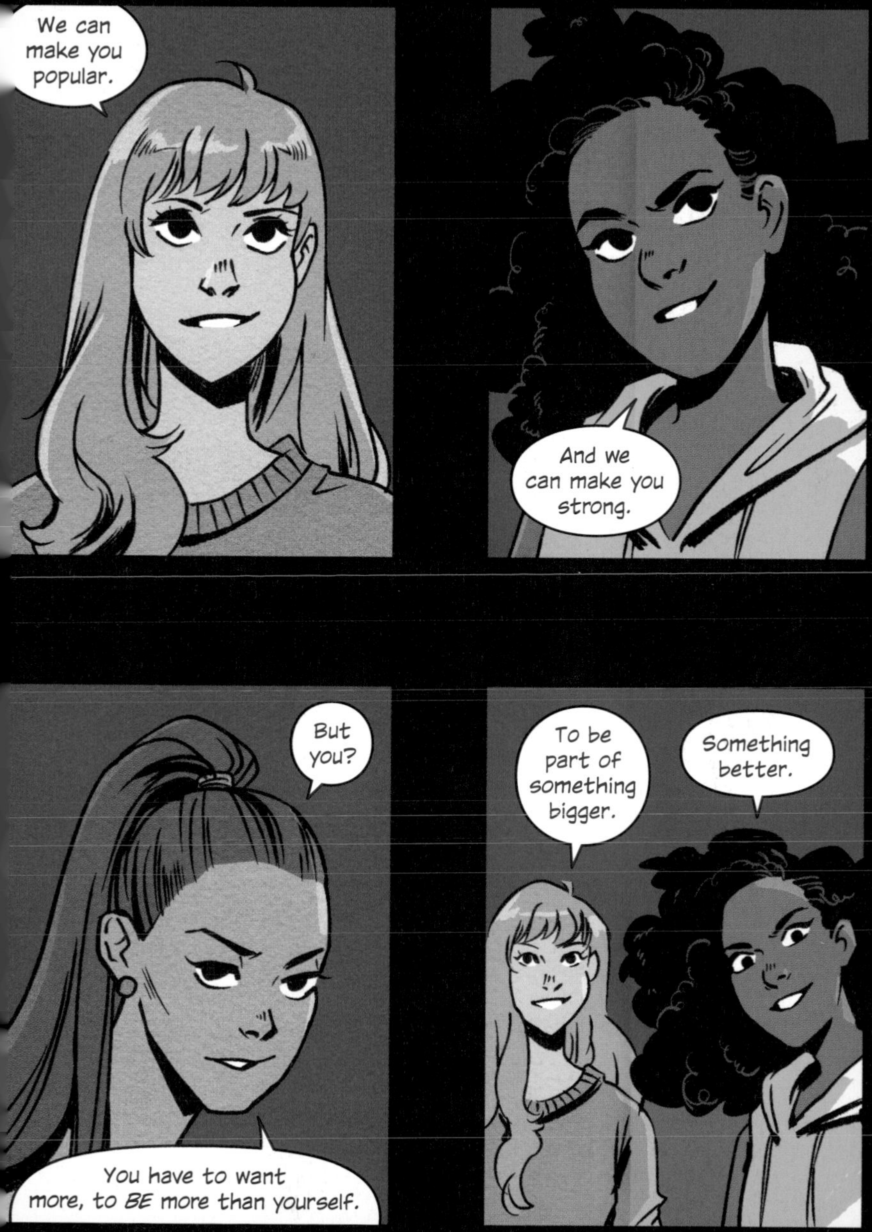
We can make you popular.
And we can make you strong.
But you?
You have to want more, to BE more than yourself.
To be part of something bigger.
Something better.

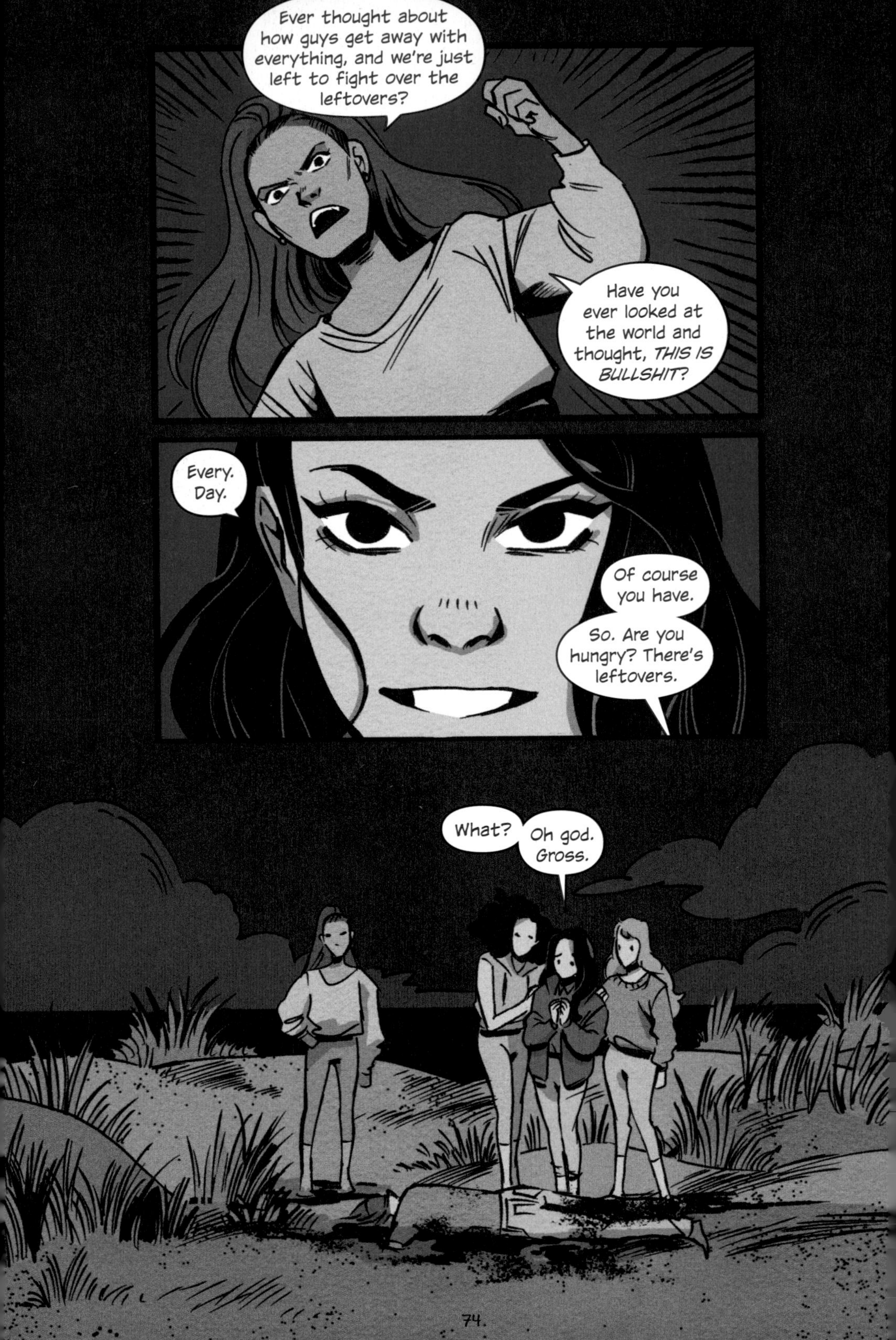
Ever thought about how guys get away with everything, and we're just left to fight over the leftovers?
Have you ever looked at the world and thought, *THIS IS BULLSHIT?*
Every. Day.
Of course you have.
So. Are you hungry? There's leftovers.
What?
Oh god. Gross.

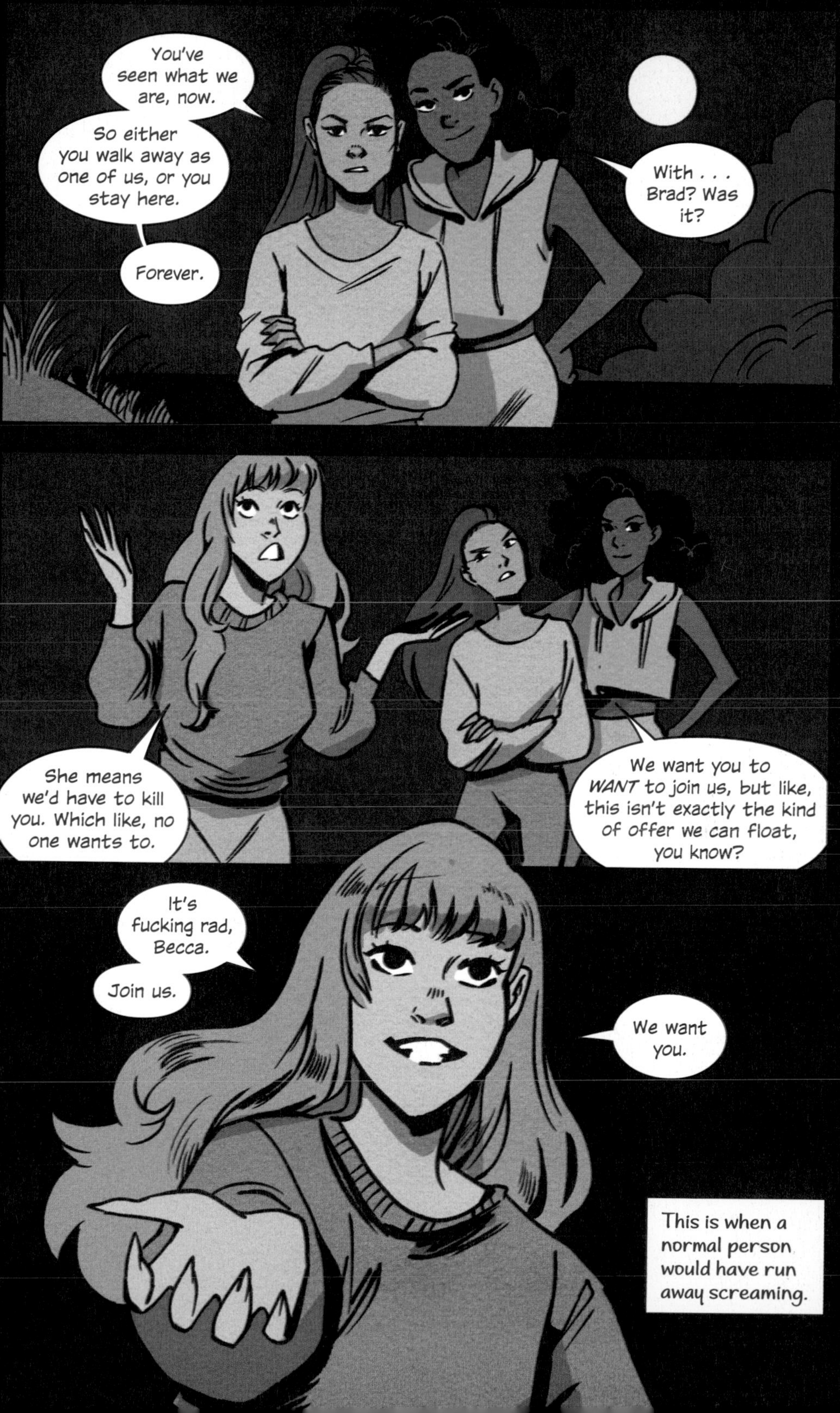
You've seen what we are, now.
So either you walk away as one of us, or you stay here.
Forever.
With . . . Brad? Was it?
She means we'd have to kill you. Which like, no one wants to.
We want you to *WANT* to join us, but like, this isn't exactly the kind of offer we can float, you know?
It's fucking rad, Becca.
Join us.
We want you.
This is when a normal person would have run away screaming.

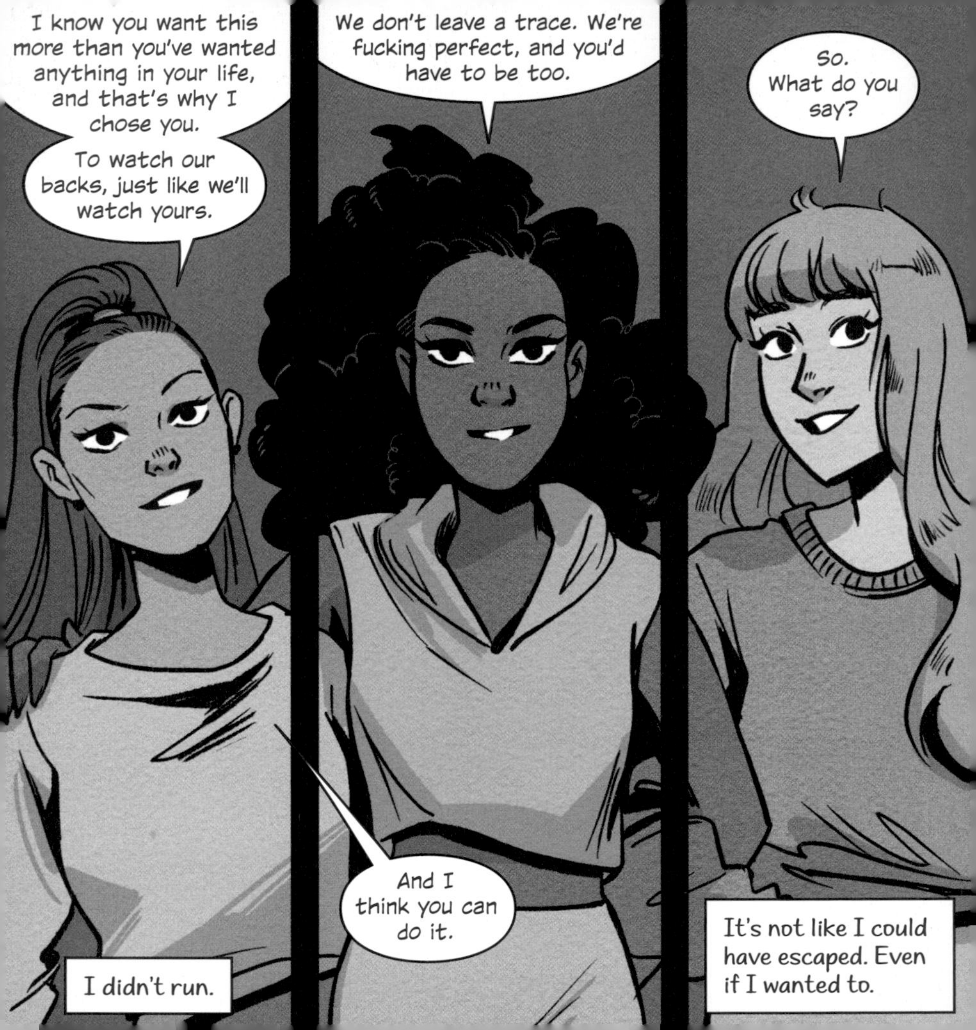

I know you want this more than you've wanted anything in your life, and that's why I chose you.
To watch our backs, just like we'll watch yours.
I didn't run.
We don't leave a trace. We're fucking perfect, and you'd have to be too.
And I think you can do it.
So. What do you say?
It's not like I could have escaped. Even if I wanted to.

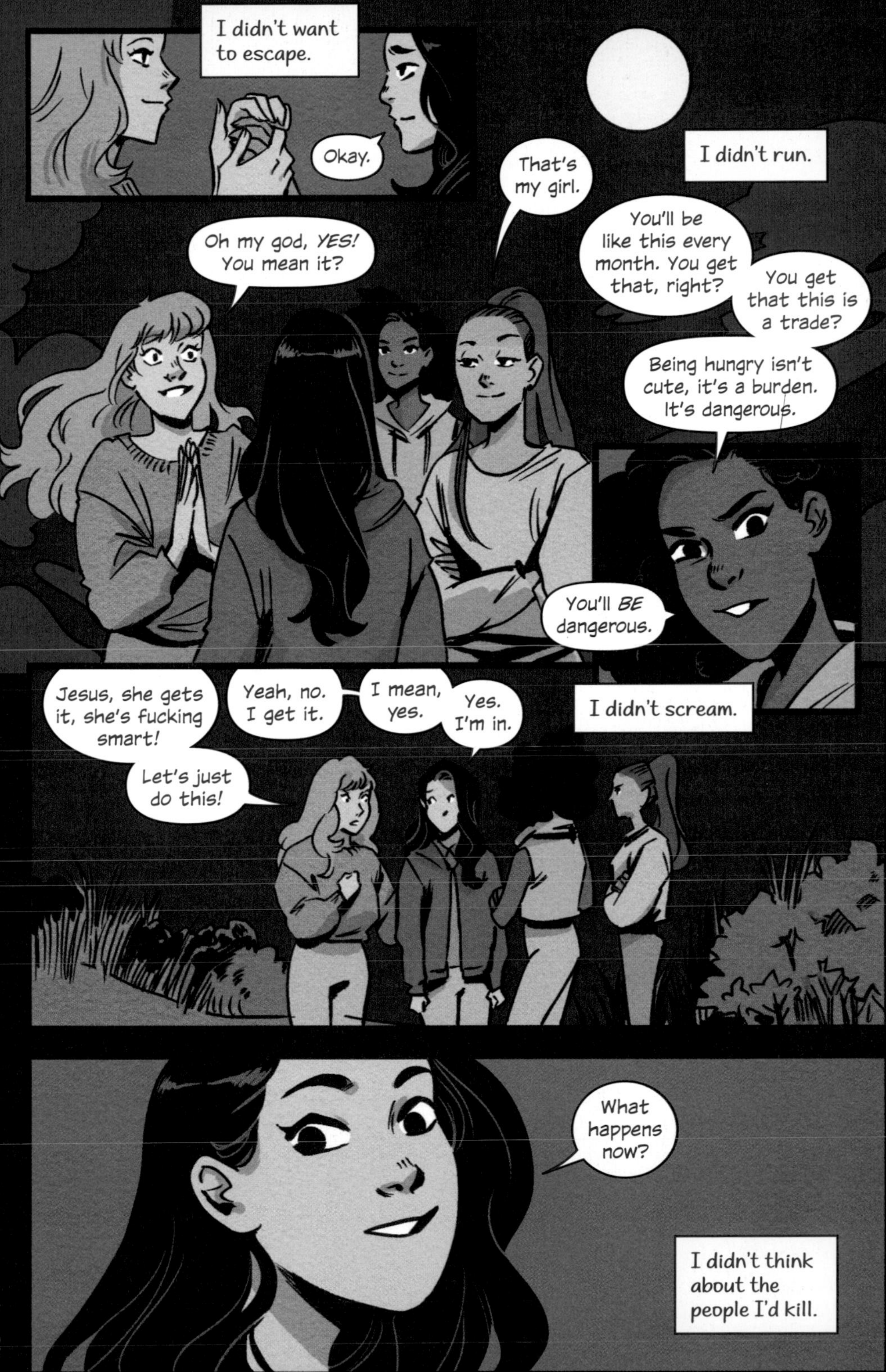

I didn't want to escape.
Okay.
I didn't run.
That's my girl.
Oh my god, YES! You mean it?
You'll be like this every month. You get that, right?
You get that this is a trade?
Being hungry isn't cute, it's a burden. It's dangerous.
You'll BE dangerous.
Jesus, she gets it, she's fucking smart!
Yeah, no. I get it.
I mean, yes.
Yes. I'm in.
I didn't scream.
Let's just do this!
What happens now?
I didn't think about the people I'd kill.

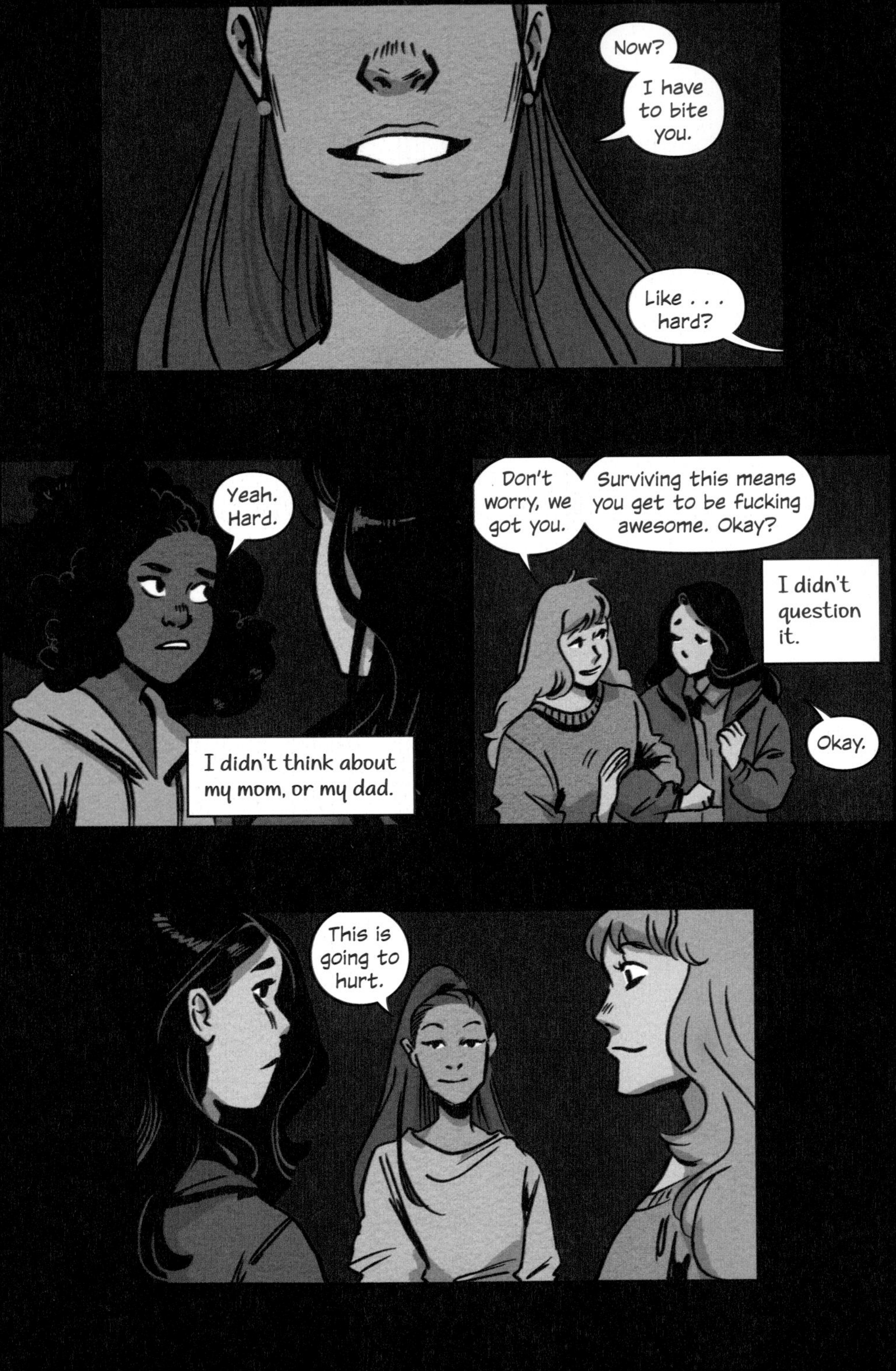
Now?
I have to bite you.
Like . . . hard?
Yeah. Hard.
I didn't think about my mom, or my dad.
Don't worry, we got you.
Surviving this means you get to be fucking awesome. Okay?
I didn't question it.
Okay.
This is going to hurt.

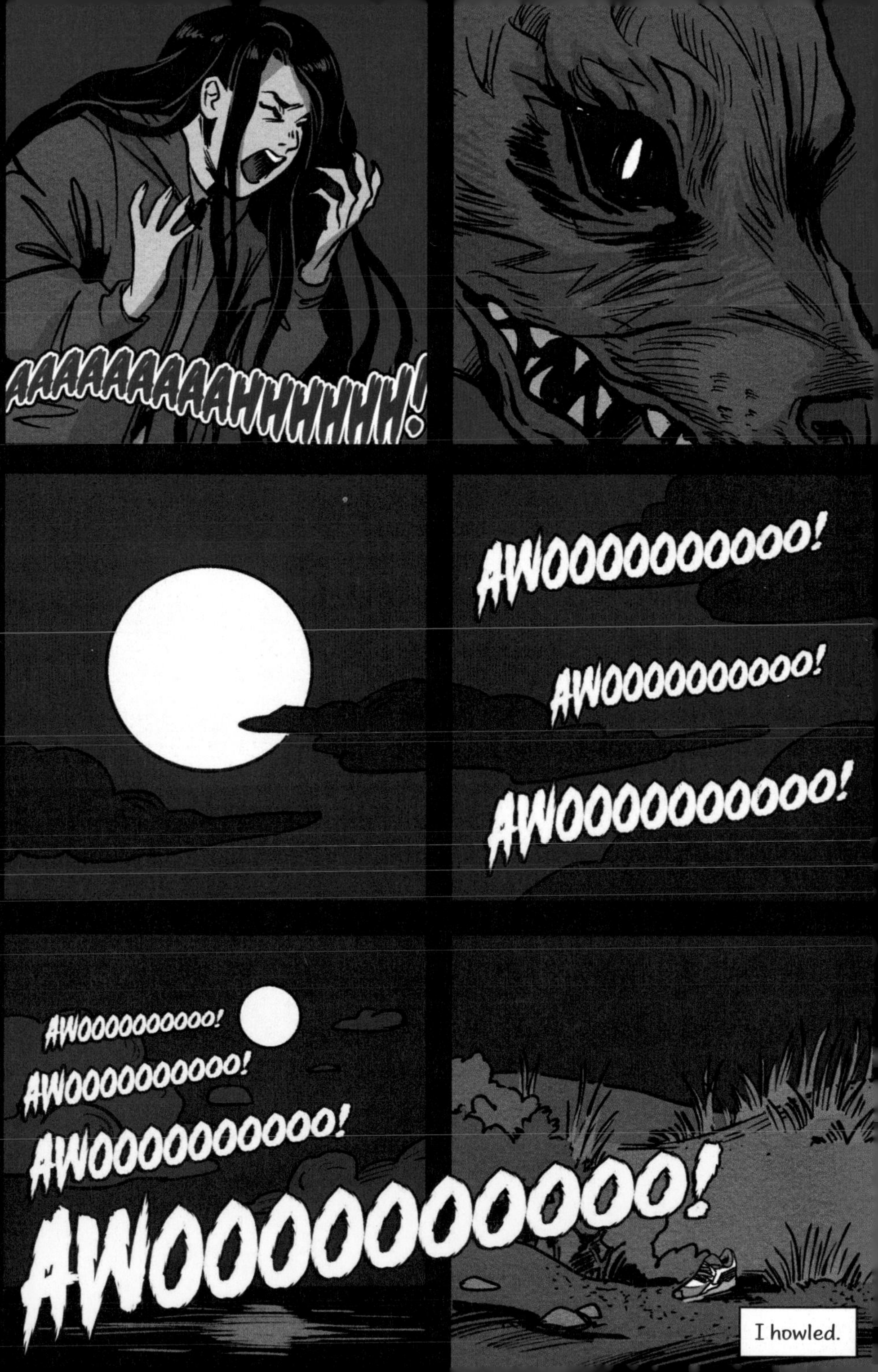
AAAAAAAAAAHHHHHHH!
AWOOOOOOOOOOO!
AWOOOOOOOOOOO!
AWOOOOOOOOOOO!
AWOOOOOOOOOO!
AWOOOOOOOOOOO!
AWOOOOOOOOOOOO!
AWOOOOOOOOOOOO!
I howled.

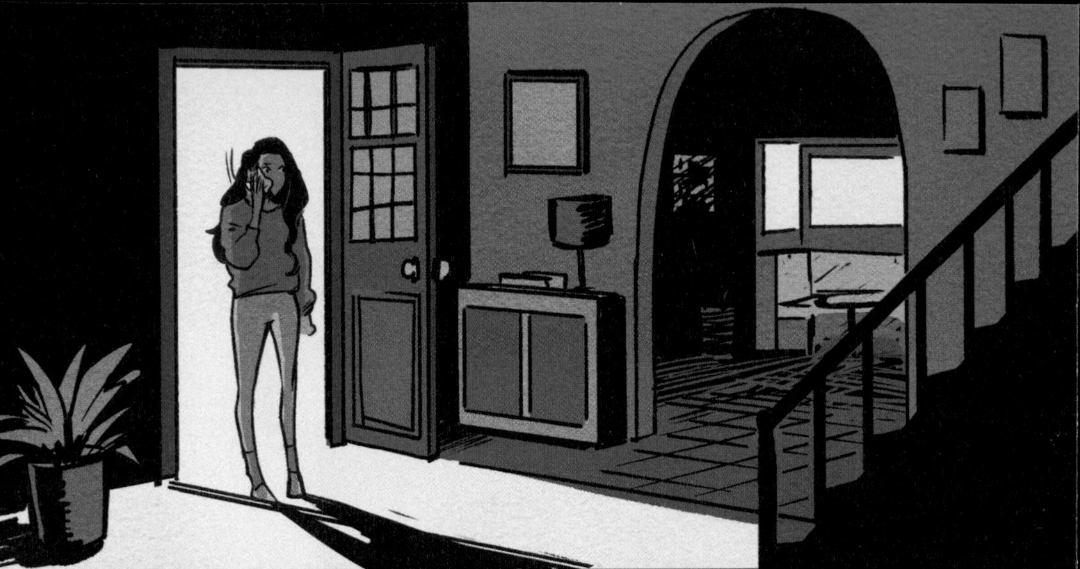

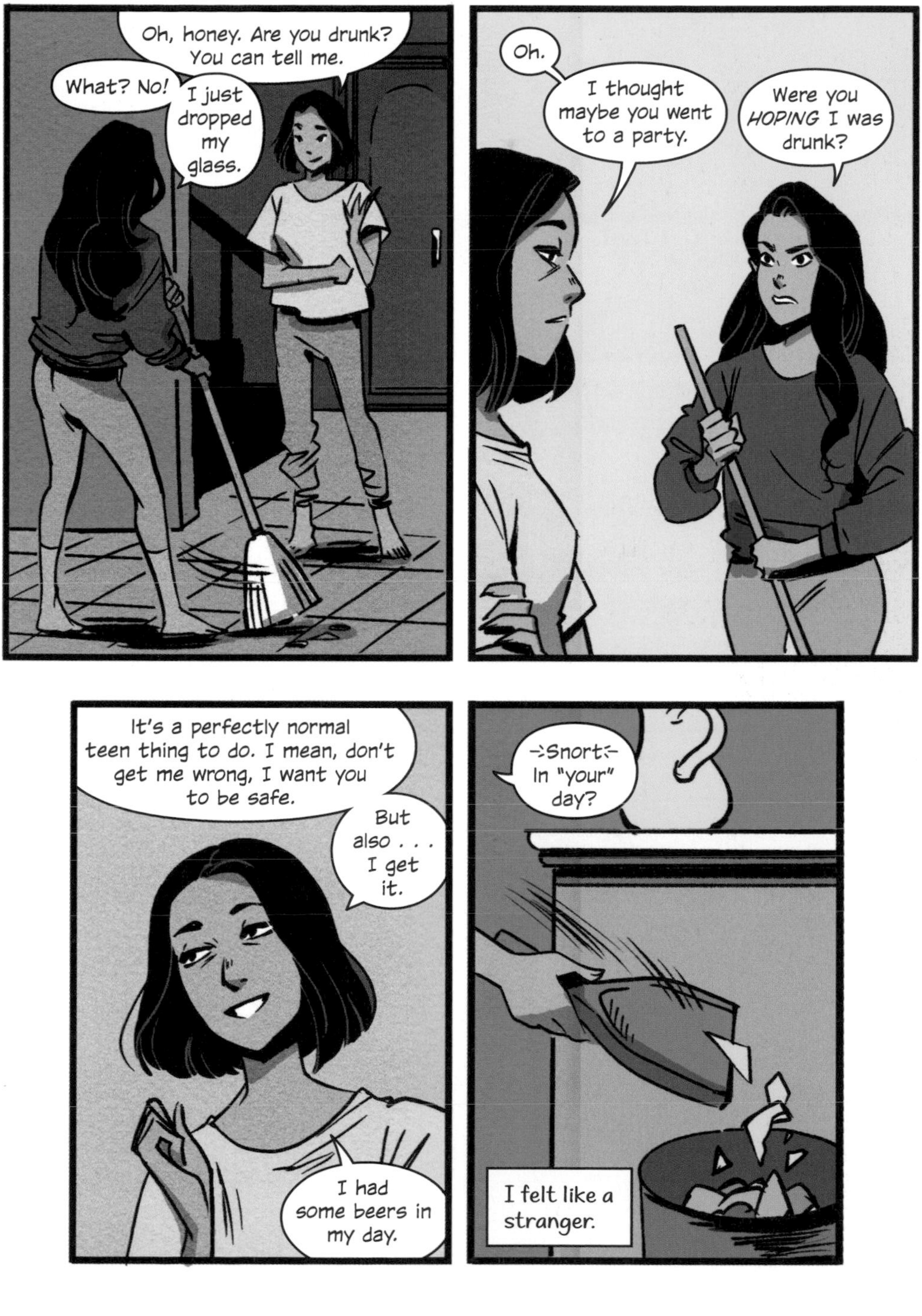
Oh, honey. Are you drunk? You can tell me.
What? No!
I just dropped my glass.
Oh.
I thought maybe you went to a party.
Were you *HOPING* I was drunk?
It's a perfectly normal teen thing to do. I mean, don't get me wrong, I want you to be safe.
But also . . . I get it.
I had some beers in my day.
-Snort- In "your" day?
I felt like a stranger.

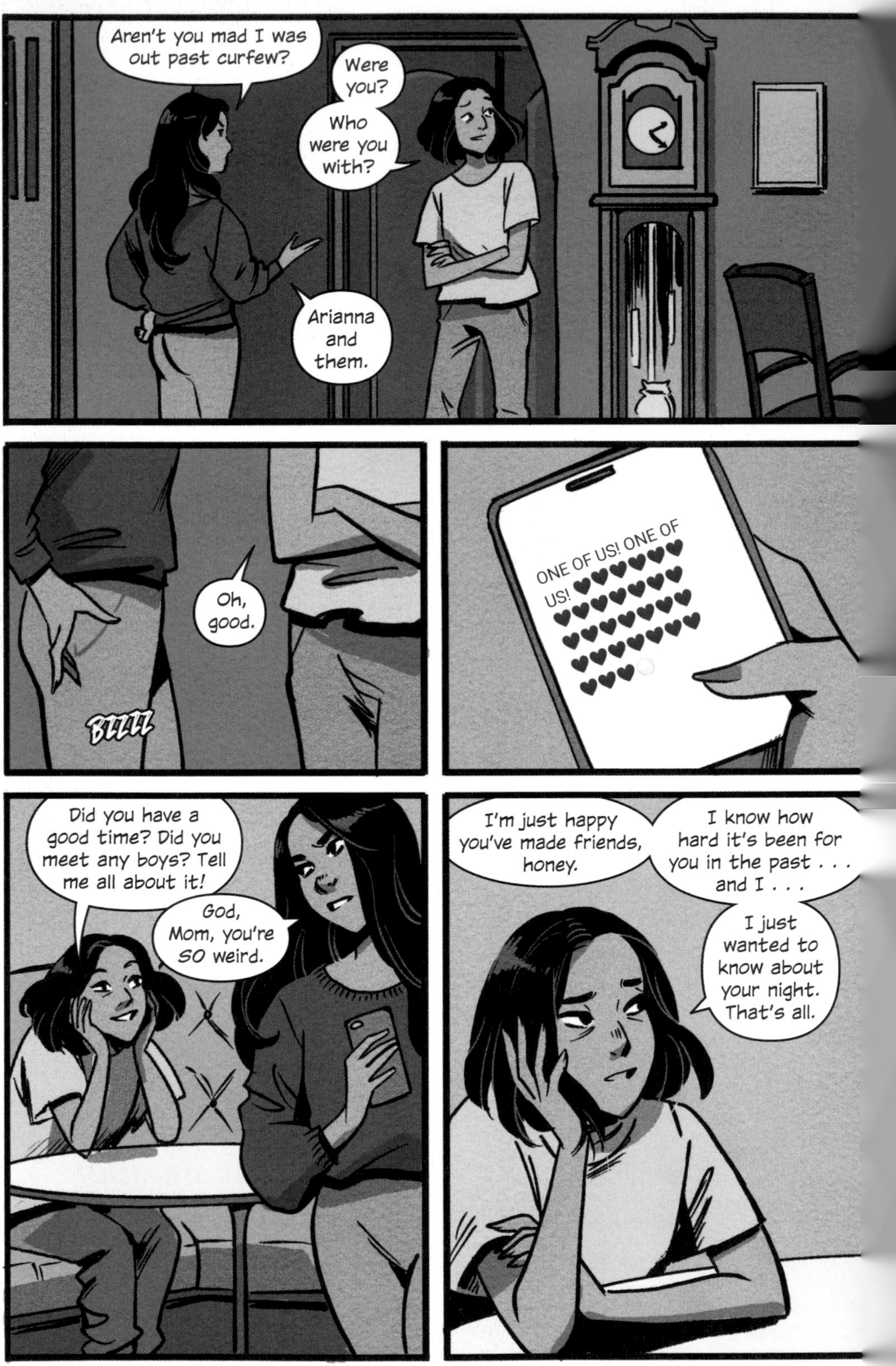
Aren't you mad I was out past curfew?
Were you?
Who were you with?
Arianna and them.
Oh, good.
BZZZZ
ONE OF US! ONE OF US! ♥♥♥♥♥♥♥♥♥♥♥♥♥♥♥♥♥♥♥♥♥♥♥♥♥♥♥♥♥♥♥♥
Did you have a good time? Did you meet any boys? Tell me all about it!
God, Mom, you're SO weird.
I'm just happy you've made friends, honey.
I know how hard it's been for you in the past . . . and I . . .
I just wanted to know about your night. That's all.

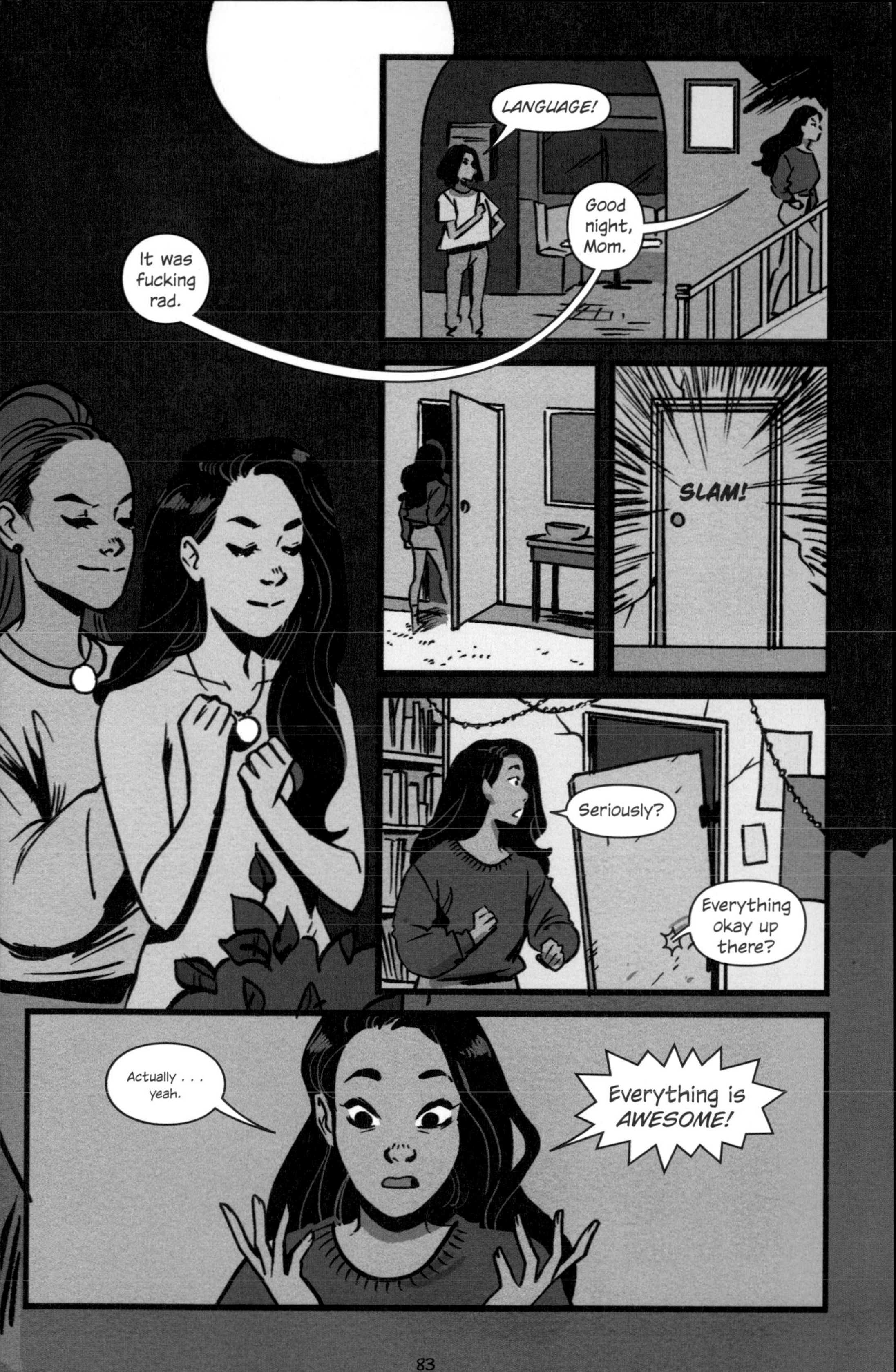
LANGUAGE!
Good night, Mom.
It was fucking rad.
SLAM!
Seriously?
Everything okay up there?
Actually . . . yeah.
Everything is AWESOME!

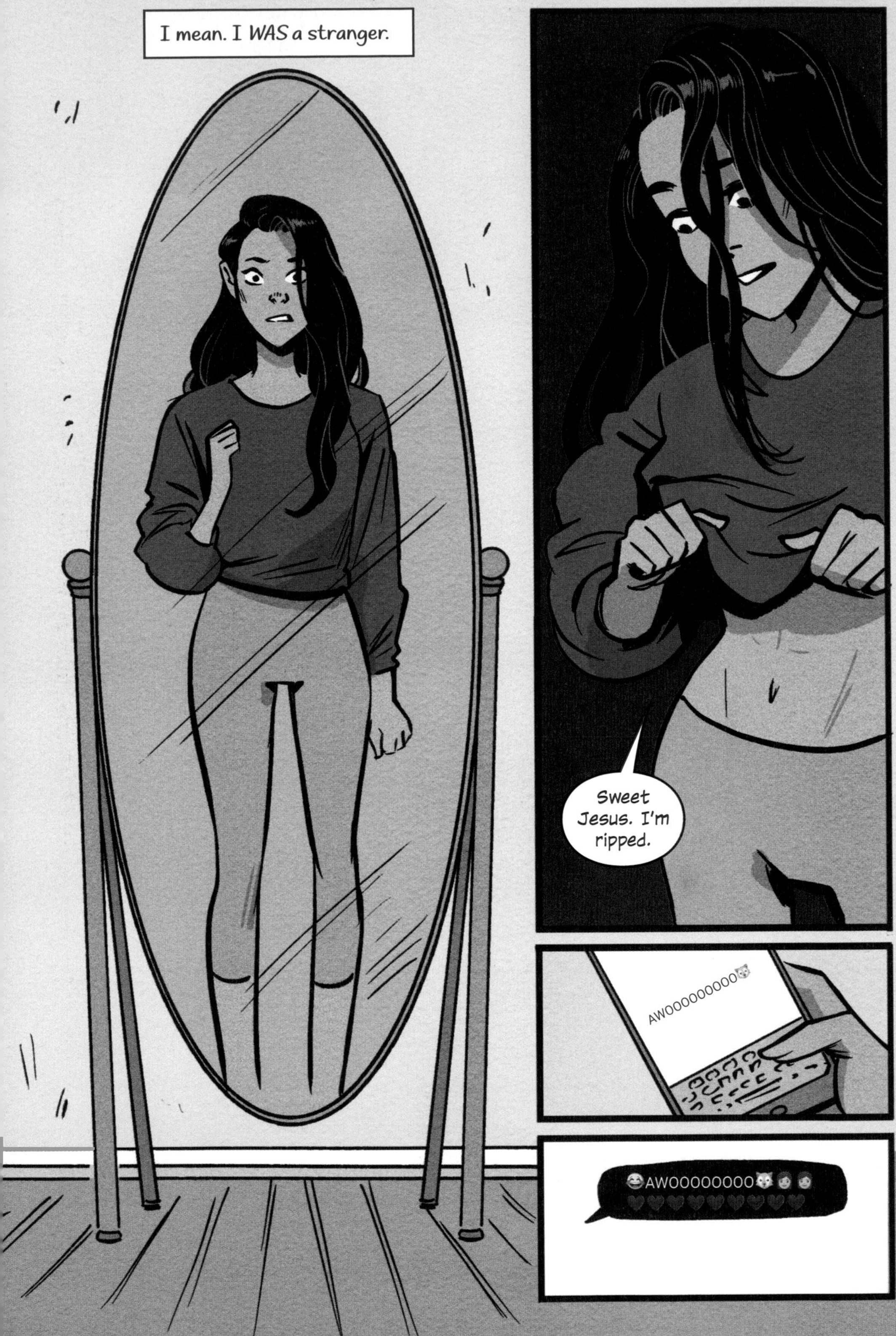
I mean. I WAS a stranger.
Sweet Jesus. I'm ripped.
AWOOOOOOOOO
AWOOOOOOOOO

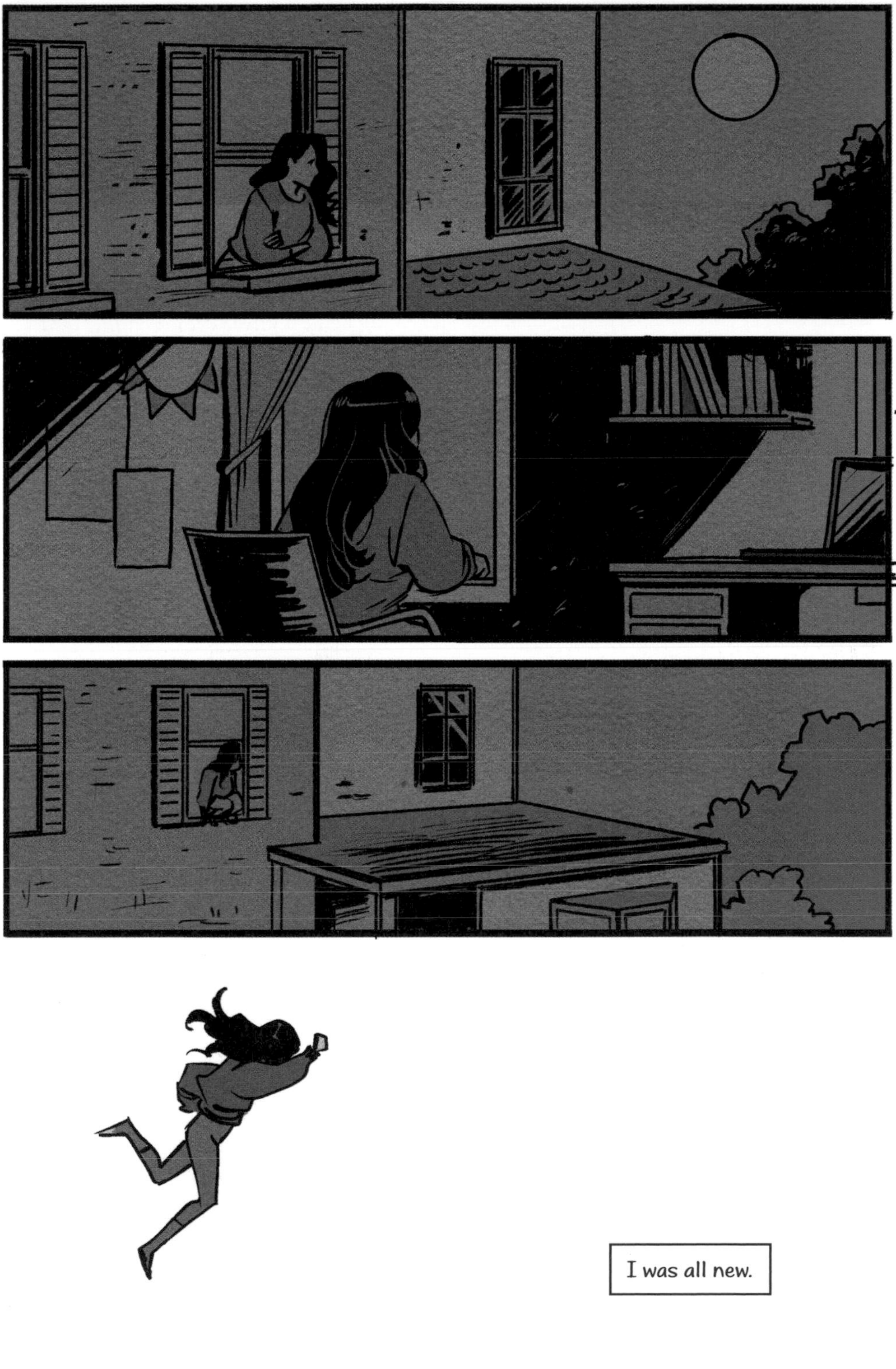
I was all new.

CHAPTER FOUR

PARTY

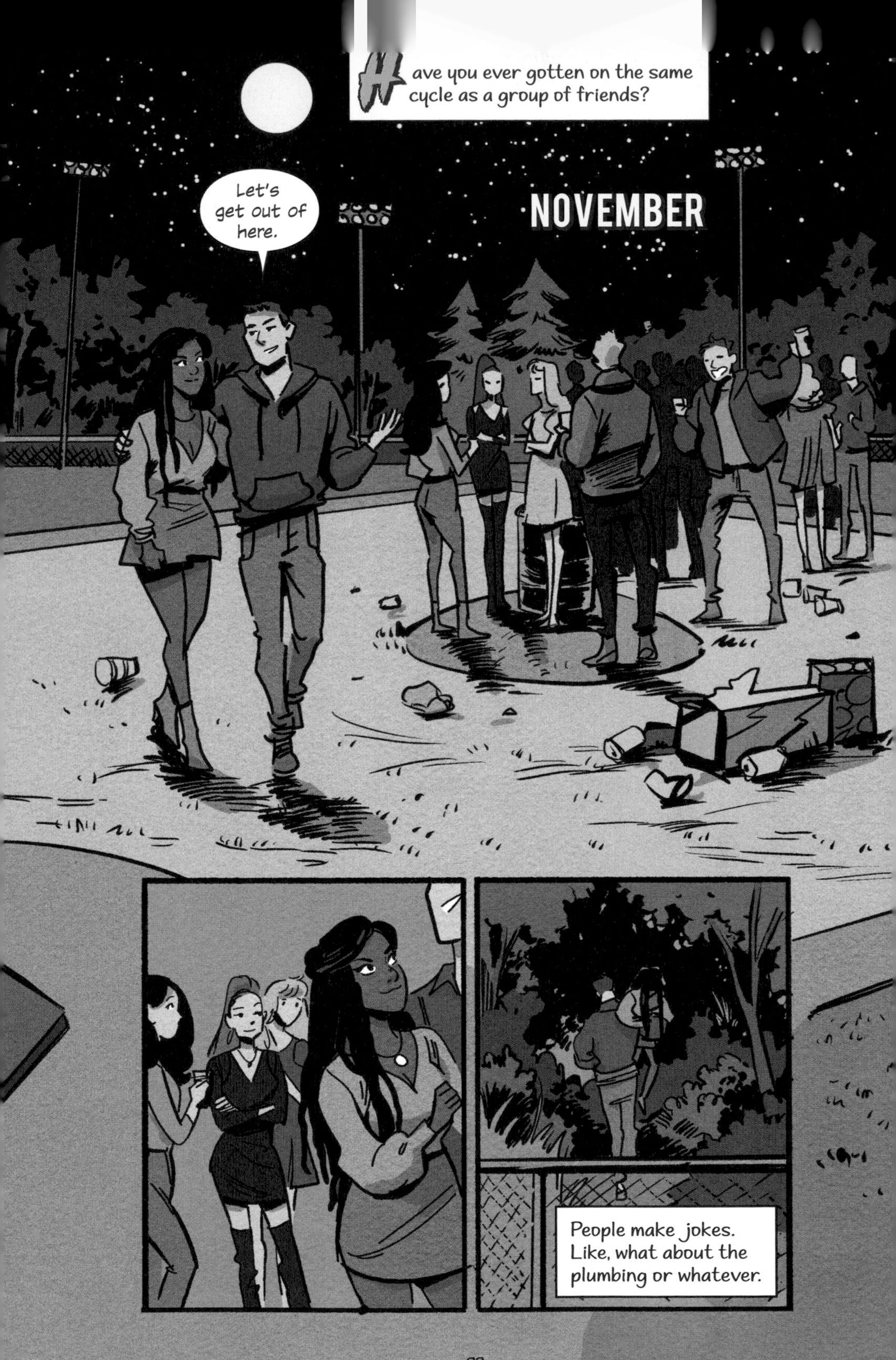
Have you ever gotten on the same cycle as a group of friends?
NOVEMBER
Let's get out of here.
People make jokes. Like, what about the plumbing or whatever.

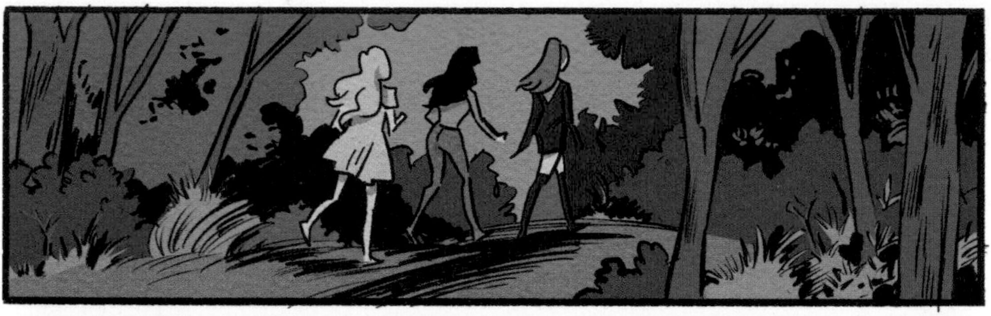

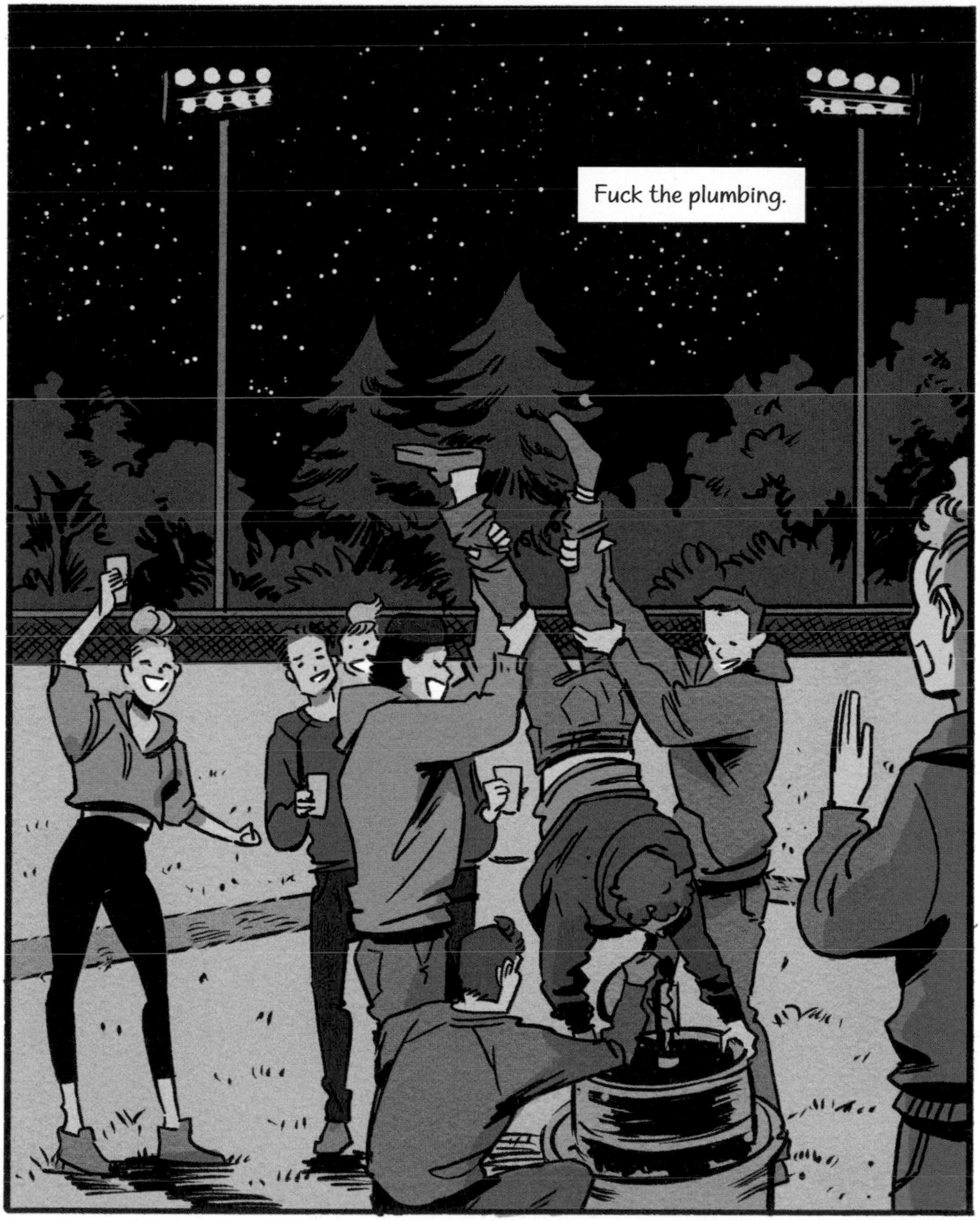
Fuck the plumbing.

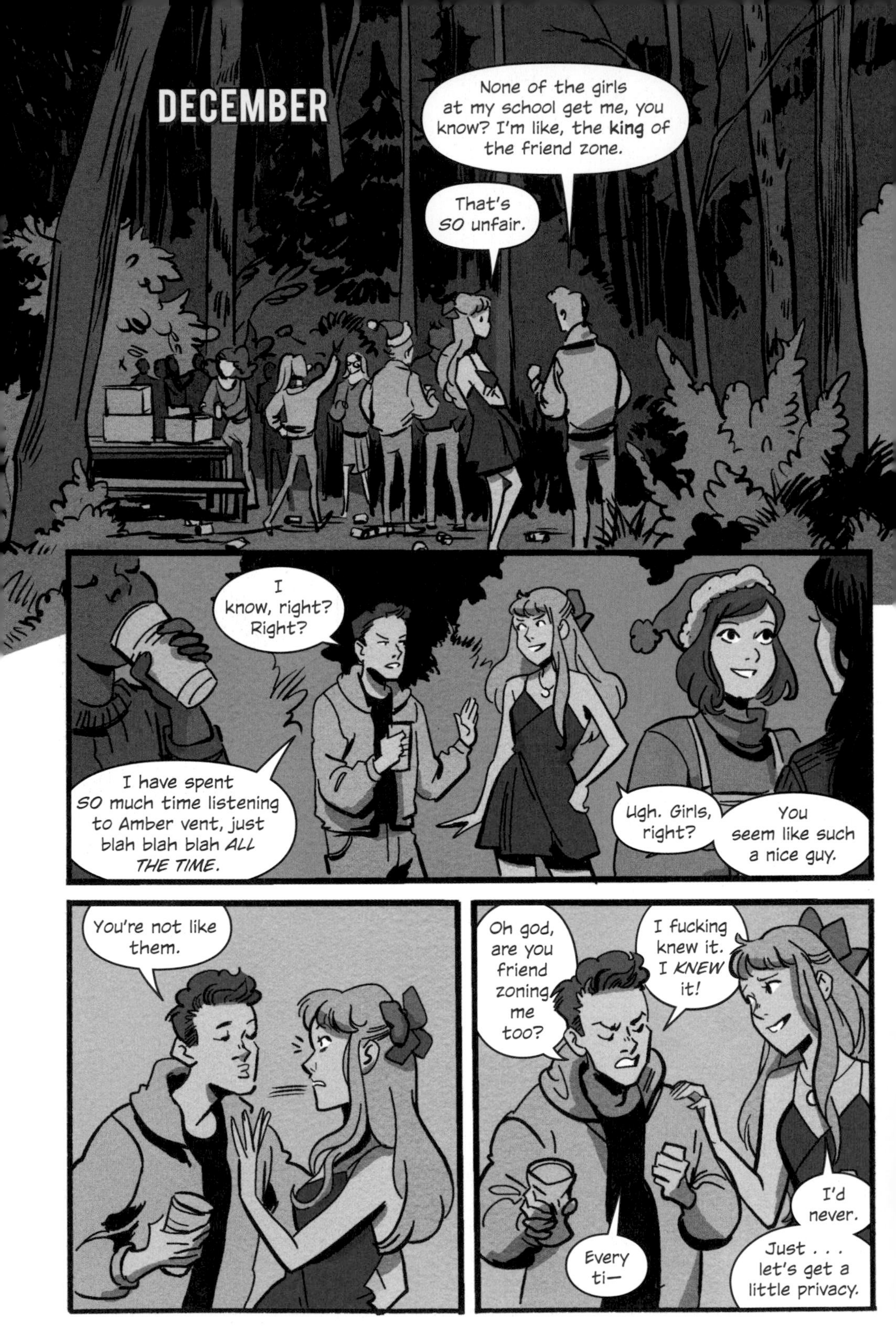
DECEMBER
None of the girls at my school get me, you know? I'm like, the **king** of the friend zone.
That's *SO* unfair.
I know, right? Right?
I have spent *SO* much time listening to Amber vent, just blah blah blah *ALL THE TIME*.
Ugh. Girls, right?
You seem like such a nice guy.
You're not like them.
Oh god, are you friend zoning me too?
I fucking knew it. I *KNEW* it!
Every ti—
I'd never.
Just . . . let's get a little privacy.

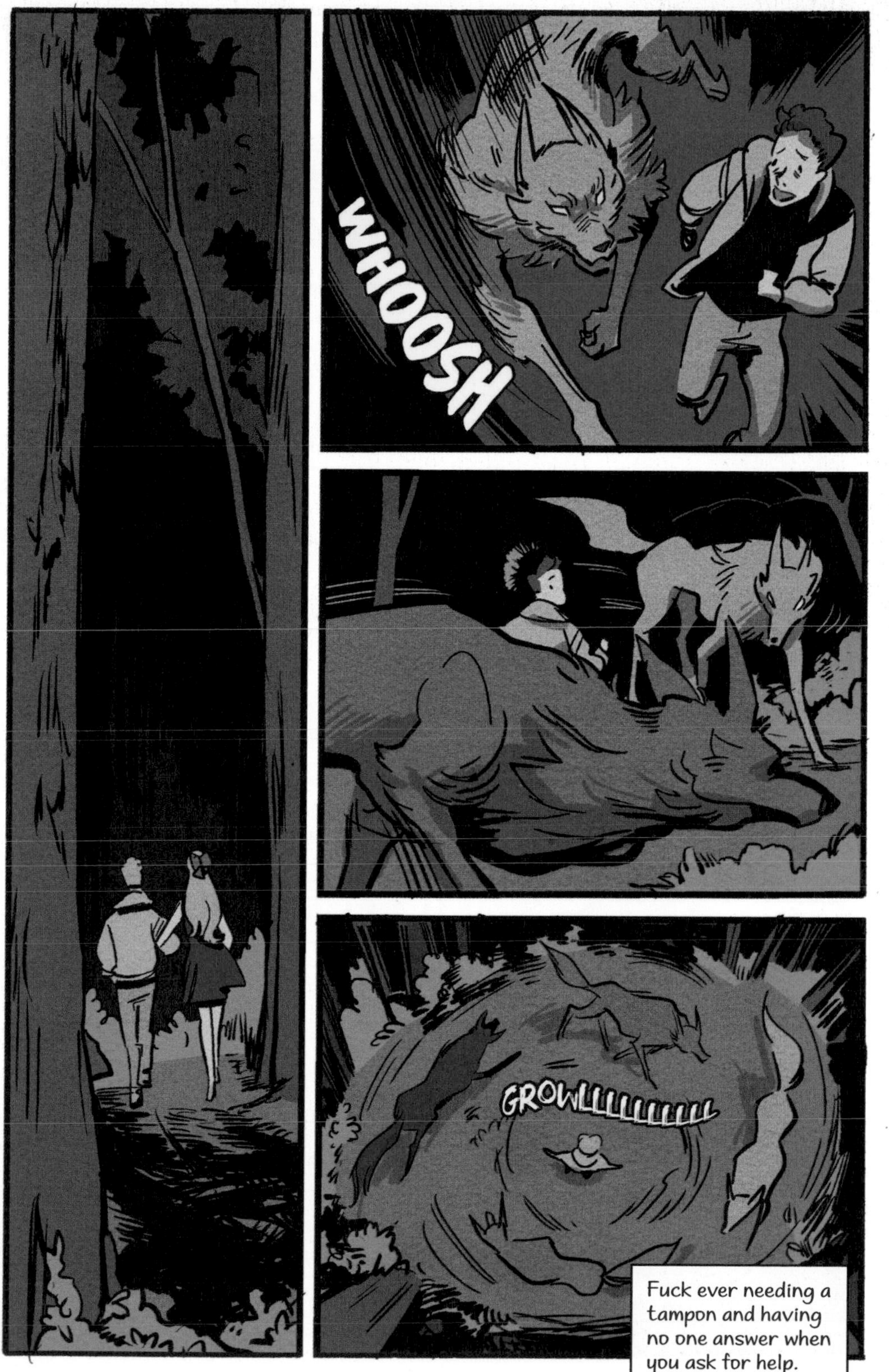
WHOOSH
GROWLLLLLLLLLL
Fuck ever needing a tampon and having no one answer when you ask for help.

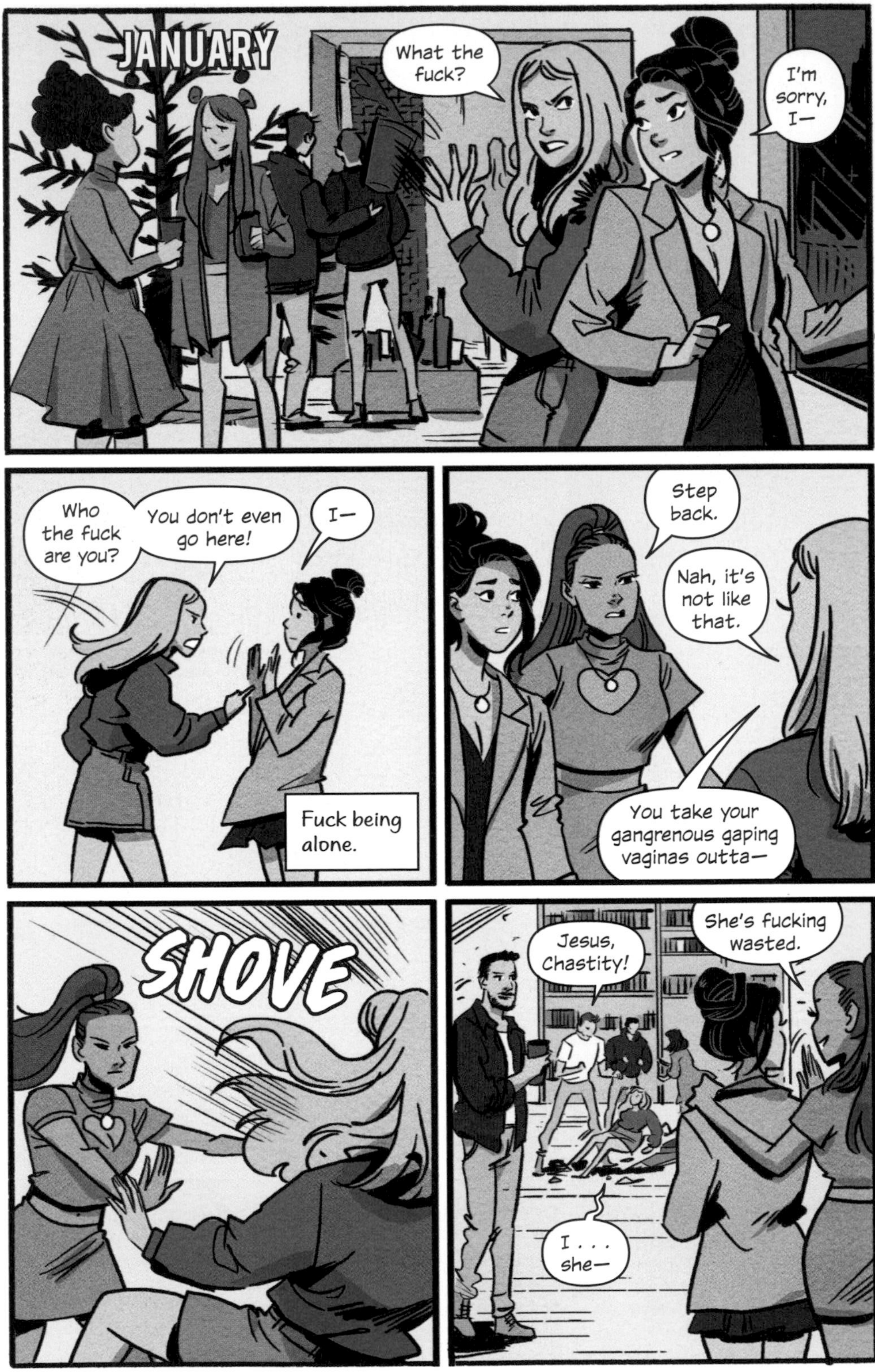
JANUARY
What the fuck?
I'm sorry, I—
Who the fuck are you?
You don't even go here!
I—
Fuck being alone.
Step back.
Nah, it's not like that.
You take your gangrenous gaping vaginas outta—
SHOVE
Jesus, Chastity!
She's fucking wasted.
I . . . she—

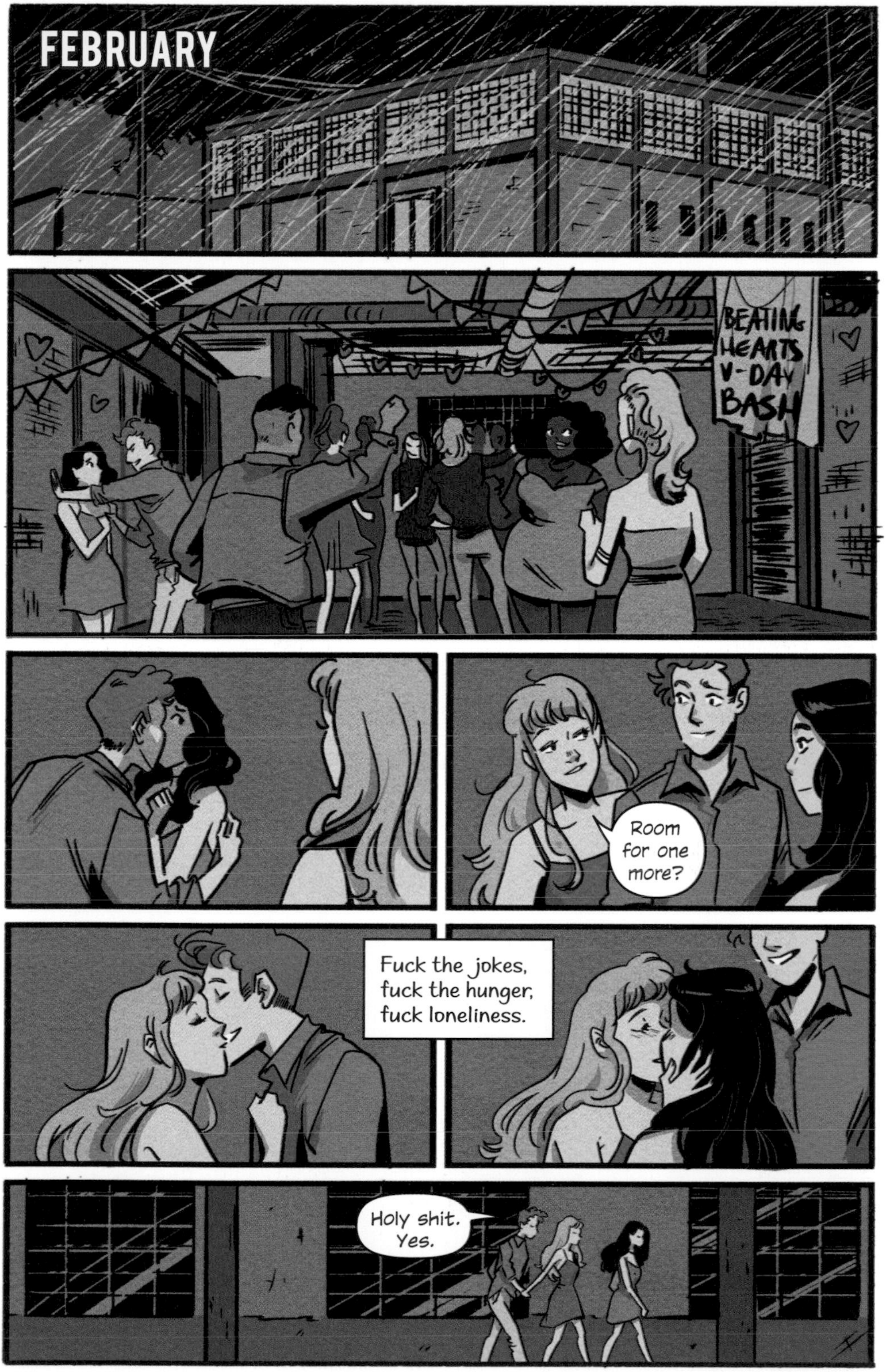
FEBRUARY
BEATING HEARTS V-DAY BASH
Room for one more?
Fuck the jokes, fuck the hunger, fuck loneliness.
Holy shit. Yes.

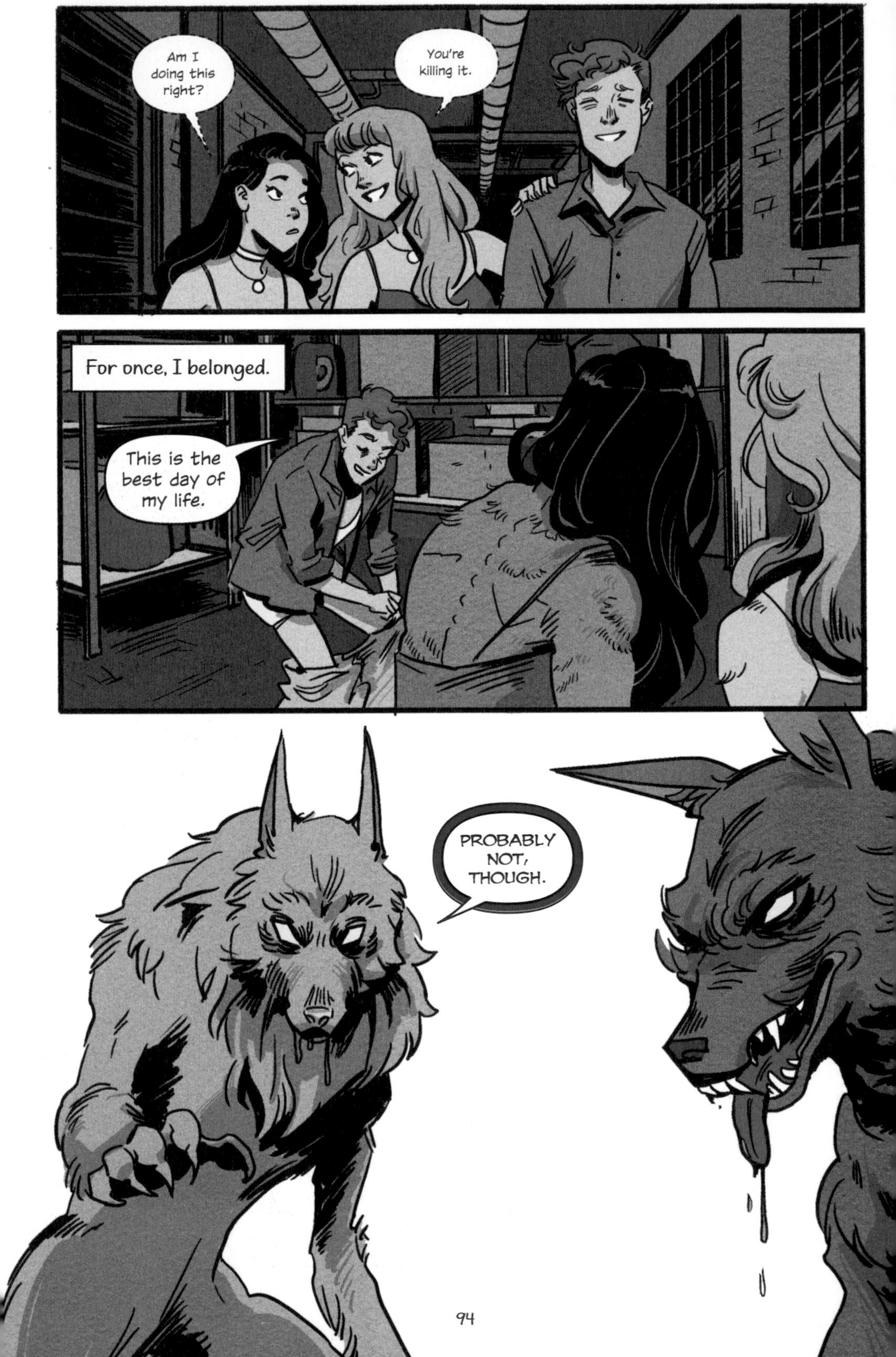
Am I doing this right?
You're killing it.
For once, I belonged.
This is the best day of my life.
PROBABLY NOT, THOUGH.

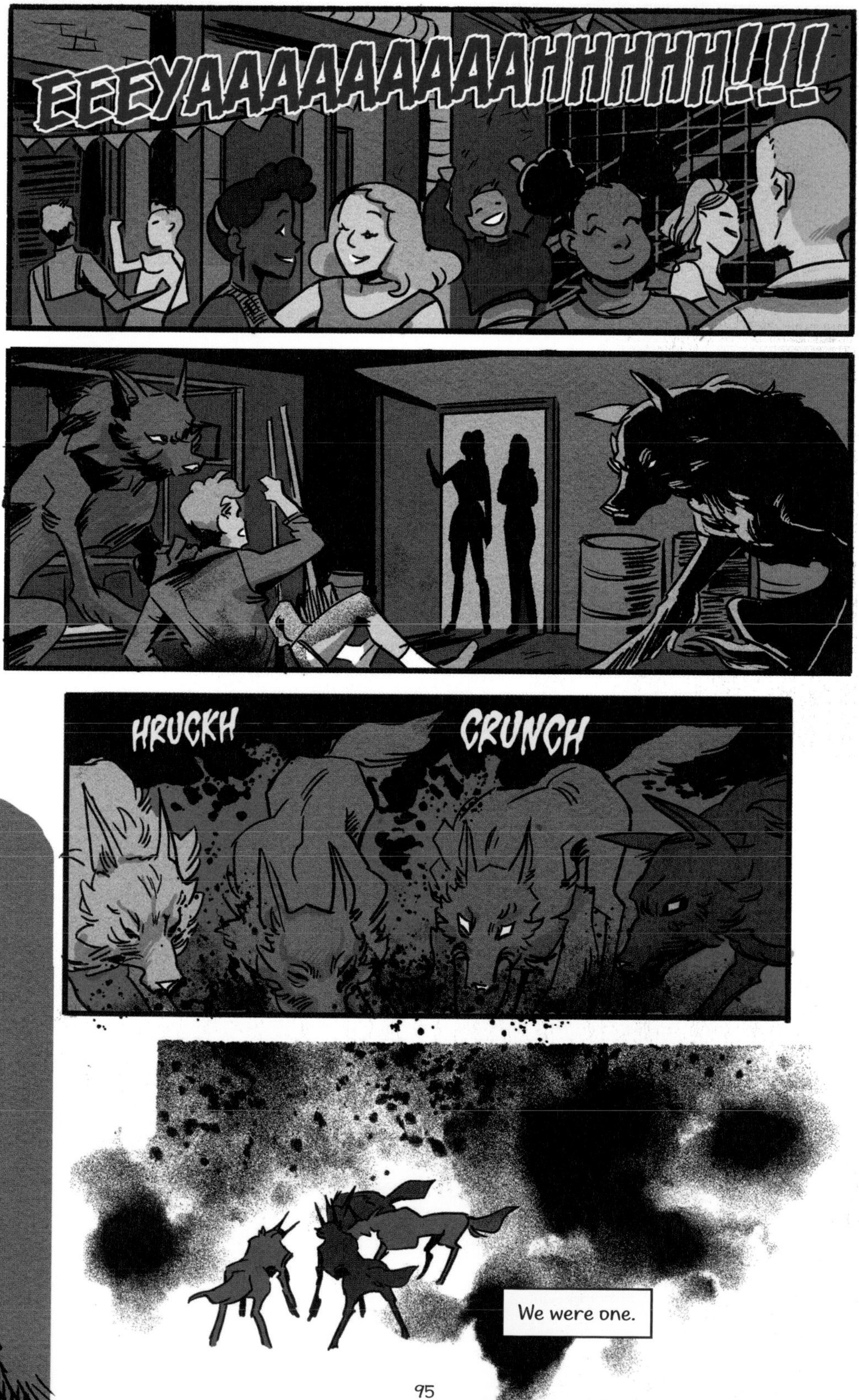
EEEYAAAAAAAAAHHHHH!!!
HRUCKH
CRUNCH
We were one.

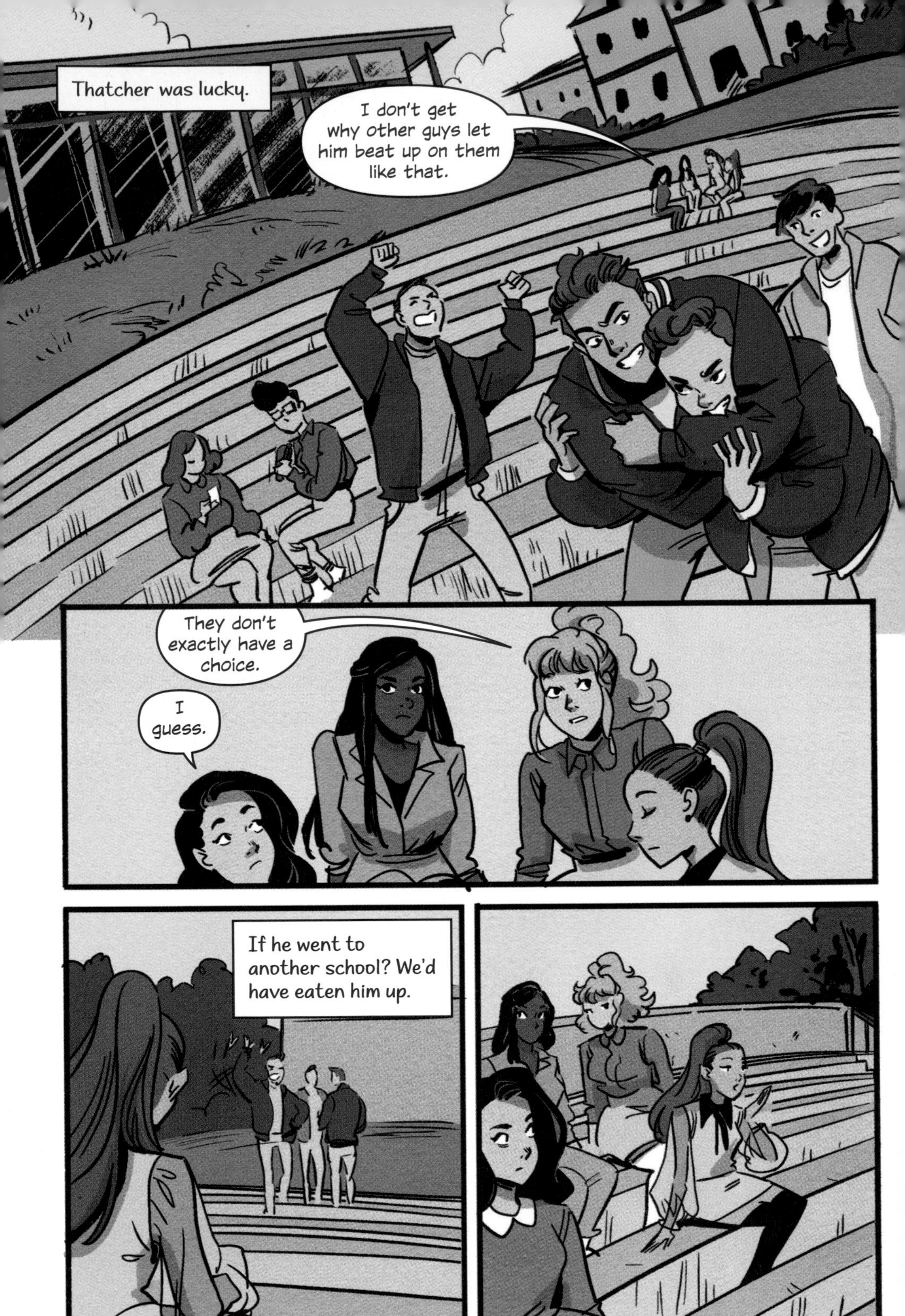
Thatcher was lucky.
I don't get why other guys let him beat up on them like that.
They don't exactly have a choice.
I guess.
If he went to another school? We'd have eaten him up.

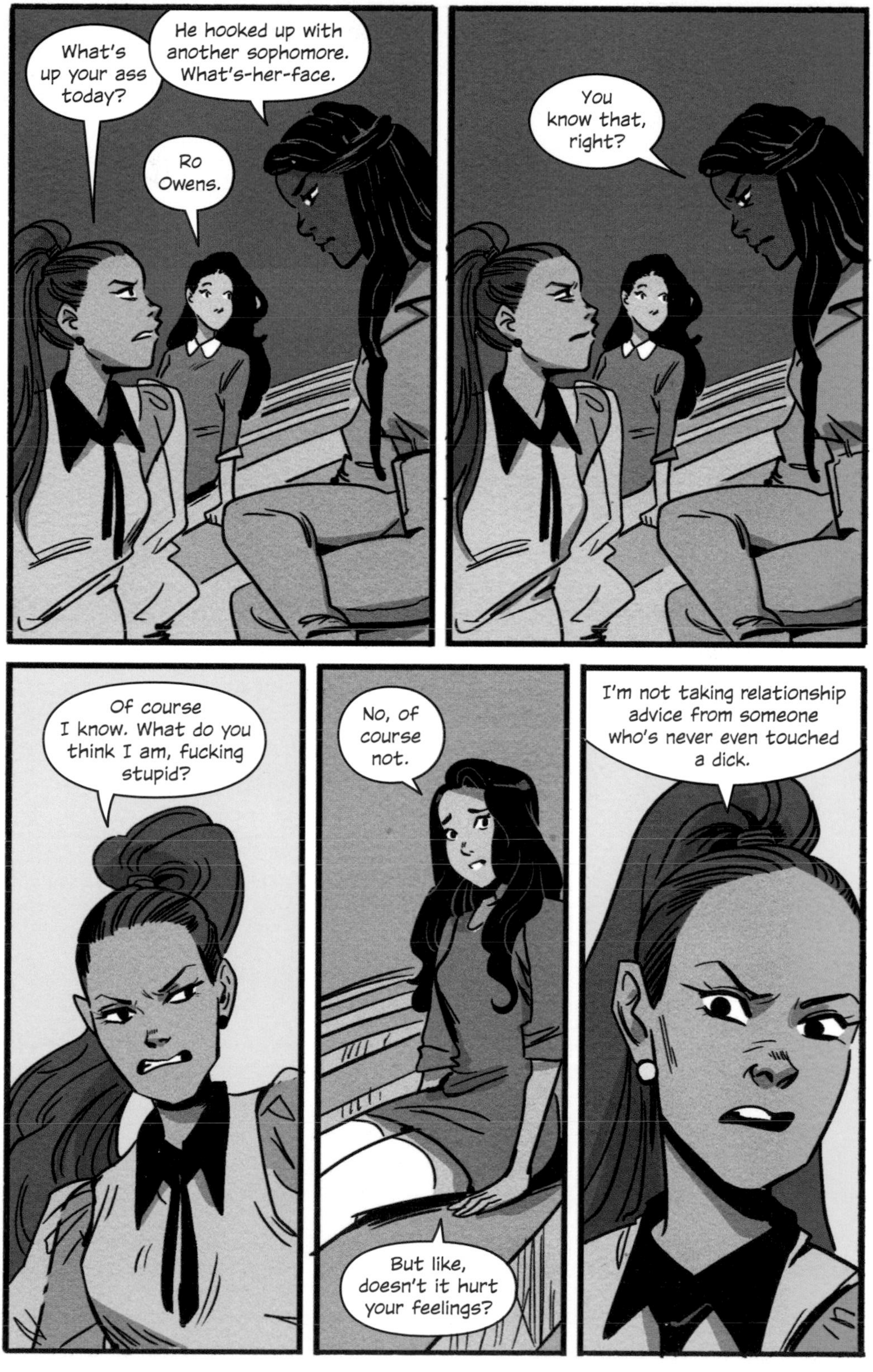
What's up your ass today?
He hooked up with another sophomore. What's-her-face.
Ro Owens.
You know that, right?
Of course I know. What do you think I am, fucking stupid?
No, of course not.
But like, doesn't it hurt your feelings?
I'm not taking relationship advice from someone who's never even touched a dick.

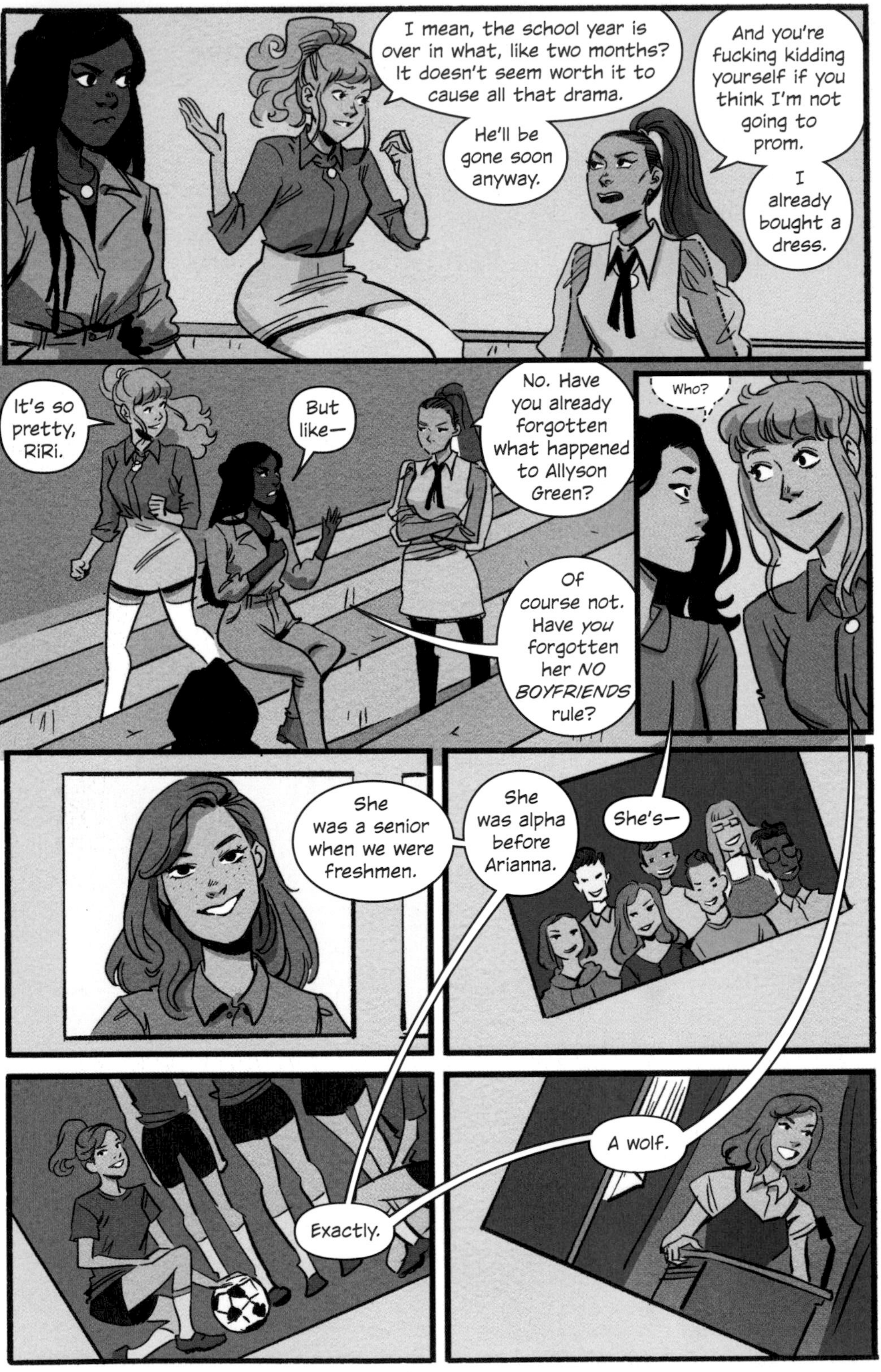
I mean, the school year is over in what, like two months? It doesn't seem worth it to cause all that drama.
He'll be gone soon anyway.
And you're fucking kidding yourself if you think I'm not going to prom.
I already bought a dress.
It's so pretty, RiRi.
But like—
No. Have you already forgotten what happened to Allyson Green?
Of course not. Have *you* forgotten her *NO BOYFRIENDS* rule?
Who?
She's—
She was alpha before Arianna.
She was a senior when we were freshmen.
A wolf.
Exactly.

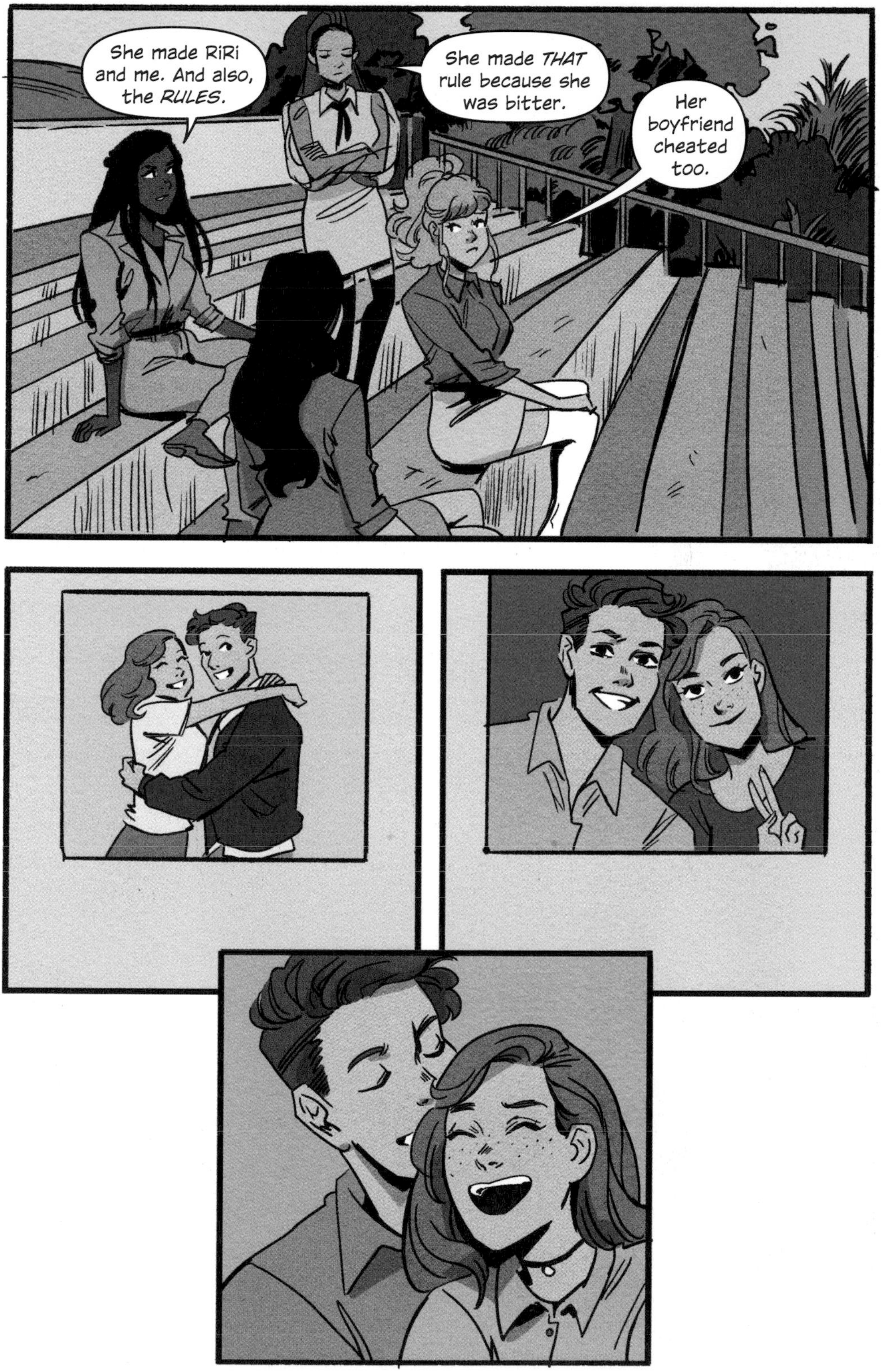
She made RiRi and me. And also, the RULES.
She made THAT rule because she was bitter.
Her boyfriend cheated too.

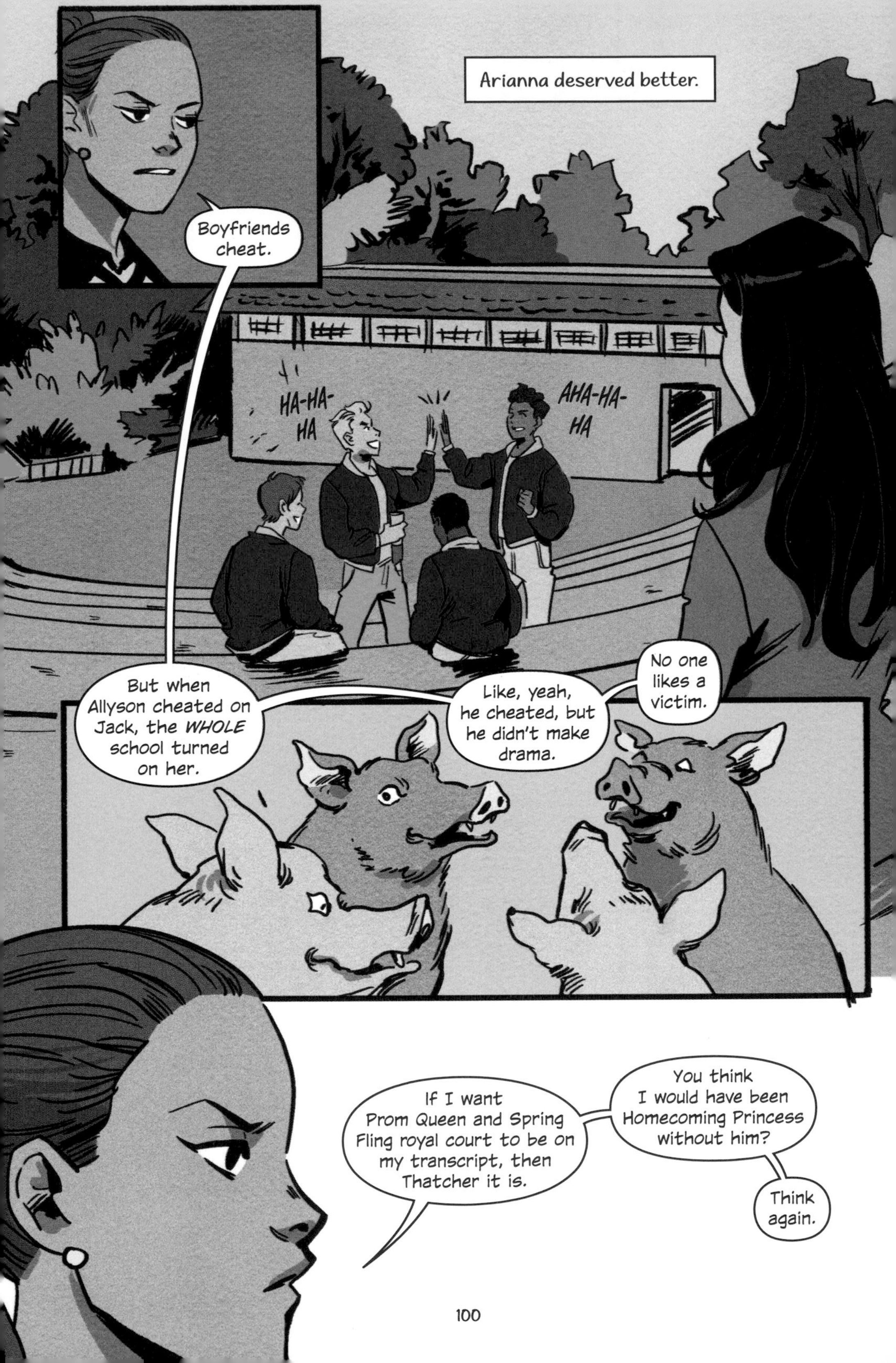
Arianna deserved better.
Boyfriends cheat.
HA-HA-HA
AHA-HA-HA
But when Allyson cheated on Jack, the *WHOLE* school turned on her.
Like, yeah, he cheated, but he didn't make drama.
No one likes a victim.
If I want Prom Queen and Spring Fling royal court to be on my transcript, then Thatcher it is.
You think I would have been Homecoming Princess without him?
Think again.

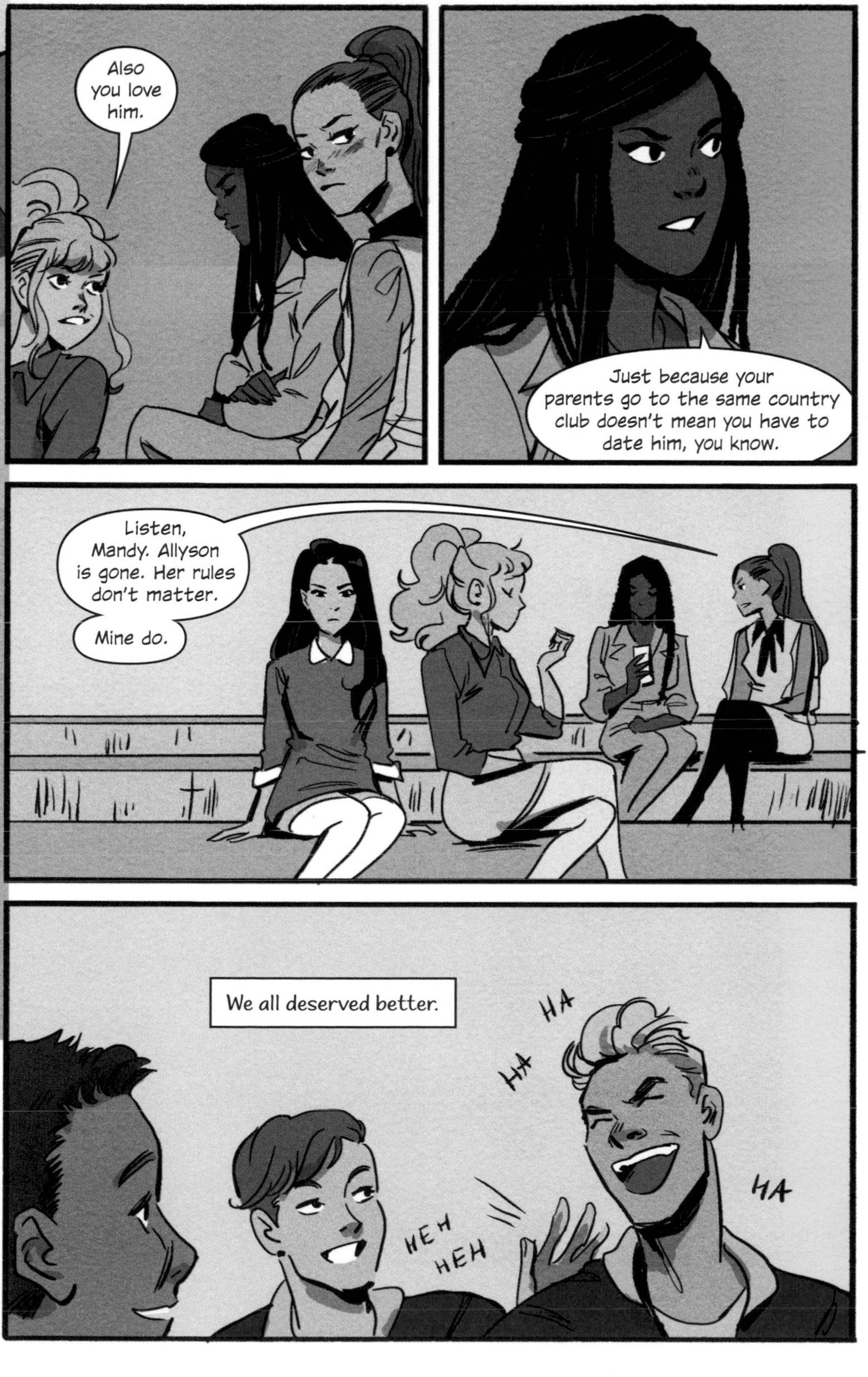
Also you love him.
Just because your parents go to the same country club doesn't mean you have to date him, you know.
Listen, Mandy. Allyson is gone. Her rules don't matter.
Mine do.
We all deserved better.
HA
HA
HA
HEH
HEH

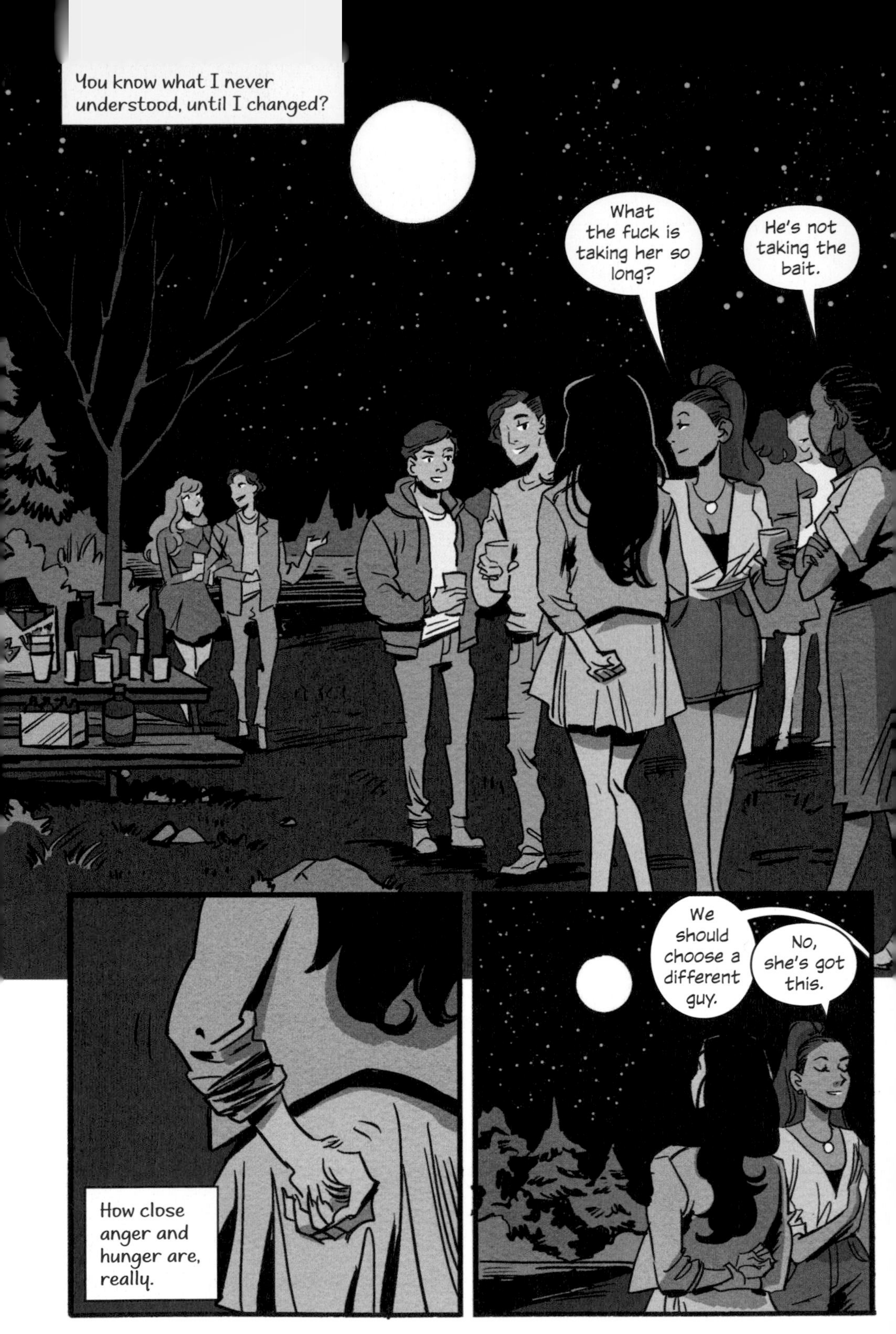
You know what I never understood, until I changed?
What the fuck is taking her so long?
He's not taking the bait.
How close anger and hunger are, really.
We should choose a different guy.
No, she's got this.

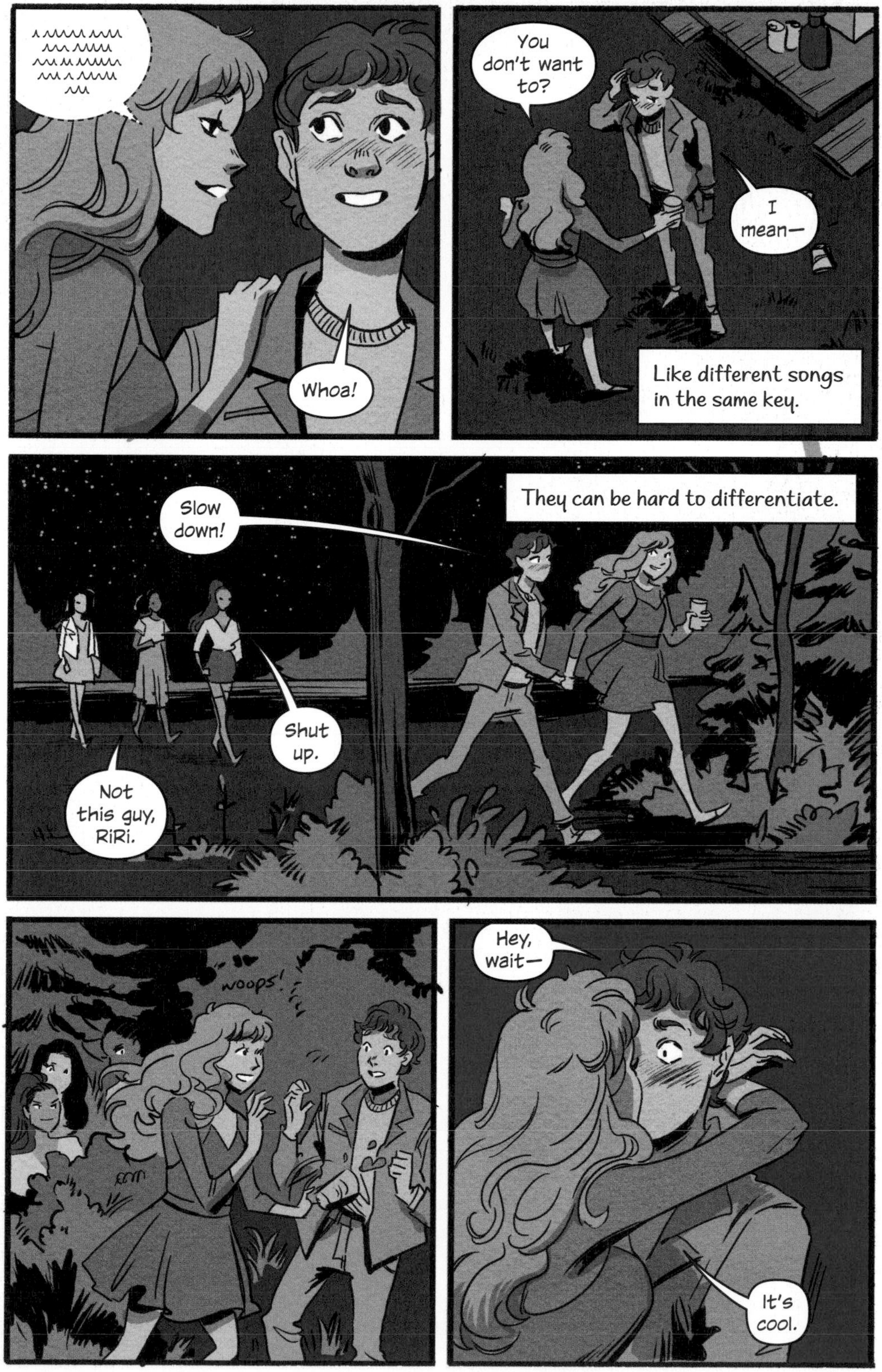

Whoa!
You don't want to?
I mean—
Like different songs in the same key.
They can be hard to differentiate.
Slow down!
Shut up.
Not this guy, RiRi.
woops!
Hey, wait—
It's cool.

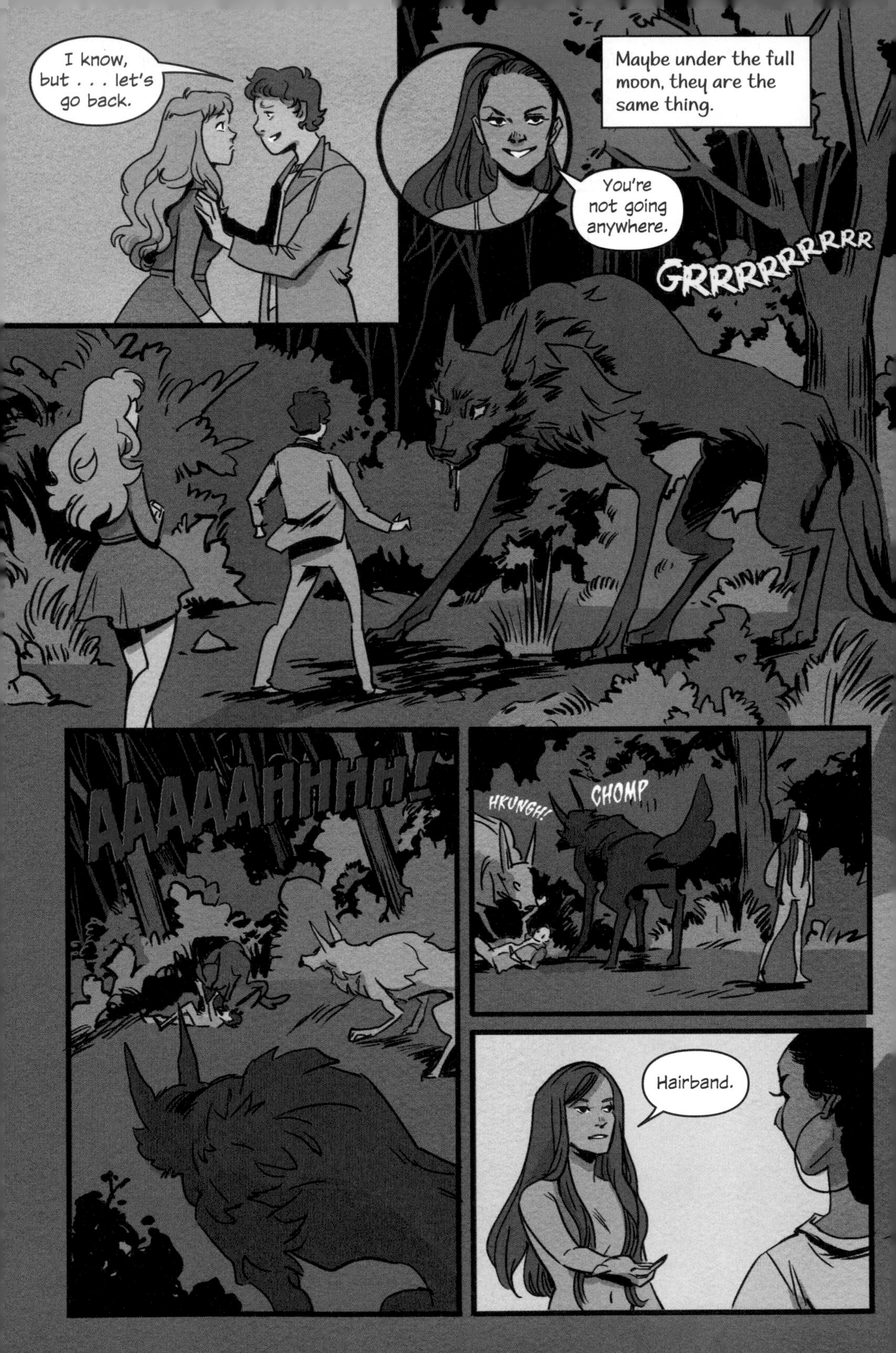
I know, but . . . let's go back.
Maybe under the full moon, they are the same thing.
You're not going anywhere.
GRRRRRRRRR
AAAAAHHHH!
HKUNGH!
CHOMP
Hairband.

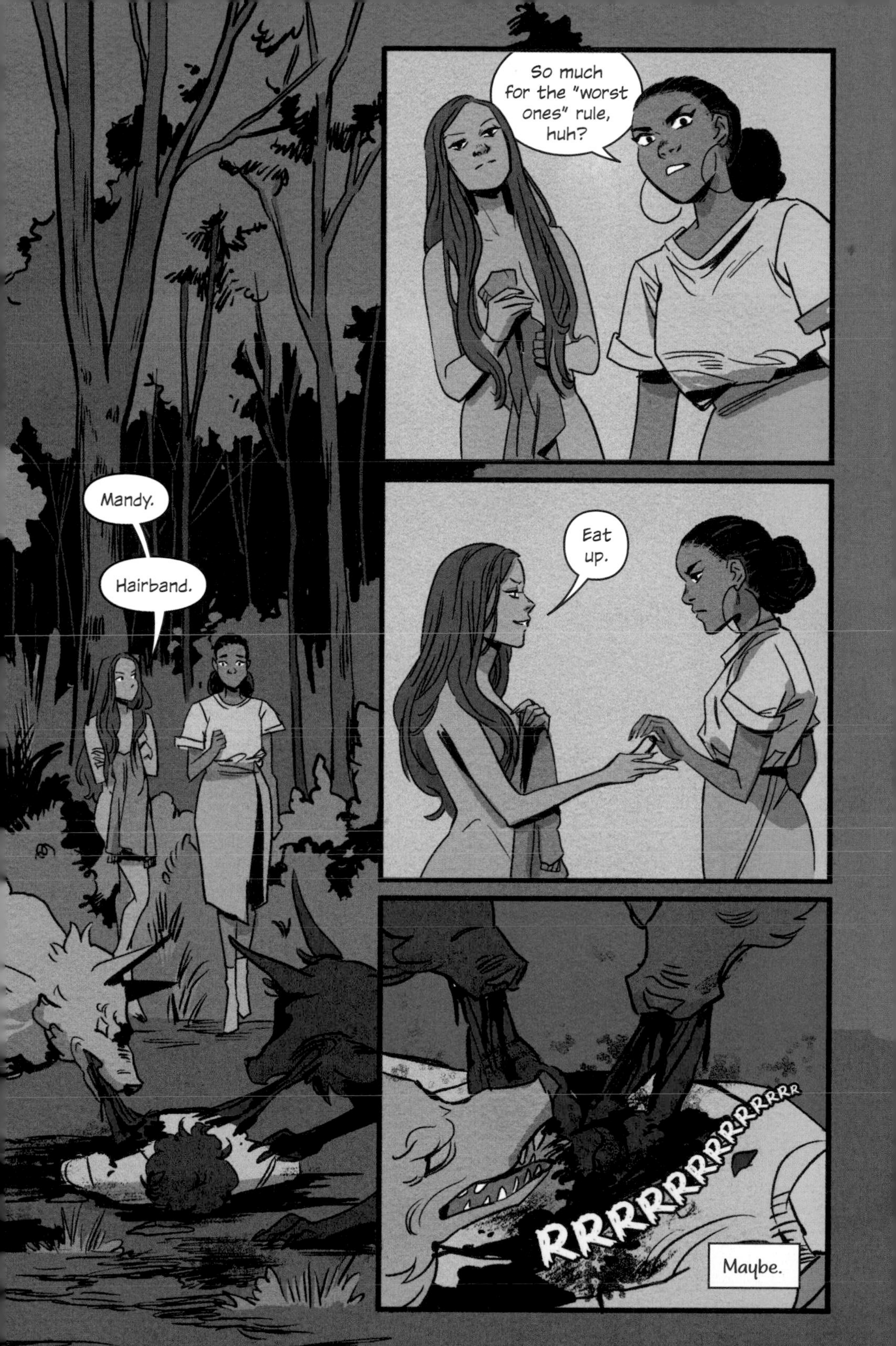
Mandy.
Hairband.
So much for the "worst ones" rule, huh?
Eat up.
RRRRRRRRRRRRRRR
Maybe.

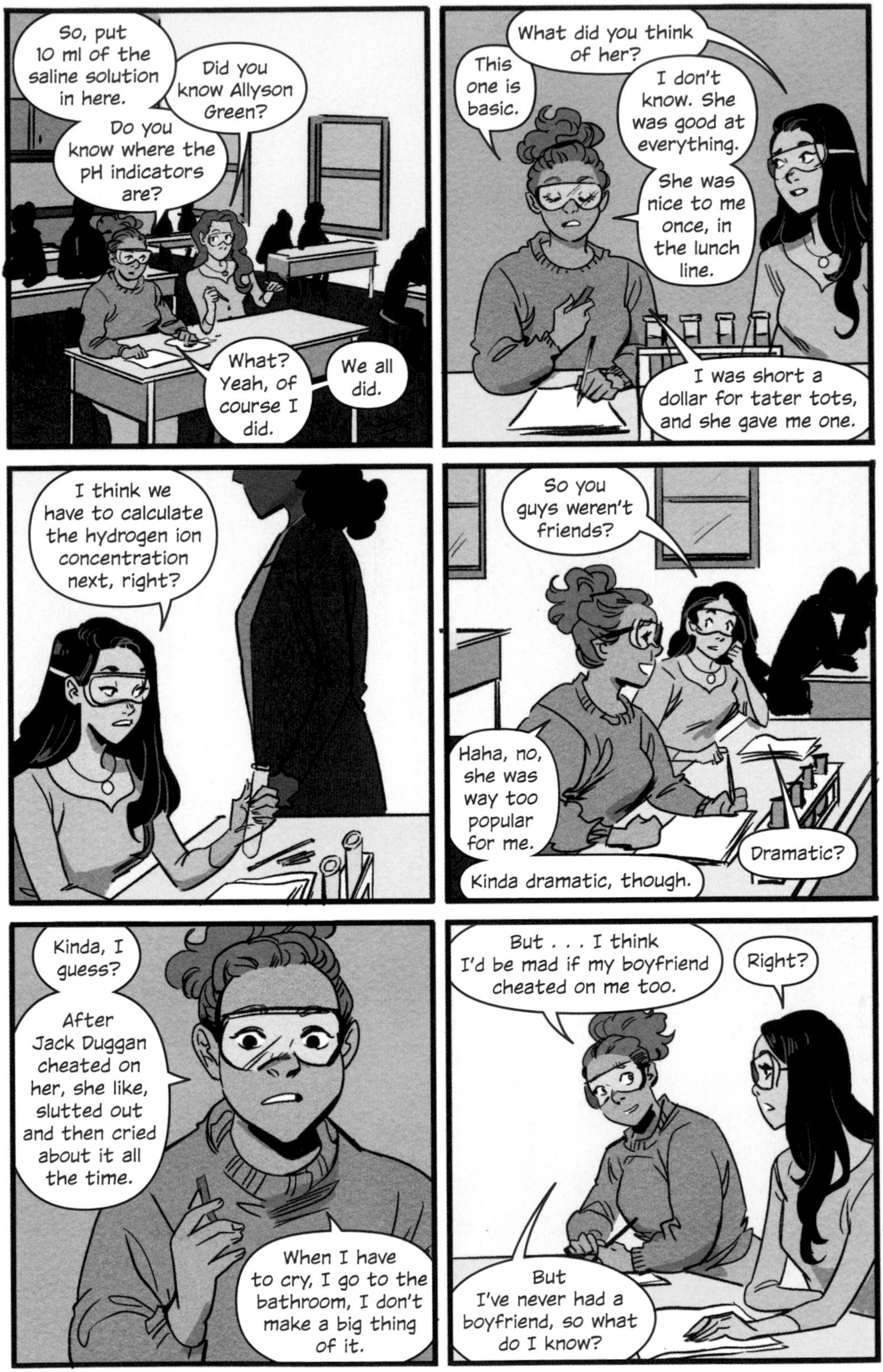
So, put 10 ml of the saline solution in here.
Did you know Allyson Green?
Do you know where the pH indicators are?
What? Yeah, of course I did.
We all did.
What did you think of her?
This one is basic.
I don't know. She was good at everything.
She was nice to me once, in the lunch line.
I was short a dollar for tater tots, and she gave me one.
I think we have to calculate the hydrogen ion concentration next, right?
So you guys weren't friends?
Haha, no, she was way too popular for me.
Kinda dramatic, though.
Dramatic?
Kinda, I guess?
After Jack Duggan cheated on her, she like, slutted out and then cried about it all the time.
When I have to cry, I go to the bathroom, I don't make a big thing of it.
But . . . I think I'd be mad if my boyfriend cheated on me too.
Right?
But I've never had a boyfriend, so what do I know?

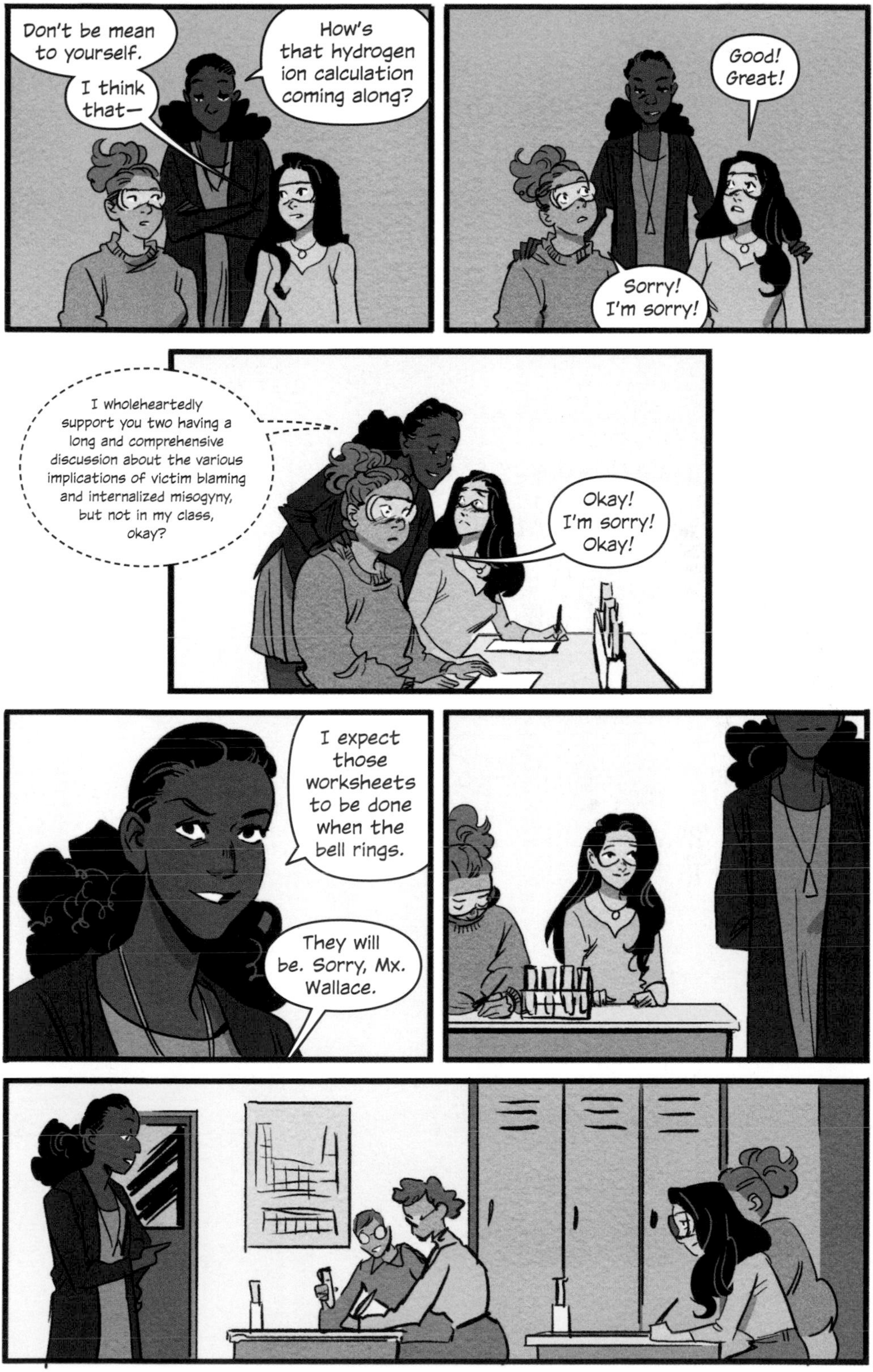
Don't be mean to yourself.
I think that—
How's that hydrogen ion calculation coming along?
Good! Great!
Sorry! I'm sorry!
I wholeheartedly support you two having a long and comprehensive discussion about the various implications of victim blaming and internalized misogyny, but not in my class, okay?
Okay! I'm sorry! Okay!
I expect those worksheets to be done when the bell rings.
They will be. Sorry, Mx. Wallace.

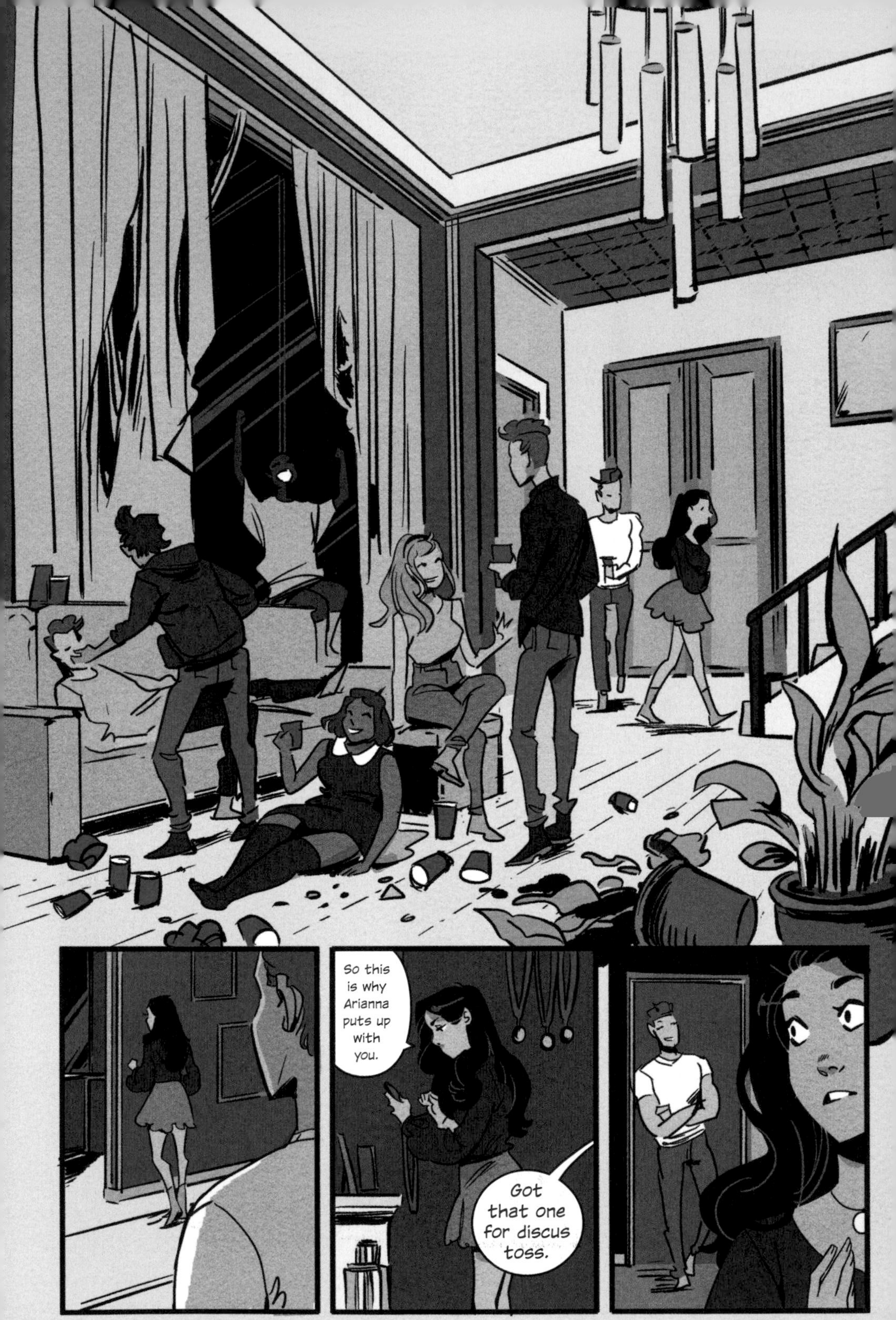
So this is why Arianna puts up with you.
Got that one for discus toss.

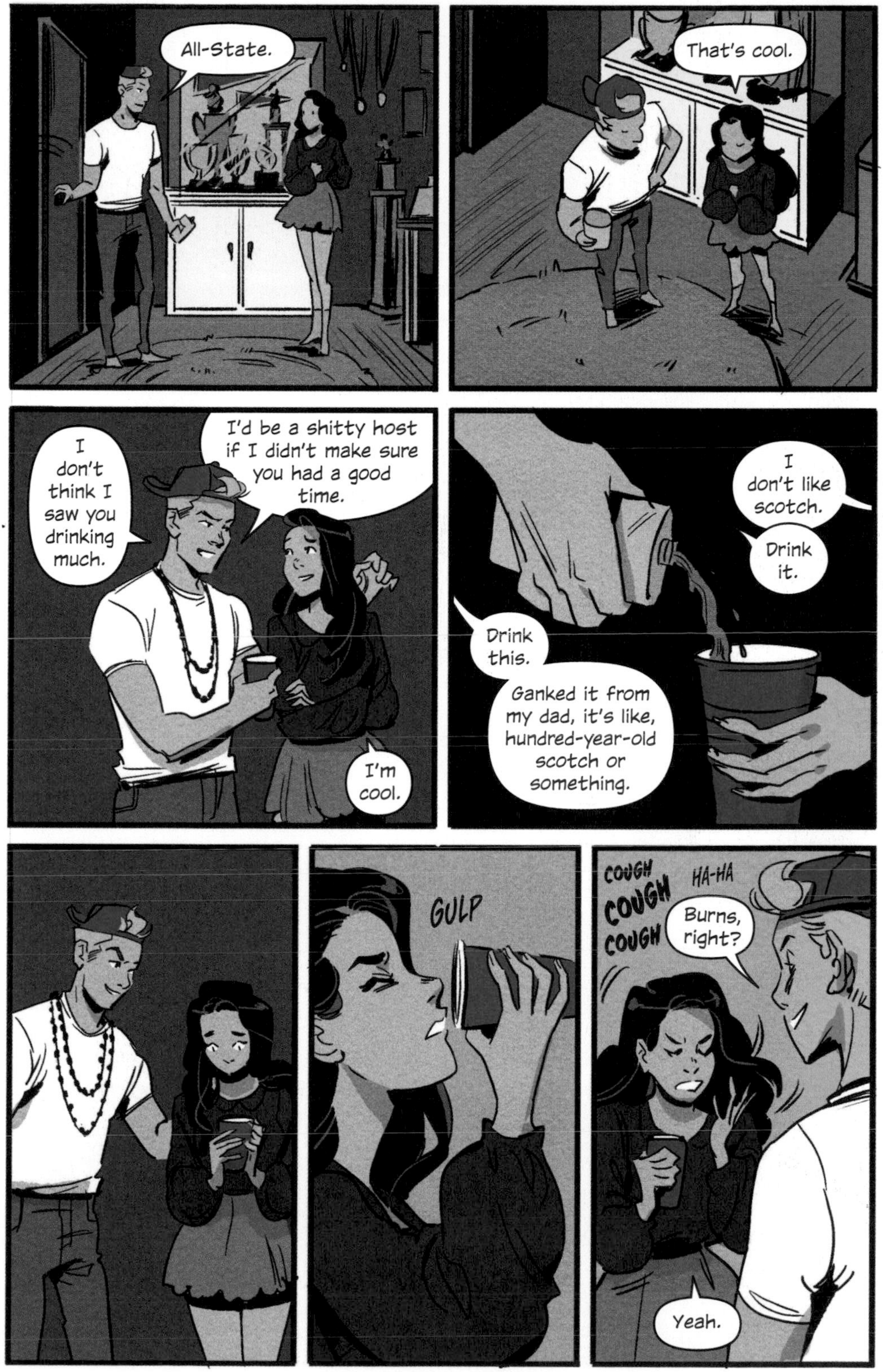
All-State.
That's cool.
I don't think I saw you drinking much.
I'd be a shitty host if I didn't make sure you had a good time.
I'm cool.
Drink this.
Ganked it from my dad, it's like, hundred-year-old scotch or something.
I don't like scotch.
Drink it.
GULP
COUGH COUGH COUGH
HA-HA
Burns, right?
Yeah.

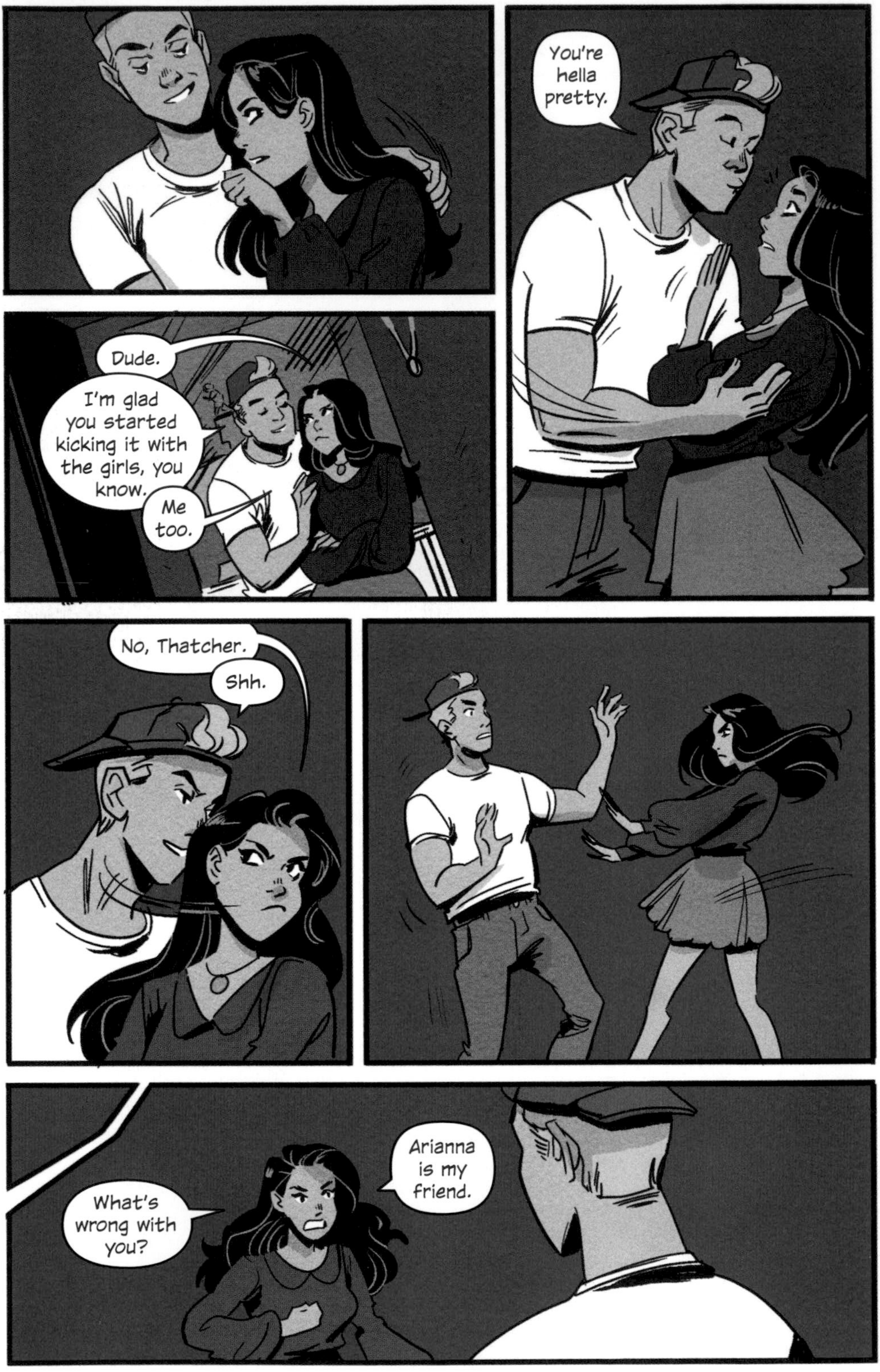
You're hella pretty.
Dude.
I'm glad you started kicking it with the girls, you know.
Me too.
No, Thatcher.
Shh.
What's wrong with you?
Arianna is my friend.

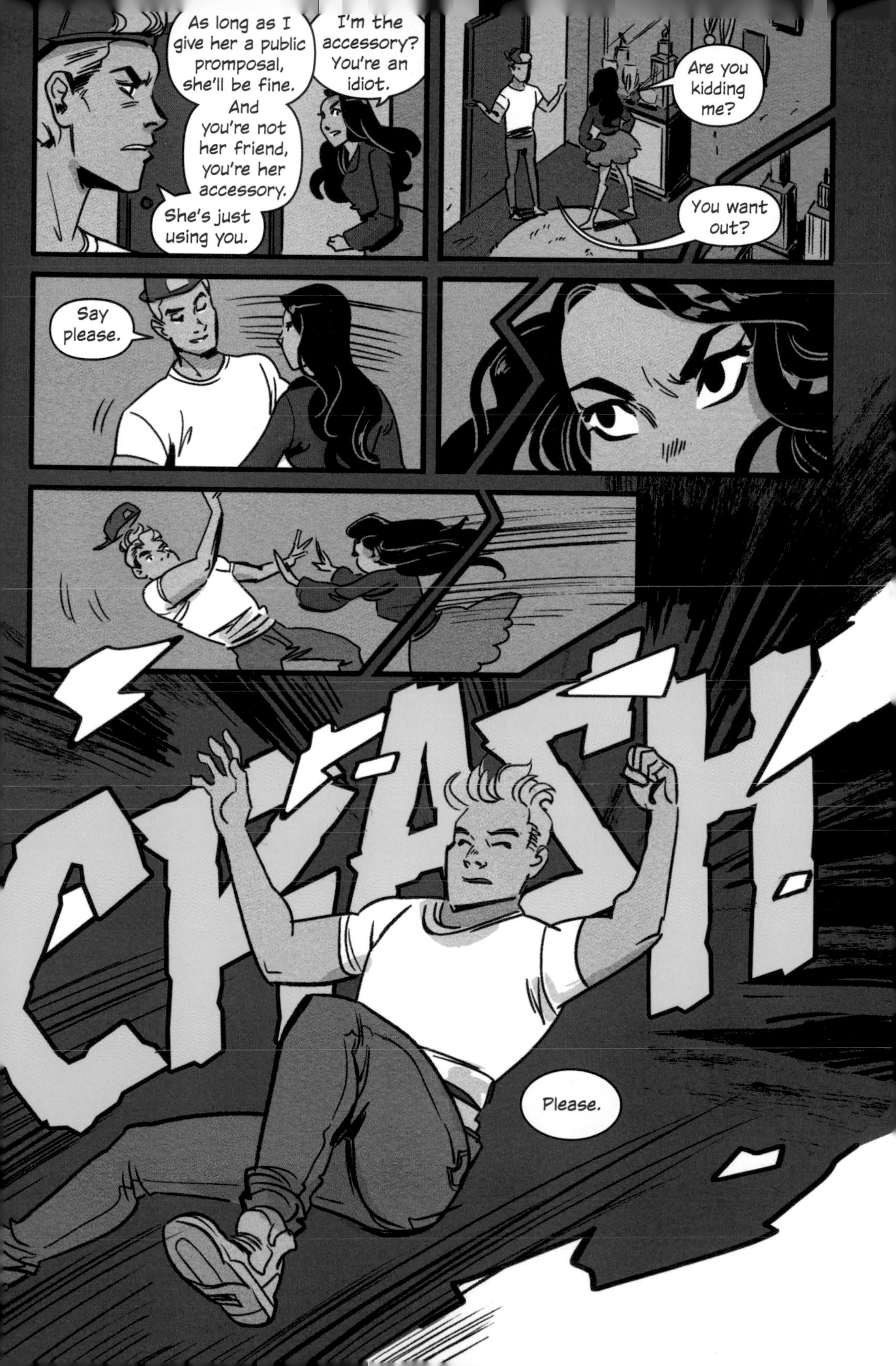

She's just using you.
As long as I give her a public promposal, she'll be fine.
And you're not her friend, you're her accessory.
I'm the accessory? You're an idiot.
Are you kidding me?
You want out?
Say please.
CRASH!
Please.

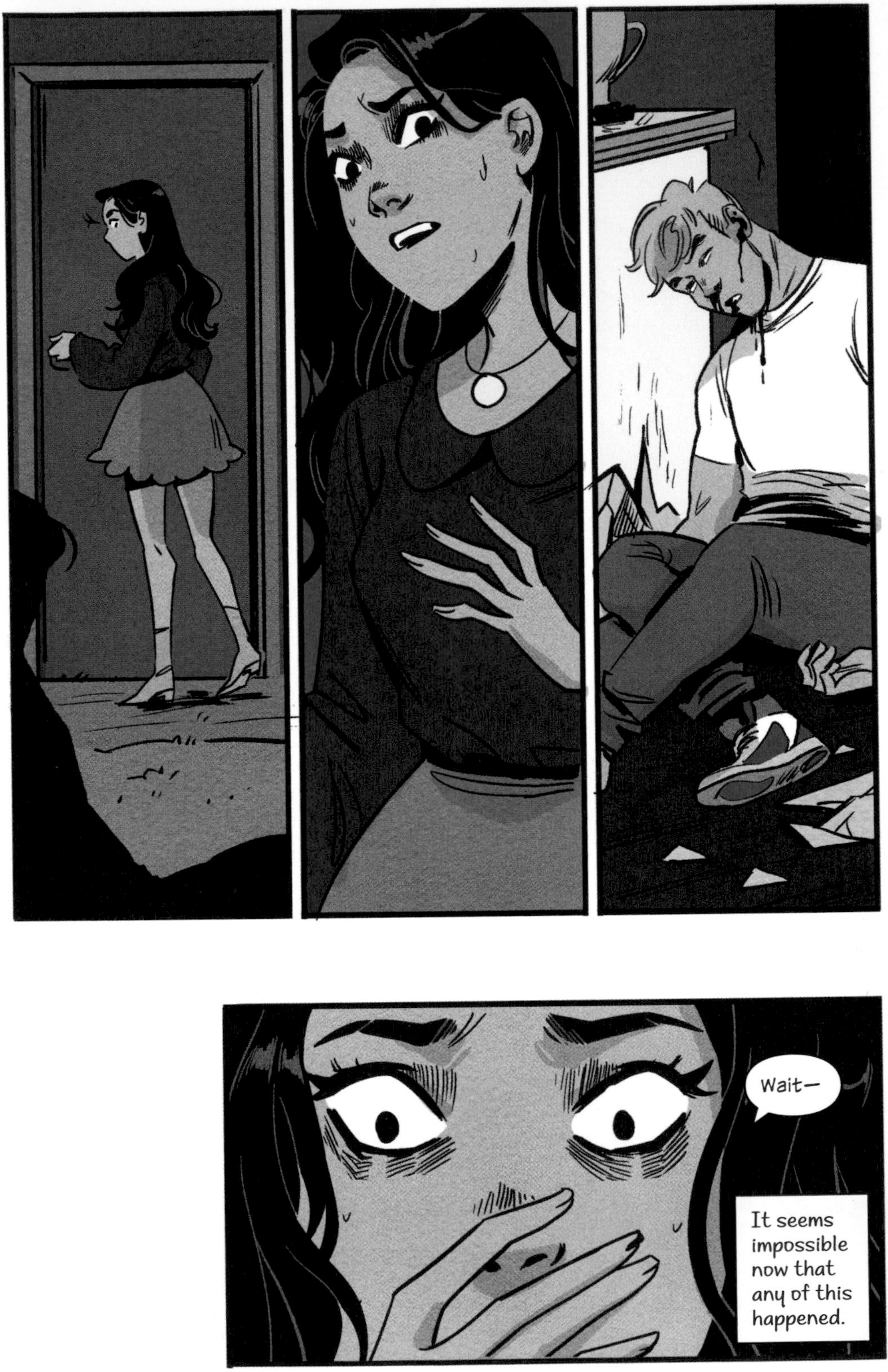
Wait—
It seems impossible now that any of this happened.

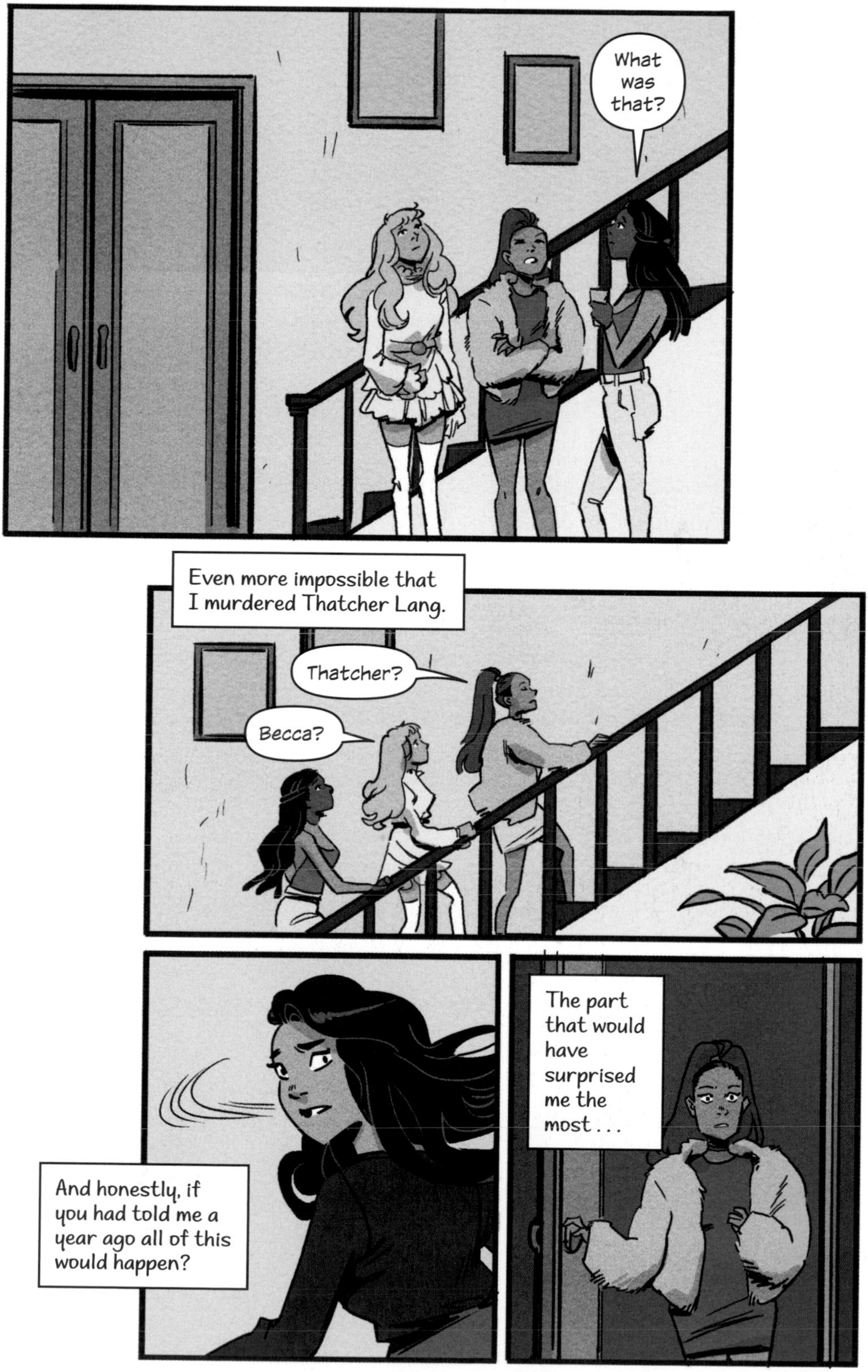
What was that?
Even more impossible that I murdered Thatcher Lang.
Thatcher?
Becca?
And honestly, if you had told me a year ago all of this would happen?
The part that would have surprised me the most . . .

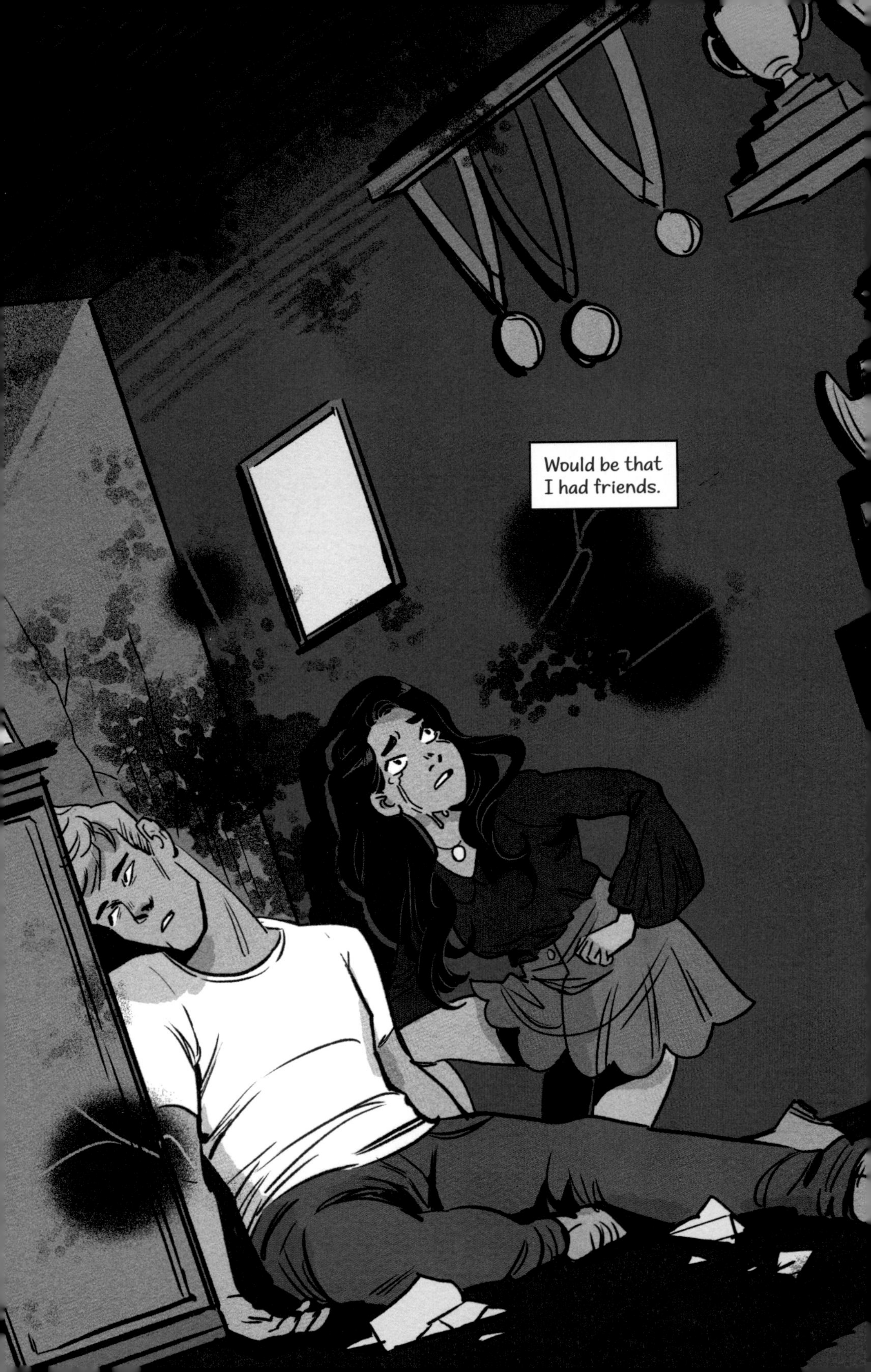
Would be that
I had friends.

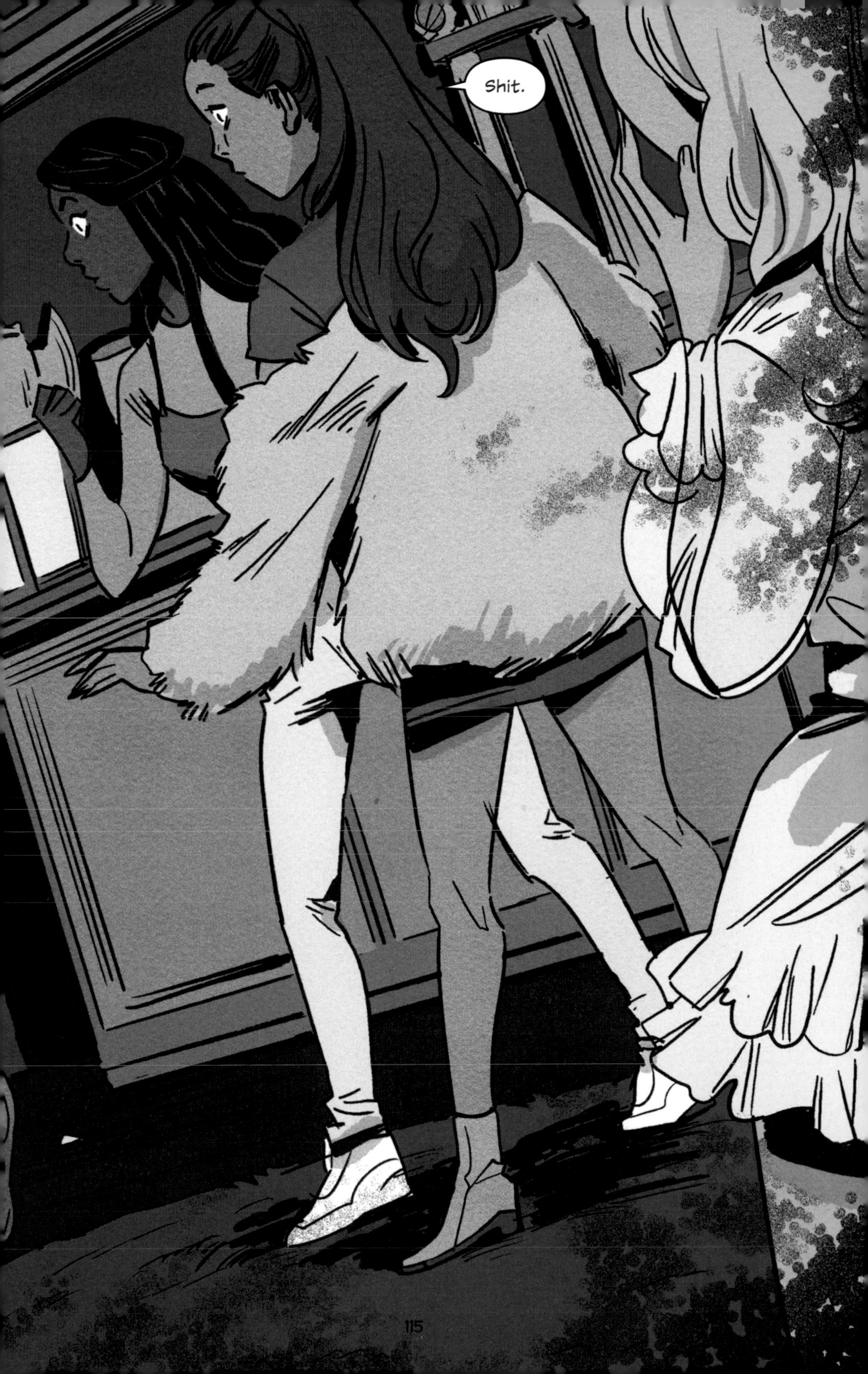
Shit.

CHAPTER FIVE

THATCHER'S BODY

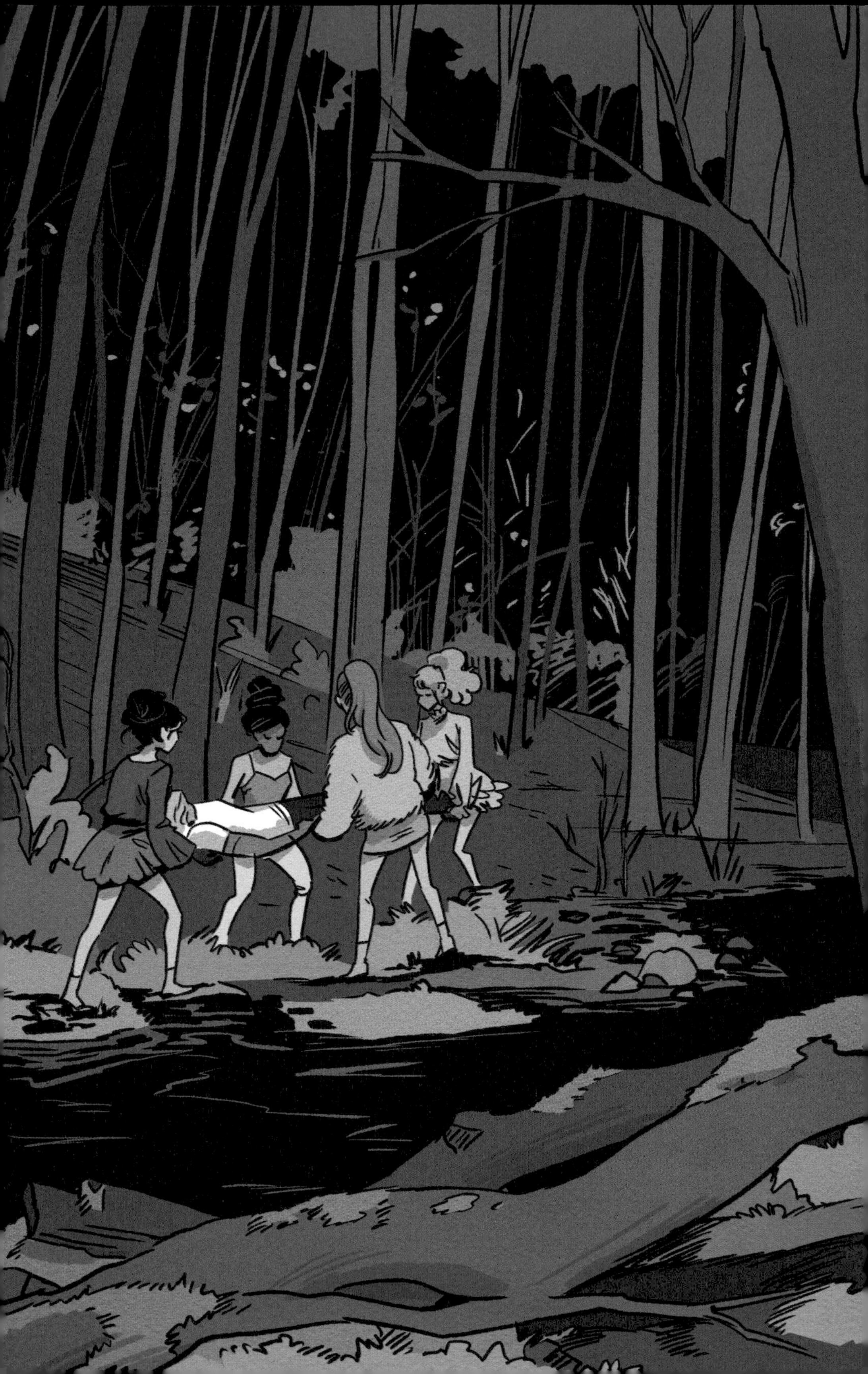

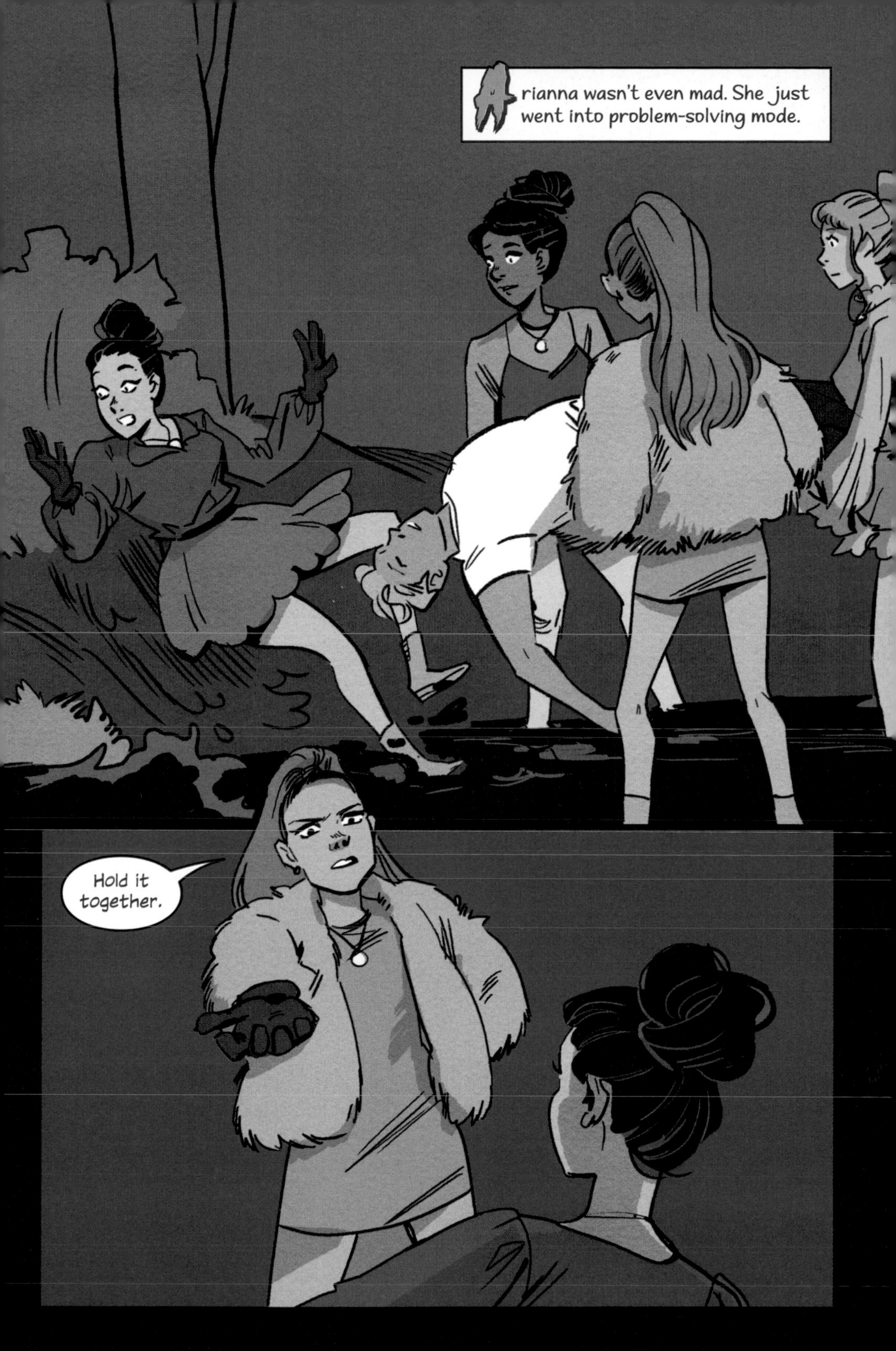
Arianna wasn't even mad. She just went into problem-solving mode.
Hold it together.

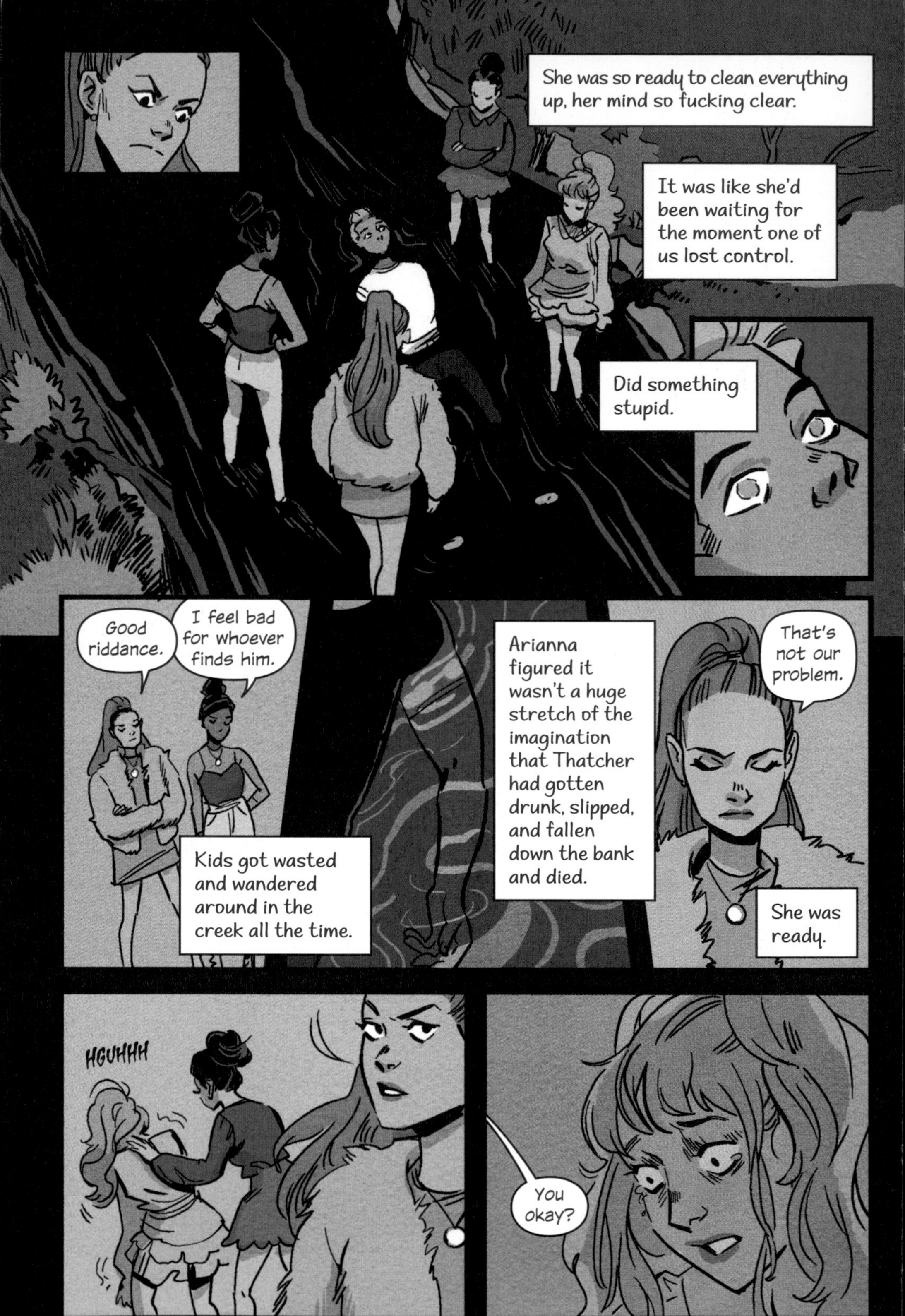
She was so ready to clean everything up, her mind so fucking clear.
It was like she'd been waiting for the moment one of us lost control.
Did something stupid.
Good riddance.
I feel bad for whoever finds him.
Kids got wasted and wandered around in the creek all the time.
Arianna figured it wasn't a huge stretch of the imagination that Thatcher had gotten drunk, slipped, and fallen down the bank and died.
That's not our problem.
She was ready.
HGUHHH
You okay?

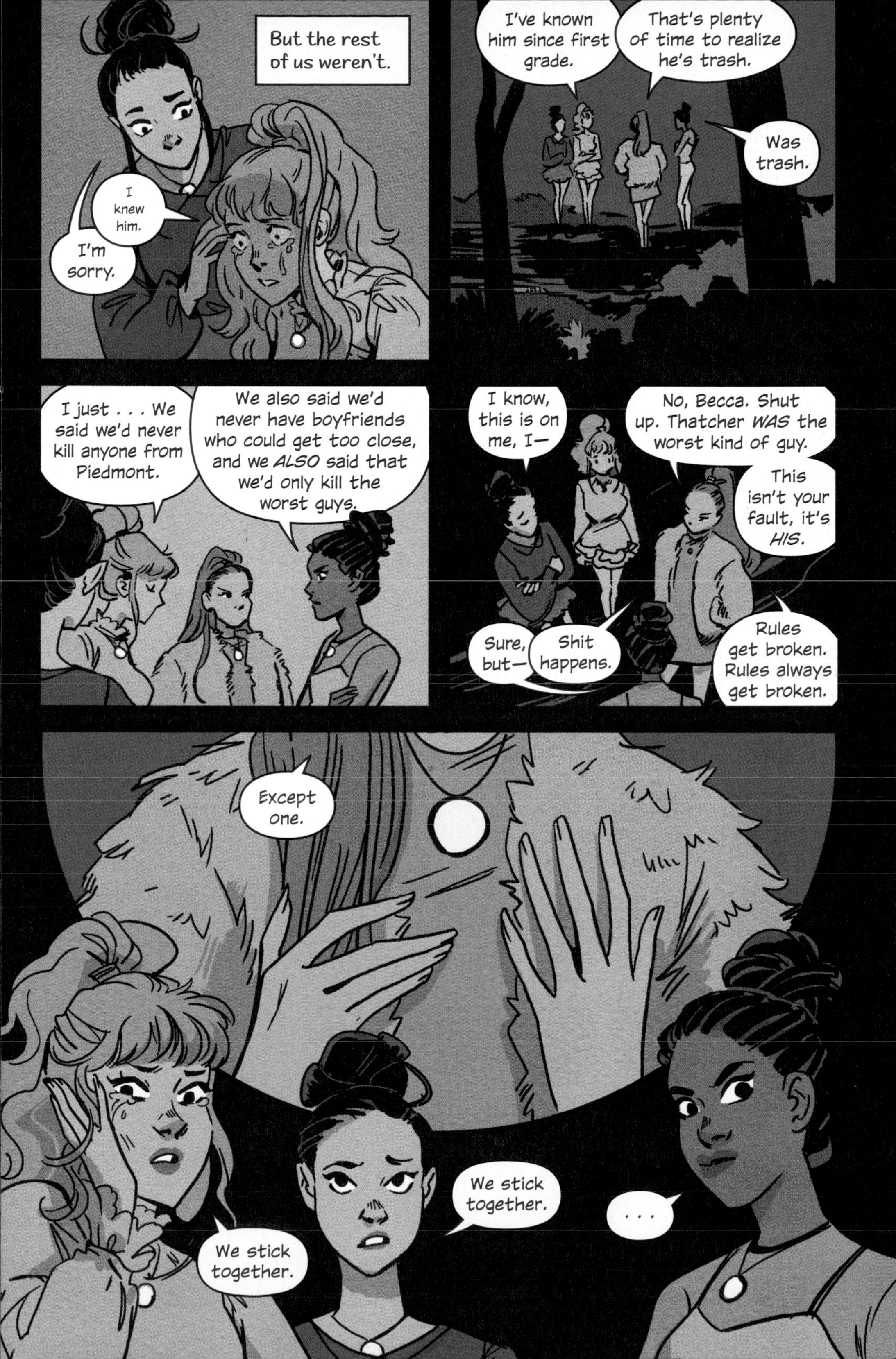

But the rest of us weren't.
I knew him.
I'm sorry.
I've known him since first grade.
That's plenty of time to realize he's trash.
Was trash.
I just . . . We said we'd never kill anyone from Piedmont.
We also said we'd never have boyfriends who could get too close, and we *ALSO* said that we'd only kill the worst guys.
I know, this is on me, I—
No, Becca. Shut up. Thatcher *WAS* the worst kind of guy.
This isn't your fault, it's *HIS*.
Sure, but—
Shit happens.
Rules get broken. Rules always get broken.
Except one.
We stick together.
We stick together.
. . .

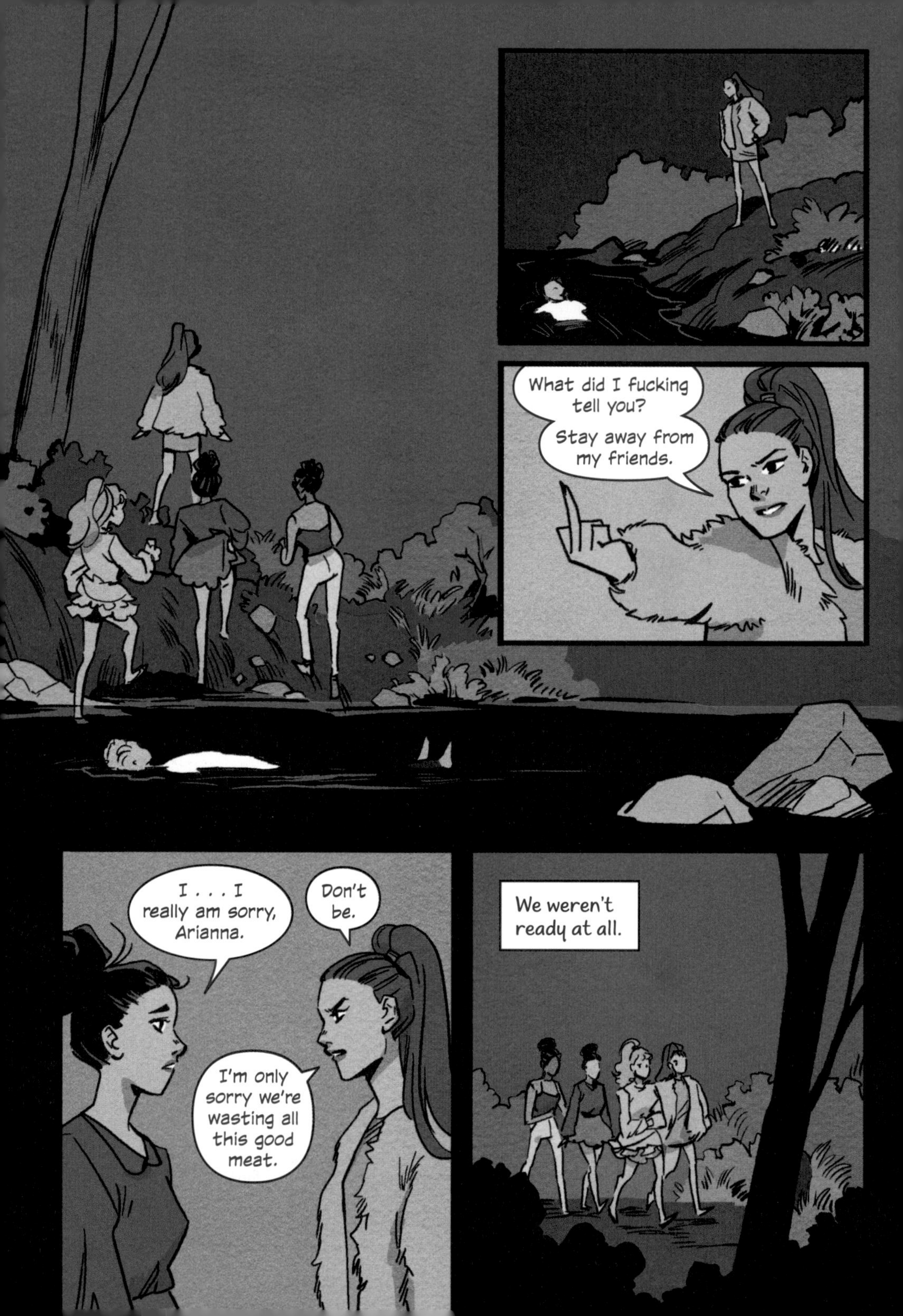
What did I fucking tell you?
Stay away from my friends.
I . . . I really am sorry, Arianna.
Don't be.
I'm only sorry we're wasting all this good meat.
We weren't ready at all.

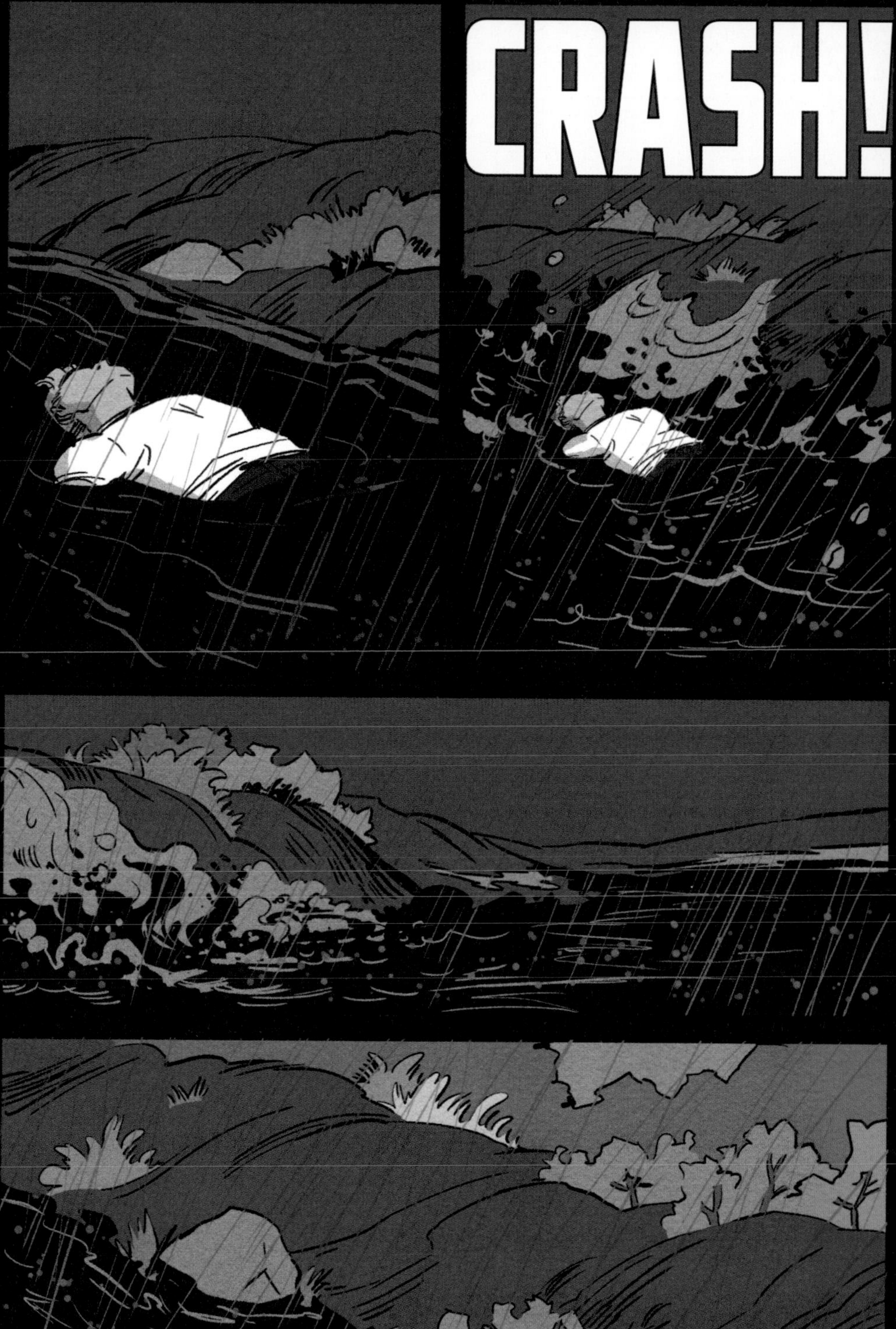
CRASH!

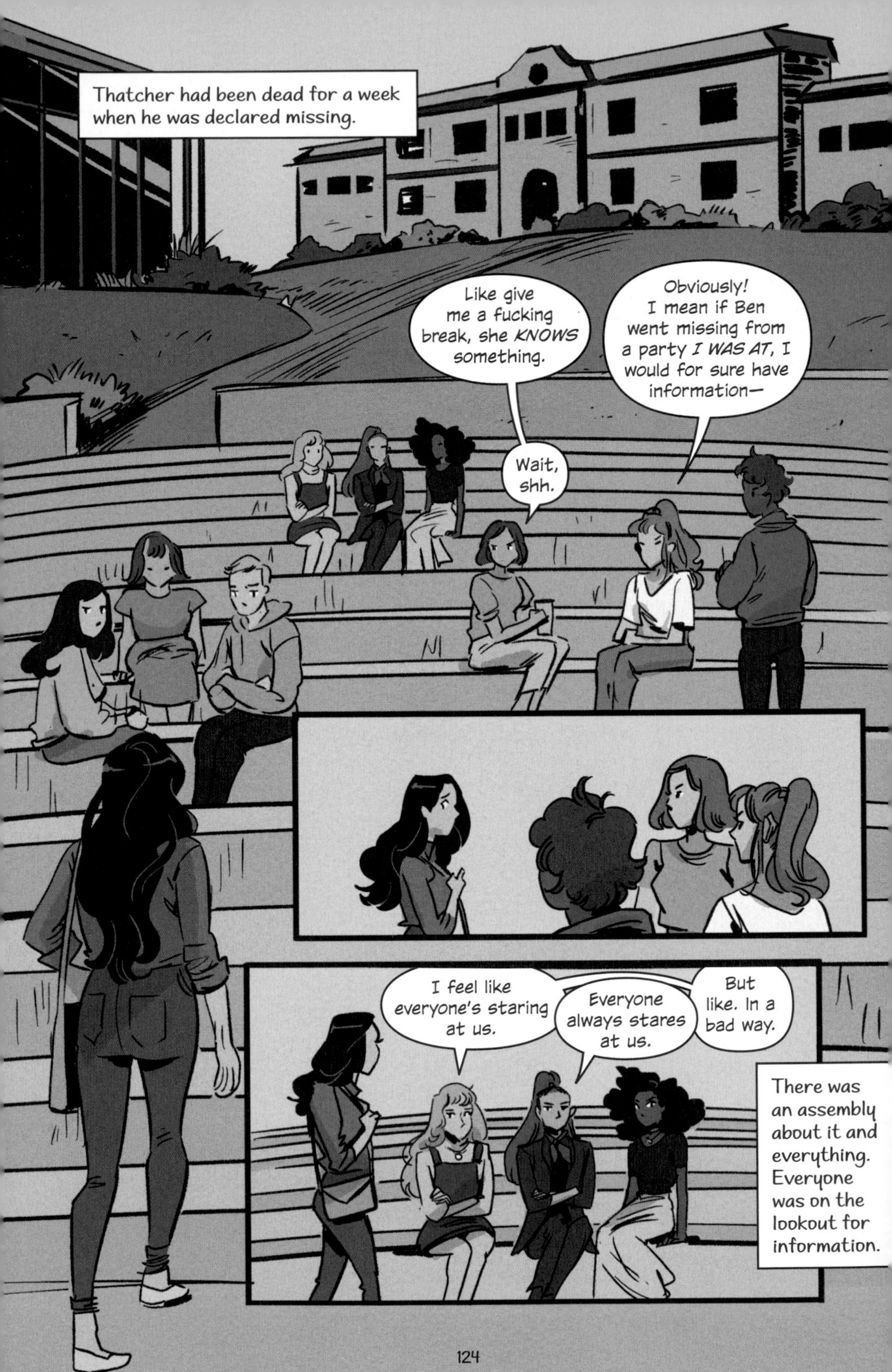
Thatcher had been dead for a week when he was declared missing.
Like give me a fucking break, she *KNOWS* something.
Obviously! I mean if Ben went missing from a party *I WAS AT*, I would for sure have information—
Wait, shh.
I feel like everyone's staring at us.
Everyone always stares at us.
But like. In a bad way.
There was an assembly about it and everything. Everyone was on the lookout for information.

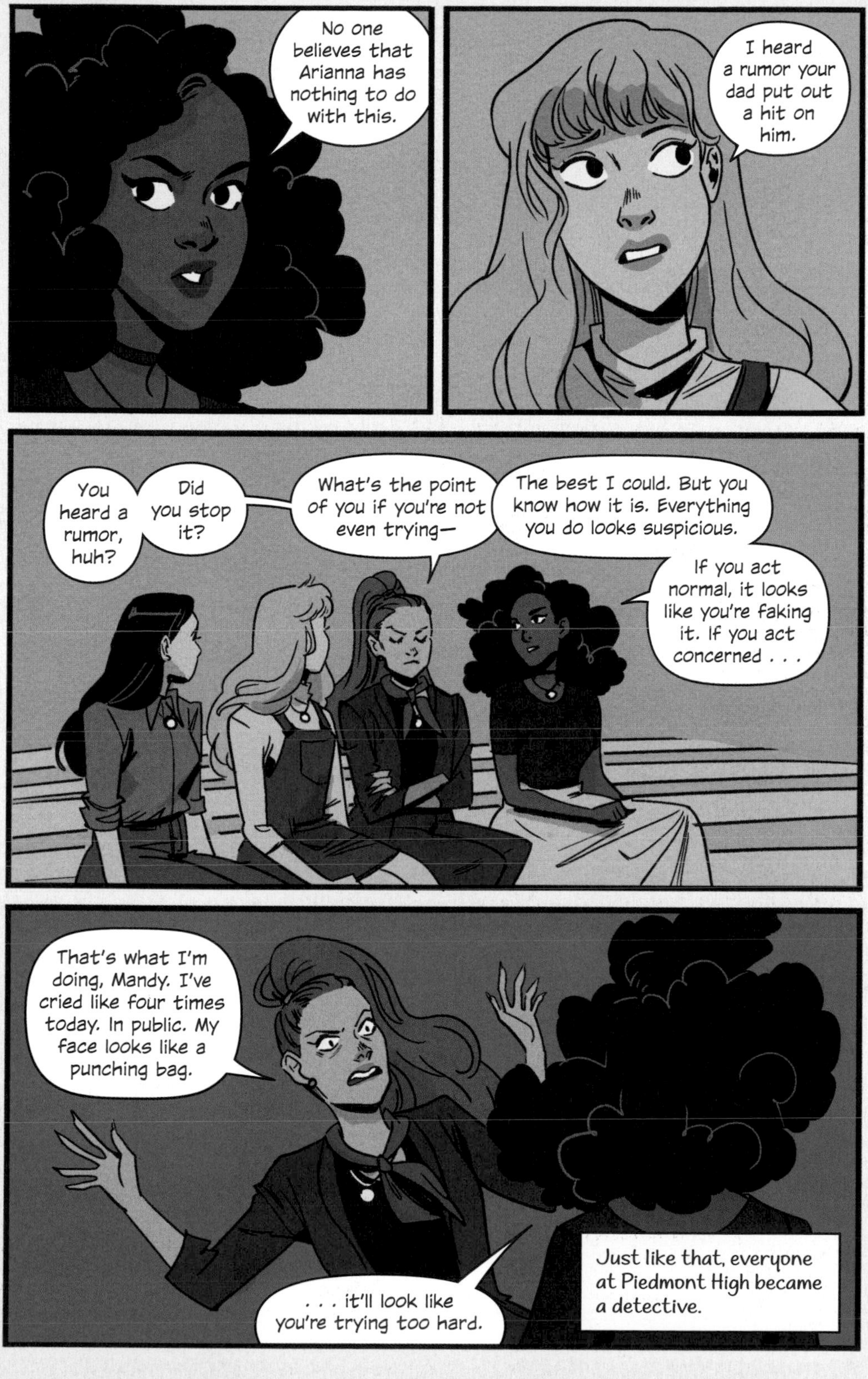
No one believes that Arianna has nothing to do with this.
I heard a rumor your dad put out a hit on him.
You heard a rumor, huh?
Did you stop it?
What's the point of you if you're not even trying—
The best I could. But you know how it is. Everything you do looks suspicious.
If you act normal, it looks like you're faking it. If you act concerned . . .
That's what I'm doing, Mandy. I've cried like four times today. In public. My face looks like a punching bag.
. . . it'll look like you're trying too hard.
Just like that, everyone at Piedmont High became a detective.

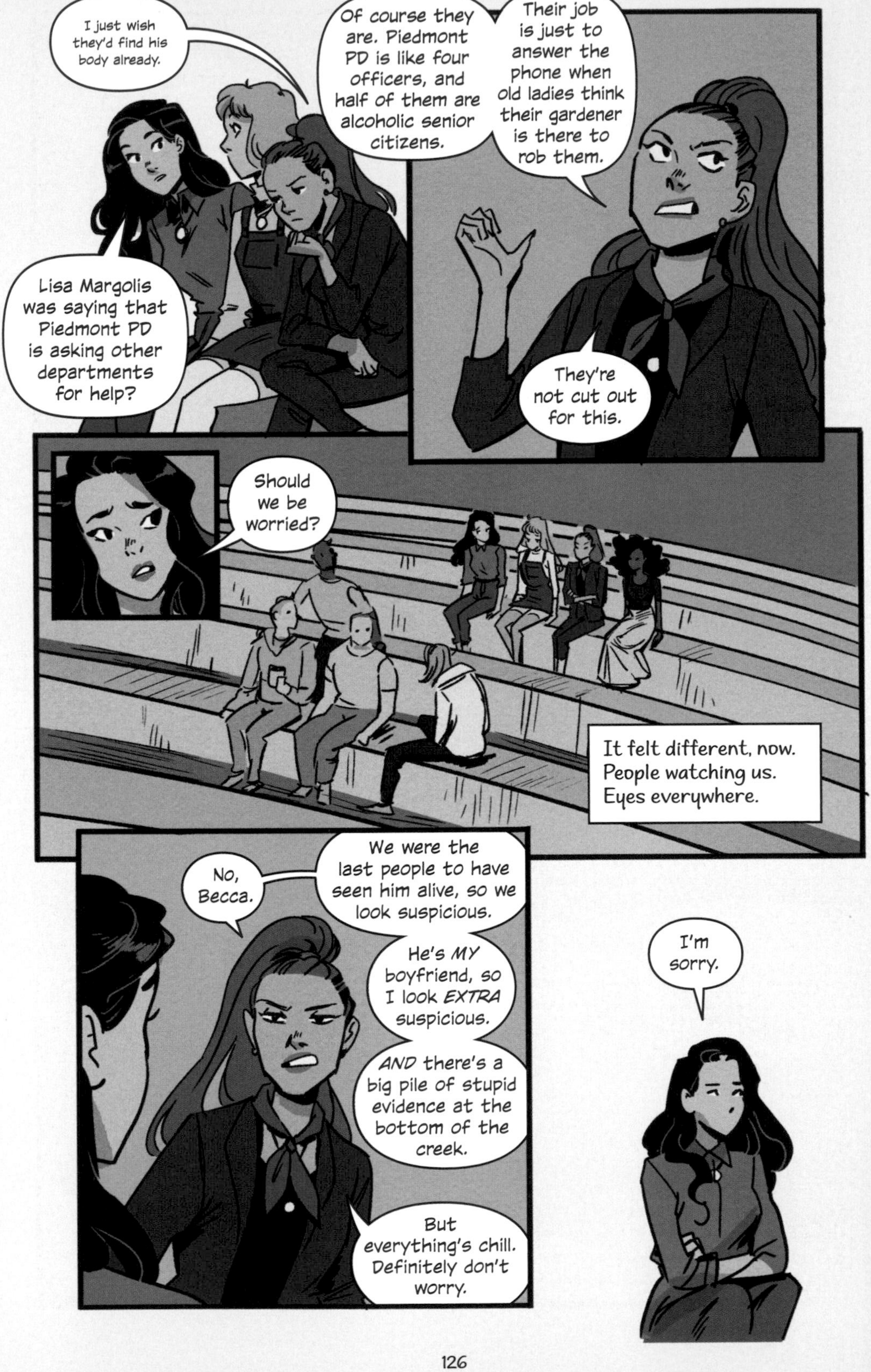
I just wish they'd find his body already.
Of course they are. Piedmont PD is like four officers, and half of them are alcoholic senior citizens.
Their job is just to answer the phone when old ladies think their gardener is there to rob them.
Lisa Margolis was saying that Piedmont PD is asking other departments for help?
They're not cut out for this.
Should we be worried?
It felt different, now. People watching us. Eyes everywhere.
No, Becca.
We were the last people to have seen him alive, so we look suspicious.
He's *MY* boyfriend, so I look *EXTRA* suspicious.
AND there's a big pile of stupid evidence at the bottom of the creek.
But everything's chill. Definitely don't worry.
I'm sorry.

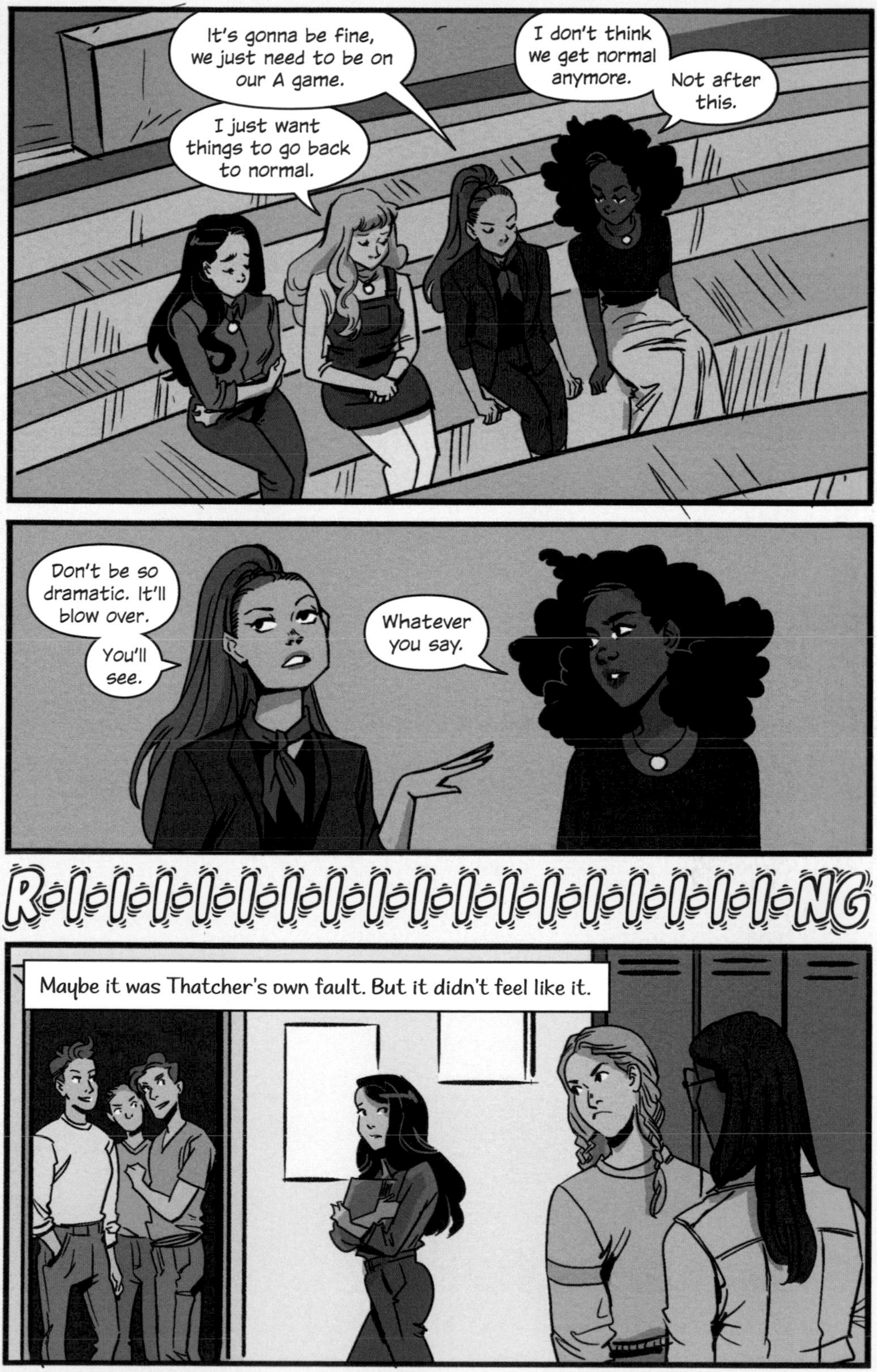
It's gonna be fine, we just need to be on our A game.
I just want things to go back to normal.
I don't think we get normal anymore.
Not after this.
Don't be so dramatic. It'll blow over.
You'll see.
Whatever you say.
RIIIIIIIIIIIIIIIIING
Maybe it was Thatcher's own fault. But it didn't feel like it.

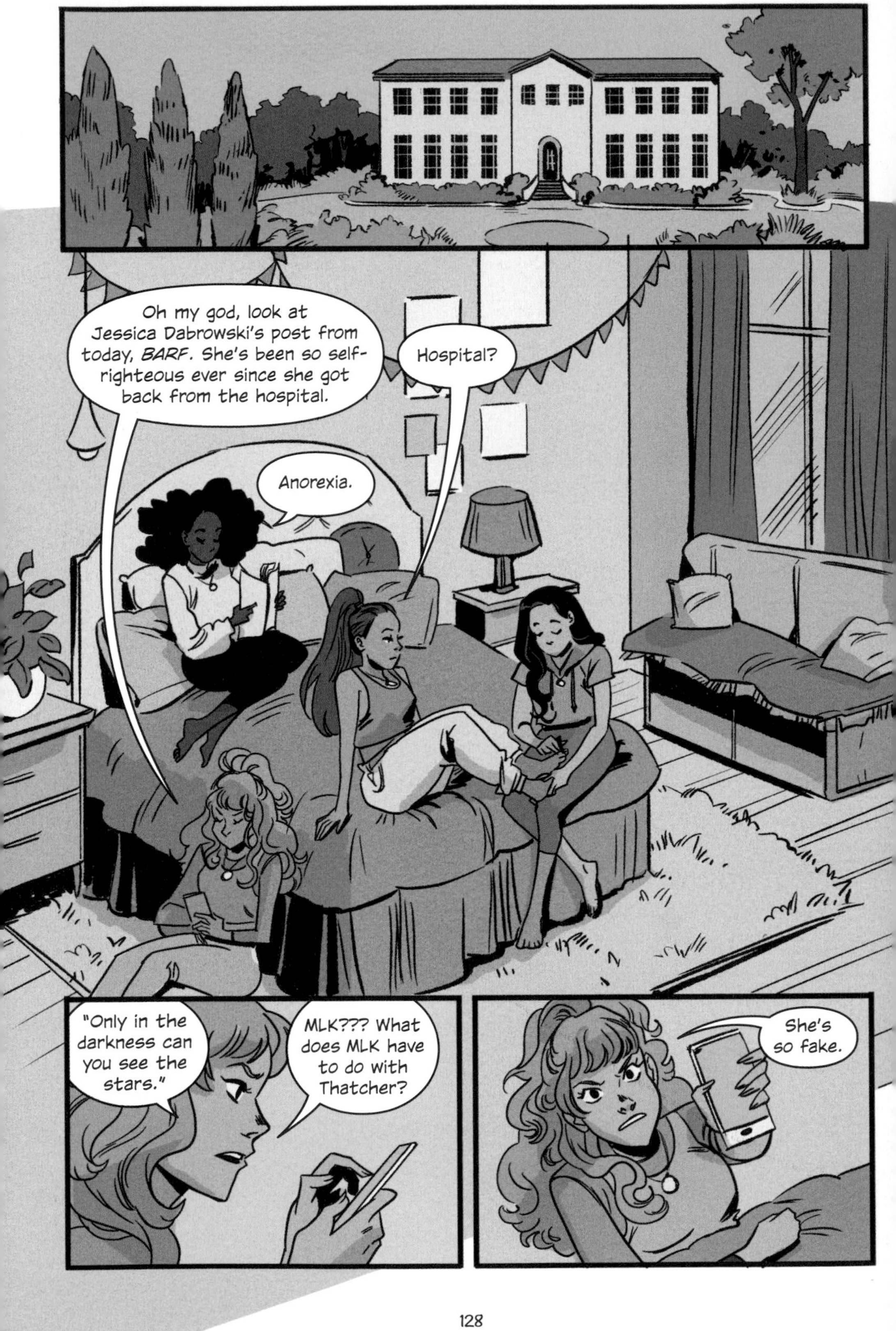
Oh my god, look at Jessica Dabrowski's post from today, *BARF*. She's been so self-righteous ever since she got back from the hospital.
Hospital?
Anorexia.
"Only in the darkness can you see the stars."
MLK??? What does MLK have to do with Thatcher?
She's so fake.

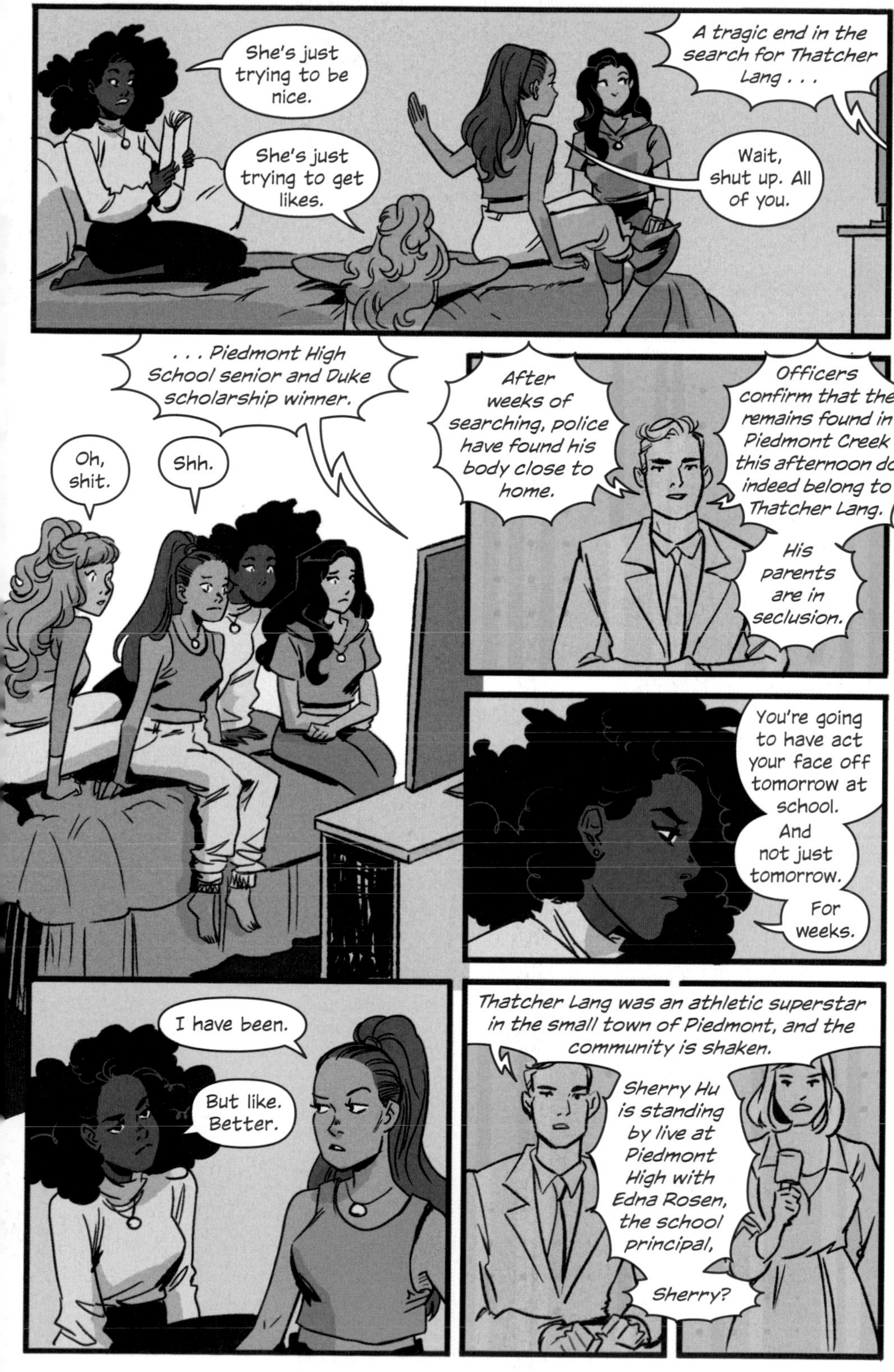
She's just trying to be nice.
She's just trying to get likes.
A tragic end in the search for Thatcher Lang . . .
Wait, shut up. All of you.
. . . Piedmont High School senior and Duke scholarship winner.
Oh, shit.
Shh.
After weeks of searching, police have found his body close to home.
Officers confirm that the remains found in Piedmont Creek this afternoon do indeed belong to Thatcher Lang.
His parents are in seclusion.
You're going to have act your face off tomorrow at school.
And not just tomorrow.
For weeks.
I have been.
But like. Better.
Thatcher Lang was an athletic superstar in the small town of Piedmont, and the community is shaken.
Sherry Hu is standing by live at Piedmont High with Edna Rosen, the school principal,
Sherry?

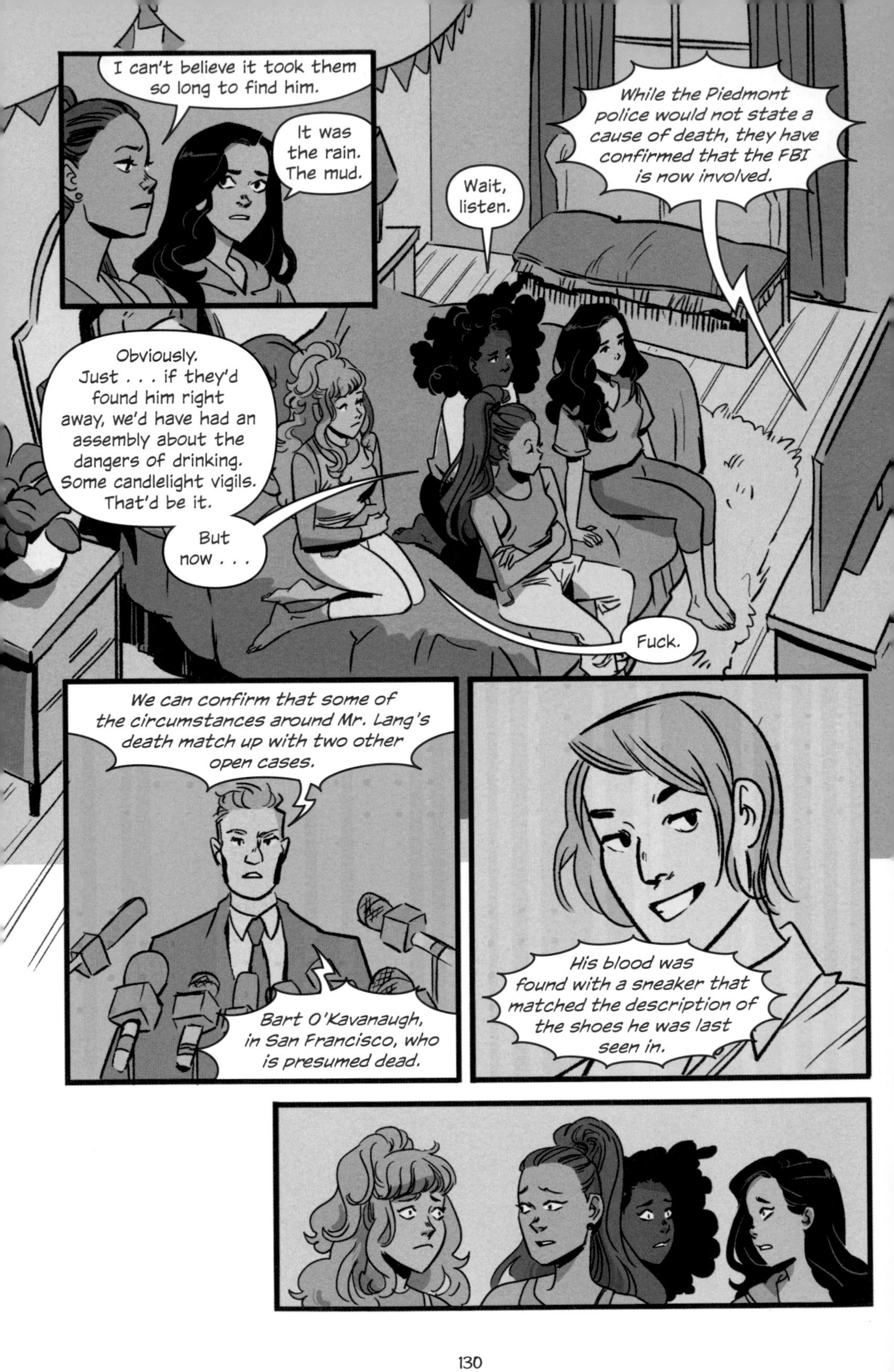
I can't believe it took them so long to find him.
It was the rain. The mud.
Wait, listen.
While the Piedmont police would not state a cause of death, they have confirmed that the FBI is now involved.
Obviously. Just . . . if they'd found him right away, we'd have had an assembly about the dangers of drinking. Some candlelight vigils. That'd be it.
But now . . .
Fuck.
We can confirm that some of the circumstances around Mr. Lang's death match up with two other open cases.
Bart O'Kavanaugh, in San Francisco, who is presumed dead.
His blood was found with a sneaker that matched the description of the shoes he was last seen in.

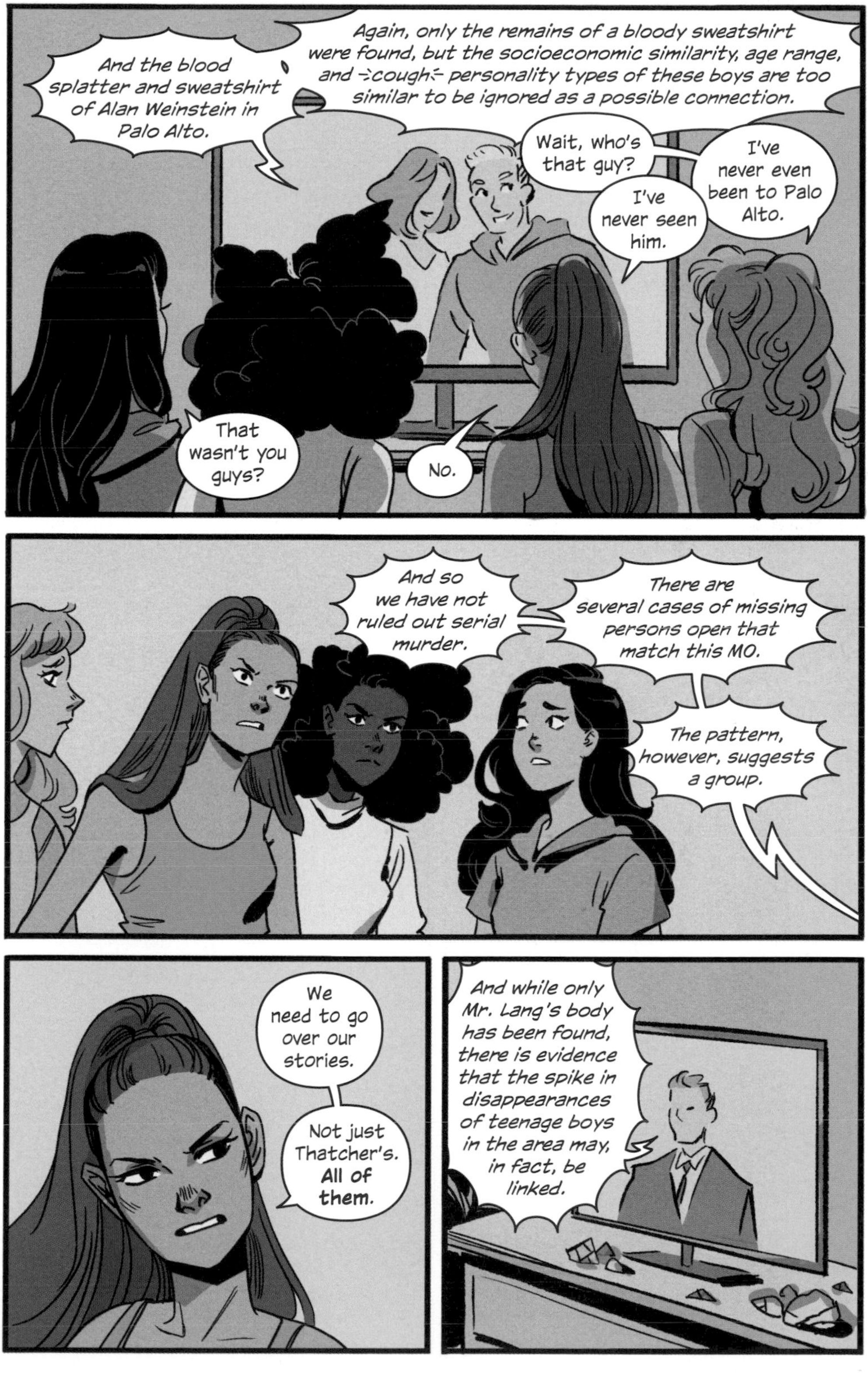
And the blood splatter and sweatshirt of Alan Weinstein in Palo Alto.
Again, only the remains of a bloody sweatshirt were found, but the socioeconomic similarity, age range, and ~cough~ personality types of these boys are too similar to be ignored as a possible connection.
Wait, who's that guy?
I've never even been to Palo Alto.
I've never seen him.
That wasn't you guys?
No.
And so we have not ruled out serial murder.
There are several cases of missing persons open that match this MO.
The pattern, however, suggests a group.
We need to go over our stories.
Not just Thatcher's. **All of them.**
And while only Mr. Lang's body has been found, there is evidence that the spike in disappearances of teenage boys in the area may, in fact, be linked.

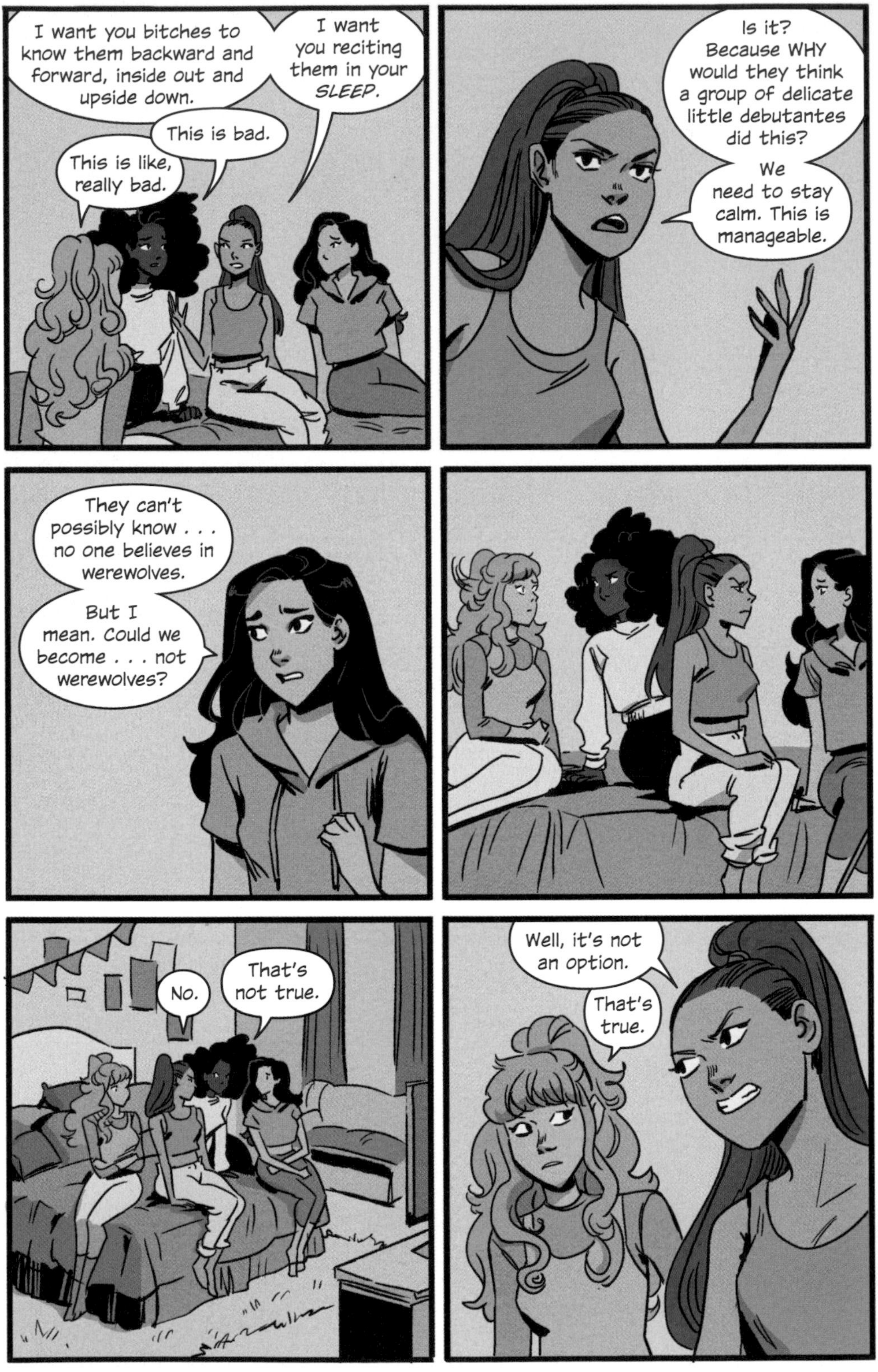
I want you bitches to know them backward and forward, inside out and upside down.
I want you reciting them in your *SLEEP*.
This is bad.
This is like, really bad.
Is it? Because WHY would they think a group of delicate little debutantes did this?
We need to stay calm. This is manageable.
They can't possibly know . . . no one believes in werewolves.
But I mean. Could we become . . . not werewolves?
No.
That's not true.
Well, it's not an option.
That's true.

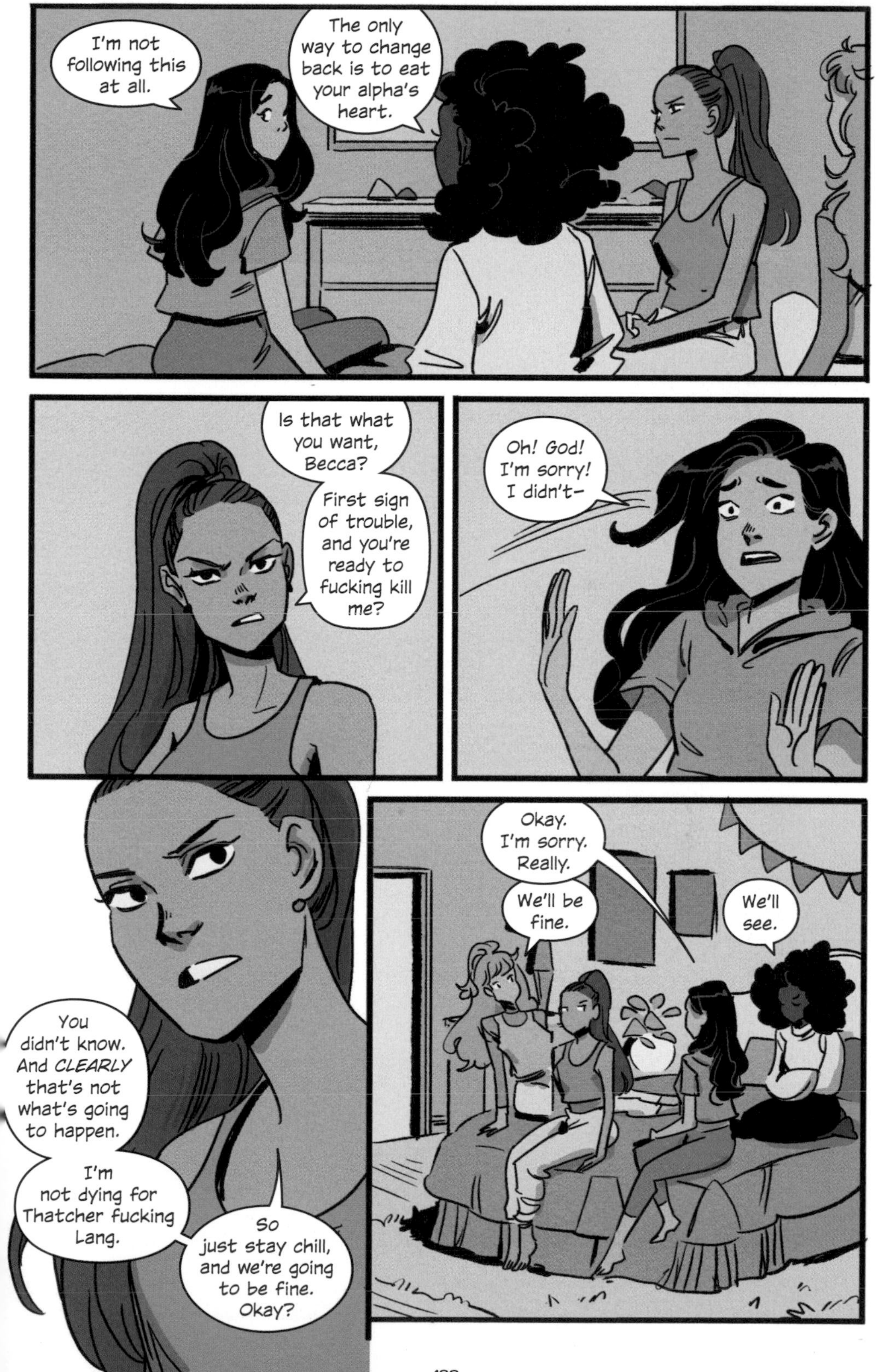

I'm not following this at all.
The only way to change back is to eat your alpha's heart.
Is that what you want, Becca?
First sign of trouble, and you're ready to fucking kill me?
Oh! God! I'm sorry! I didn't–
You didn't know. And CLEARLY that's not what's going to happen.
I'm not dying for Thatcher fucking Lang.
So just stay chill, and we're going to be fine. Okay?
Okay. I'm sorry. Really.
We'll be fine.
We'll see.

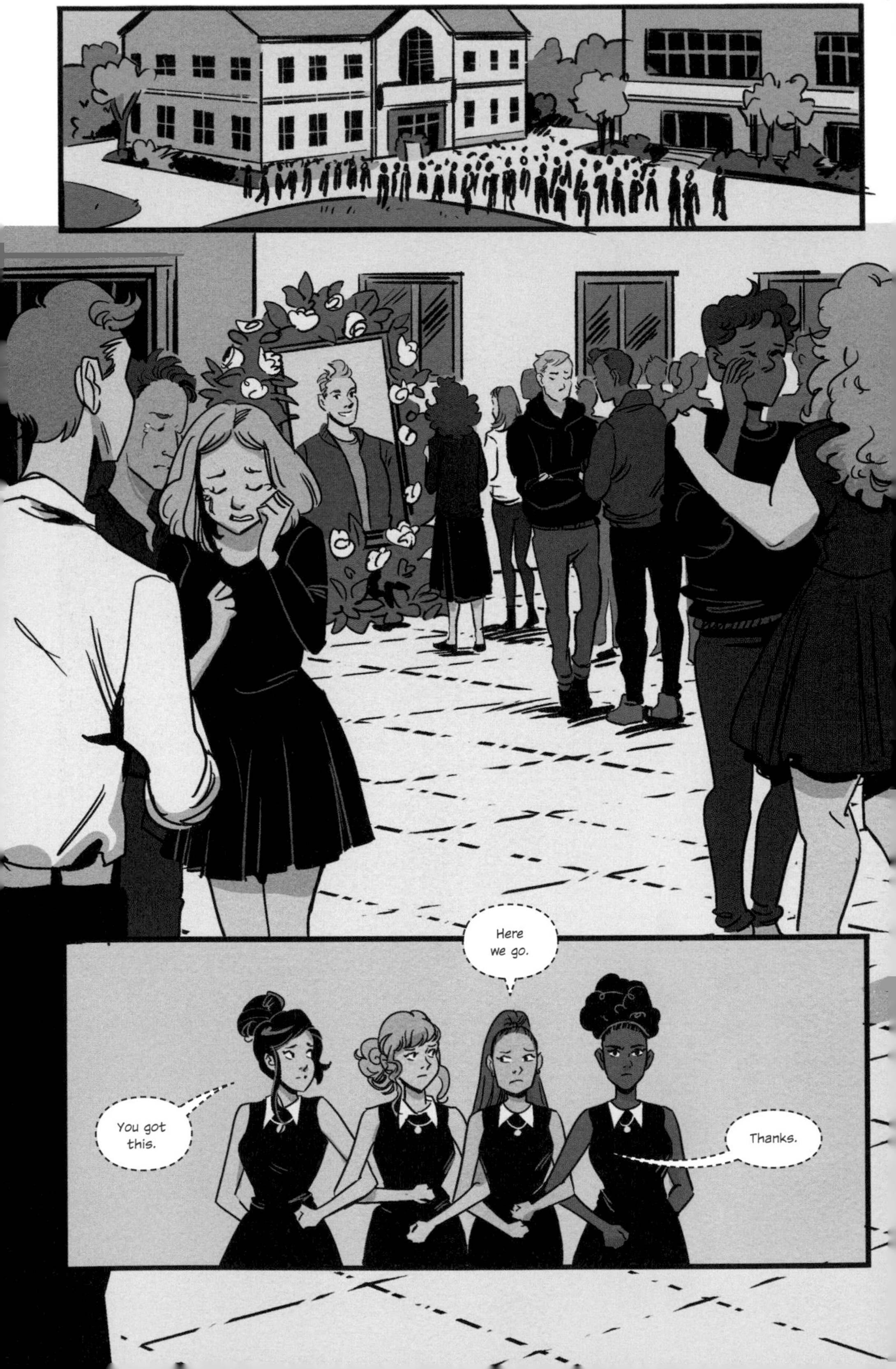
Here we go.
You got this.
Thanks.

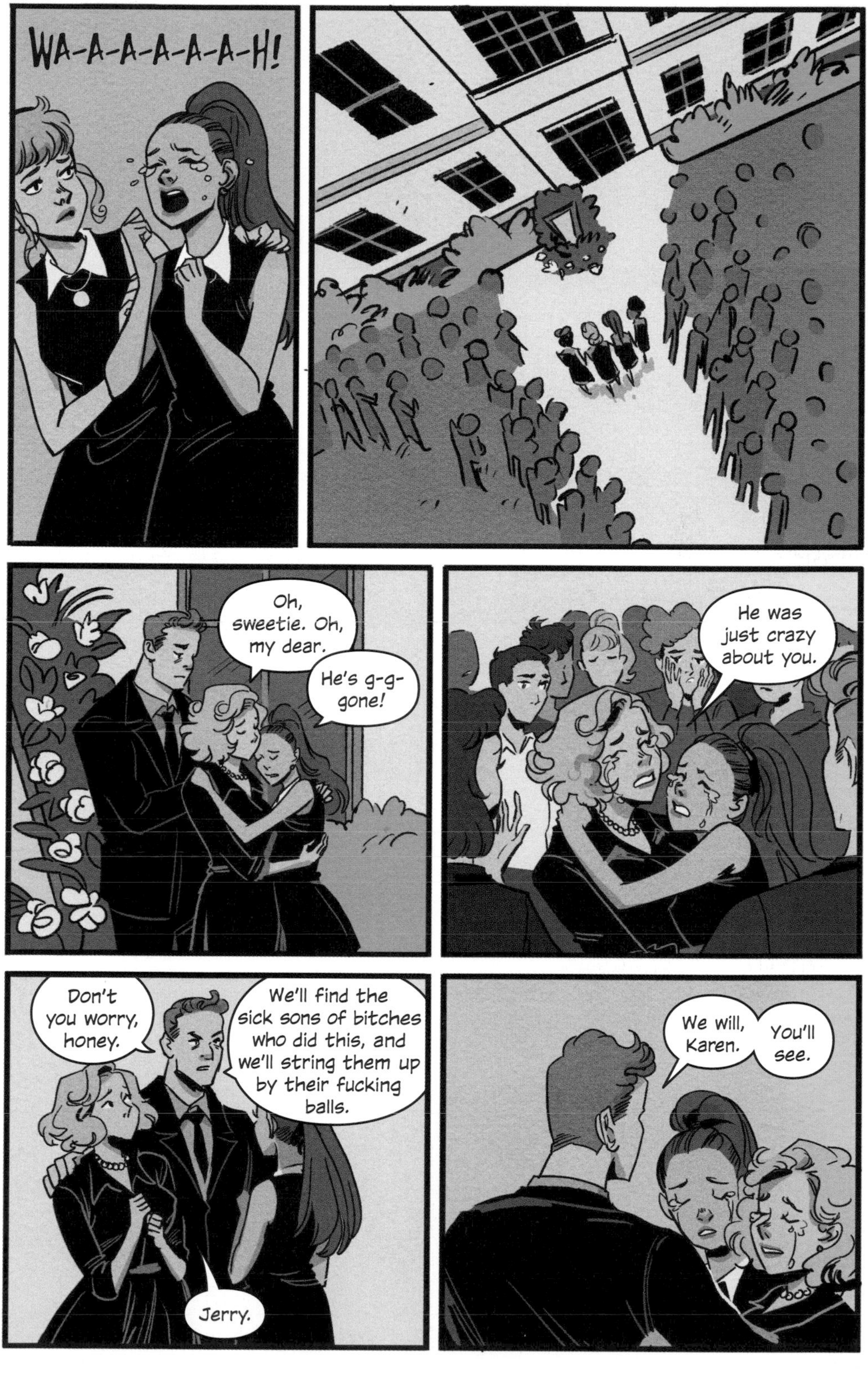
WA-A-A-A-A-A-H!
Oh, sweetie. Oh, my dear.
He's g-g-gone!
He was just crazy about you.
Don't you worry, honey.
We'll find the sick sons of bitches who did this, and we'll string them up by their fucking balls.
Jerry.
We will, Karen.
You'll see.

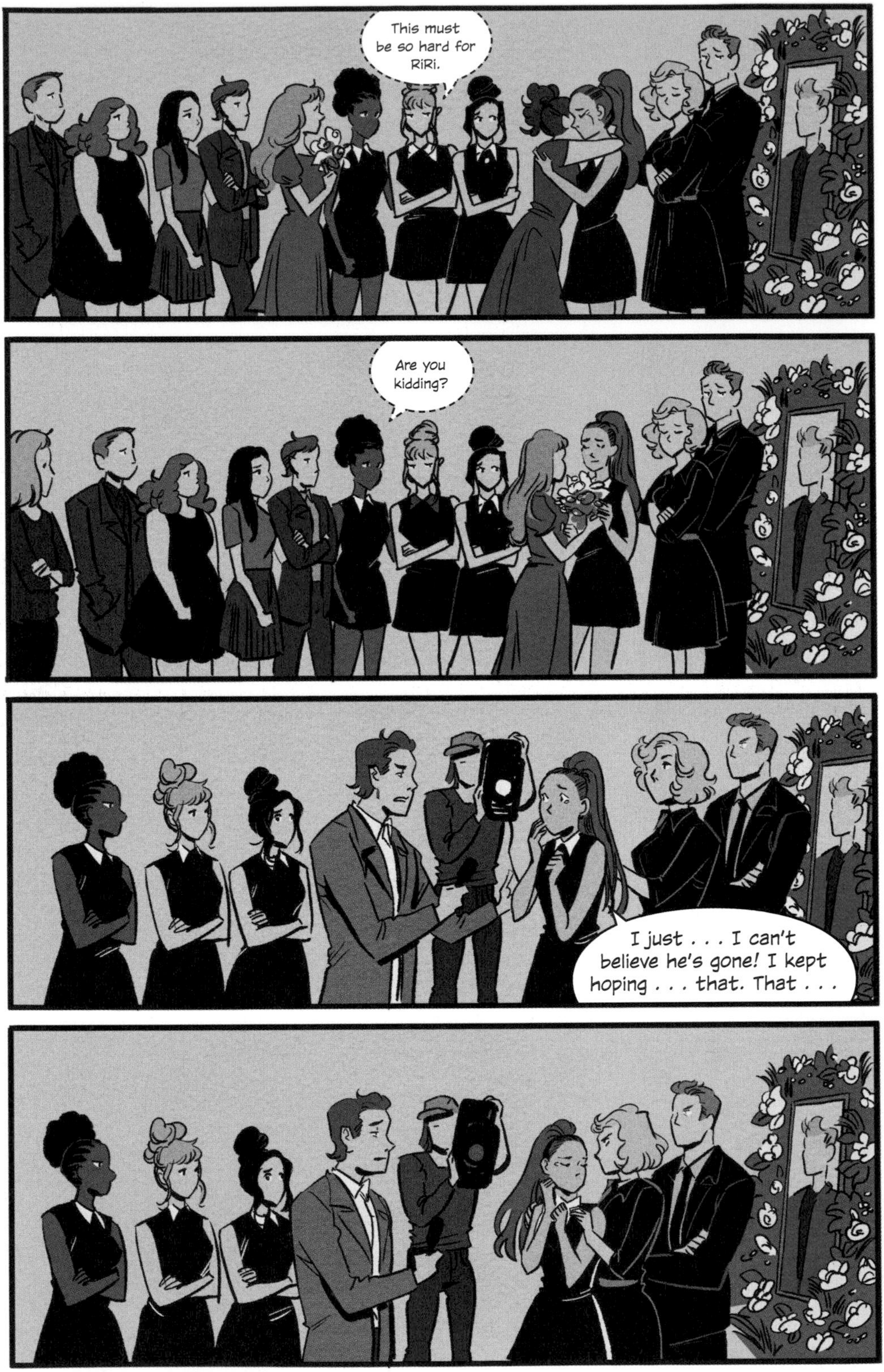
This must be so hard for RiRi.
Are you kidding?
I just . . . I can't believe he's gone! I kept hoping . . . that. That . . .

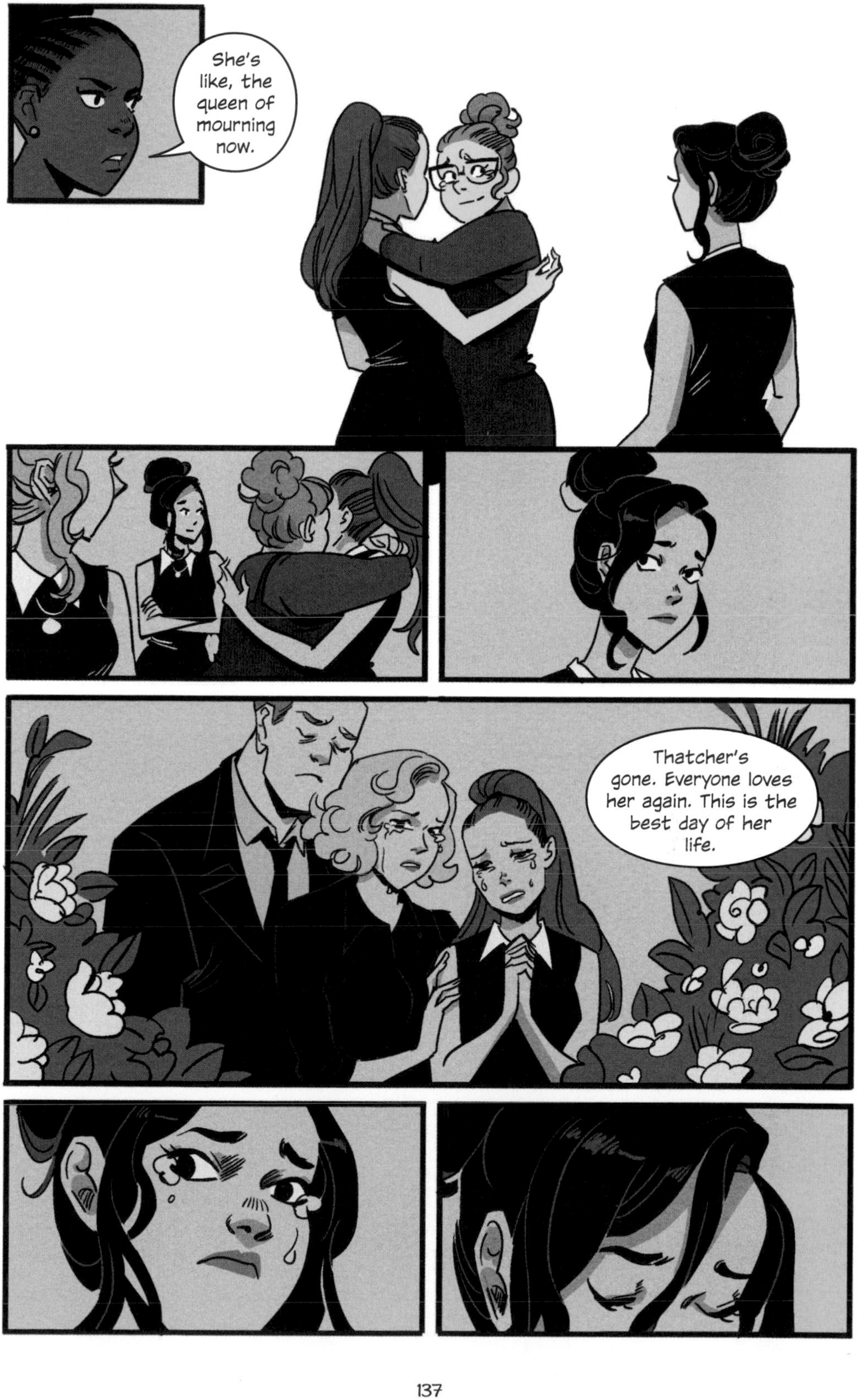
She's like, the queen of mourning now.
Thatcher's gone. Everyone loves her again. This is the best day of her life.

CHAPTER SIX

THINGS FALL APART

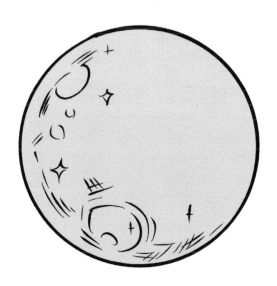

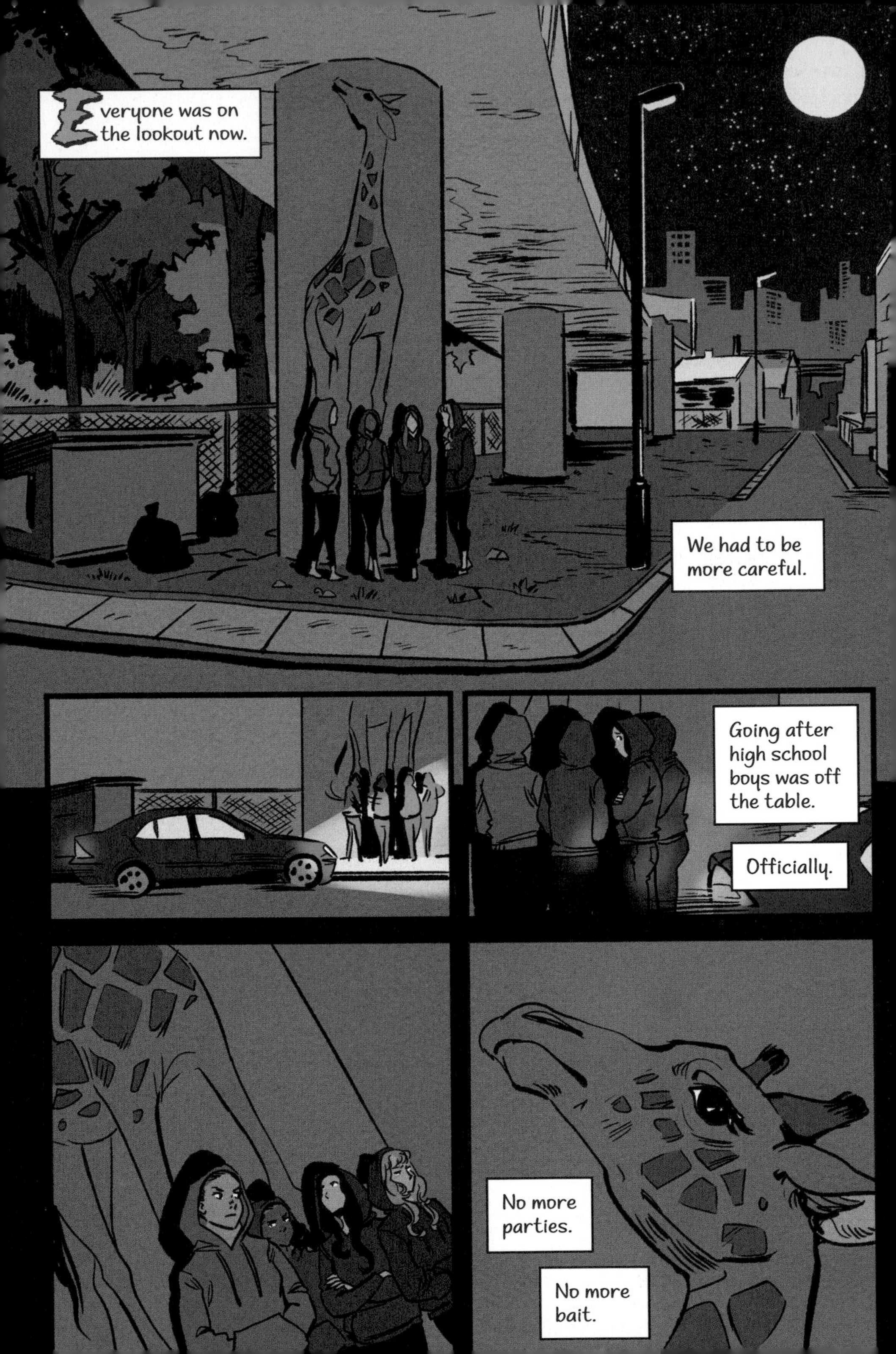
Everyone was on the lookout now.
We had to be more careful.
Going after high school boys was off the table.
Officially.
No more parties.
No more bait.

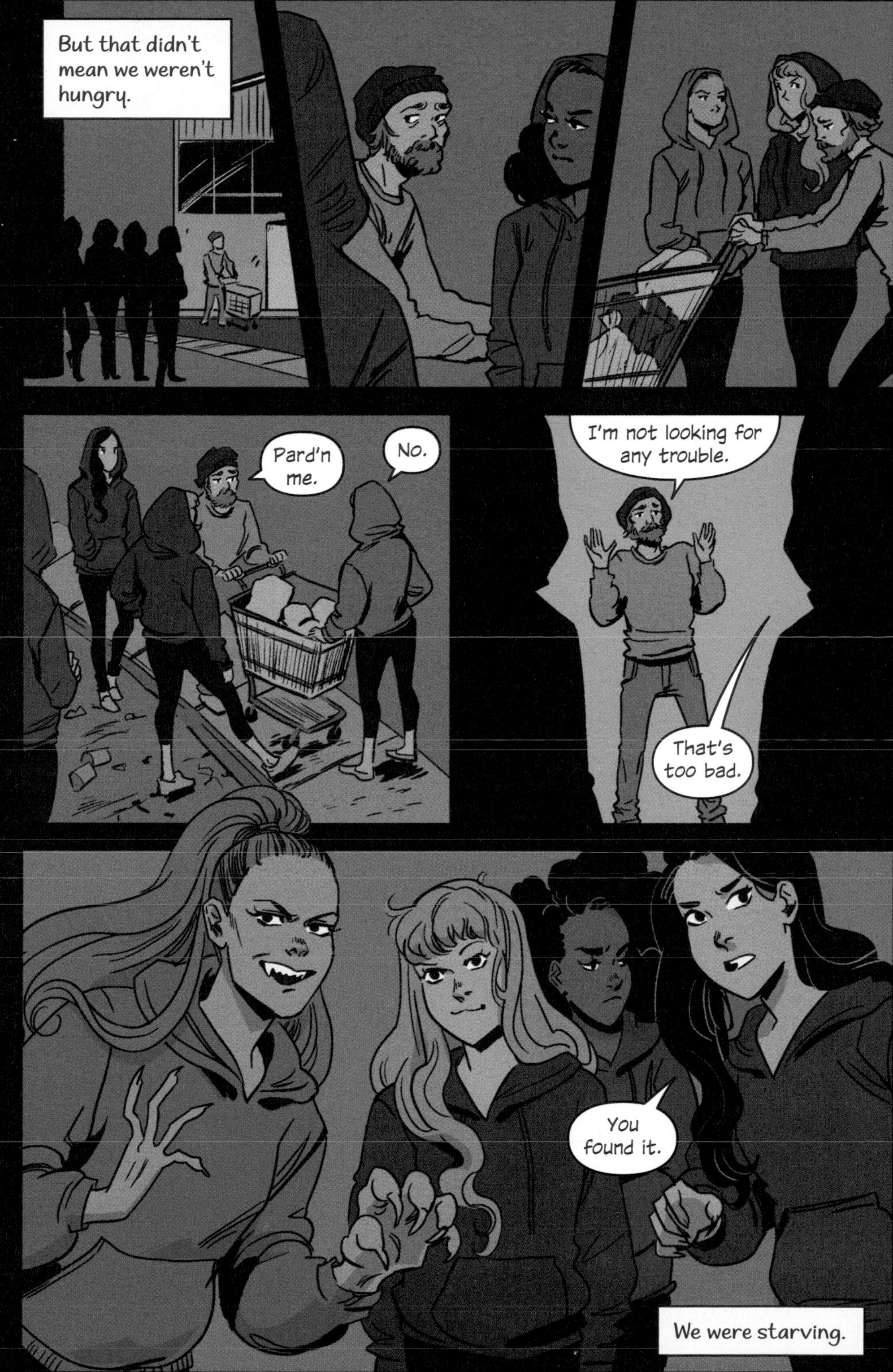
But that didn't mean we weren't hungry.
Pard'n me.
No.
I'm not looking for any trouble.
That's too bad.
You found it.
We were starving.

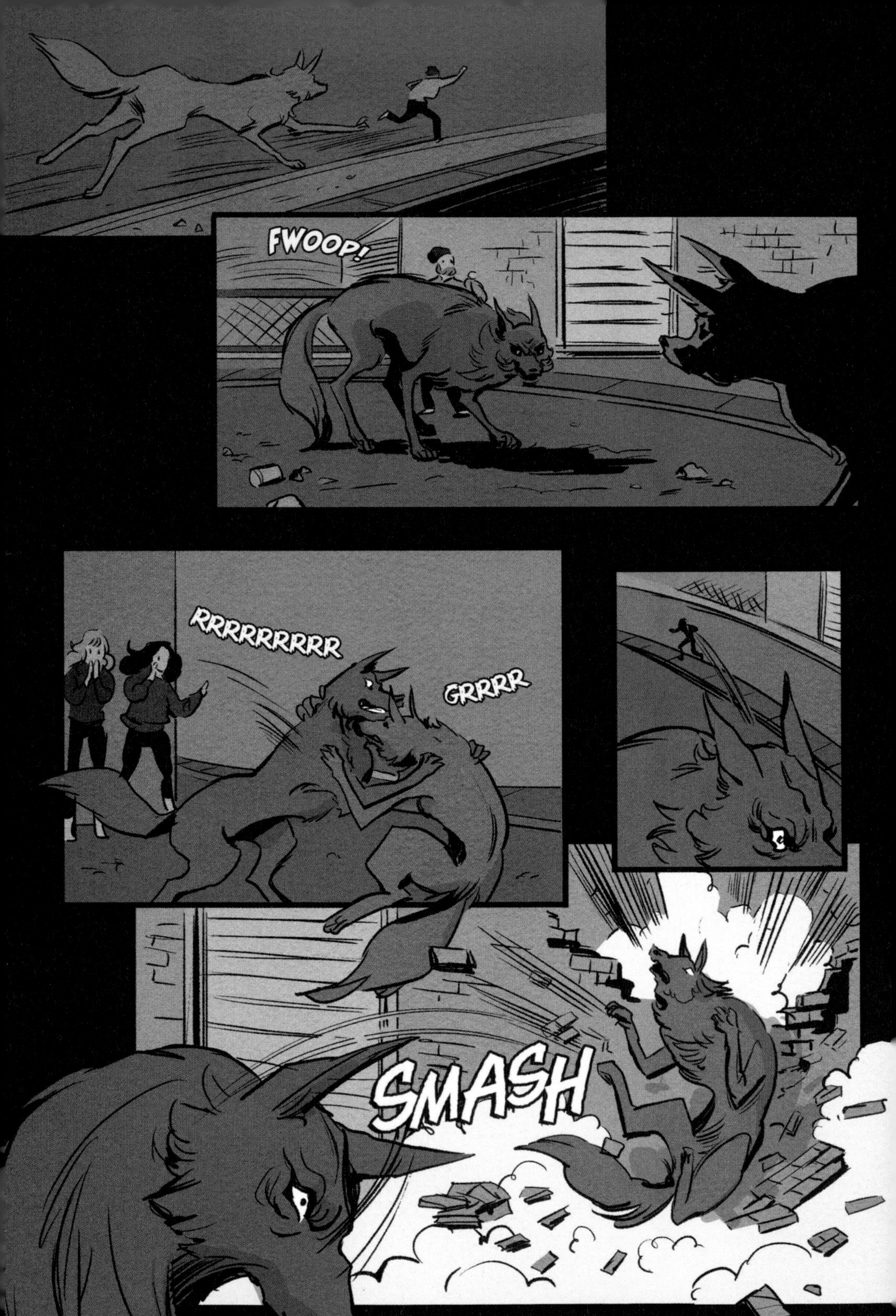
FWOOP!
RRRRRRRRRR
GRRRR
SMASH

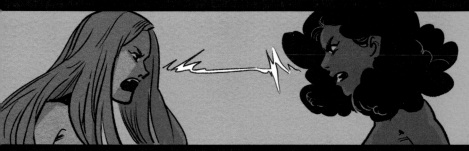

What the actual and entire living *FUCK*, Amanda.

We *HAVE* to eat.

Not like this.

You're not in charge!

Maybe I should be! Maybe if I was in charge *NONE OF THIS* would have happened!

We wouldn't have to worry about a dead boyfriend *OR* the FBI!

We wouldn't be hunting homeless people when there are like, *REAL* assholes out there, just for us!

You're messing it all up, you're messing it all up for *ALL OF US*, do you even *GET* that?

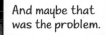

And maybe that was the problem.

Maybe we were just too hungry.

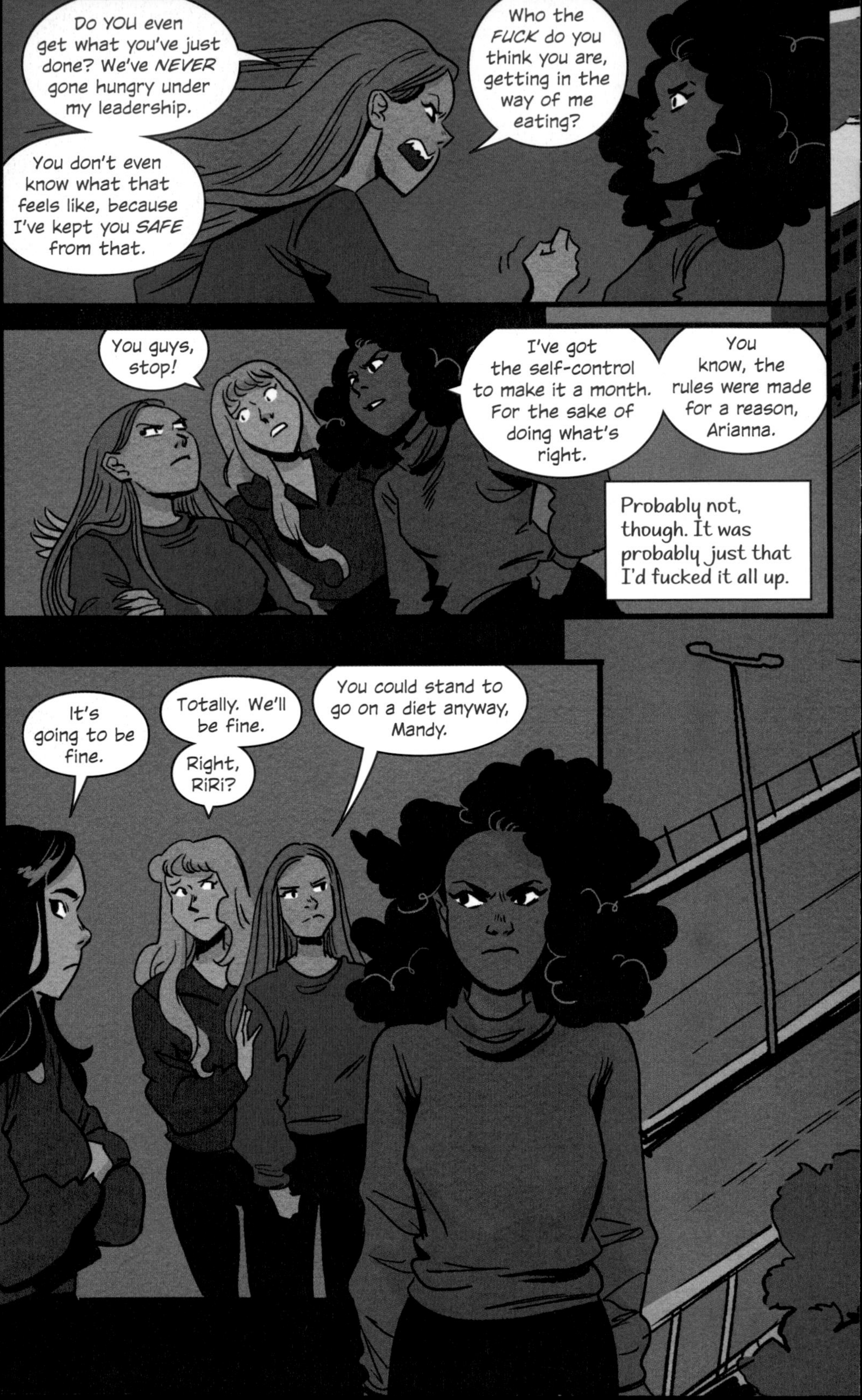
Do YOU even get what you've just done? We've NEVER gone hungry under my leadership.
You don't even know what that feels like, because I've kept you SAFE from that.
Who the FUCK do you think you are, getting in the way of me eating?
You guys, stop!
I've got the self-control to make it a month. For the sake of doing what's right.
You know, the rules were made for a reason, Arianna.
Probably not, though. It was probably just that I'd fucked it all up.
It's going to be fine.
Totally. We'll be fine.
Right, RiRi?
You could stand to go on a diet anyway, Mandy.

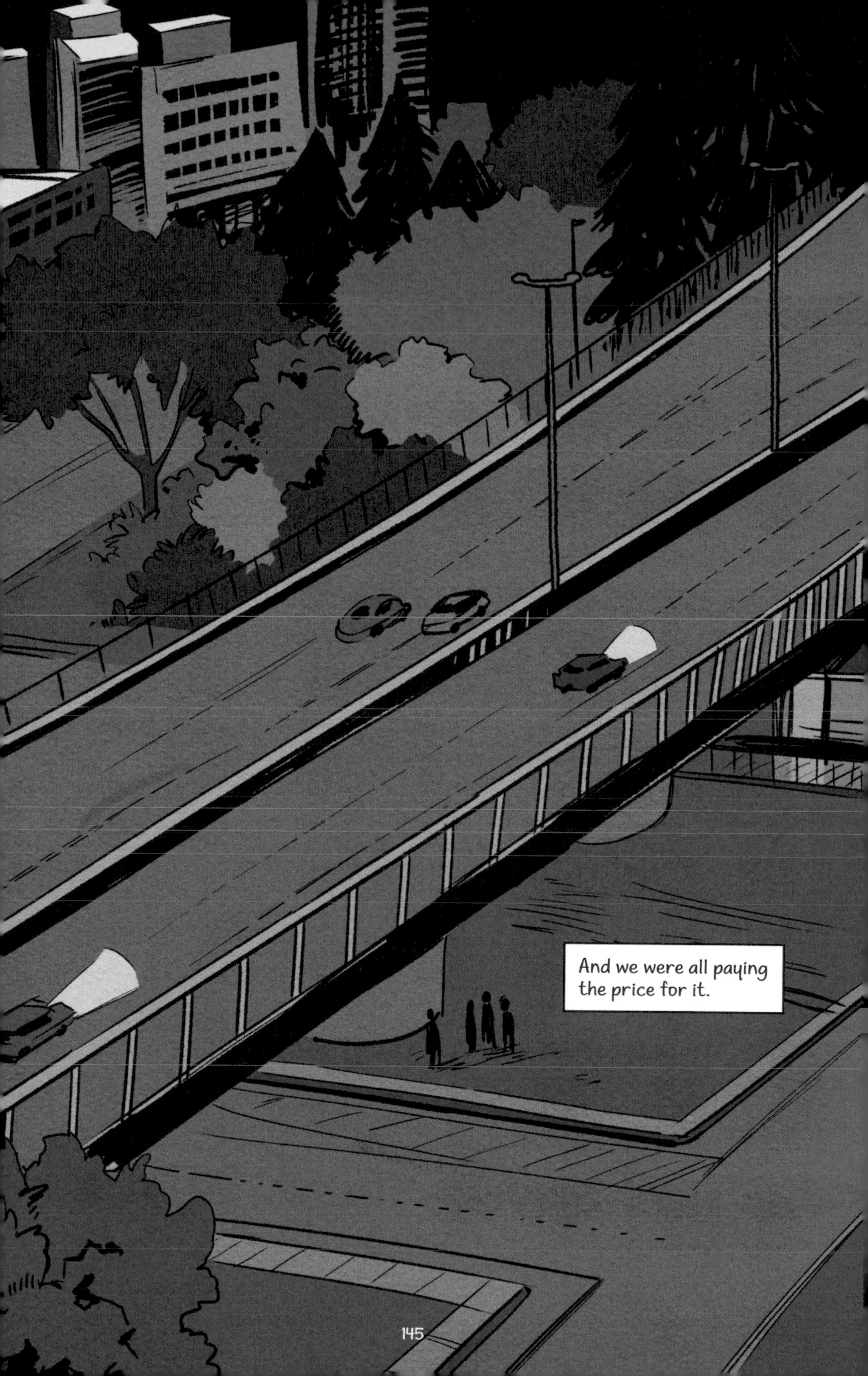
And we were all paying the price for it.

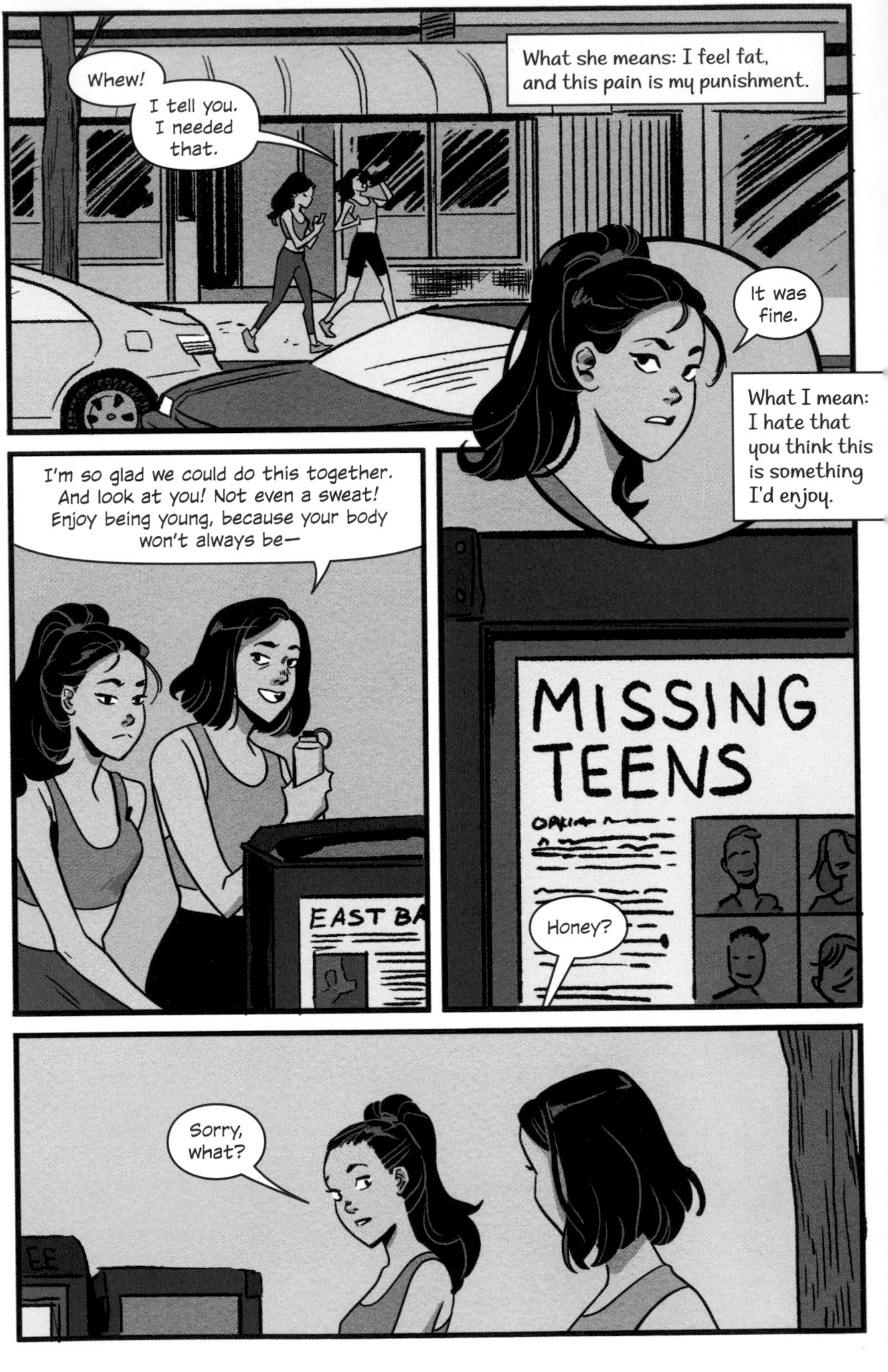
Whew!
I tell you. I needed that.
What she means: I feel fat, and this pain is my punishment.
It was fine.
What I mean: I hate that you think this is something I'd enjoy.
I'm so glad we could do this together. And look at you! Not even a sweat! Enjoy being young, because your body won't always be—
EAST BA
MISSING TEENS
Honey?
Sorry, what?

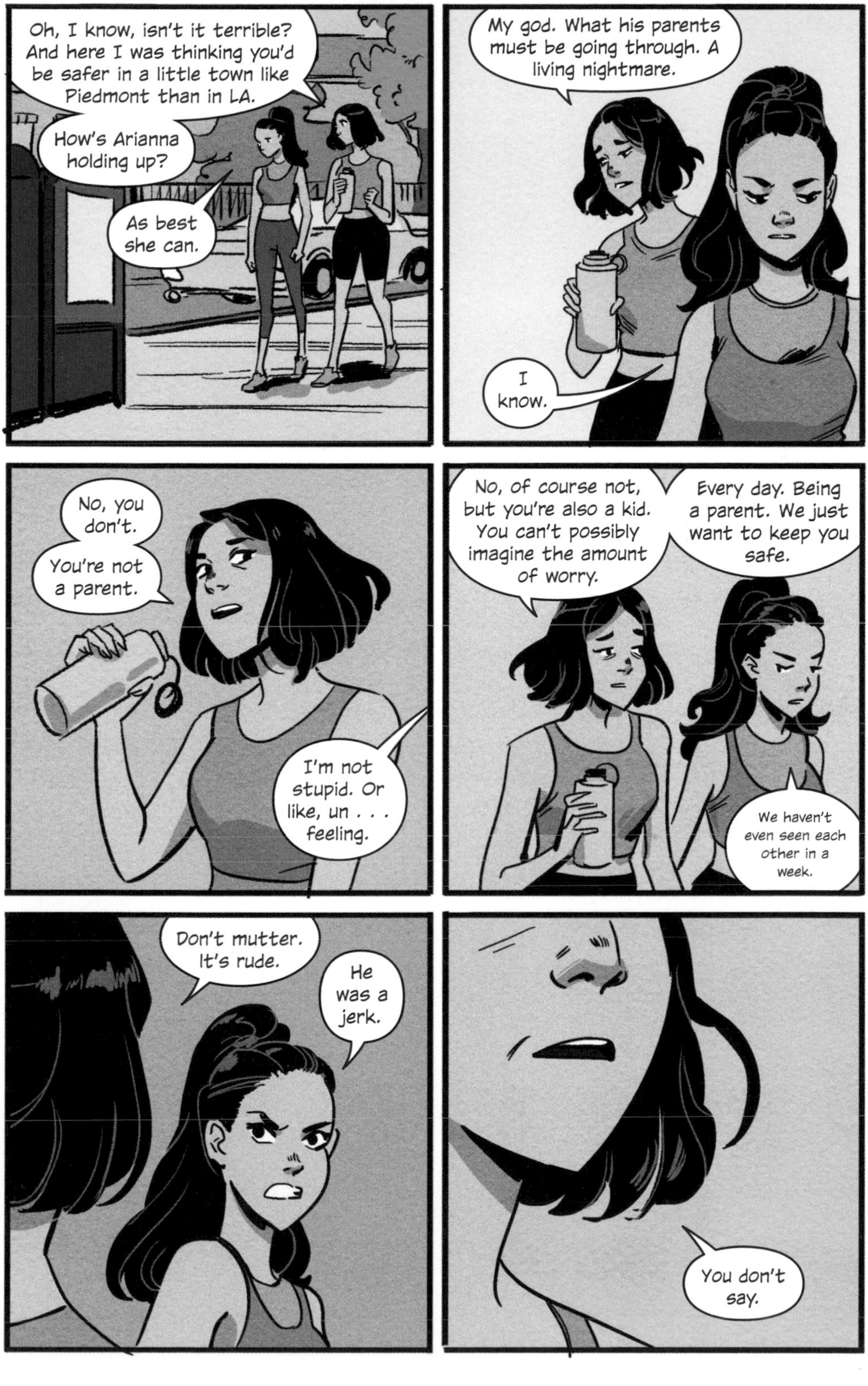
Oh, I know, isn't it terrible? And here I was thinking you'd be safer in a little town like Piedmont than in LA.
How's Arianna holding up?
As best she can.
My god. What his parents must be going through. A living nightmare.
I know.
No, you don't.
You're not a parent.
I'm not stupid. Or like, un . . . feeling.
No, of course not, but you're also a kid. You can't possibly imagine the amount of worry.
Every day. Being a parent. We just want to keep you safe.
We haven't even seen each other in a week.
Don't mutter. It's rude.
He was a jerk.
You don't say.

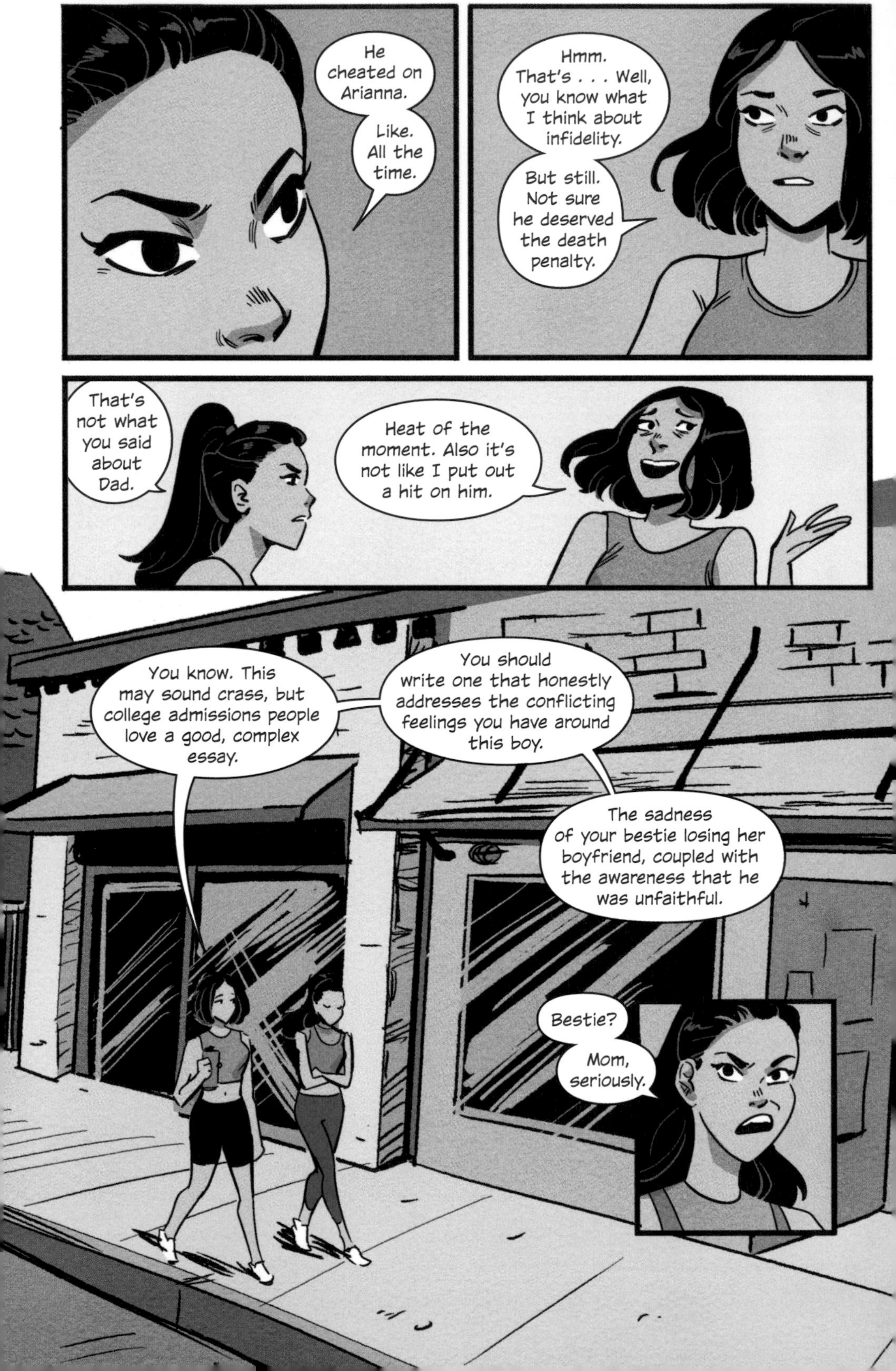
He cheated on Arianna.
Like. All the time.
Hmm. That's . . . Well, you know what I think about infidelity.
But still. Not sure he deserved the death penalty.
That's not what you said about Dad.
Heat of the moment. Also it's not like I put out a hit on him.
You know. This may sound crass, but college admissions people love a good, complex essay.
You should write one that honestly addresses the conflicting feelings you have around this boy.
The sadness of your bestie losing her boyfriend, coupled with the awareness that he was unfaithful.
Bestie?
Mom, seriously.

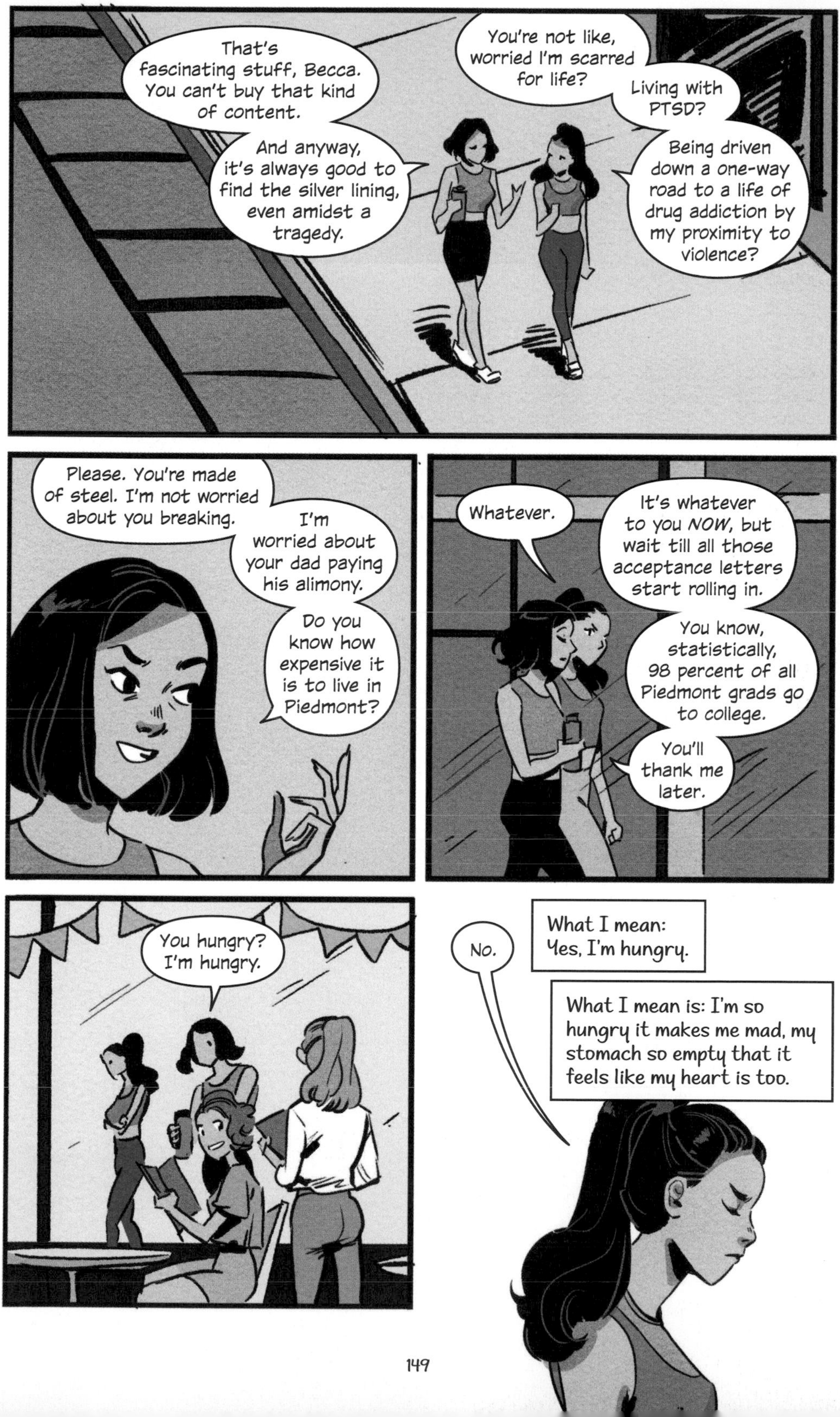
That's fascinating stuff, Becca. You can't buy that kind of content.
And anyway, it's always good to find the silver lining, even amidst a tragedy.
You're not like, worried I'm scarred for life?
Living with PTSD?
Being driven down a one-way road to a life of drug addiction by my proximity to violence?
Please. You're made of steel. I'm not worried about you breaking.
I'm worried about your dad paying his alimony.
Do you know how expensive it is to live in Piedmont?
Whatever.
It's whatever to you *NOW*, but wait till all those acceptance letters start rolling in.
You know, statistically, 98 percent of all Piedmont grads go to college.
You'll thank me later.
You hungry? I'm hungry.
No.
What I mean: Yes, I'm hungry.
What I mean is: I'm so hungry it makes me mad, my stomach so empty that it feels like my heart is too.

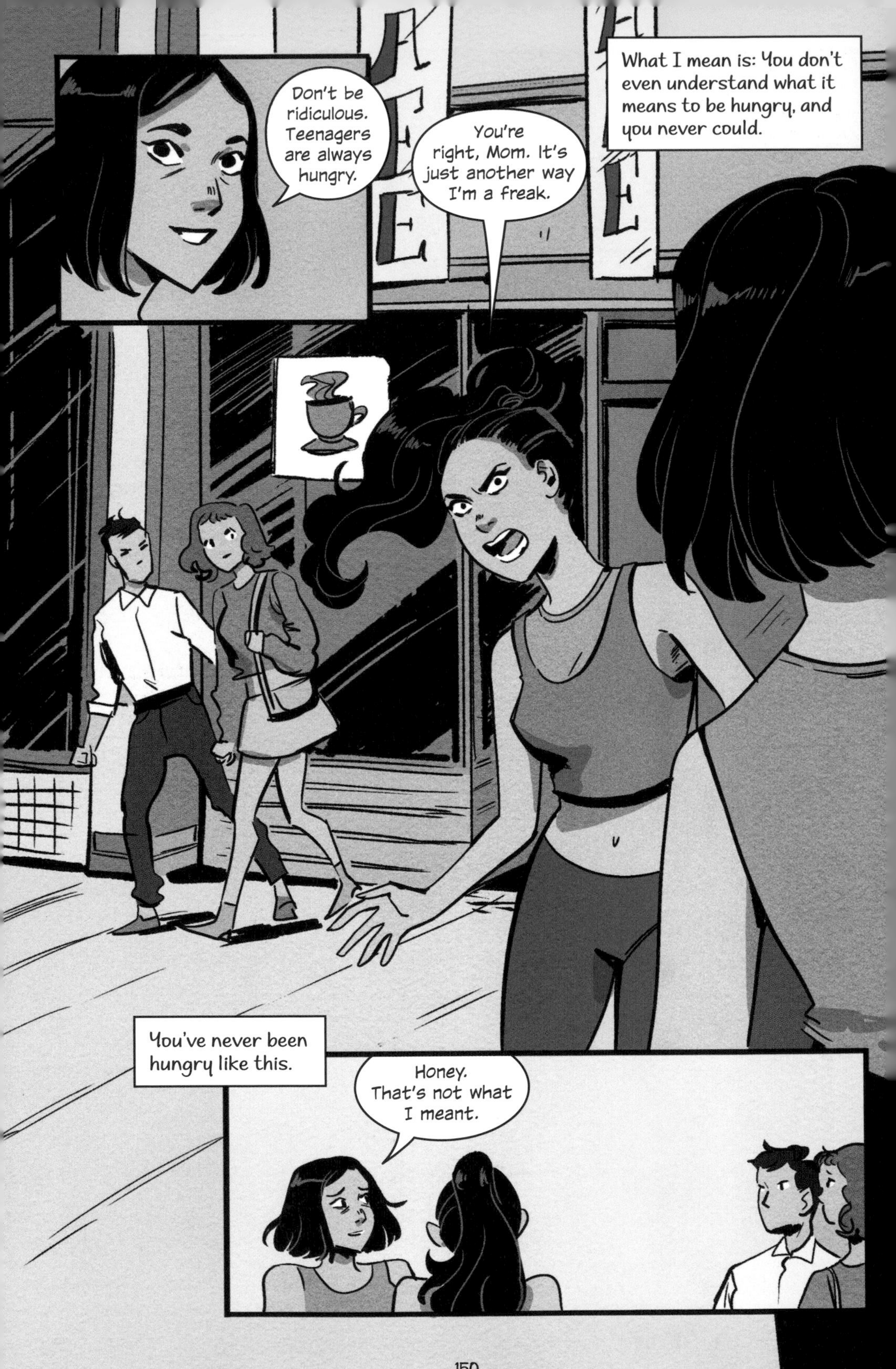
Don't be ridiculous. Teenagers are always hungry.
You're right, Mom. It's just another way I'm a freak.
What I mean is: You don't even understand what it means to be hungry, and you never could.
You've never been hungry like this.
Honey. That's not what I meant.

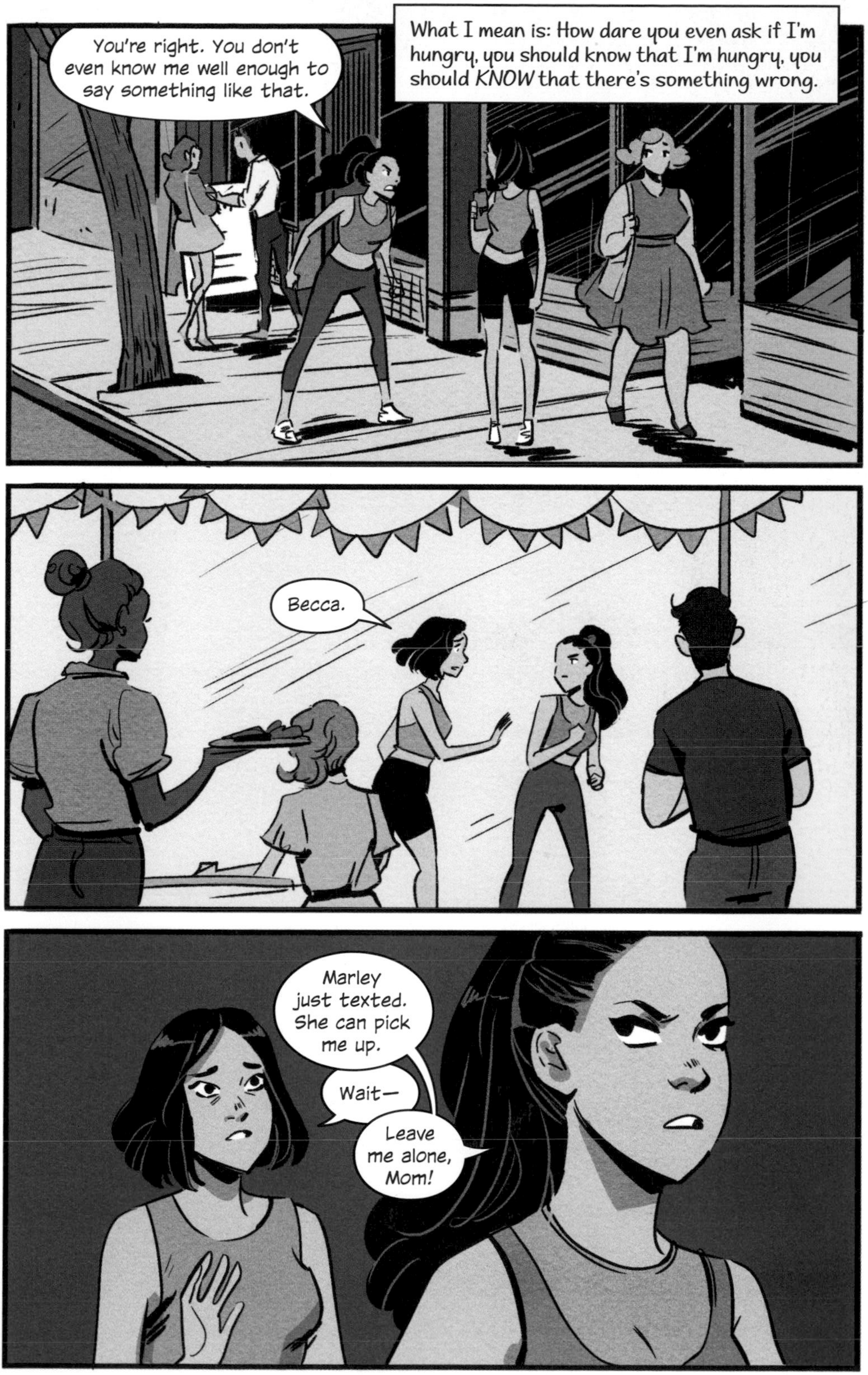
You're right. You don't even know me well enough to say something like that.
What I mean is: How dare you even ask if I'm hungry, you should know that I'm hungry, you should *KNOW* that there's something wrong.
Becca.
Marley just texted. She can pick me up.
Wait—
Leave me alone, Mom!

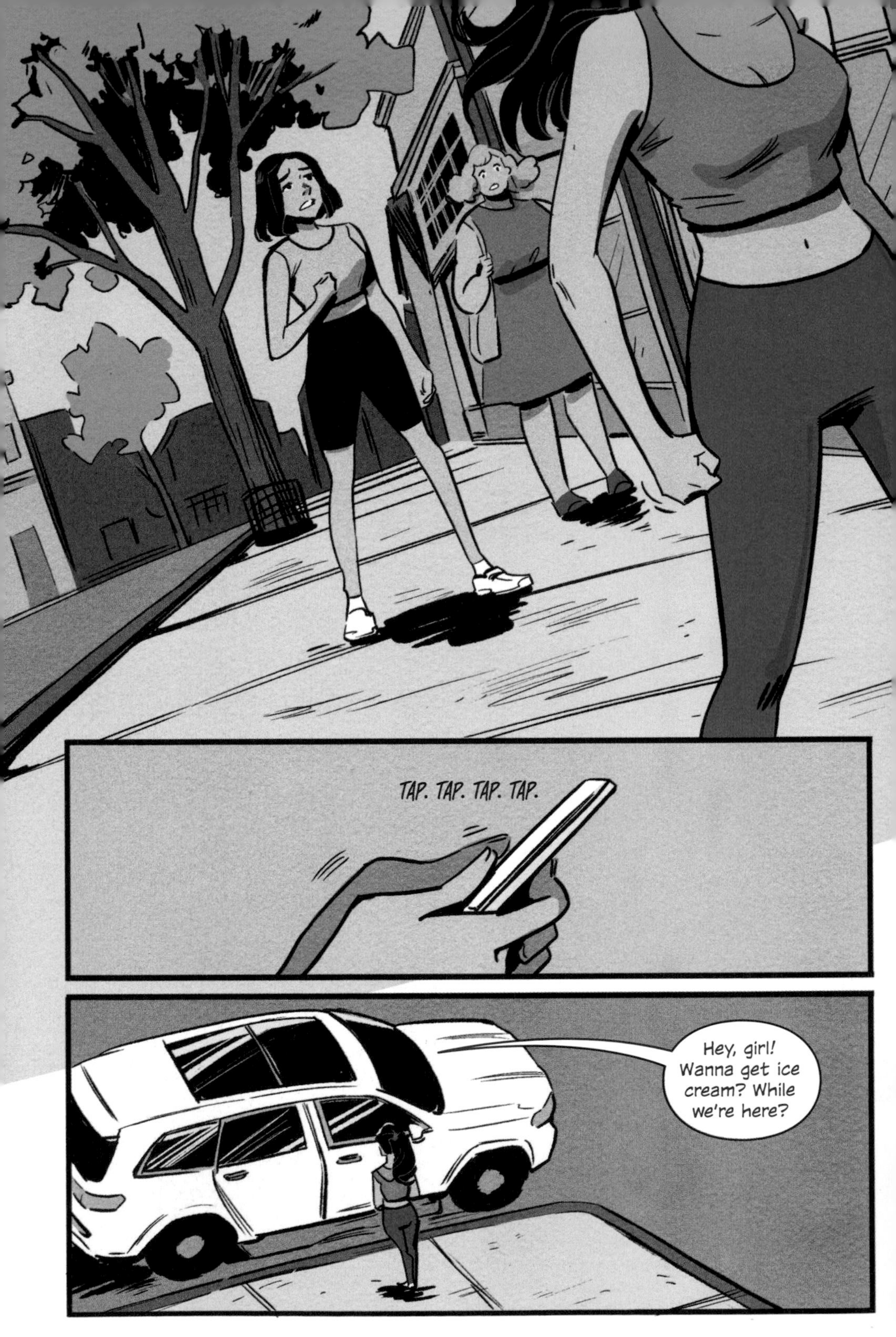
TAP. TAP. TAP. TAP.
Hey, girl! Wanna get ice cream? While we're here?

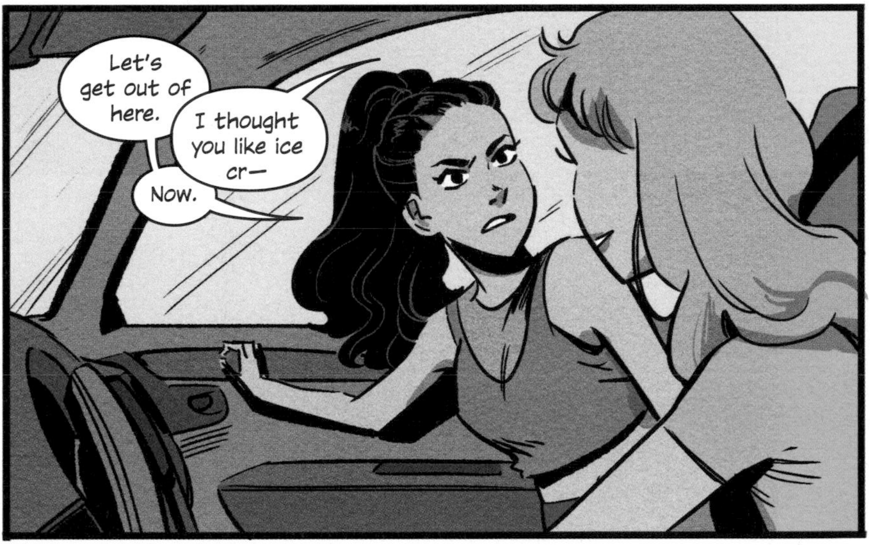
Let's get out of here.
I thought you like ice cr—
Now.

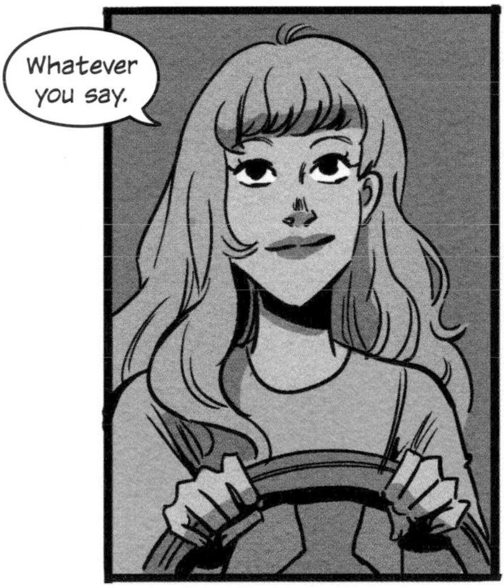
Whatever you say.

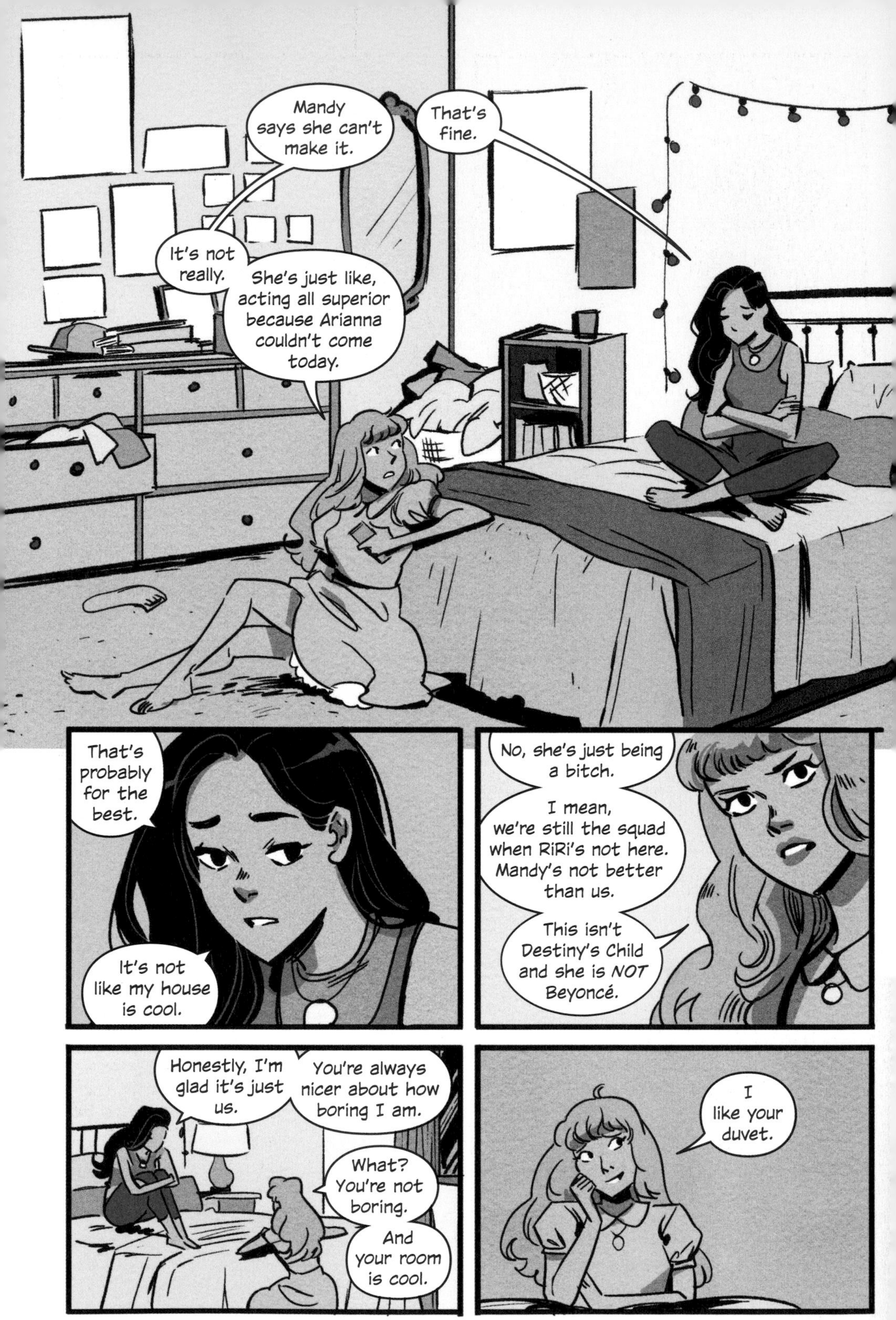

Mandy says she can't make it.
That's fine.
It's not really.
She's just like, acting all superior because Arianna couldn't come today.
That's probably for the best.
It's not like my house is cool.
No, she's just being a bitch.
I mean, we're still the squad when RiRi's not here. Mandy's not better than us.
This isn't Destiny's Child and she is *NOT* Beyoncé.
Honestly, I'm glad it's just us.
You're always nicer about how boring I am.
What? You're not boring.
And your room is cool.
I like your duvet.

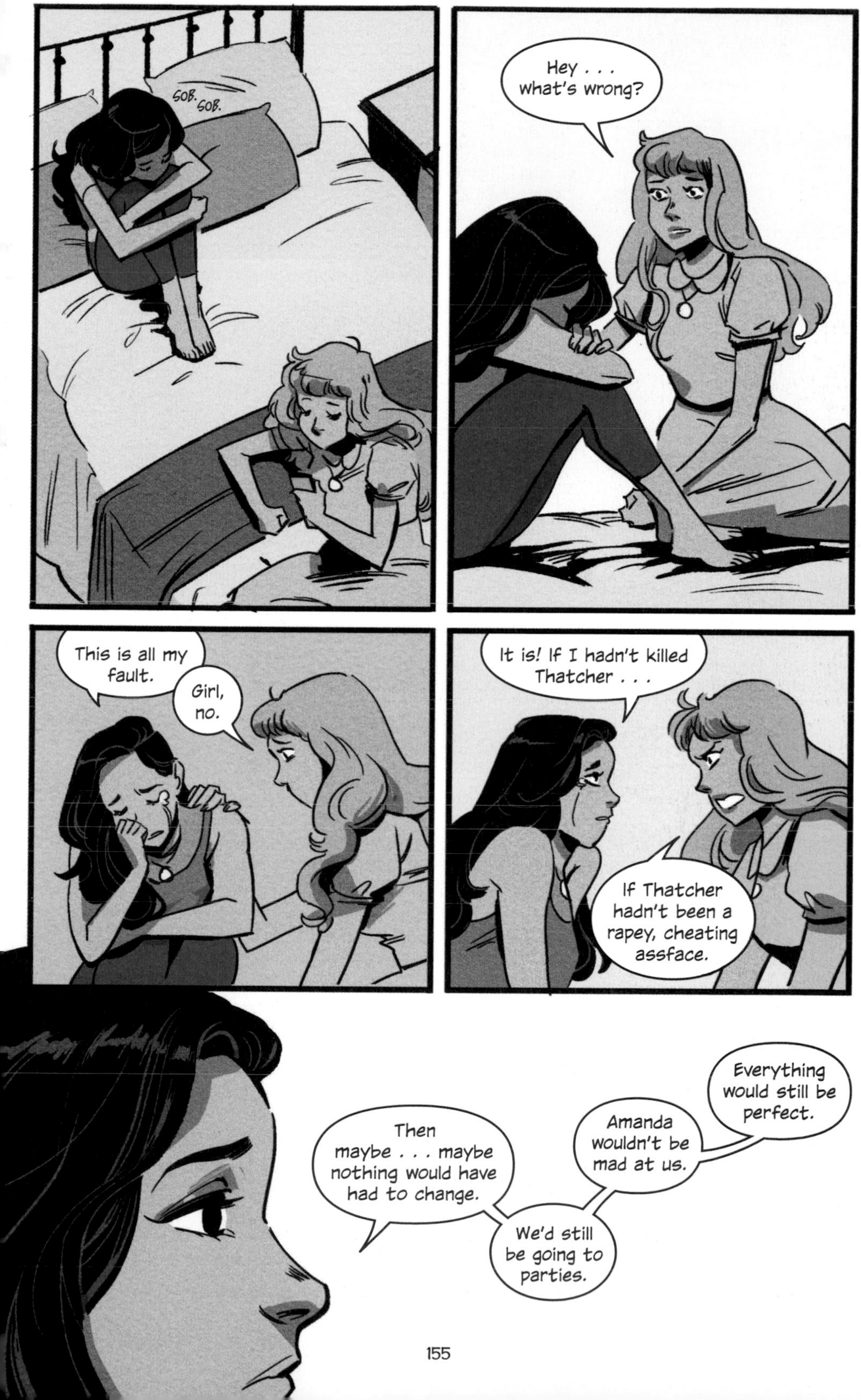
SOB. SOB.
Hey . . . what's wrong?
This is all my fault.
Girl, no.
It is! If I hadn't killed Thatcher . . .
If Thatcher hadn't been a rapey, cheating assface.
Then maybe . . . maybe nothing would have had to change.
We'd still be going to parties.
Amanda wouldn't be mad at us.
Everything would still be perfect.

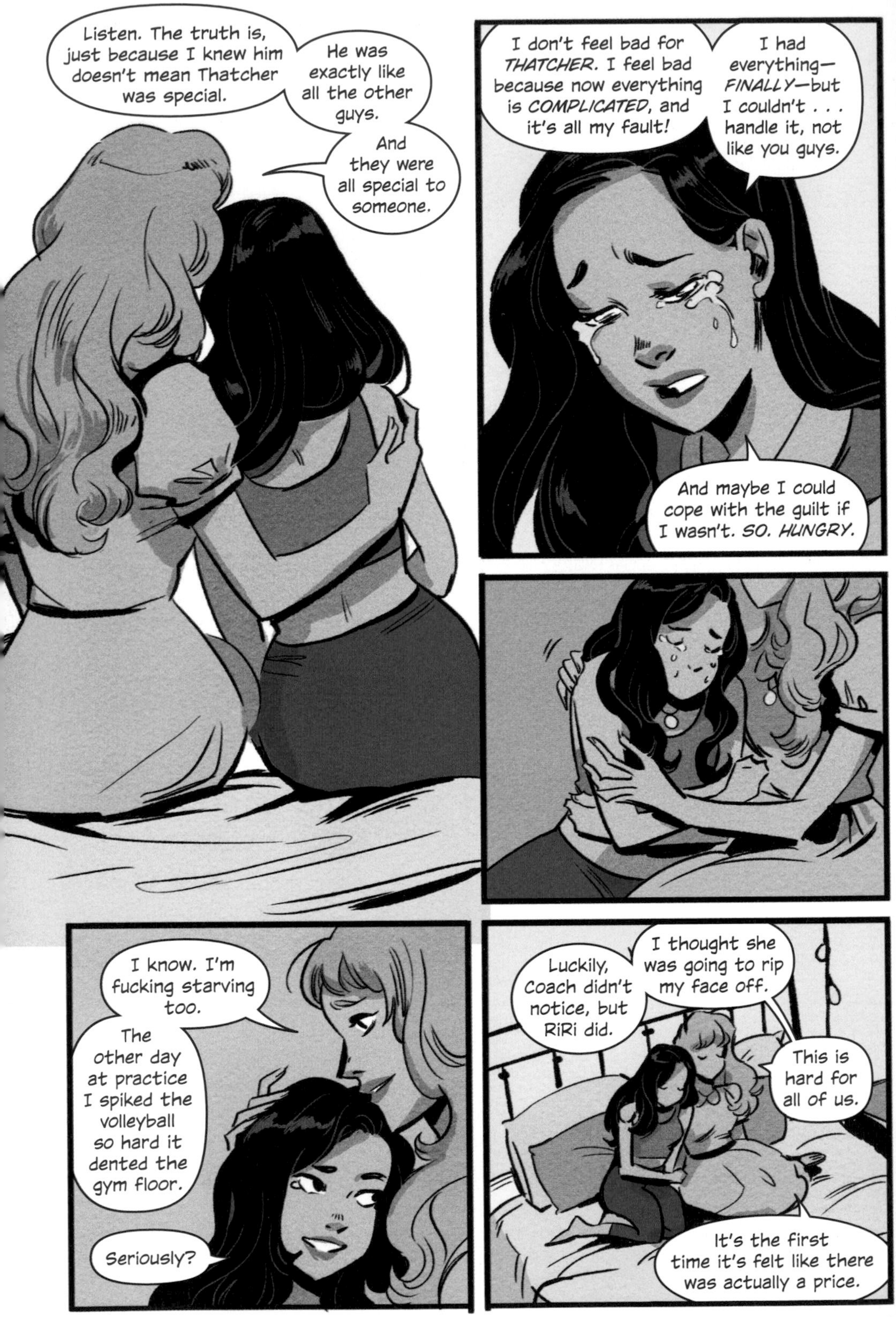
Listen. The truth is, just because I knew him doesn't mean Thatcher was special.
He was exactly like all the other guys.
And they were all special to someone.
I don't feel bad for *THATCHER*. I feel bad because now everything is *COMPLICATED*, and it's all my fault!
I had everything—*FINALLY*—but I couldn't . . . handle it, not like you guys.
And maybe I could cope with the guilt if I wasn't. *SO. HUNGRY.*
I know. I'm fucking starving too.
The other day at practice I spiked the volleyball so hard it dented the gym floor.
Seriously?
Luckily, Coach didn't notice, but RiRi did.
I thought she was going to rip my face off.
This is hard for all of us.
It's the first time it's felt like there was actually a price.

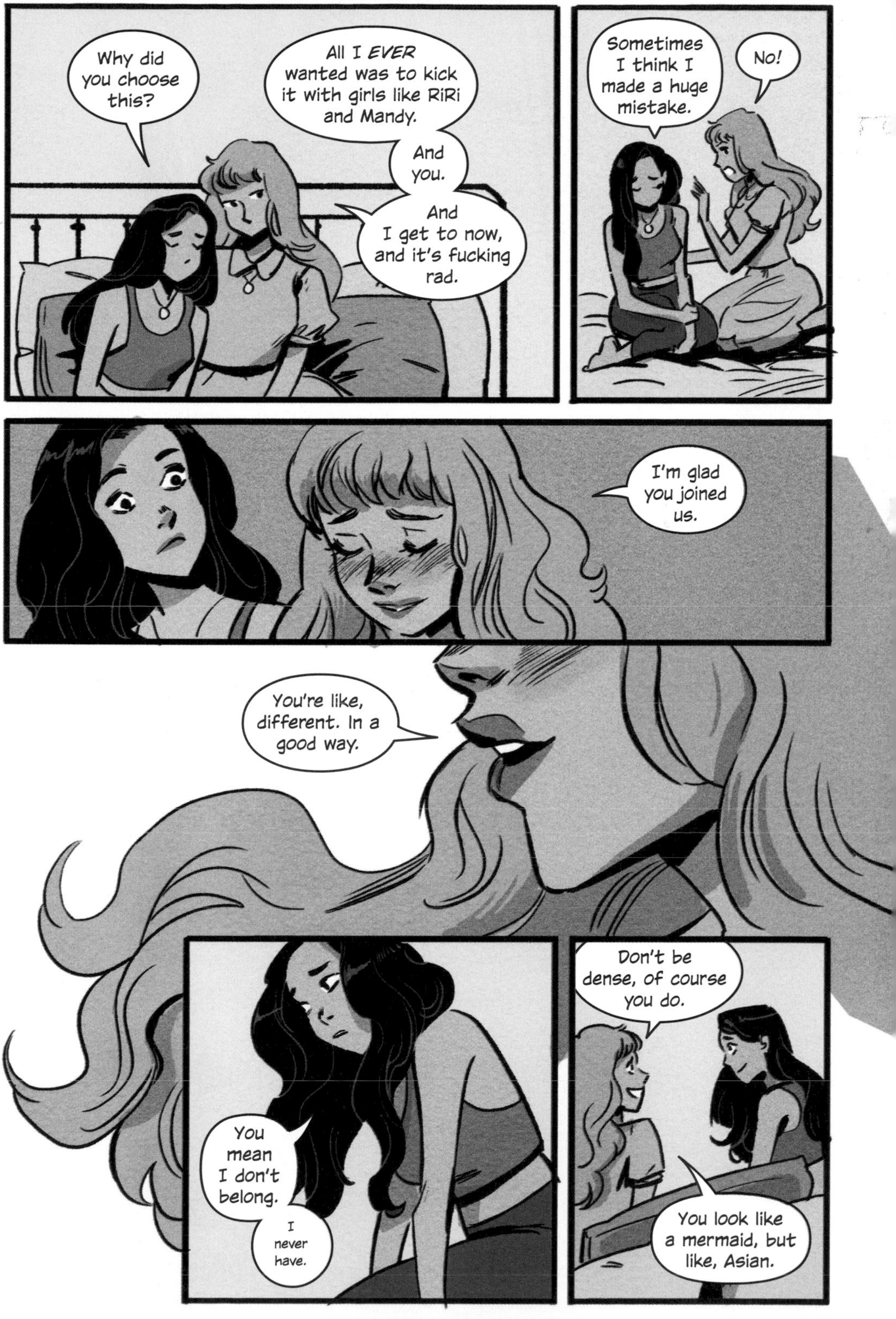
Why did you choose this?
All I EVER wanted was to kick it with girls like RiRi and Mandy.
And you.
And I get to now, and it's fucking rad.
Sometimes I think I made a huge mistake.
No!
I'm glad you joined us.
You're like, different. In a good way.
You mean I don't belong.
I never have.
Don't be dense, of course you do.
You look like a mermaid, but like, Asian.

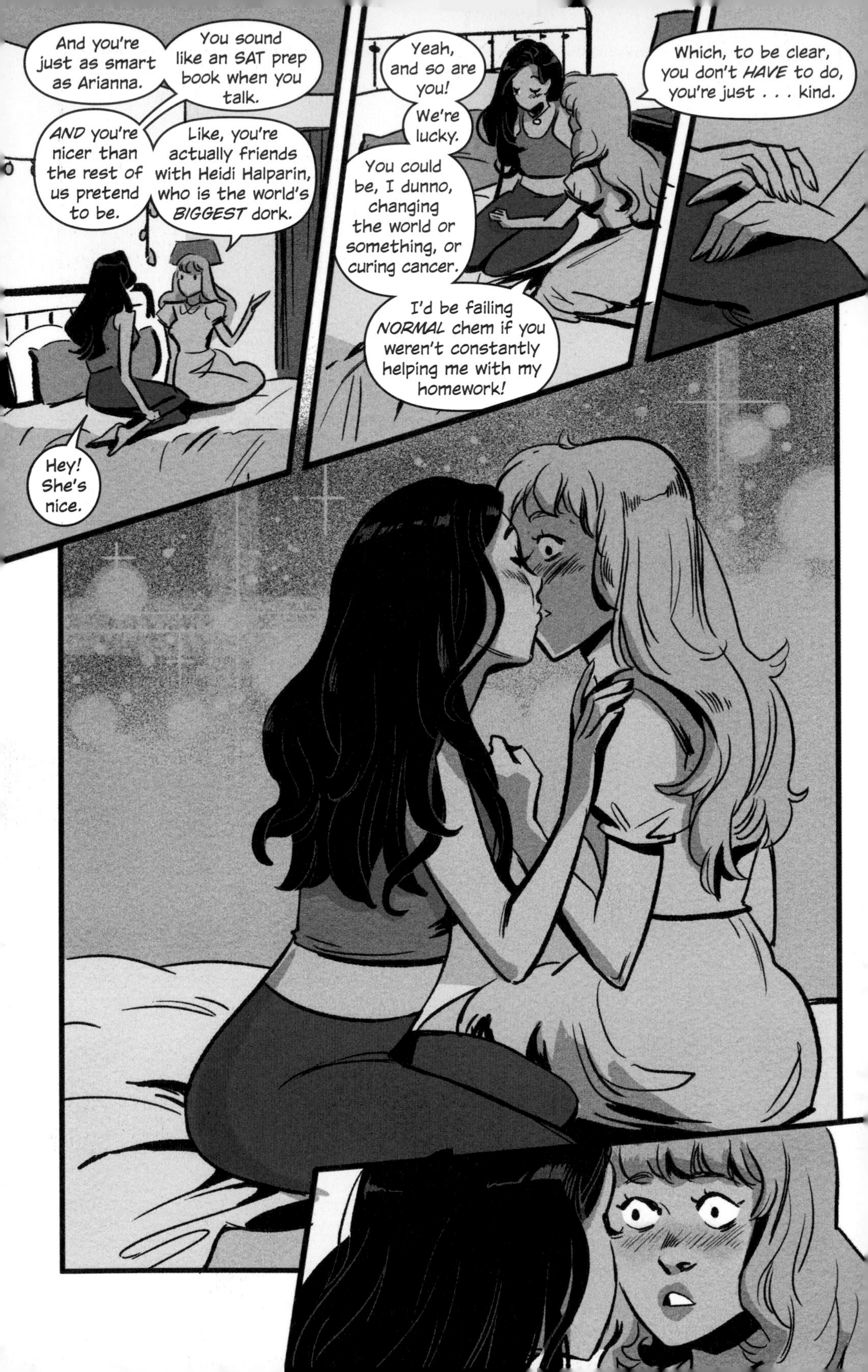
And you're just as smart as Arianna.
You sound like an SAT prep book when you talk.
AND you're nicer than the rest of us pretend to be.
Like, you're actually friends with Heidi Halparin, who is the world's BIGGEST dork.
Hey! She's nice.
Yeah, and so are you!
We're lucky.
You could be, I dunno, changing the world or something, or curing cancer.
I'd be failing NORMAL chem if you weren't constantly helping me with my homework!
Which, to be clear, you don't HAVE to do, you're just . . . kind.

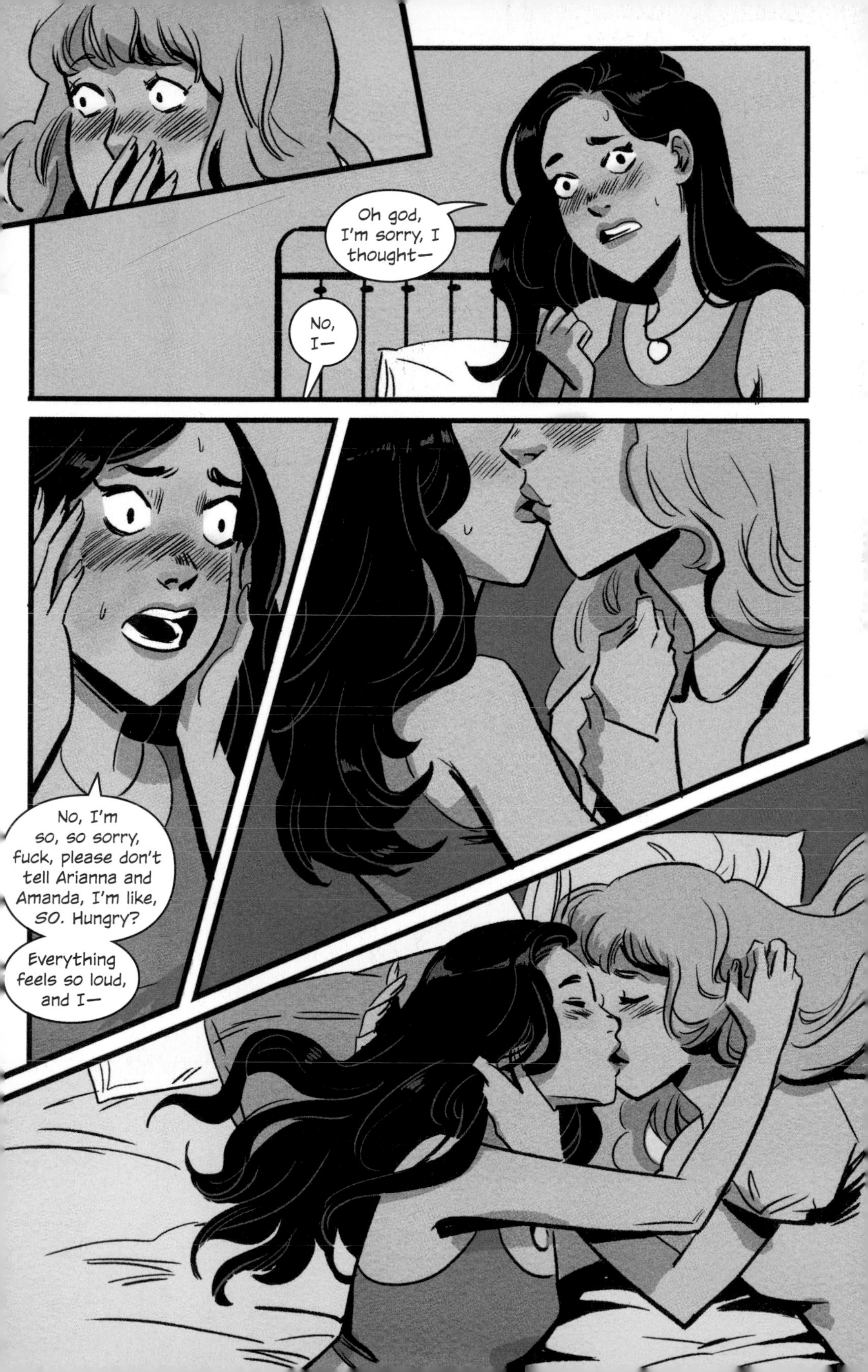

Oh god, I'm sorry, I thought—
No, I—
No, I'm so, so sorry, fuck, please don't tell Arianna and Amanda, I'm like, SO. Hungry?
Everything feels so loud, and I—

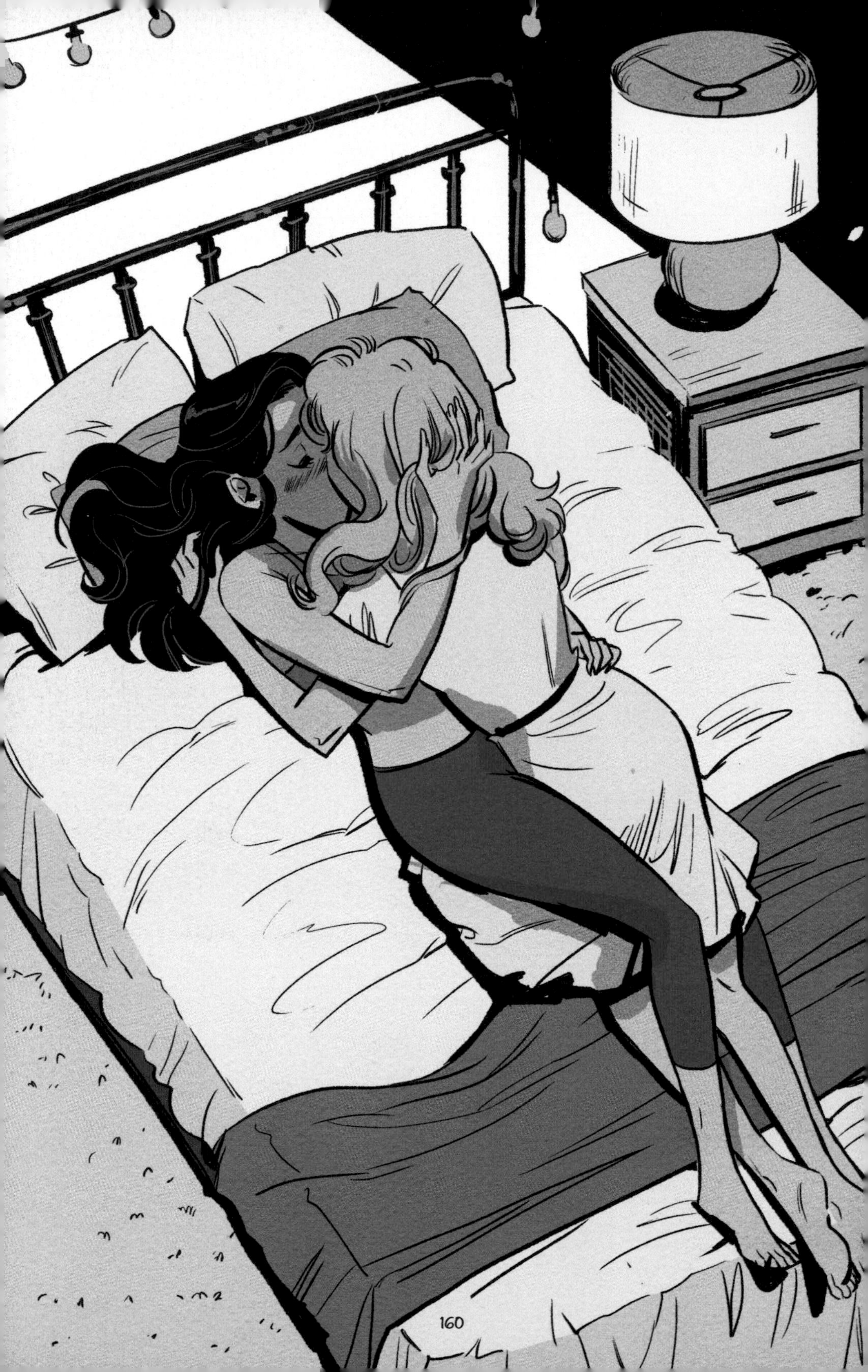

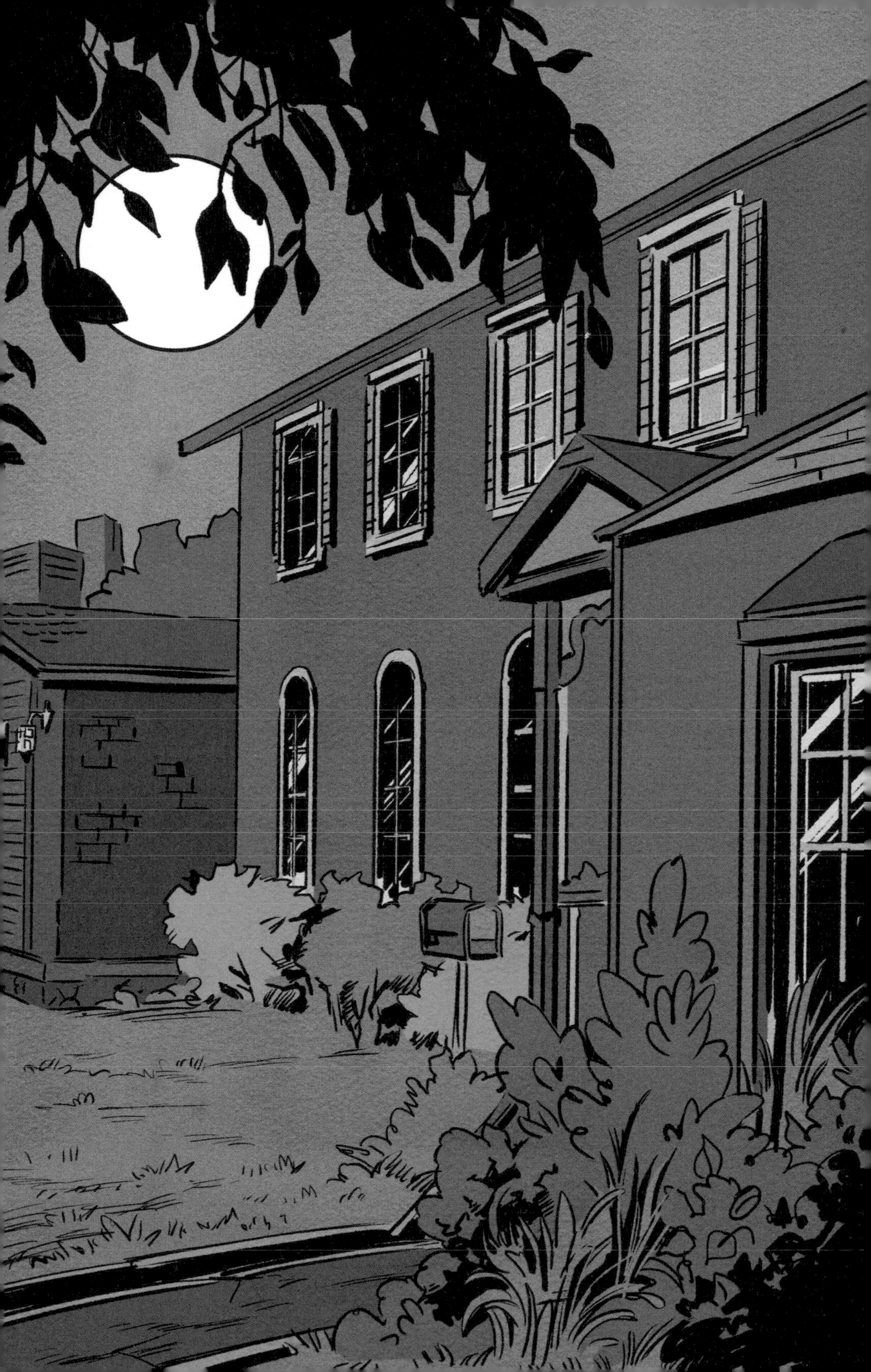

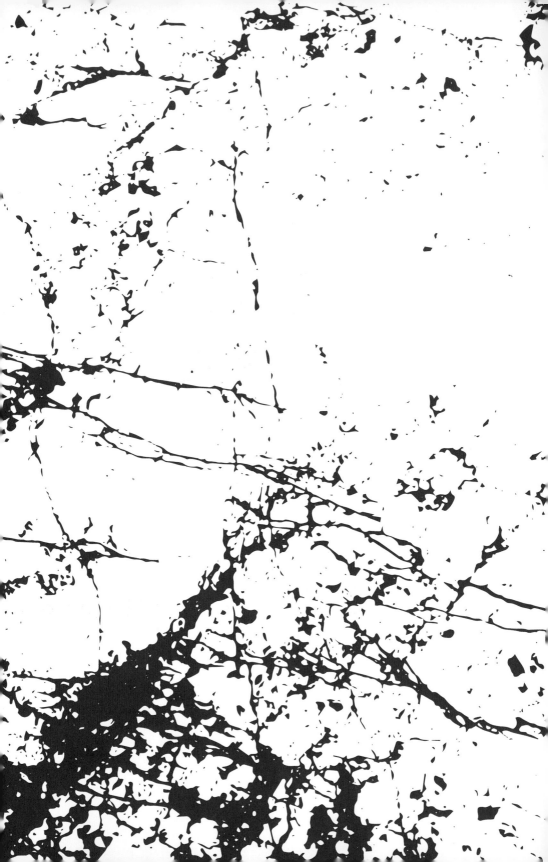

CHAPTER SEVEN

END OF THE ROAD

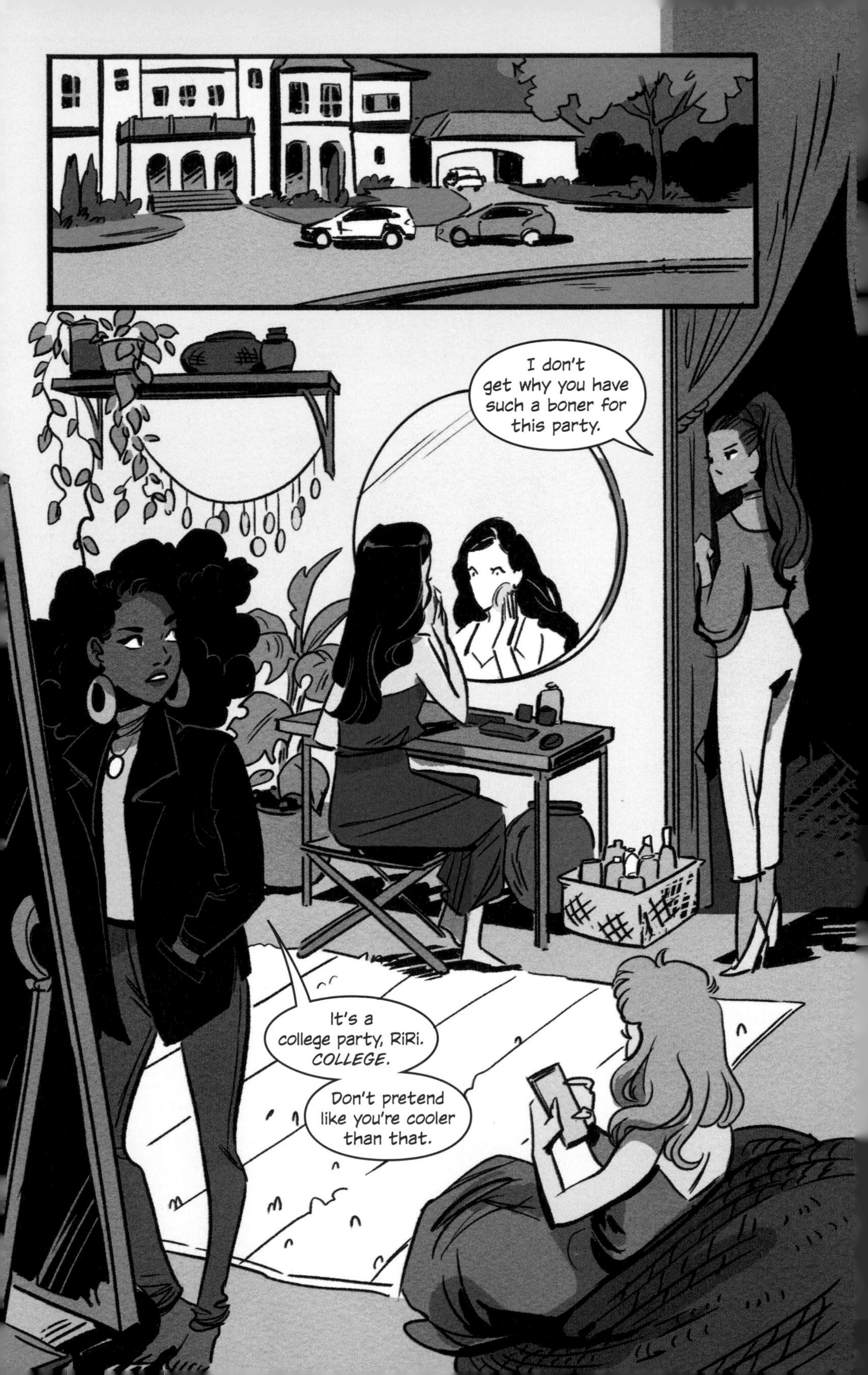
I don't get why you have such a boner for this party.
It's a college party, RiRi. COLLEGE.
Don't pretend like you're cooler than that.

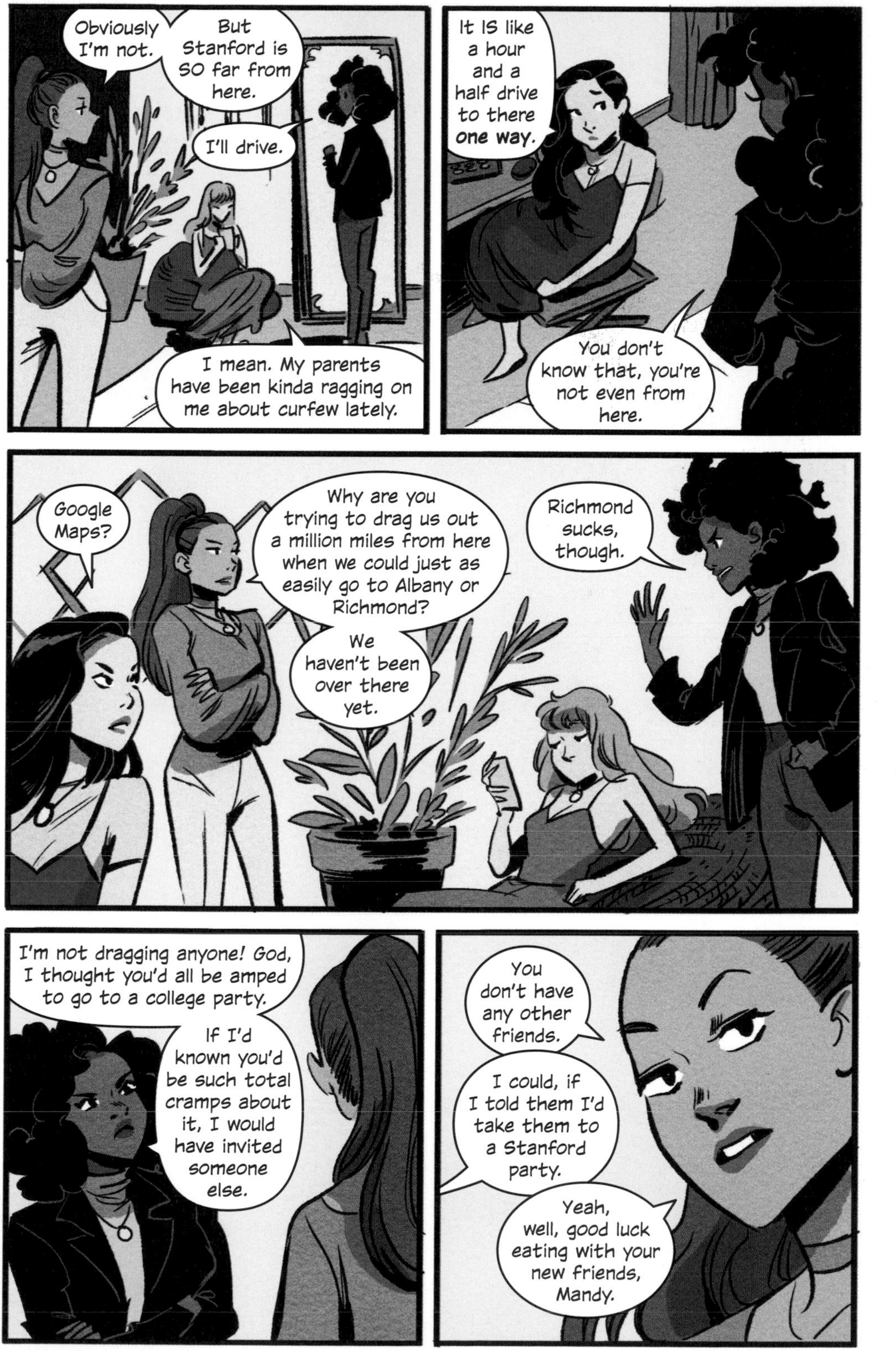
Obviously I'm not.
But Stanford is SO far from here.
I'll drive.
I mean. My parents have been kinda ragging on me about curfew lately.
It IS like a hour and a half drive to there **one way.**
You don't know that, you're not even from here.
Google Maps?
Why are you trying to drag us out a million miles from here when we could just as easily go to Albany or Richmond?
We haven't been over there yet.
Richmond sucks, though.
I'm not dragging anyone! God, I thought you'd all be amped to go to a college party.
If I'd known you'd be such total cramps about it, I would have invited someone else.
You don't have any other friends.
I could, if I told them I'd take them to a Stanford party.
Yeah, well, good luck eating with your new friends, Mandy.

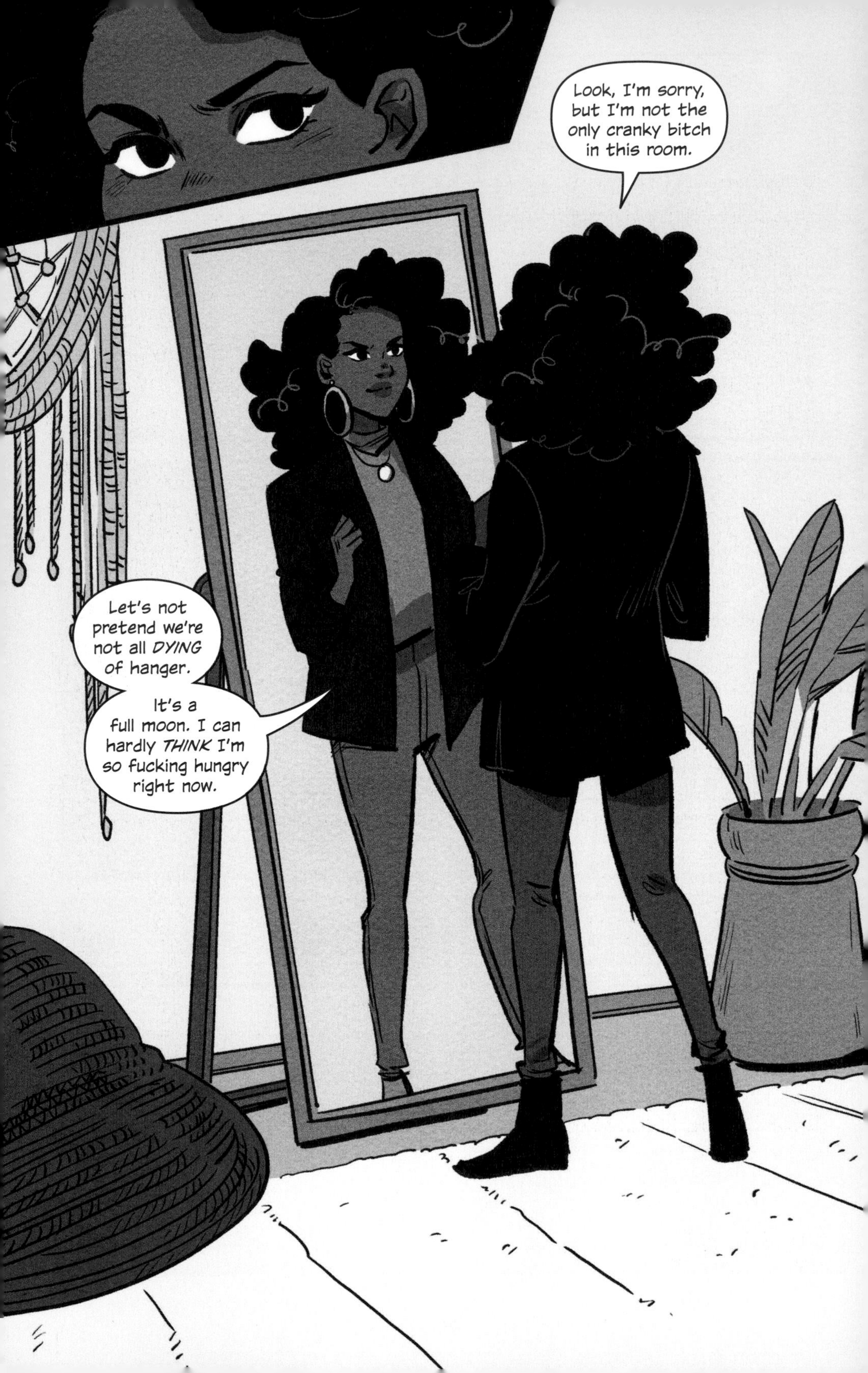
Look, I'm sorry, but I'm not the only cranky bitch in this room.
Let's not pretend we're not all *DYING* of hanger.
It's a full moon. I can hardly *THINK* I'm so fucking hungry right now.

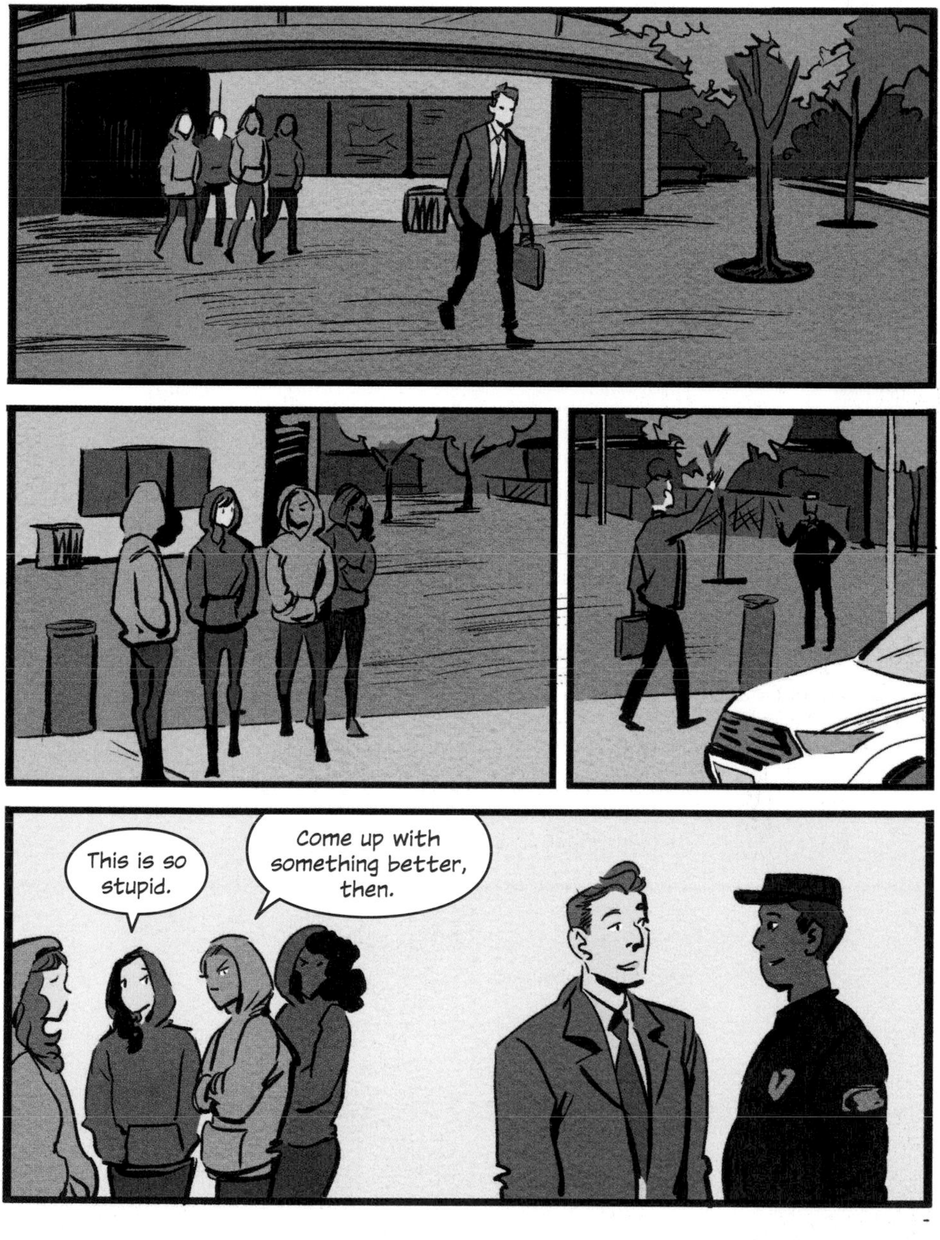
This is so stupid.
Come up with something better, then.

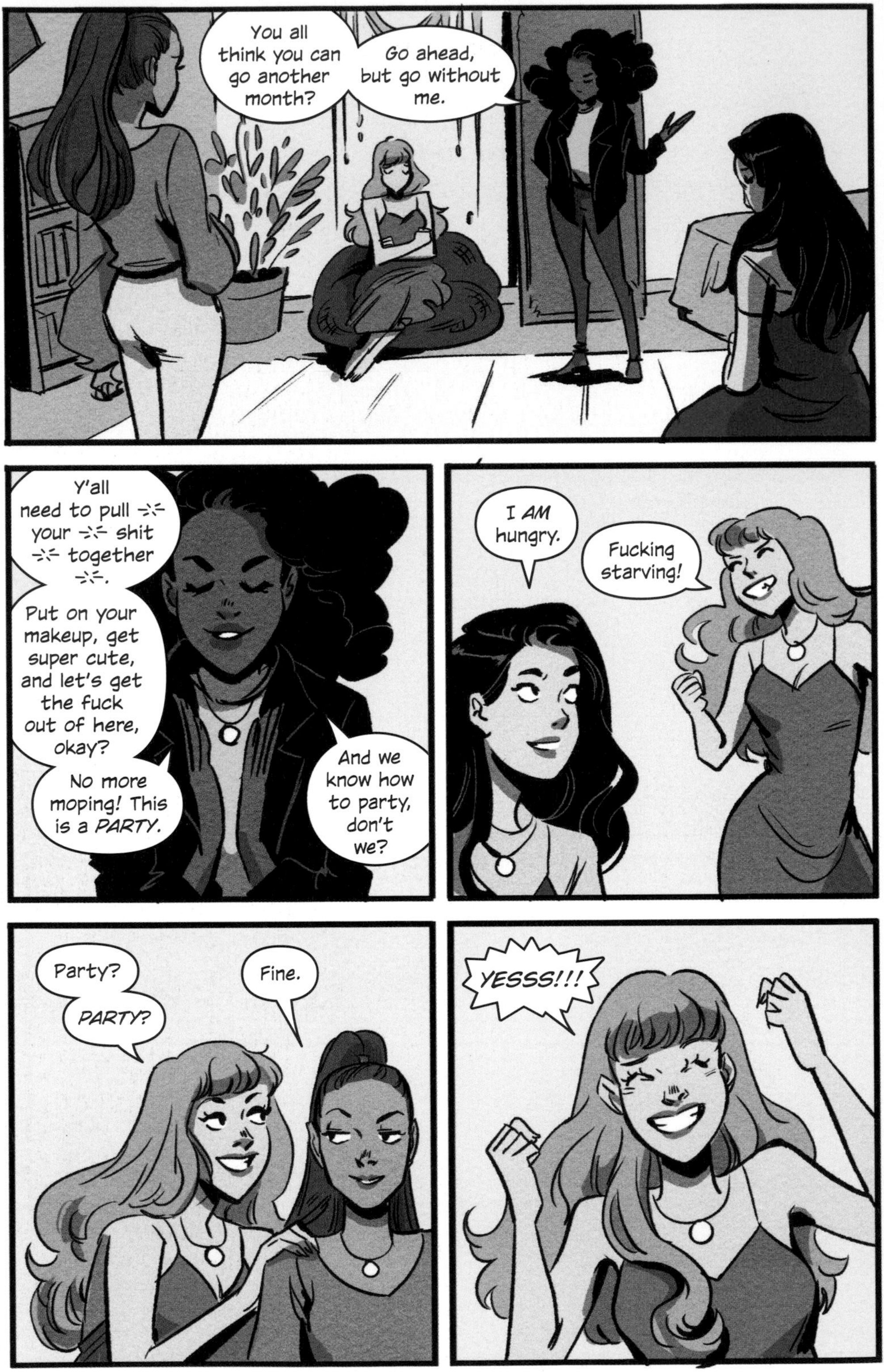
You all think you can go another month?
Go ahead, but go without me.
Y'all need to pull your shit together.
Put on your makeup, get super cute, and let's get the fuck out of here, okay?
No more moping! This is a *PARTY*.
And we know how to party, don't we?
I *AM* hungry.
Fucking starving!
Party?
PARTY?
Fine.
YESSS!!!

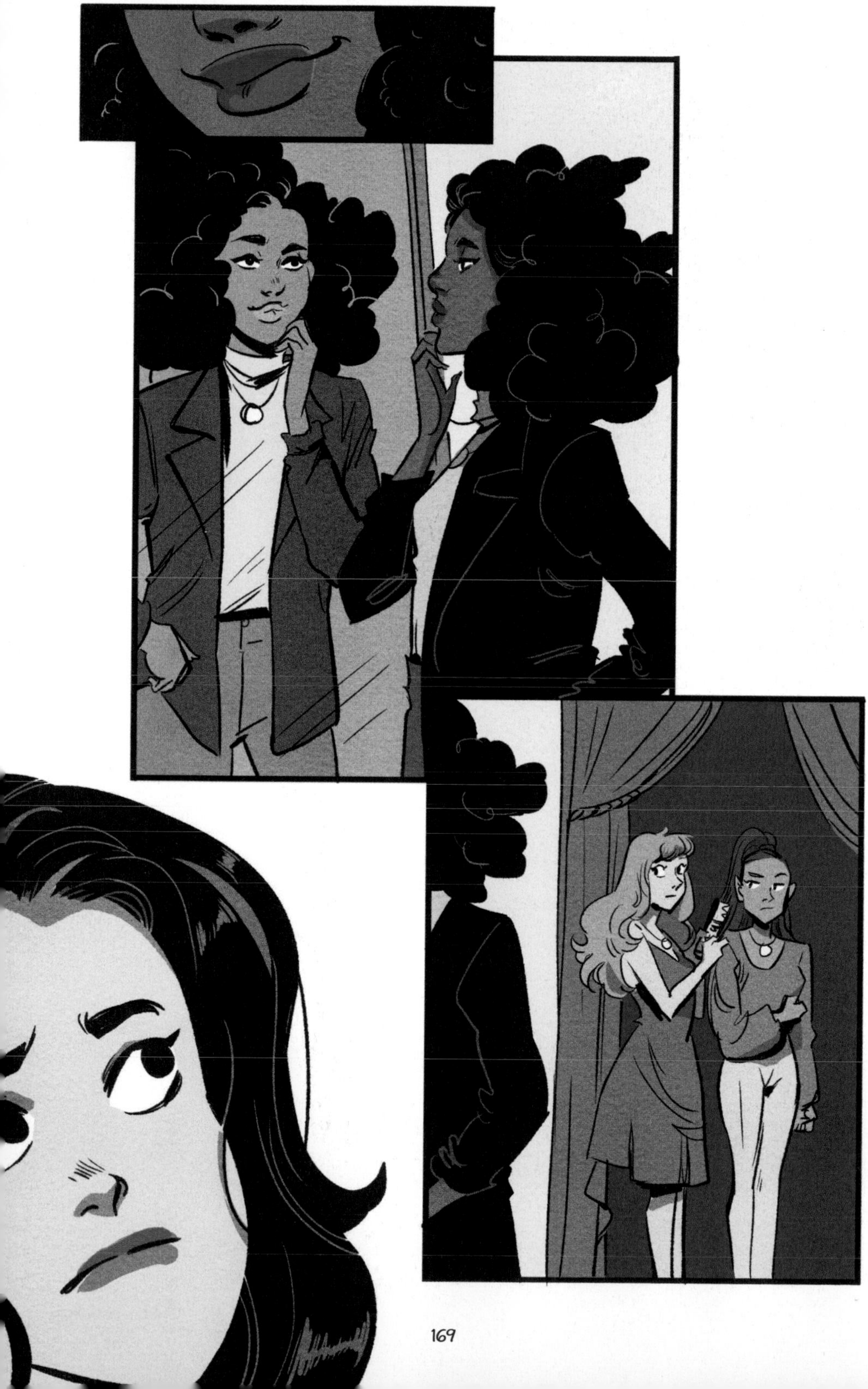

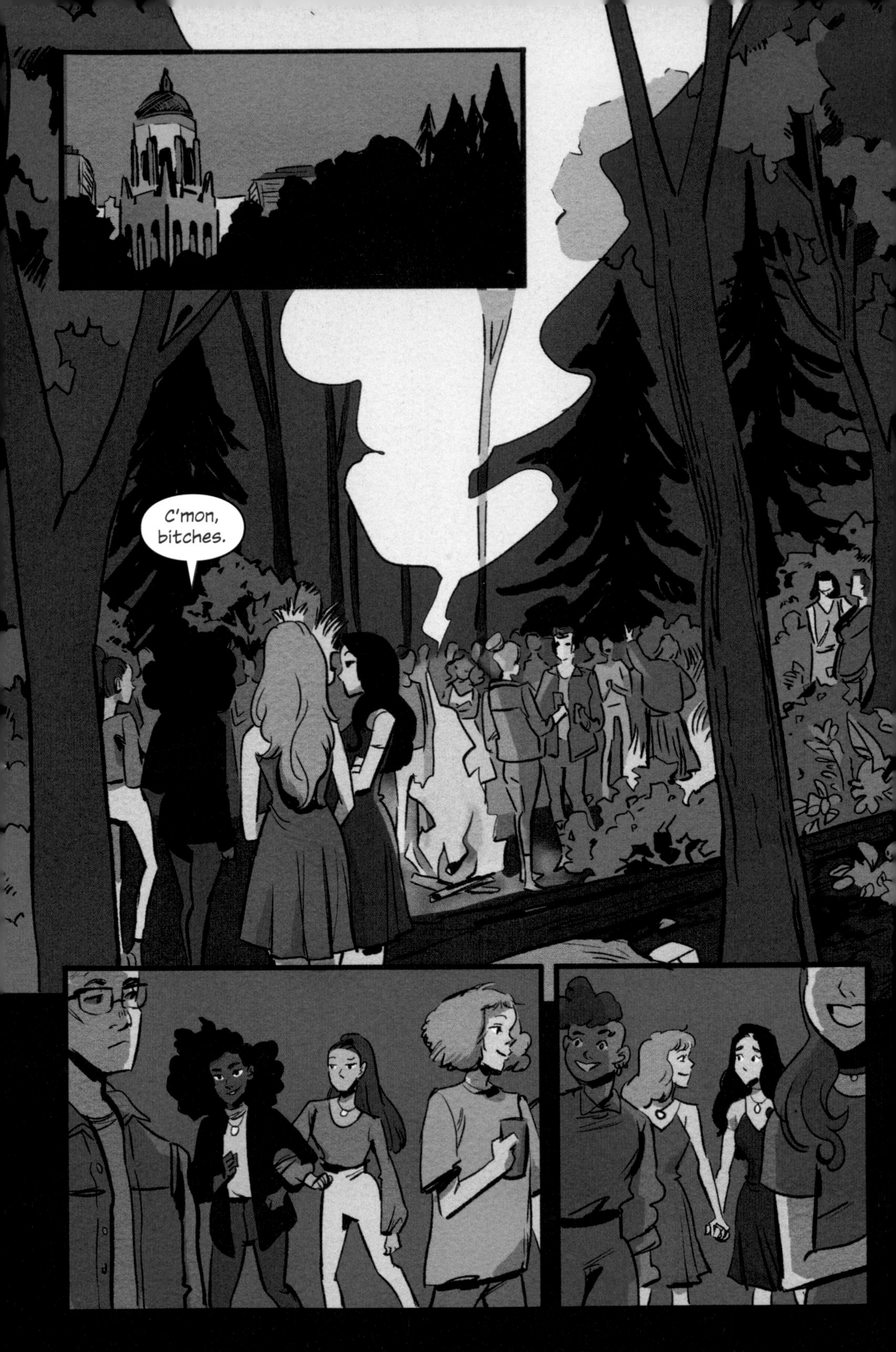
C'mon, bitches.

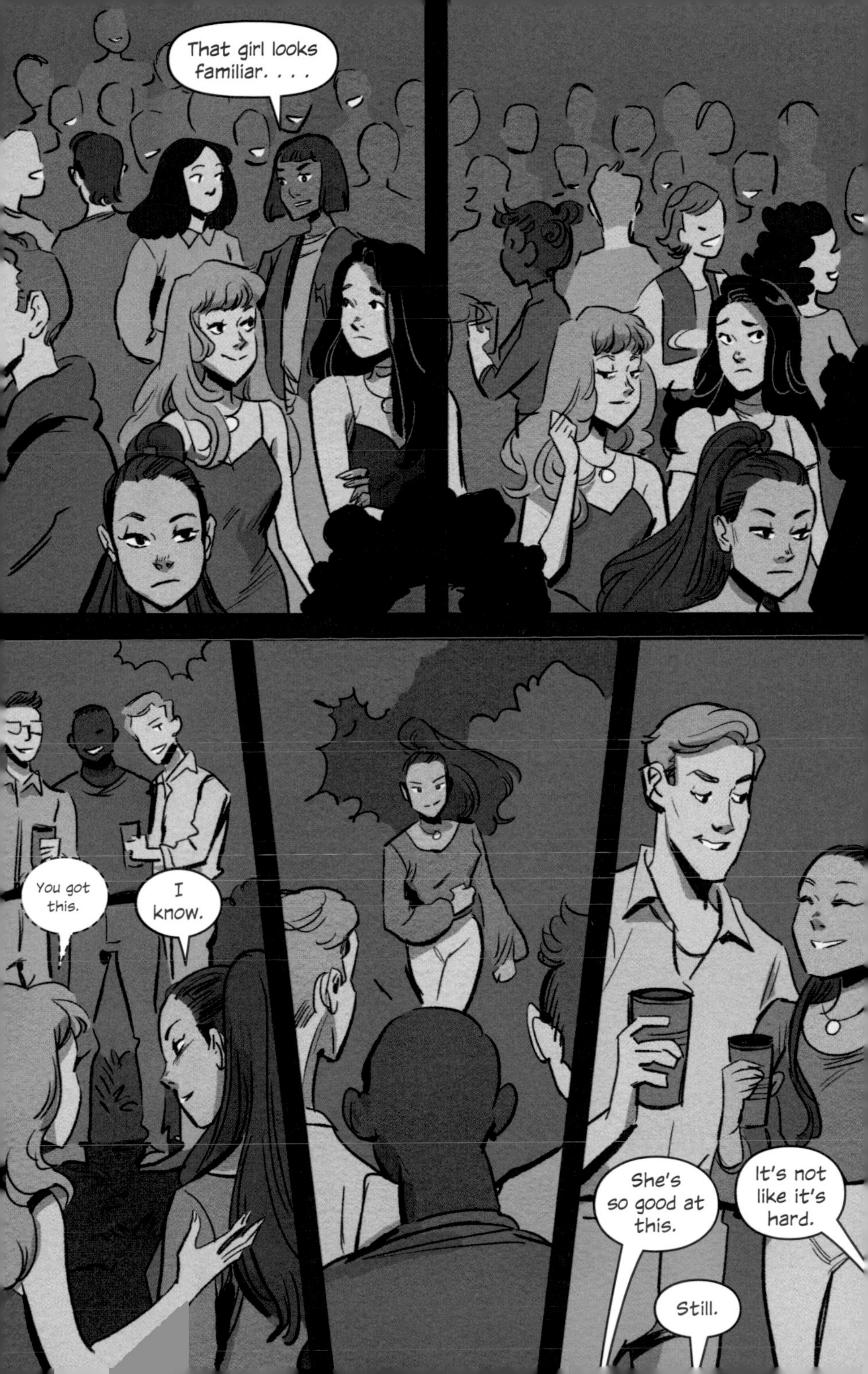
That girl looks familiar. . . .
You got this.
I know.
She's so good at this.
It's not like it's hard.
Still.

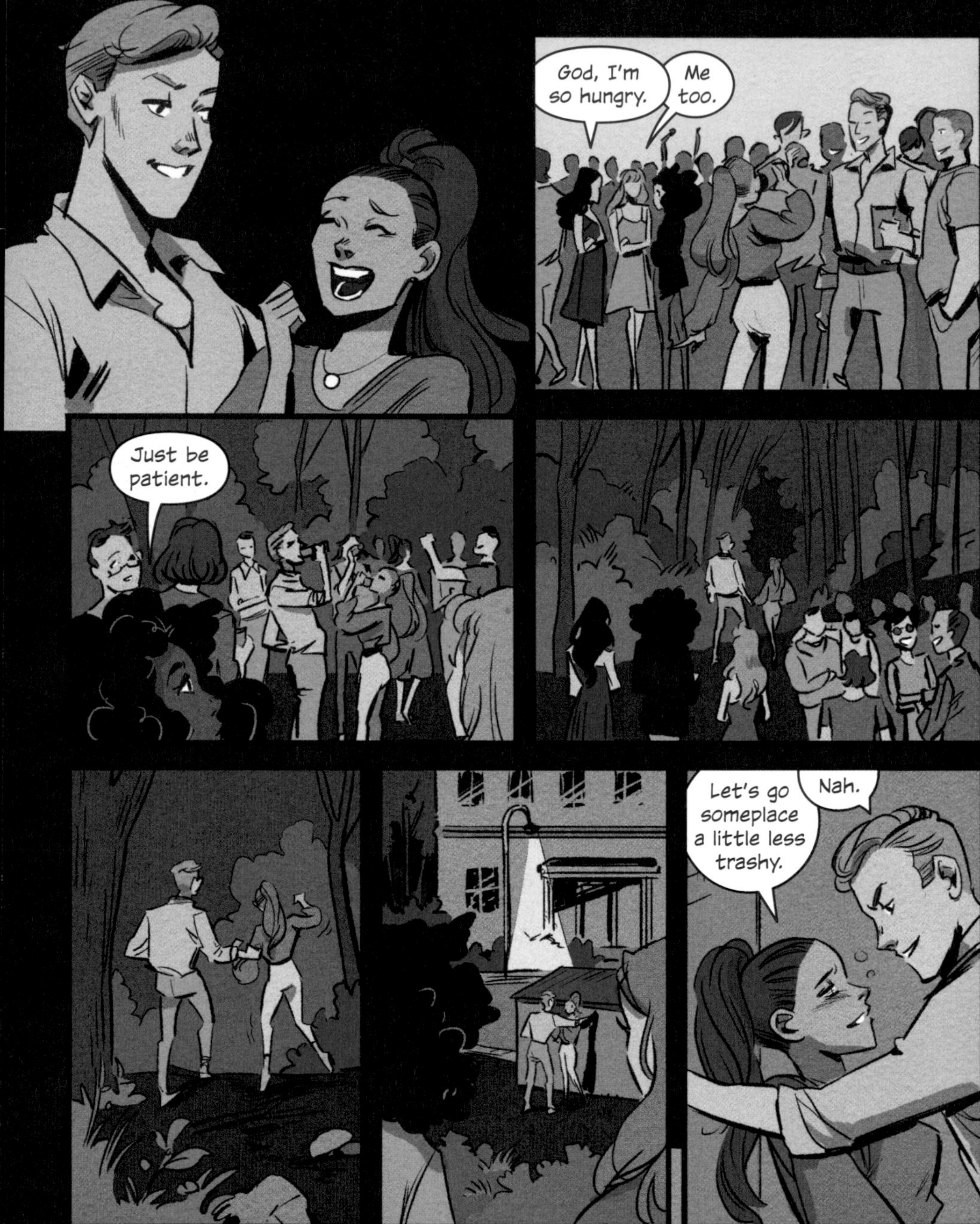

God, I'm so hungry.
Me too.
Just be patient.
Let's go someplace a little less trashy.
Nah.

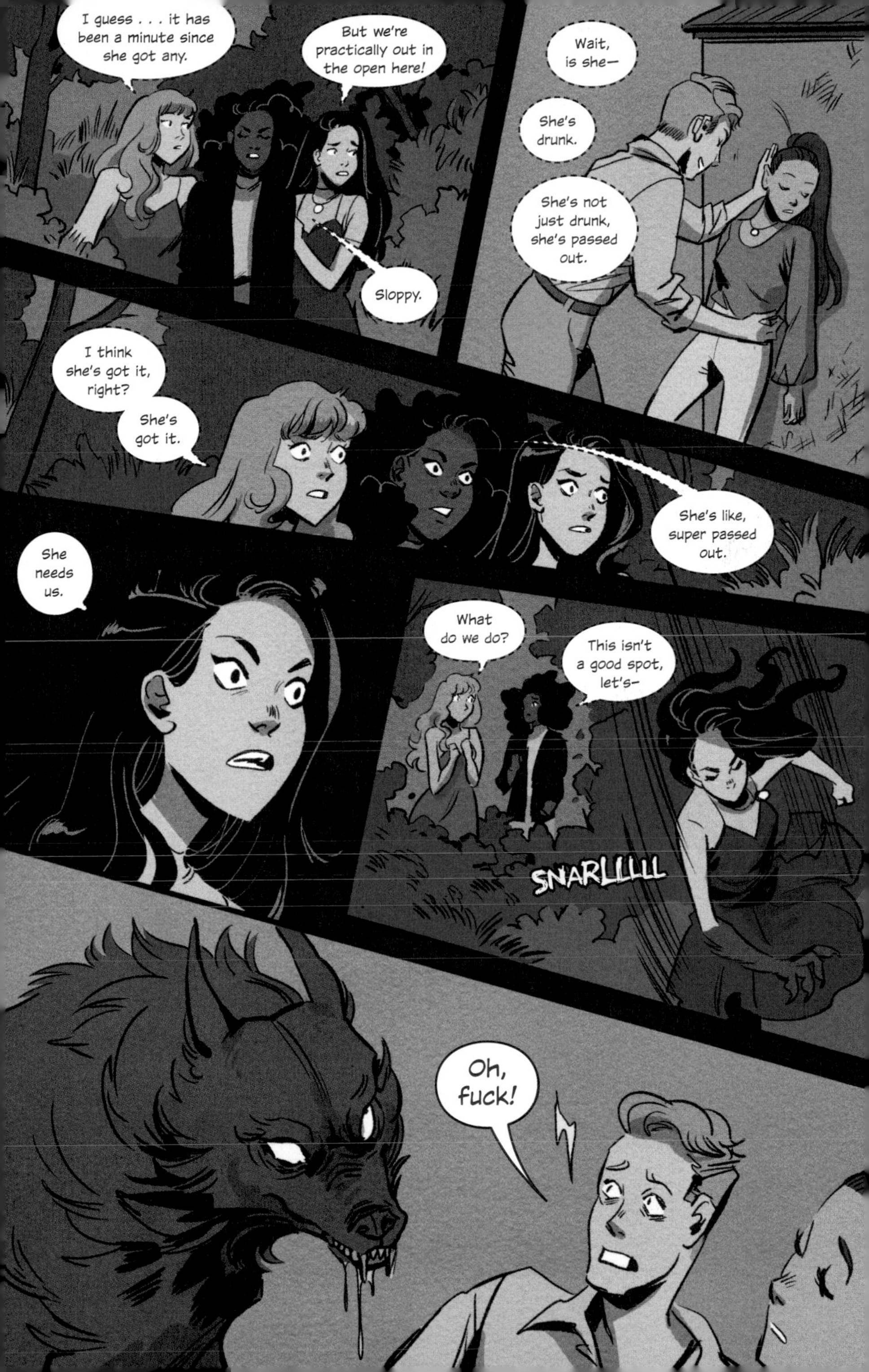
I guess . . . it has been a minute since she got any.
But we're practically out in the open here!
Sloppy.
Wait, is she—
She's drunk.
She's not just drunk, she's passed out.
I think she's got it, right?
She's got it.
She's like, super passed out.
She needs us.
What do we do?
This isn't a good spot, let's–
SNARLLLLL
Oh, fuck!

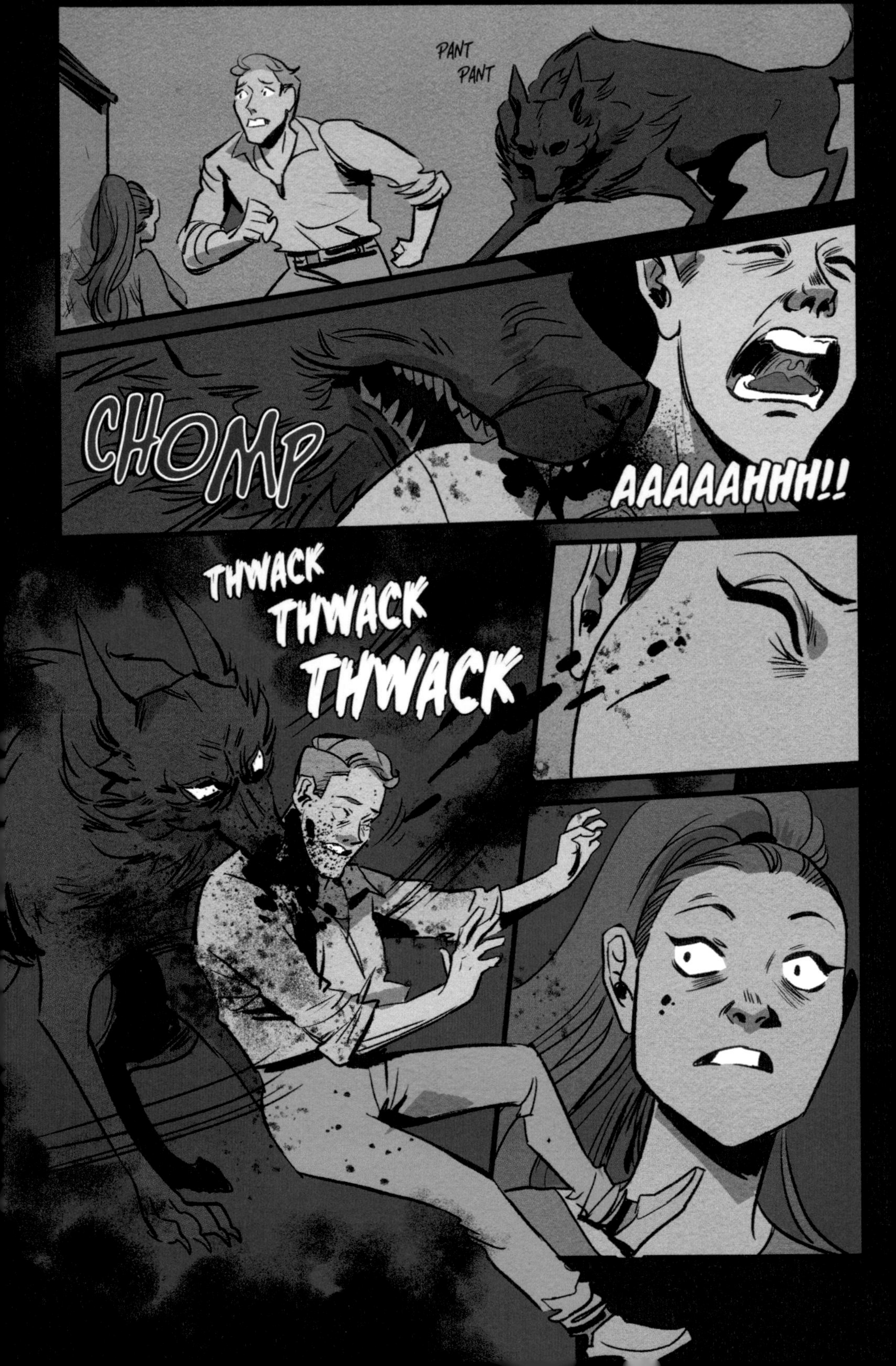
PANT
PANT
CHOMP
AAAAAHHH!!
THWACK
THWACK
THWACK

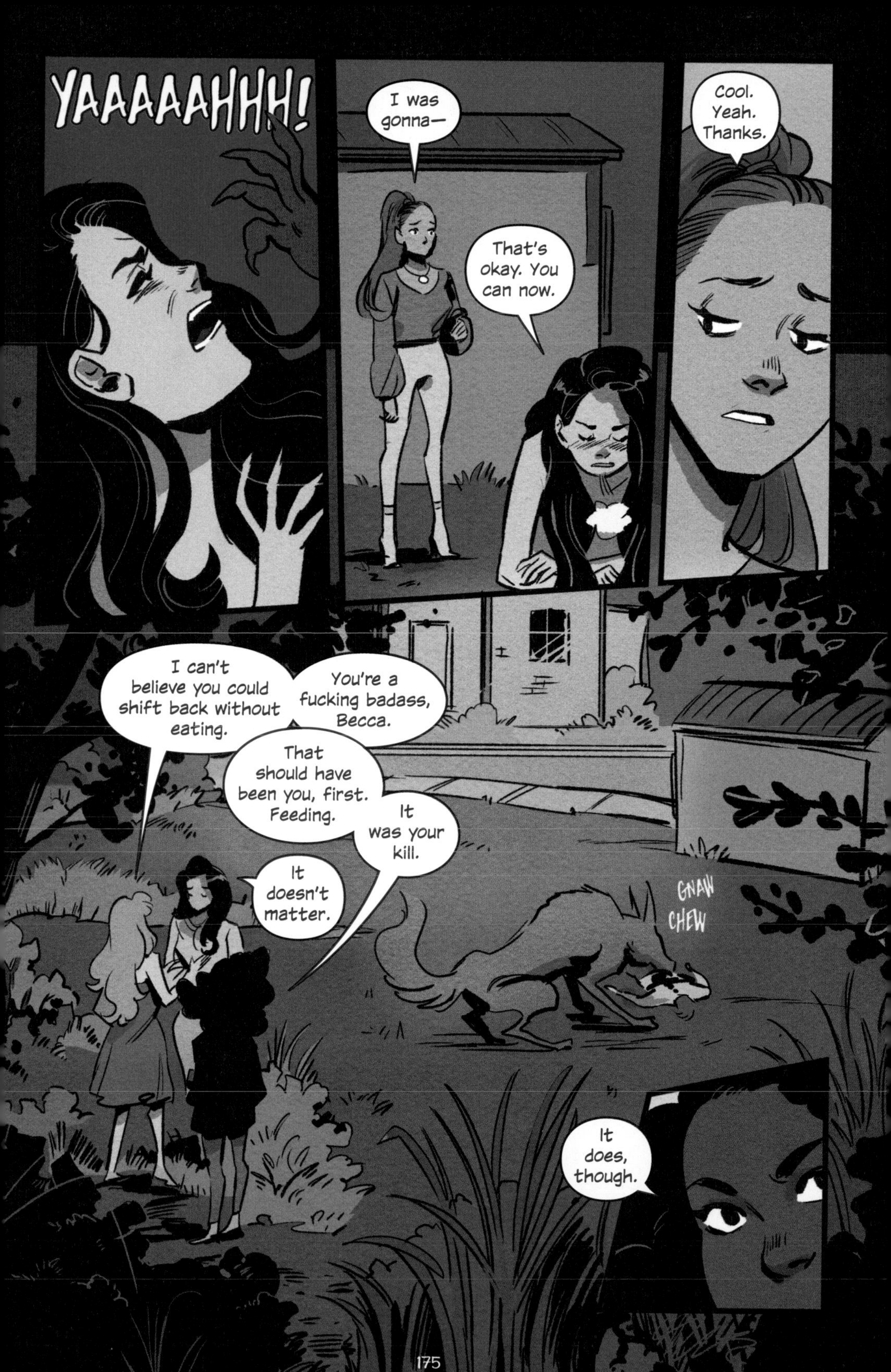
YAAAAAHHH!
I was gonna—
That's okay. You can now.
Cool. Yeah. Thanks.
I can't believe you could shift back without eating.
You're a fucking badass, Becca.
That should have been you, first. Feeding.
It was your kill.
It doesn't matter.
GNAW
CHEW
It does, though.

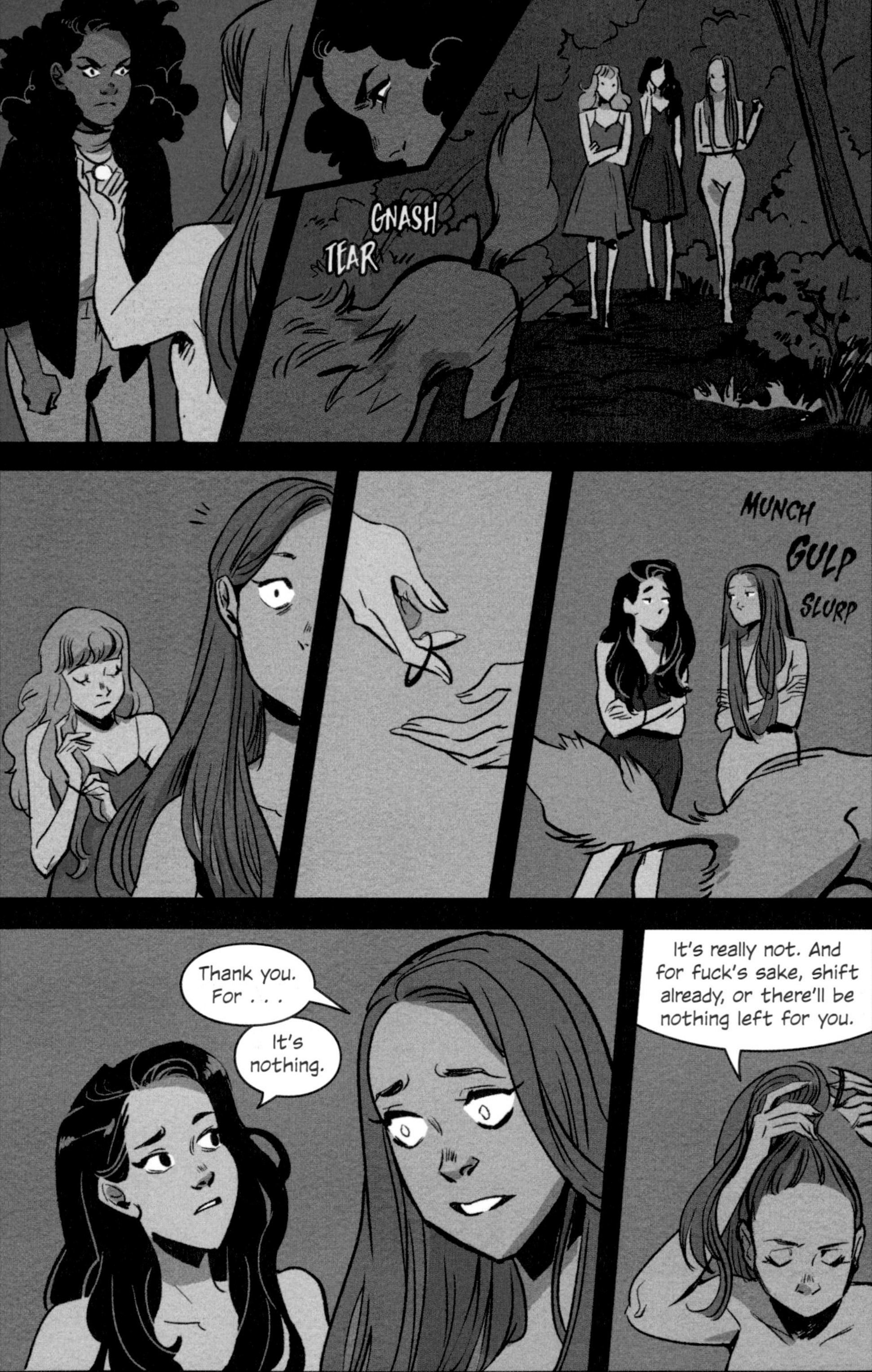
GNASH
TEAR
MUNCH
GULP
SLURP
Thank you. For . . .
It's nothing.
It's really not. And for fuck's sake, shift already, or there'll be nothing left for you.

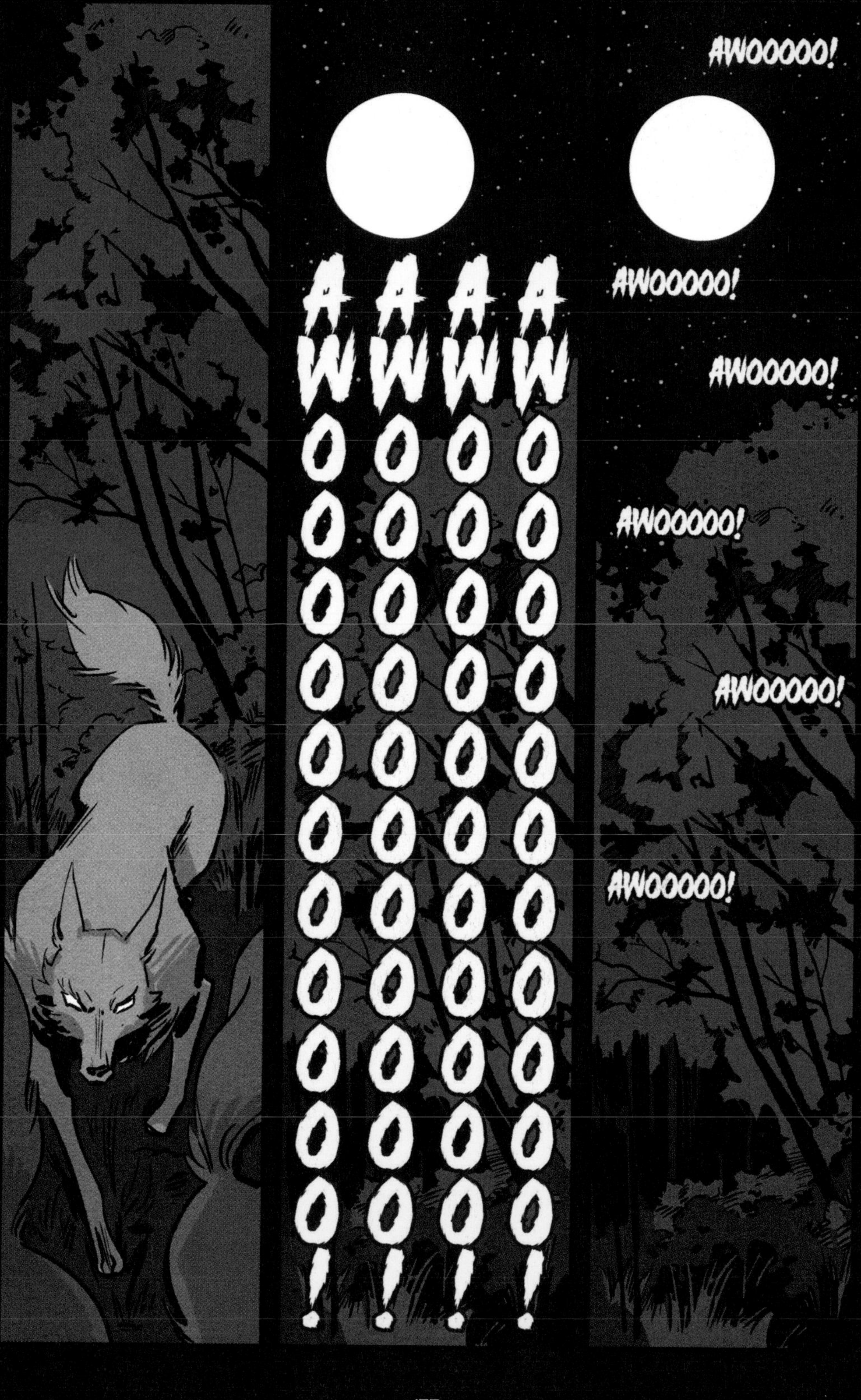
AWOOOOO!
AWOOOOOOOOOOOOO!
AWOOOOOOOOOOOOO!
AWOOOOOOOOOOOOO!
AWOOOOOOOOOOOOO!
AWOOOOO!
AWOOOOO!
AWOOOOO!
AWOOOOO!
AWOOOOO!

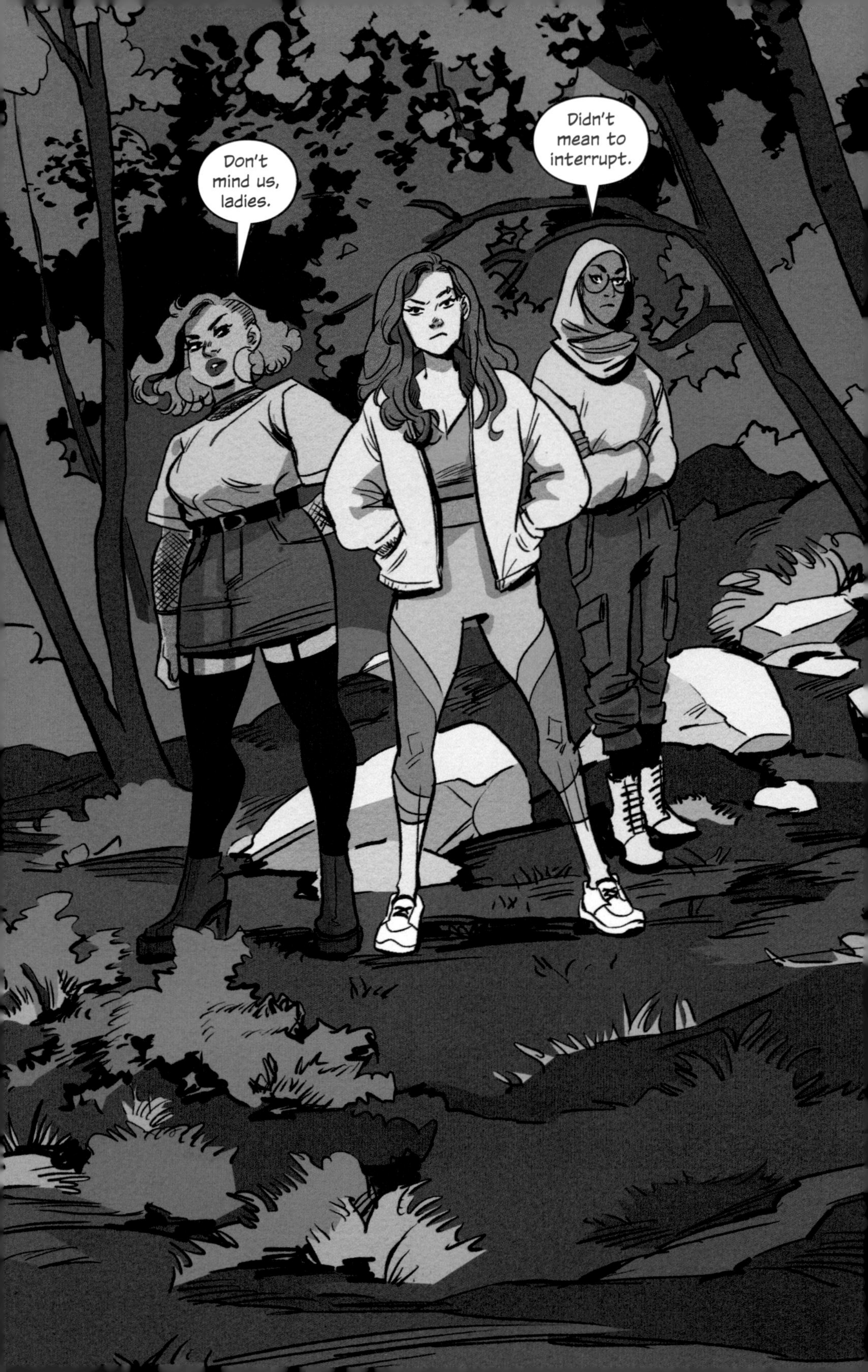
Don't mind us, ladies.
Didn't mean to interrupt.

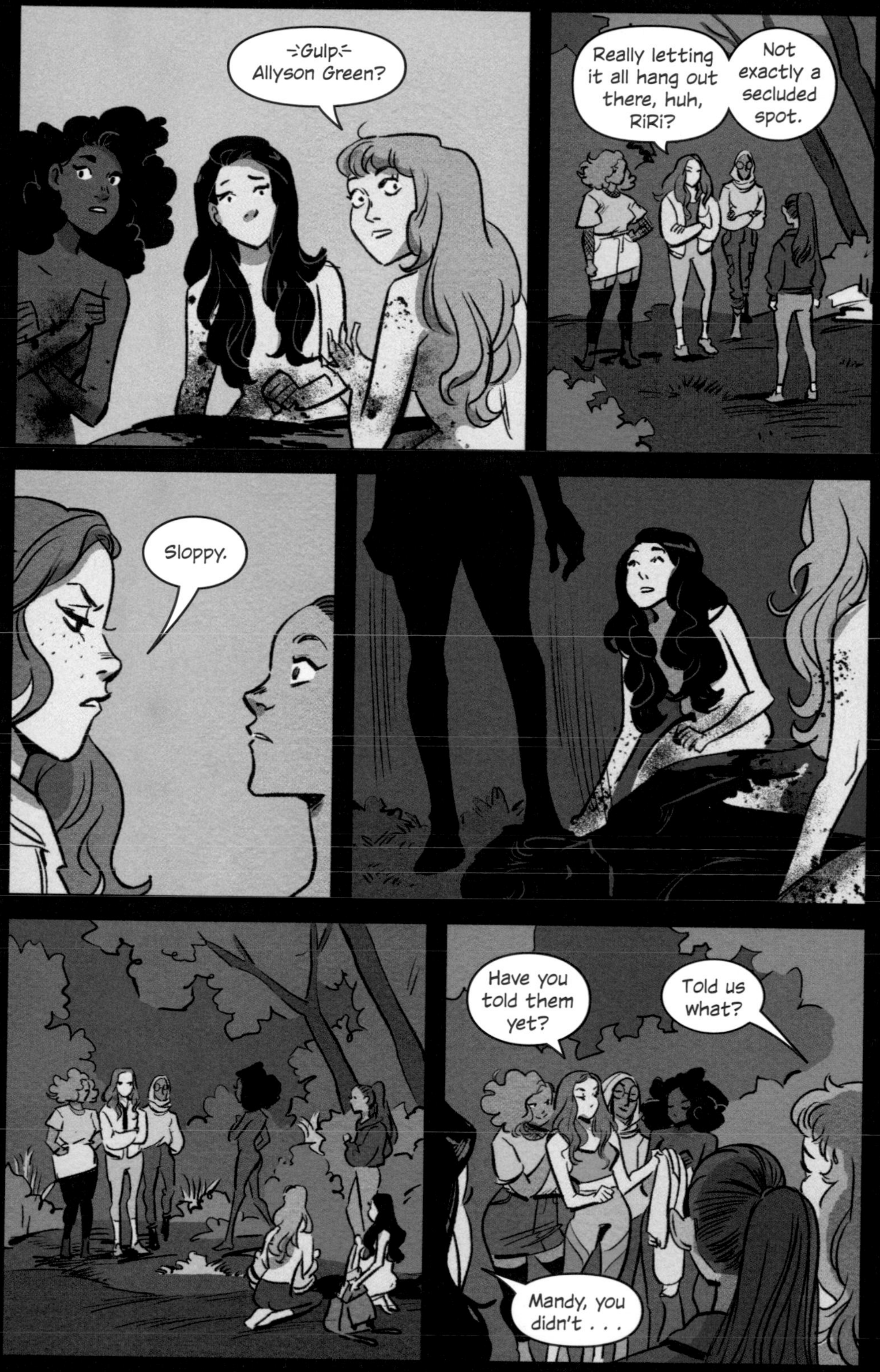

=Gulp= Allyson Green?
Really letting it all hang out there, huh, RiRi?
Not exactly a secluded spot.
Sloppy.
Have you told them yet?
Told us what?
Mandy, you didn't . . .

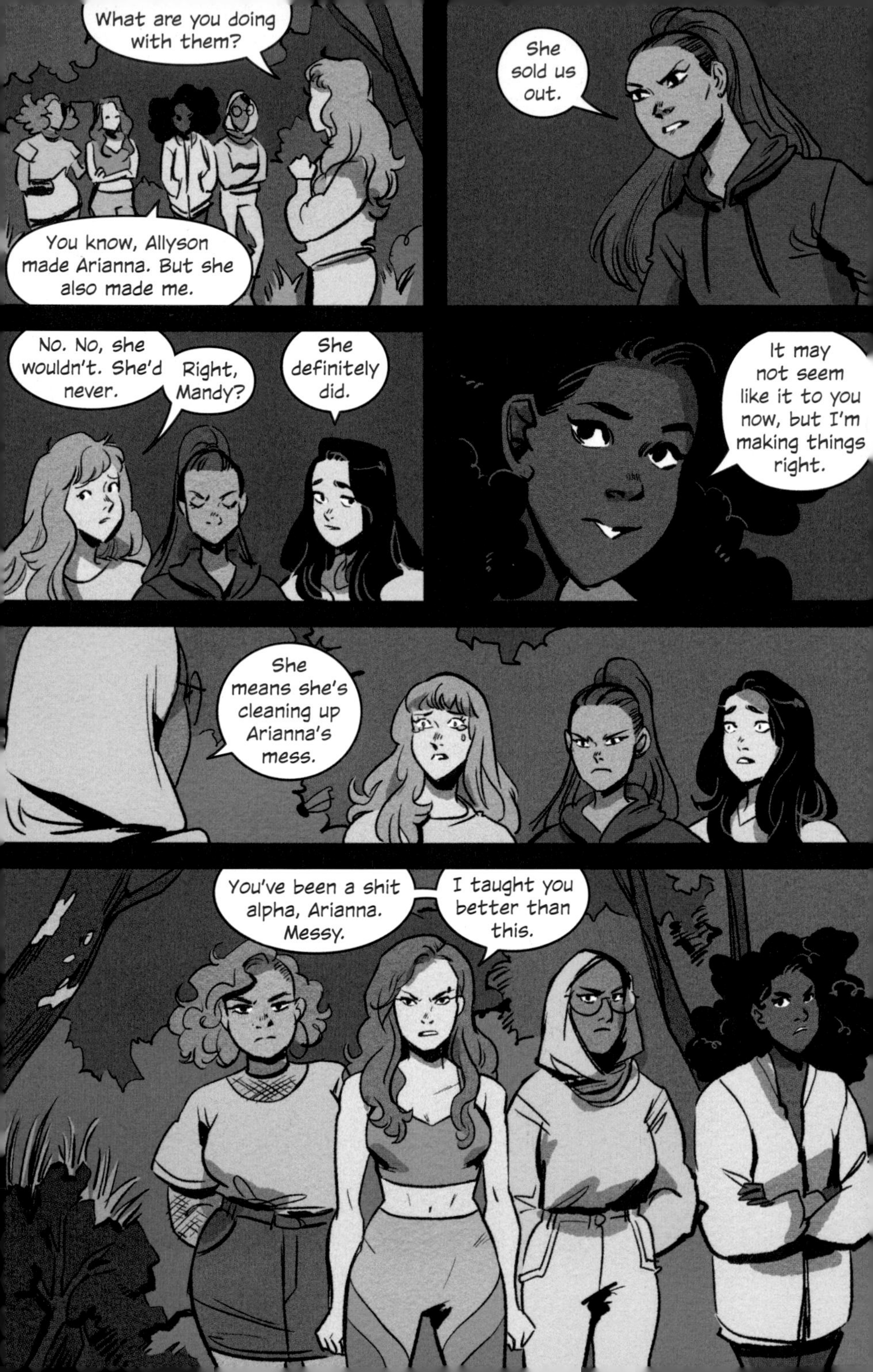
What are you doing with them?
You know, Allyson made Arianna. But she also made me.
She sold us out.
No. No, she wouldn't. She'd never.
Right, Mandy?
She definitely did.
It may not seem like it to you now, but I'm making things right.
She means she's cleaning up Arianna's mess.
You've been a shit alpha, Arianna. Messy.
I taught you better than this.

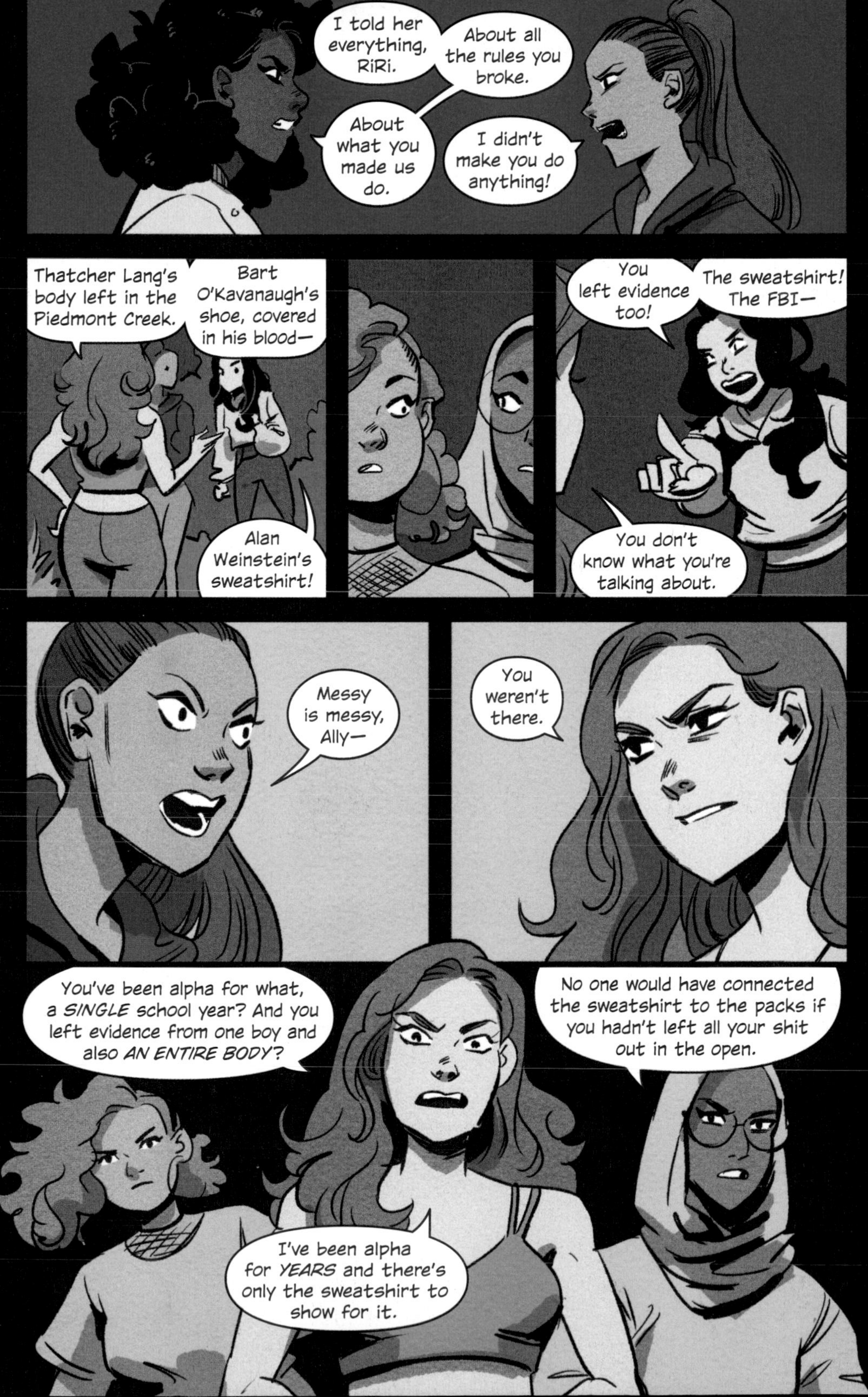
I told her everything, RiRi.
About all the rules you broke.
About what you made us do.
I didn't make you do anything!
Thatcher Lang's body left in the Piedmont Creek.
Bart O'Kavanaugh's shoe, covered in his blood—
Alan Weinstein's sweatshirt!
You left evidence too!
The sweatshirt! The FBI—
You don't know what you're talking about.
Messy is messy, Ally—
You weren't there.
You've been alpha for what, a *SINGLE* school year? And you left evidence from one boy and also *AN ENTIRE BODY*?
No one would have connected the sweatshirt to the packs if you hadn't left all your shit out in the open.
I've been alpha for *YEARS* and there's only the sweatshirt to show for it.

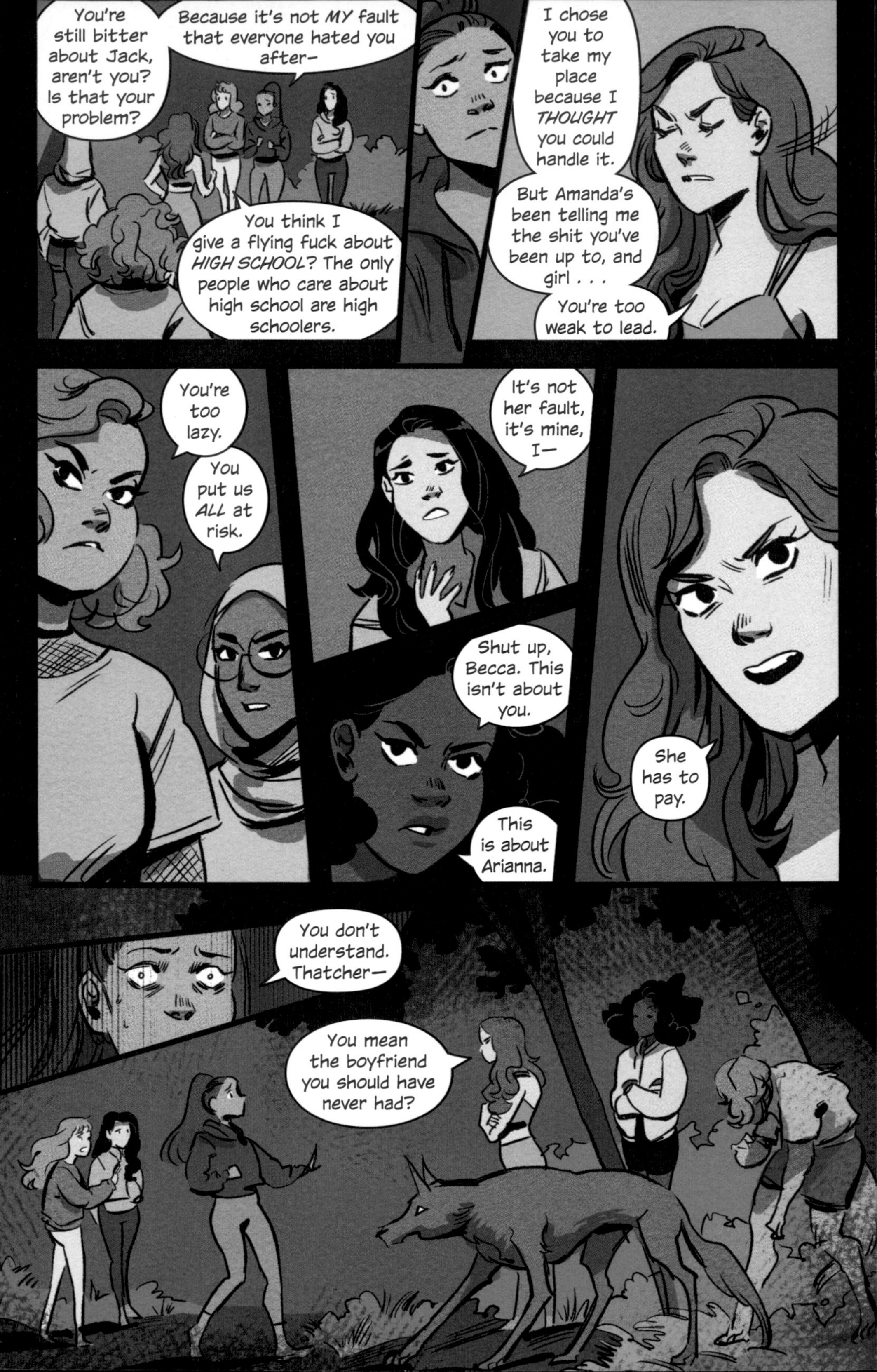
You're still bitter about Jack, aren't you? Is that your problem?
Because it's not MY fault that everyone hated you after–
You think I give a flying fuck about HIGH SCHOOL? The only people who care about high school are high schoolers.
I chose you to take my place because I THOUGHT you could handle it.
But Amanda's been telling me the shit you've been up to, and girl . . .
You're too weak to lead.
You're too lazy.
You put us ALL at risk.
It's not her fault, it's mine, I—
Shut up, Becca. This isn't about you.
This is about Arianna.
She has to pay.
You don't understand. Thatcher—
You mean the boyfriend you should have never had?

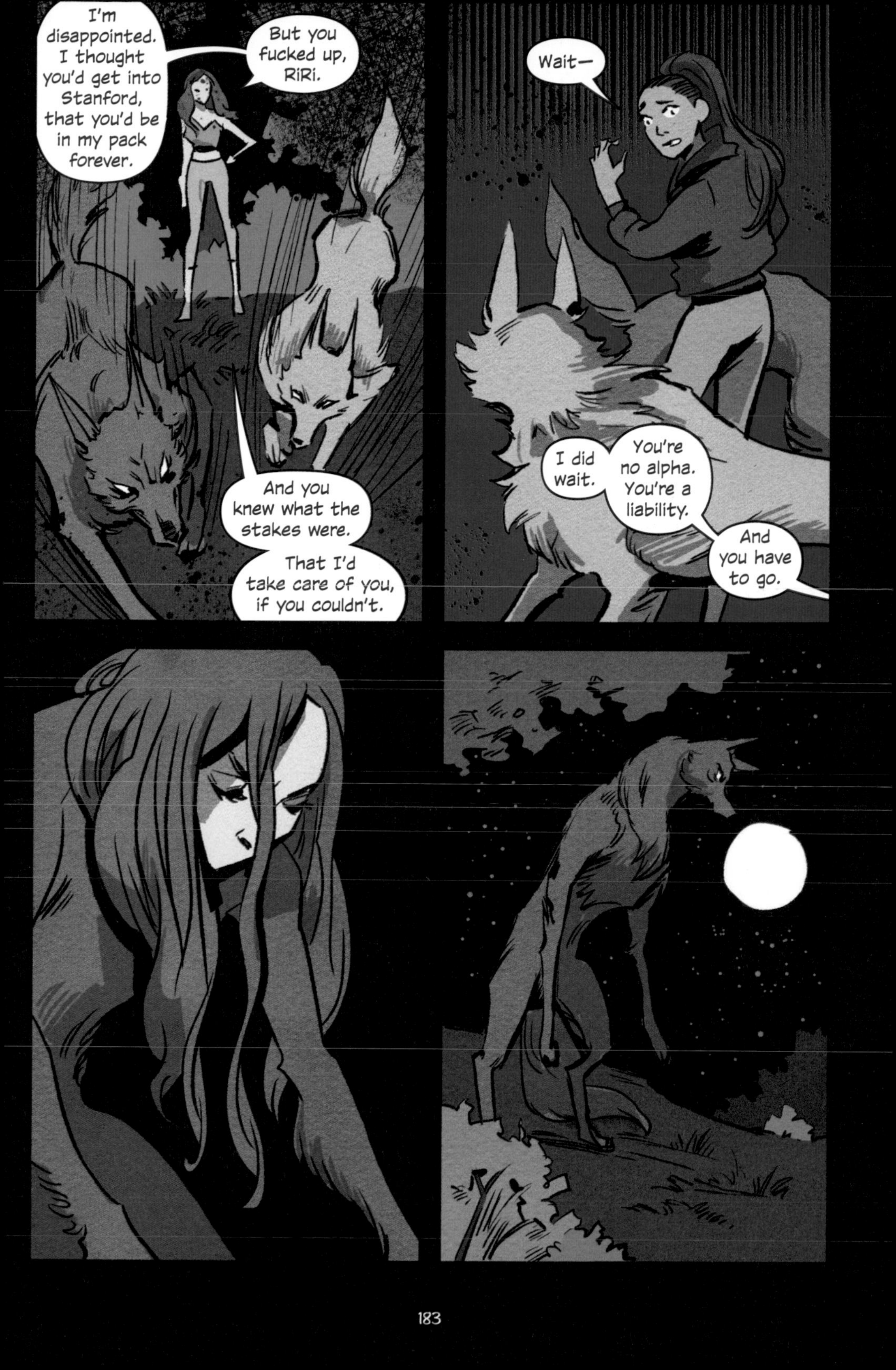
I'm disappointed. I thought you'd get into Stanford, that you'd be in my pack forever.
But you fucked up, RiRi.
And you knew what the stakes were.
That I'd take care of you, if you couldn't.
Wait—
I did wait.
You're no alpha. You're a liability.
And you have to go.

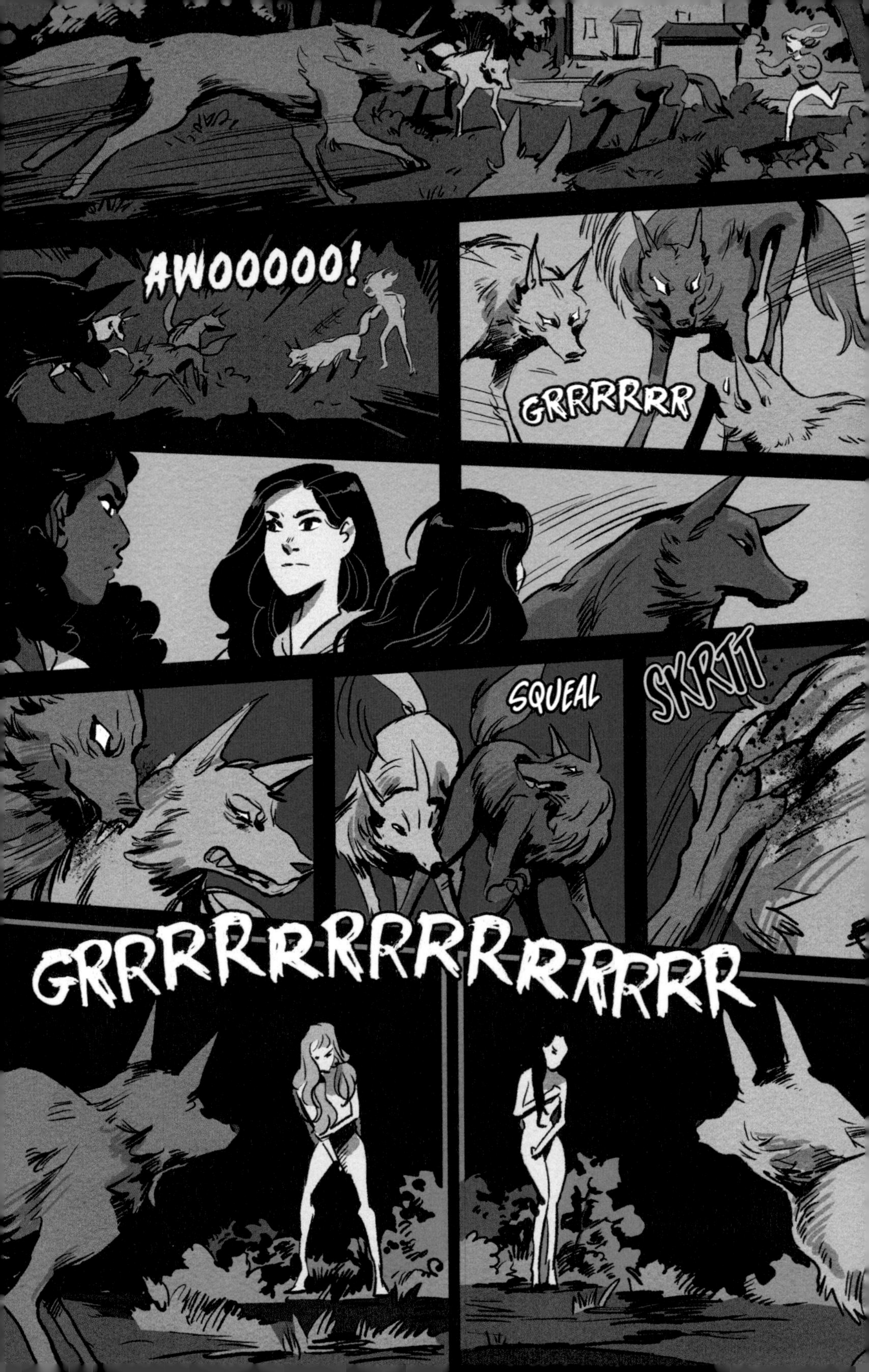
AWOOOOO!
GRRRRRR
SQUEAL
SKRTT
GRRRRRRRRRRRRRRR

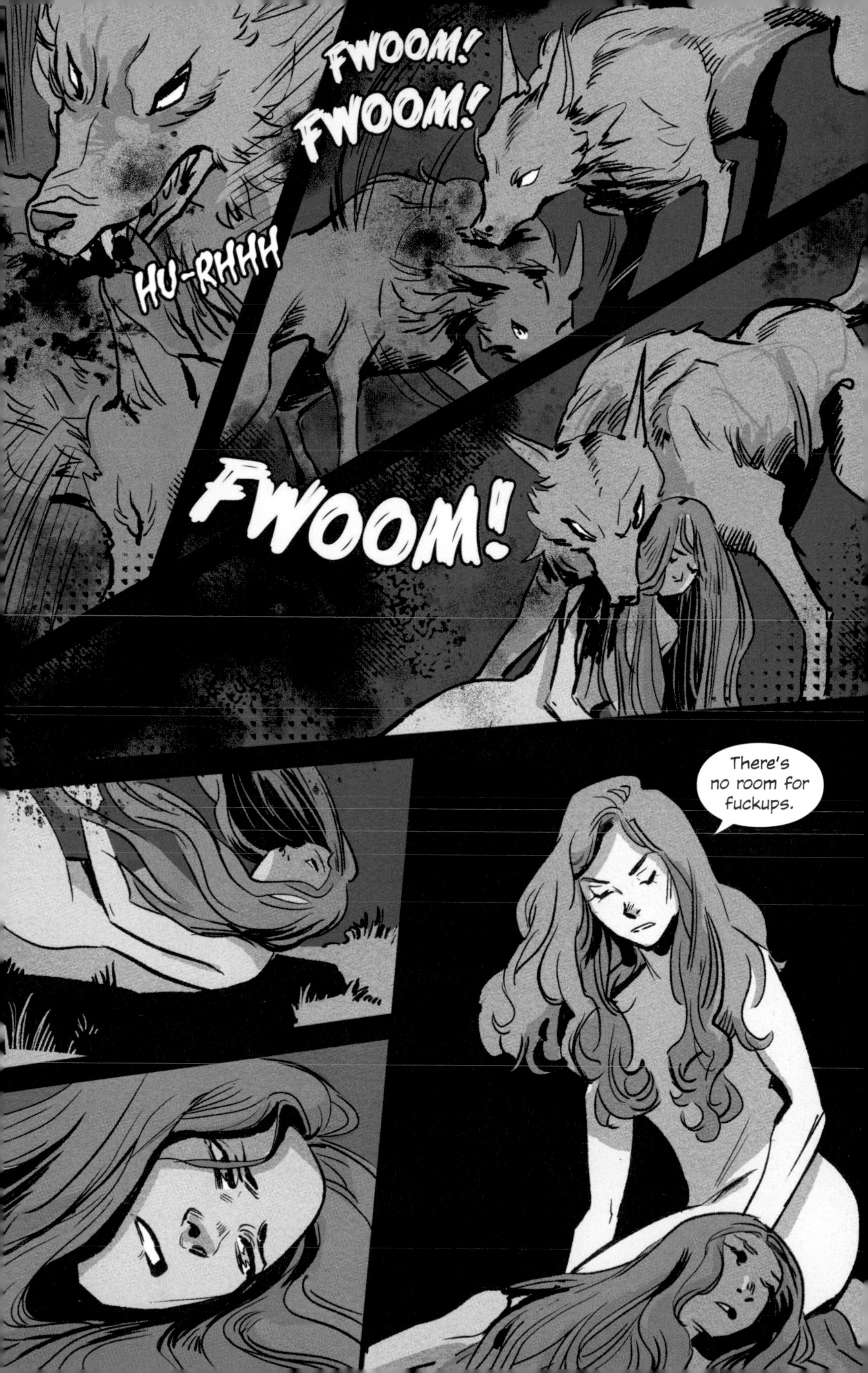
HU-RHHH
FWOOM!
FWOOM!
FWOOM!
There's no room for fuckups.

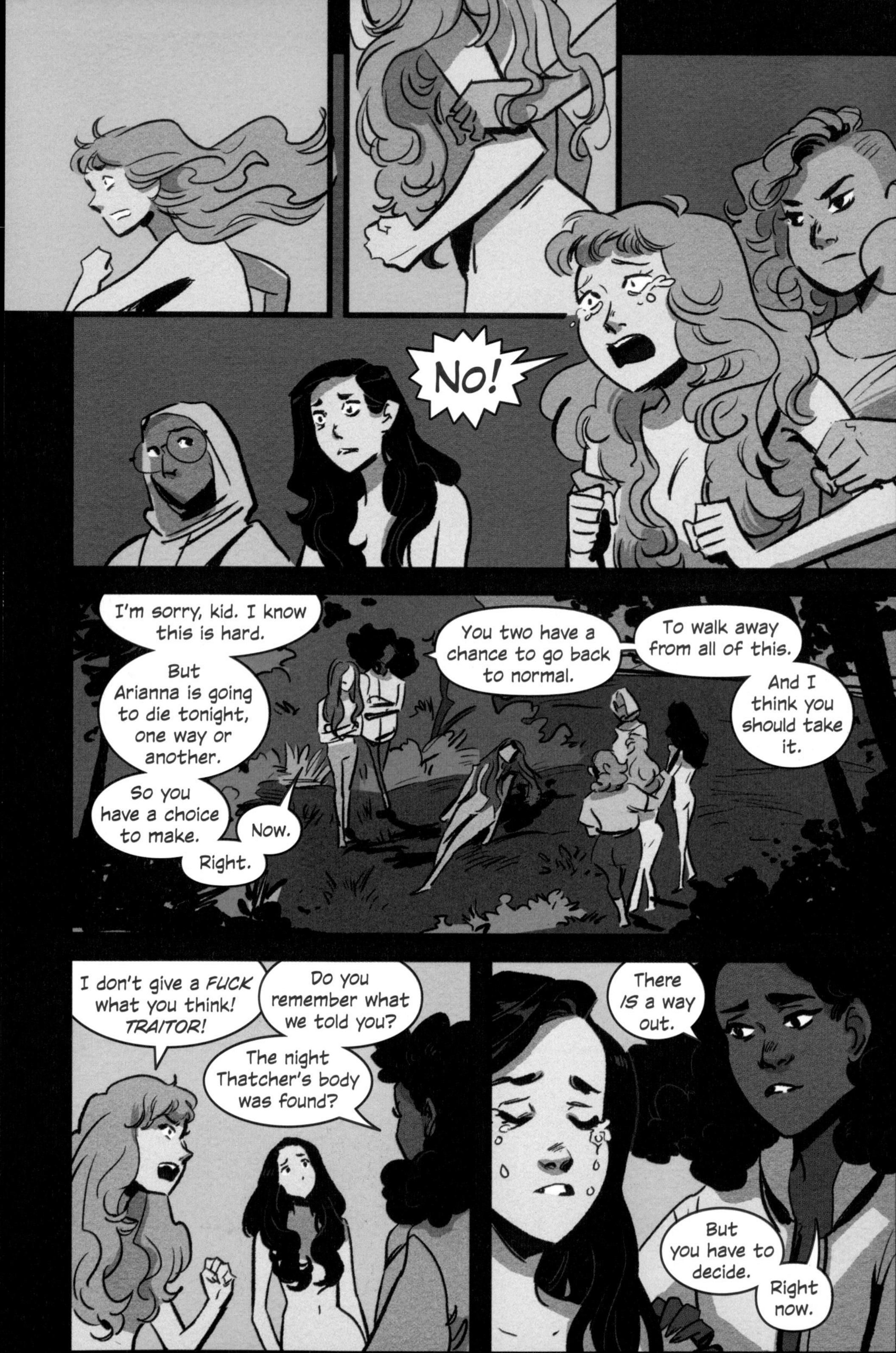
No!
I'm sorry, kid. I know this is hard.
But Arianna is going to die tonight, one way or another.
So you have a choice to make.
Now.
Right.
You two have a chance to go back to normal.
To walk away from all of this.
And I think you should take it.
I don't give a *FUCK* what you think! *TRAITOR!*
Do you remember what we told you?
The night Thatcher's body was found?
There *IS* a way out.
But you have to decide.
Right now.

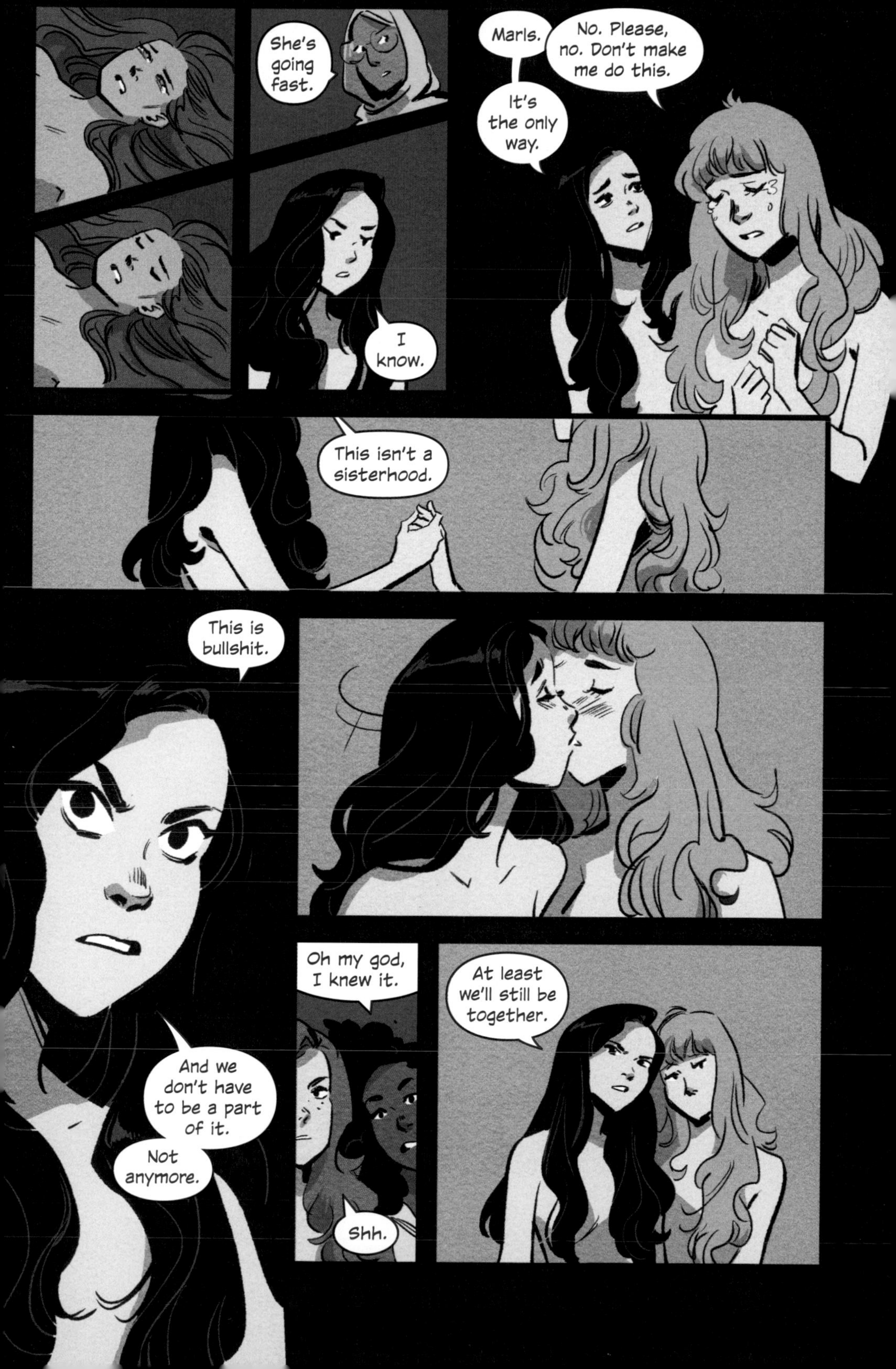
She's going fast.
I know.
Marls.
No. Please, no. Don't make me do this.
It's the only way.
This isn't a sisterhood.
This is bullshit.
And we don't have to be a part of it.
Not anymore.
Oh my god, I knew it.
Shh.
At least we'll still be together.

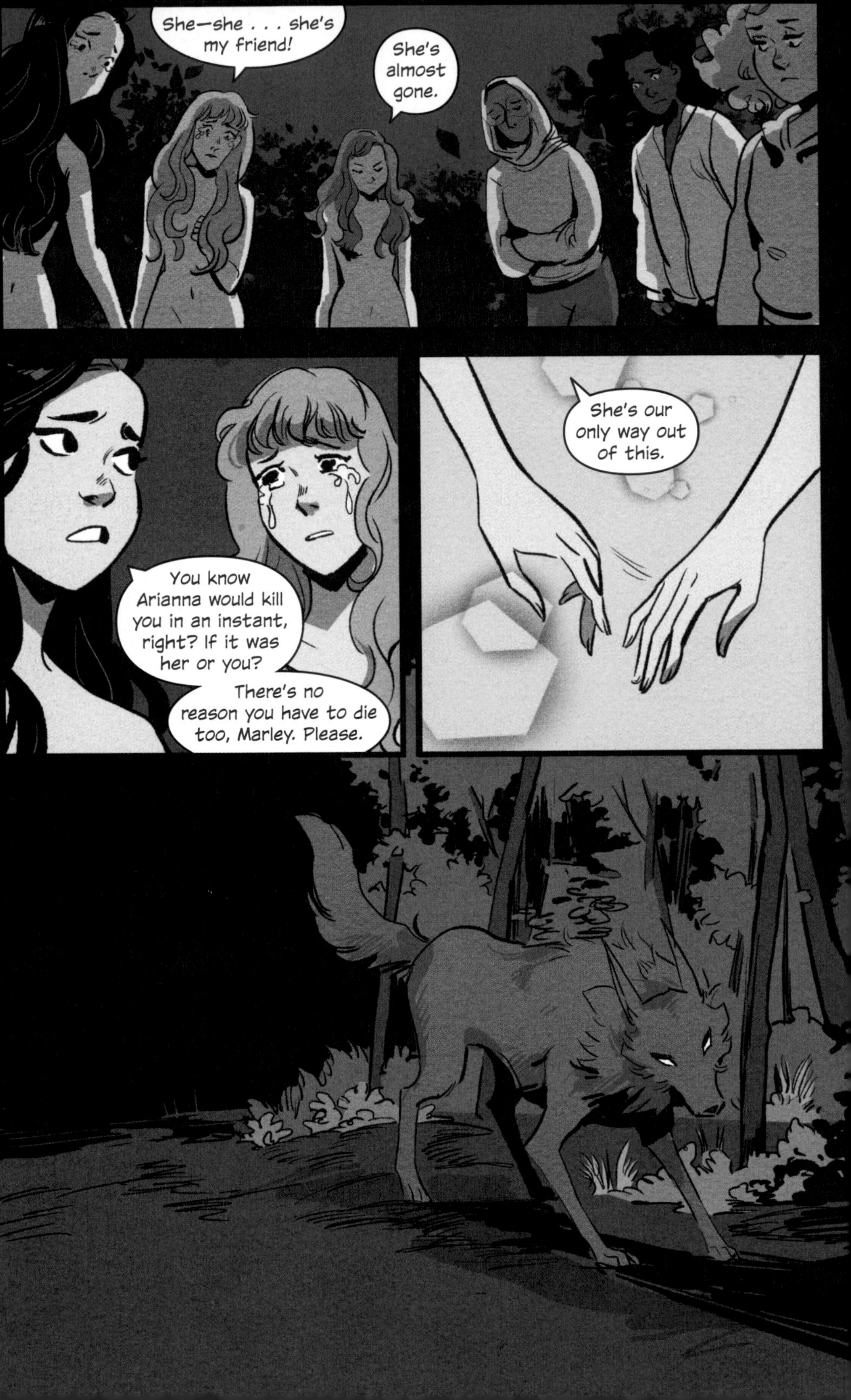
She—she . . . she's my friend!
She's almost gone.
You know Arianna would kill you in an instant, right? If it was her or you?
There's no reason you have to die too, Marley. Please.
She's our only way out of this.

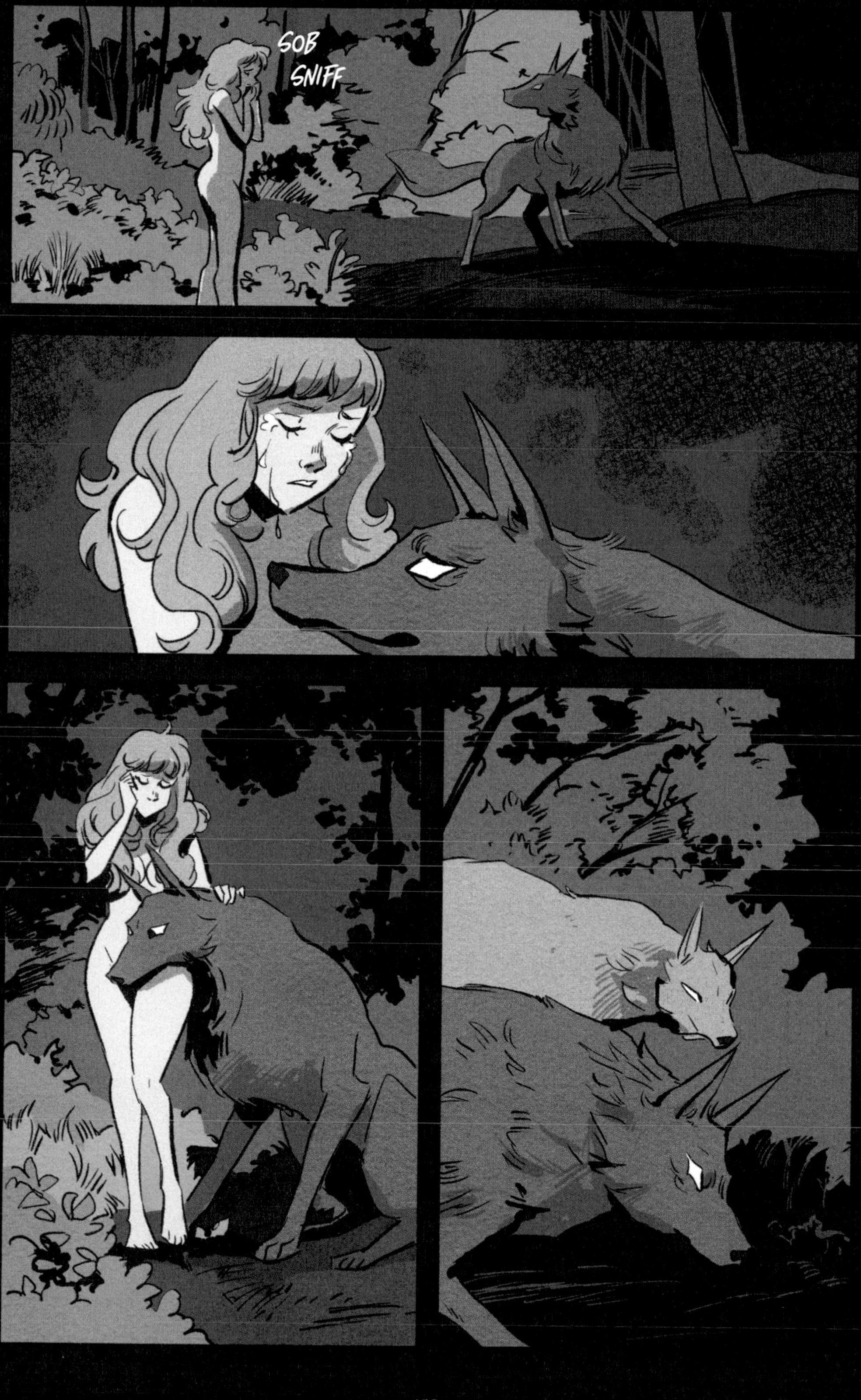
SOB
SNIFF

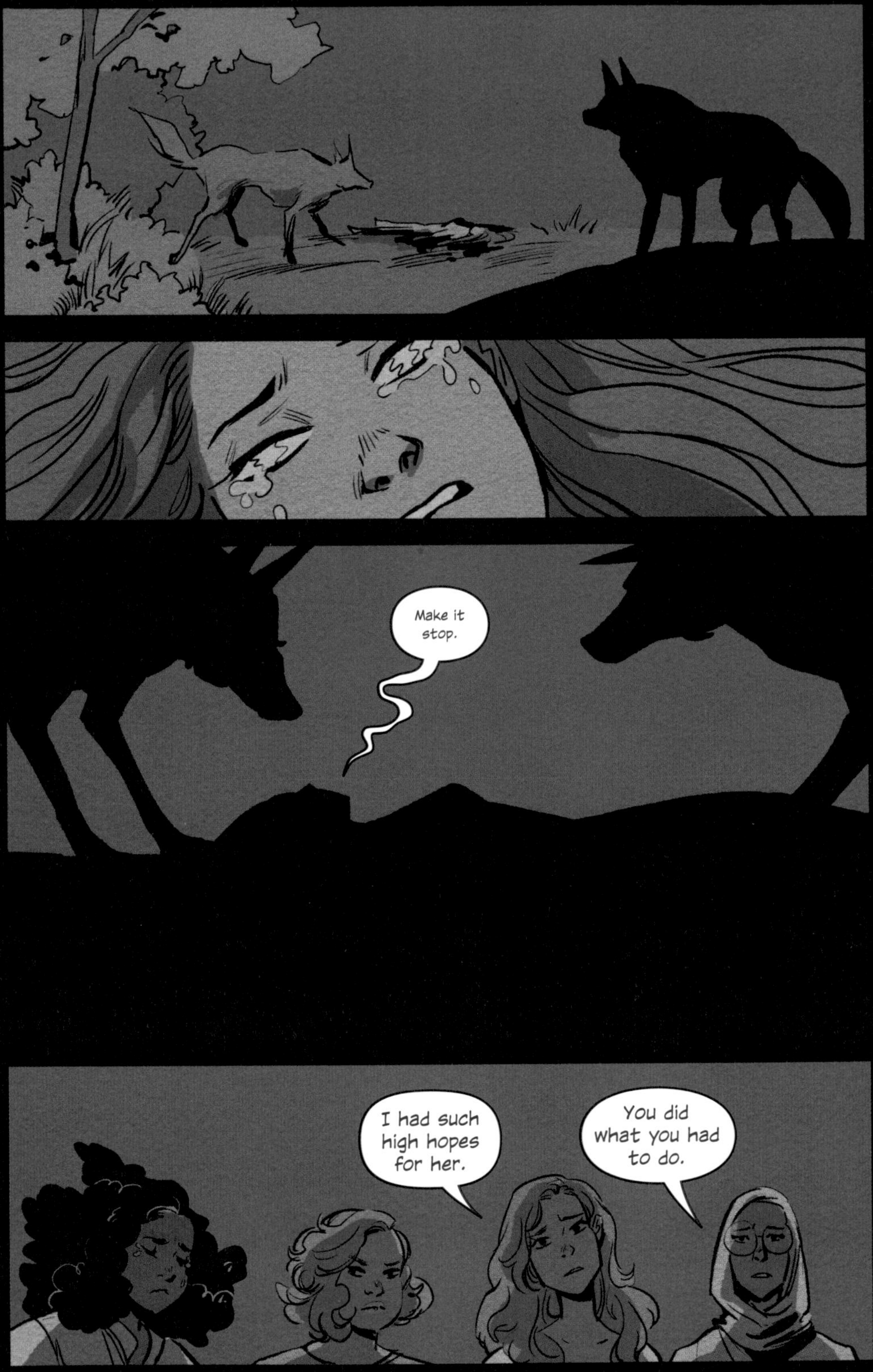
Make it stop.
I had such high hopes for her.
You did what you had to do.

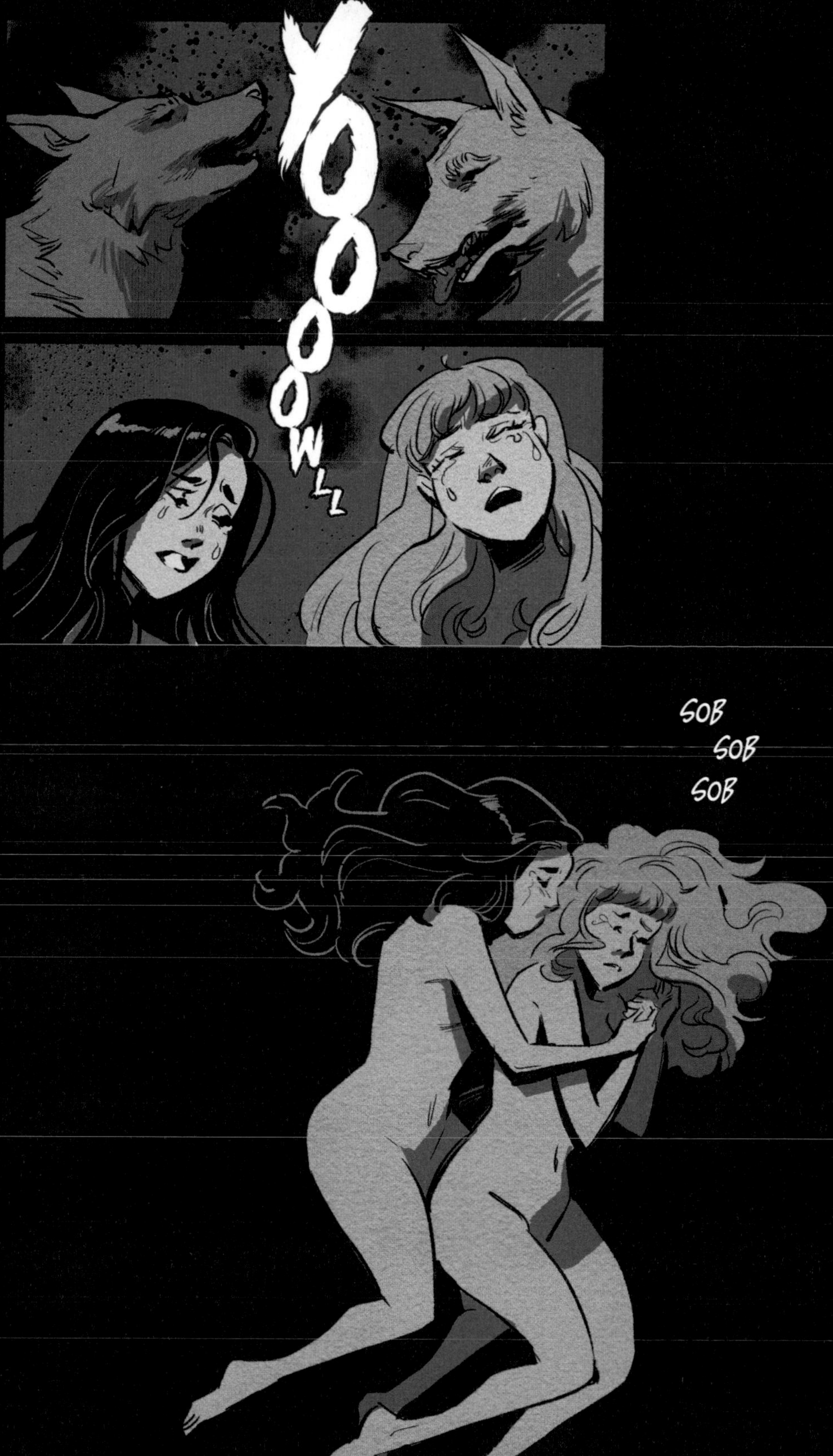
YOOOOOOWLL
SOB
SOB
SOB

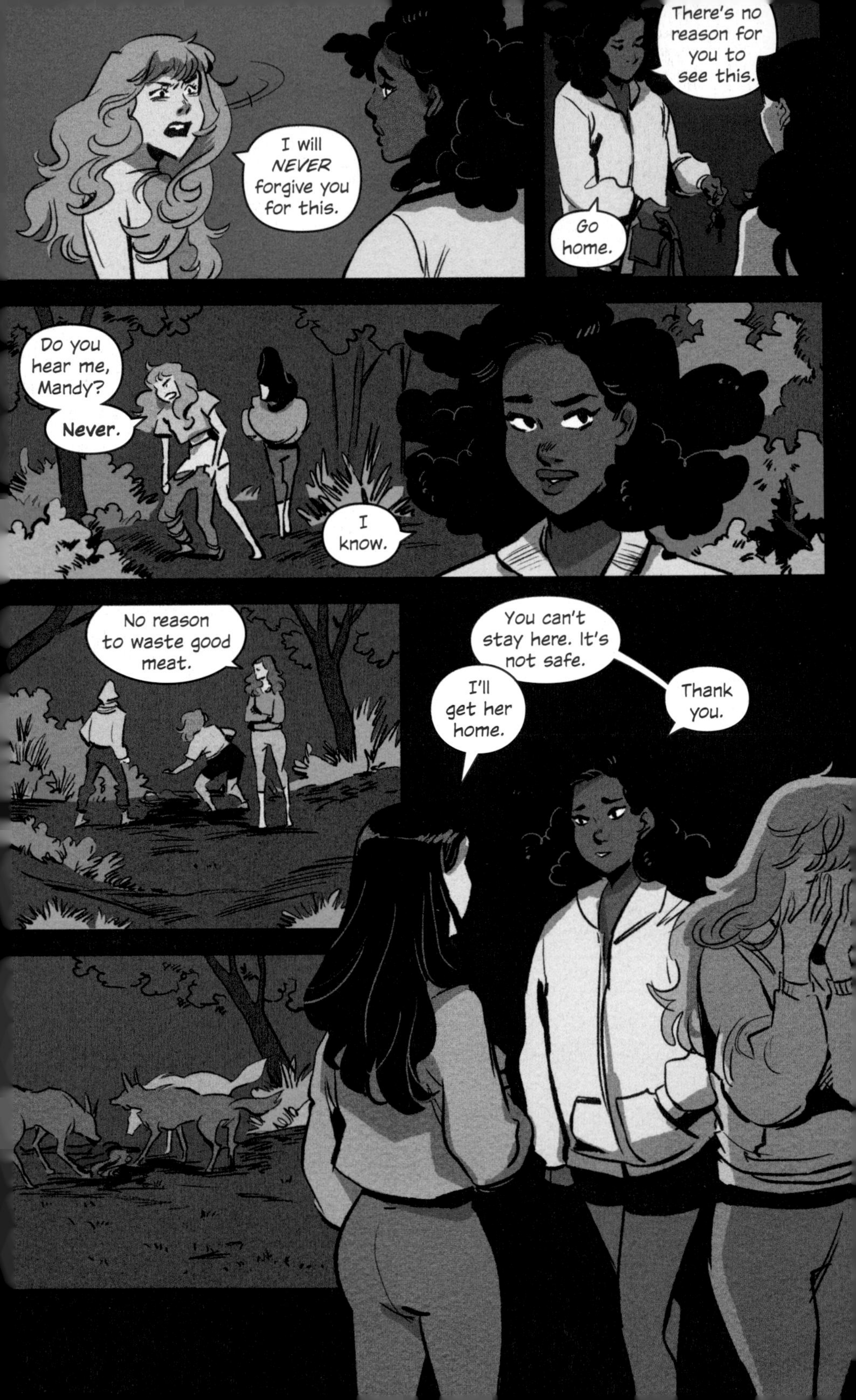
I will NEVER forgive you for this.
There's no reason for you to see this.
Go home.
Do you hear me, Mandy?
Never.
I know.
No reason to waste good meat.
You can't stay here. It's not safe.
I'll get her home.
Thank you.

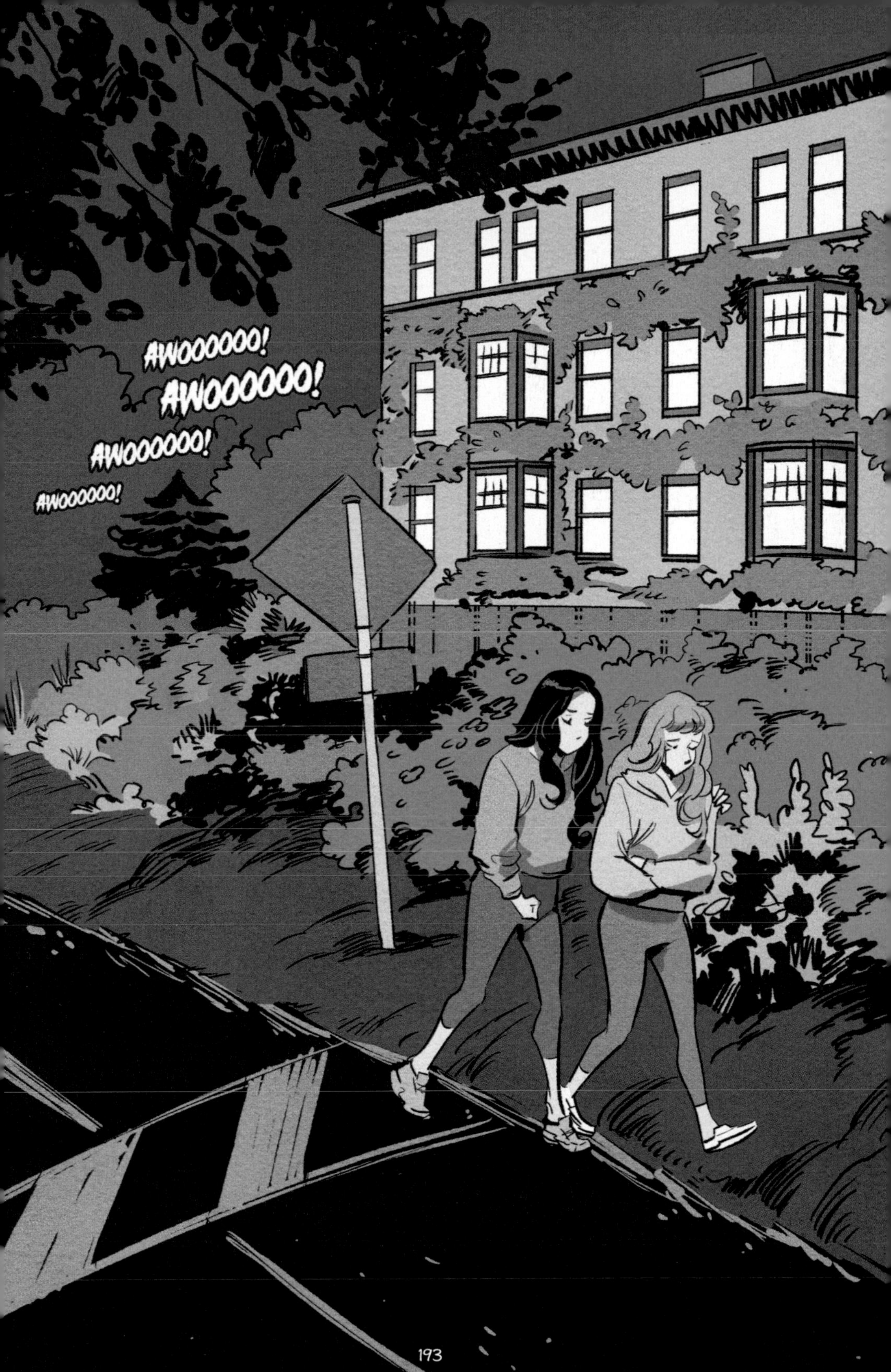
AWOOOOOO!
AWOOOOOO!
AWOOOOOO!
AWOOOOOO!

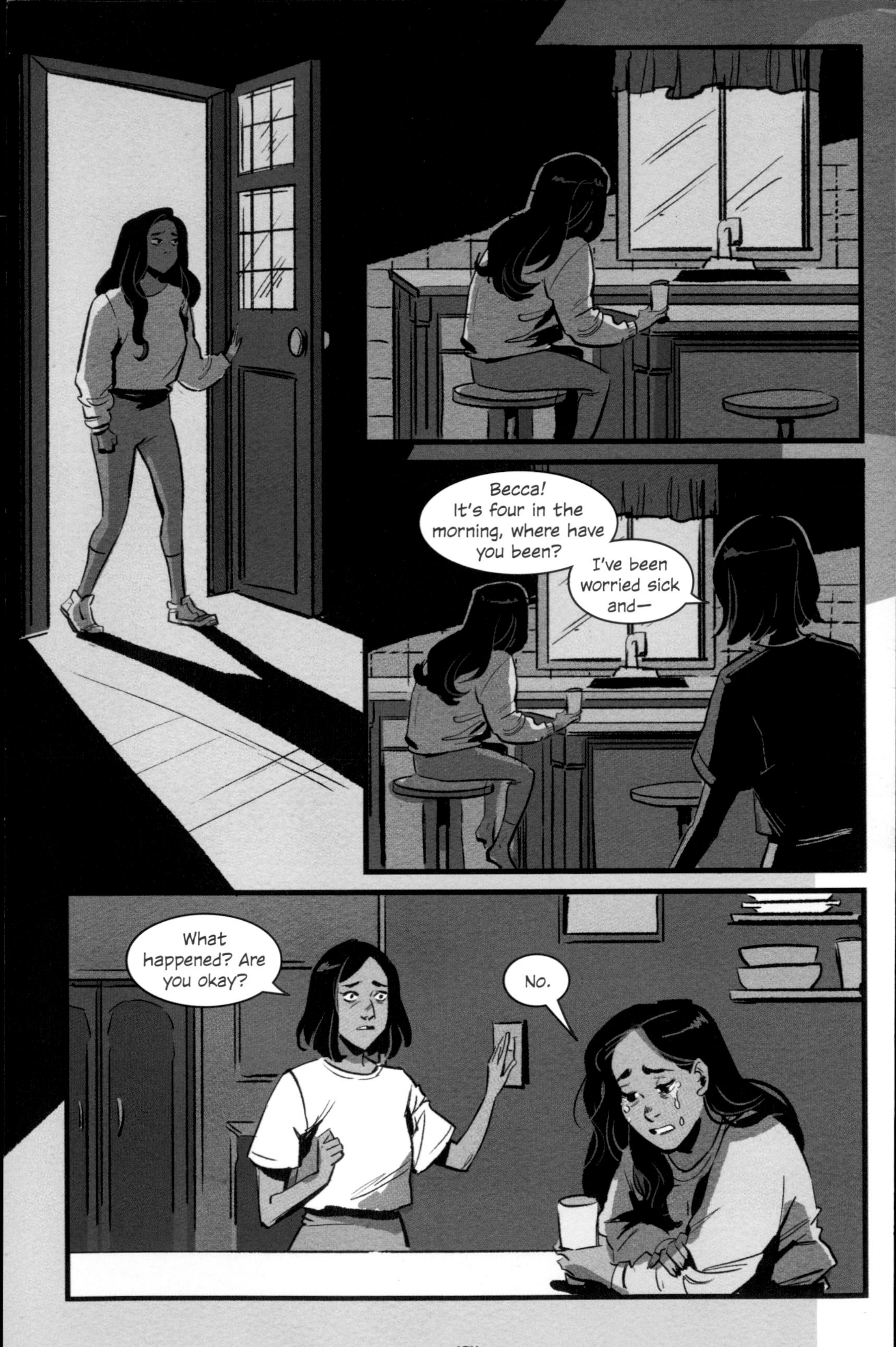
Becca! It's four in the morning, where have you been?
I've been worried sick and—
What happened? Are you okay?
No.

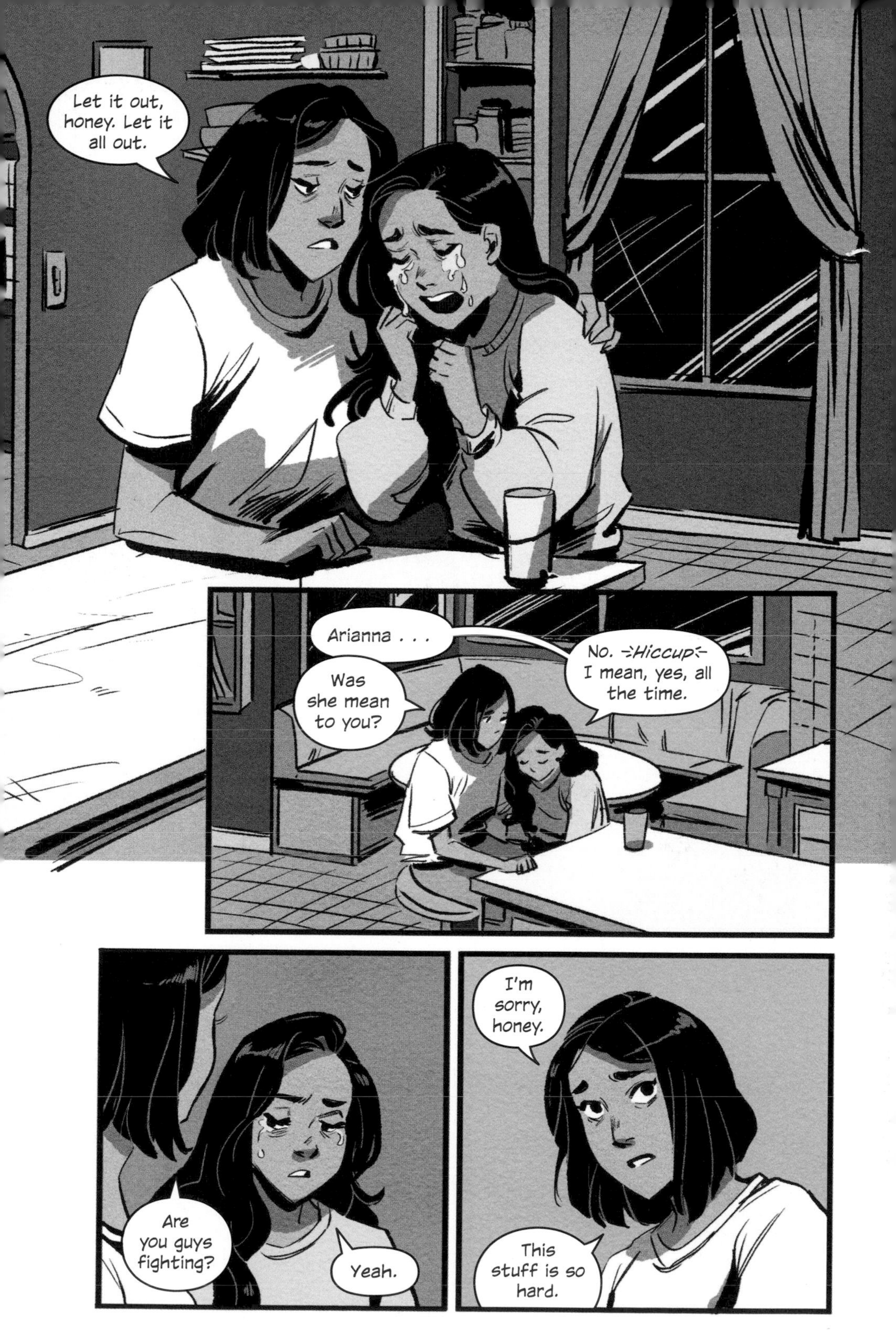
Let it out, honey. Let it all out.
Arianna . . .
Was she mean to you?
No. Hiccup I mean, yes, all the time.
Are you guys fighting?
Yeah.
I'm sorry, honey.
This stuff is so hard.

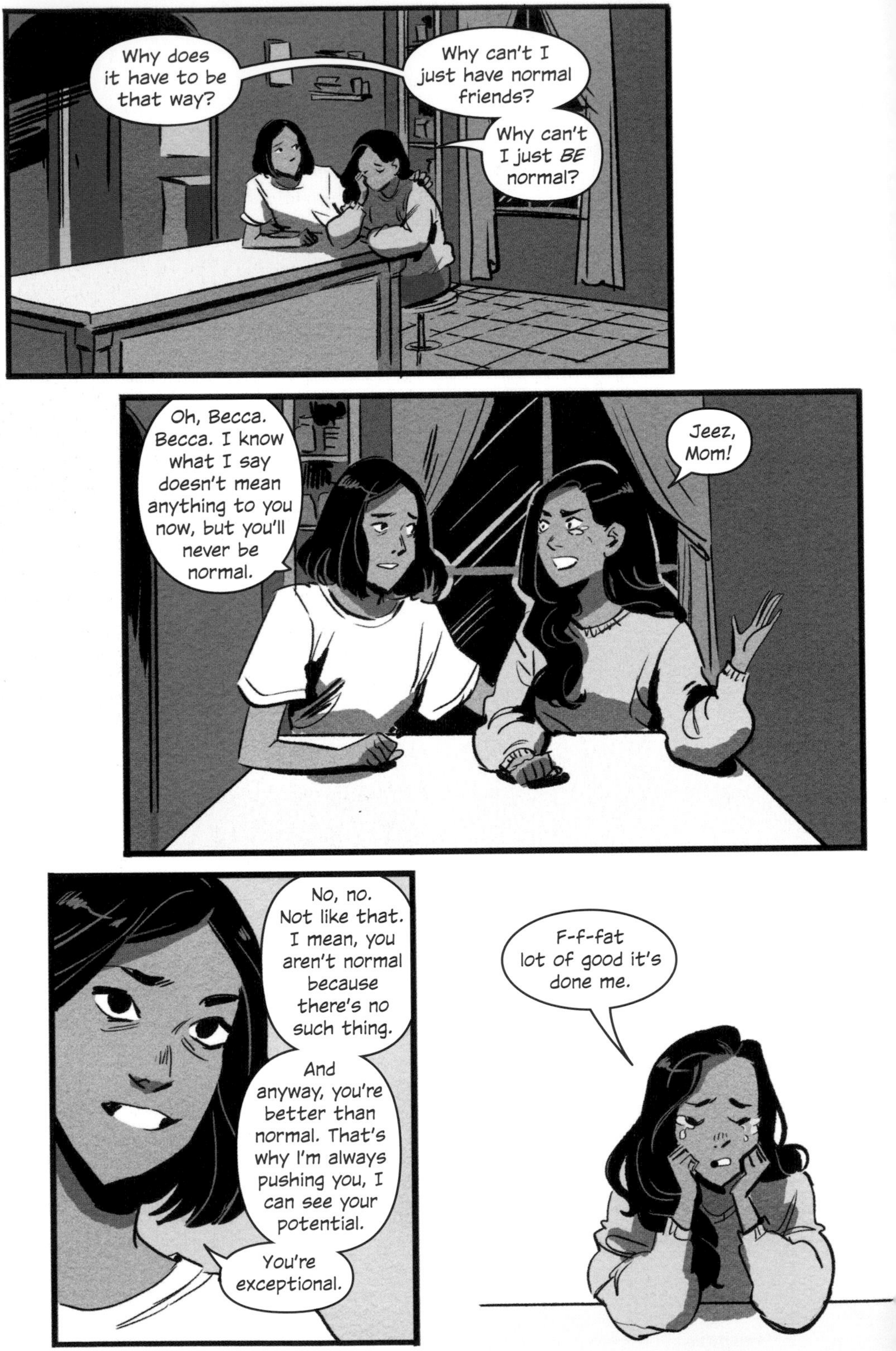
Why does it have to be that way?
Why can't I just have normal friends?
Why can't I just *BE* normal?
Oh, Becca. Becca. I know what I say doesn't mean anything to you now, but you'll never be normal.
Jeez, Mom!
No, no. Not like that. I mean, you aren't normal because there's no such thing.
And anyway, you're better than normal. That's why I'm always pushing you, I can see your potential.
You're exceptional.
F-f-fat lot of good it's done me.

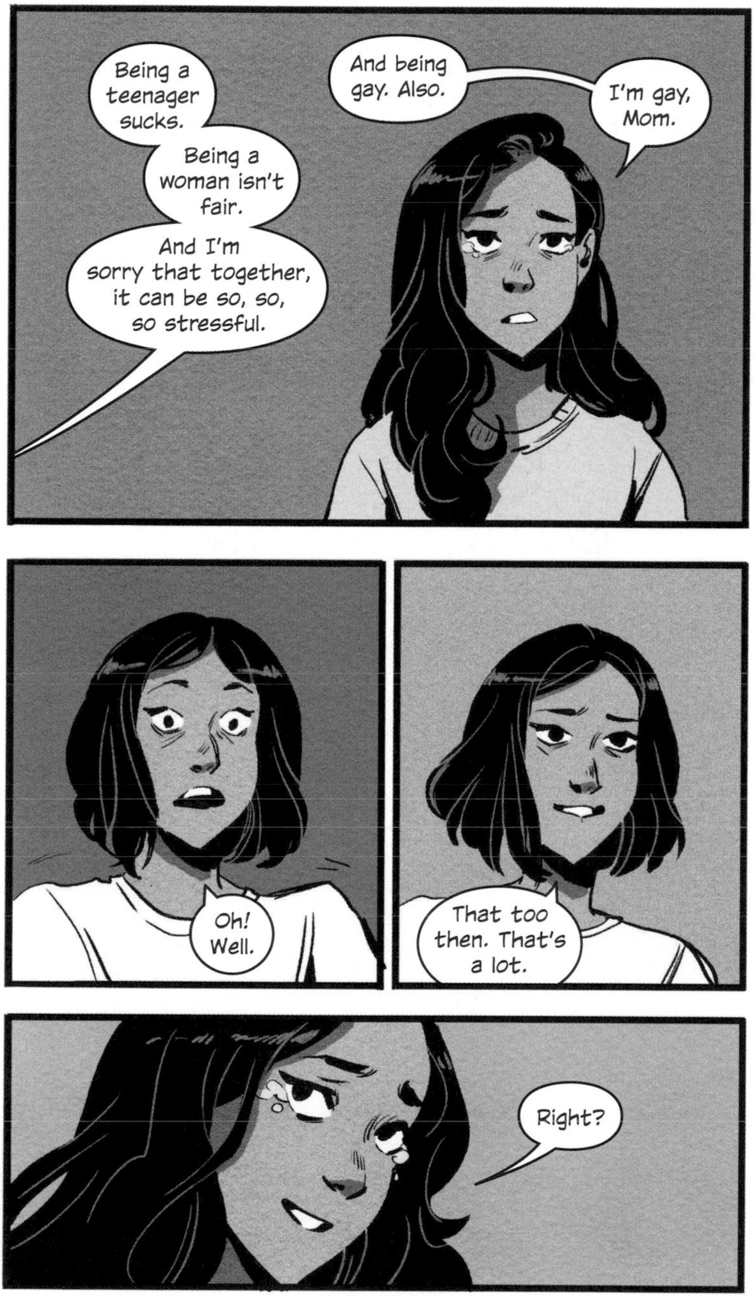
Being a teenager sucks.
Being a woman isn't fair.
And I'm sorry that together, it can be so, so, so stressful.
And being gay. Also.
I'm gay, Mom.
Oh! Well.
That too then. That's a lot.
Right?

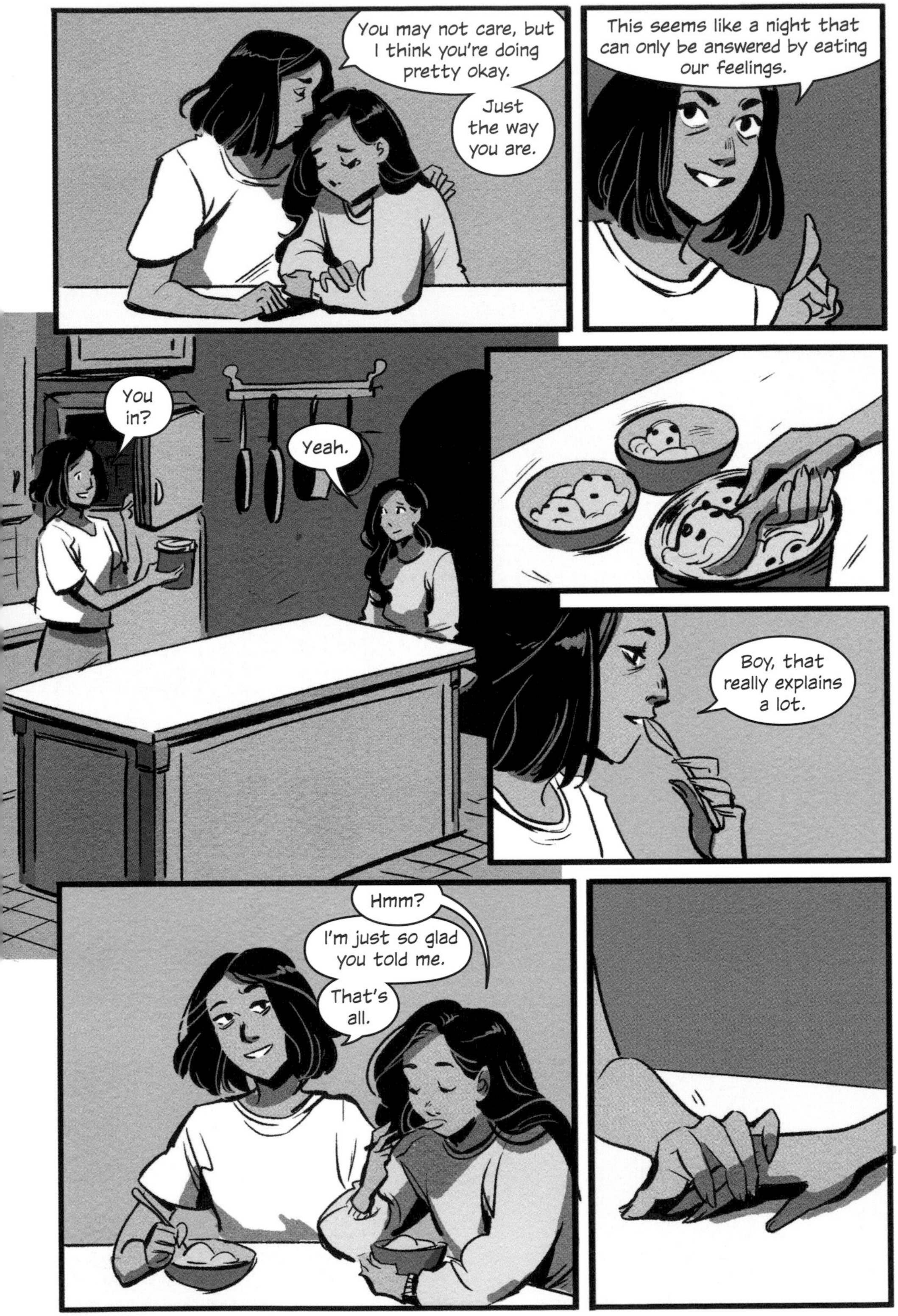
You may not care, but I think you're doing pretty okay.
Just the way you are.
This seems like a night that can only be answered by eating our feelings.
You in?
Yeah.
Boy, that really explains a lot.
Hmm?
I'm just so glad you told me.
That's all.

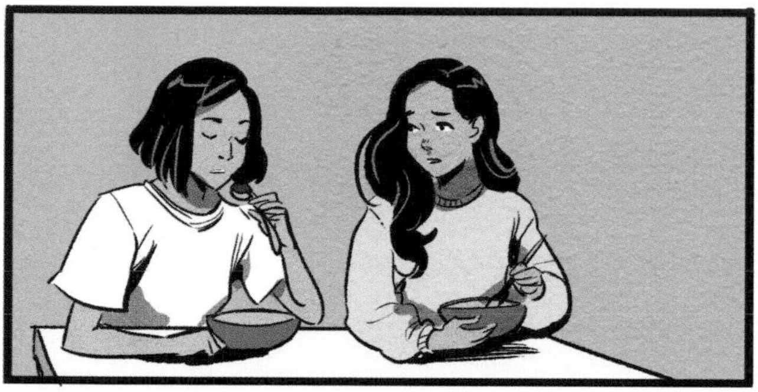

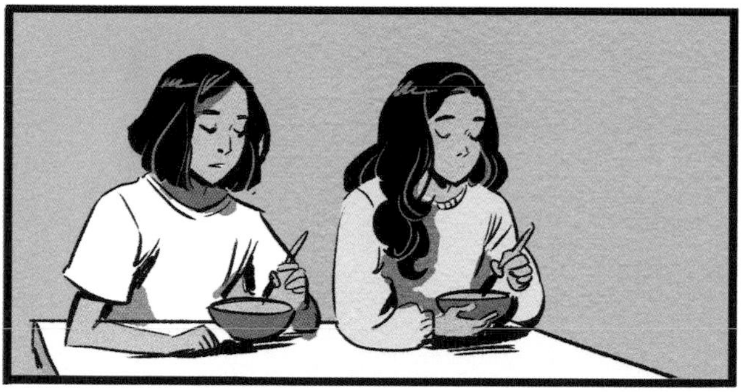

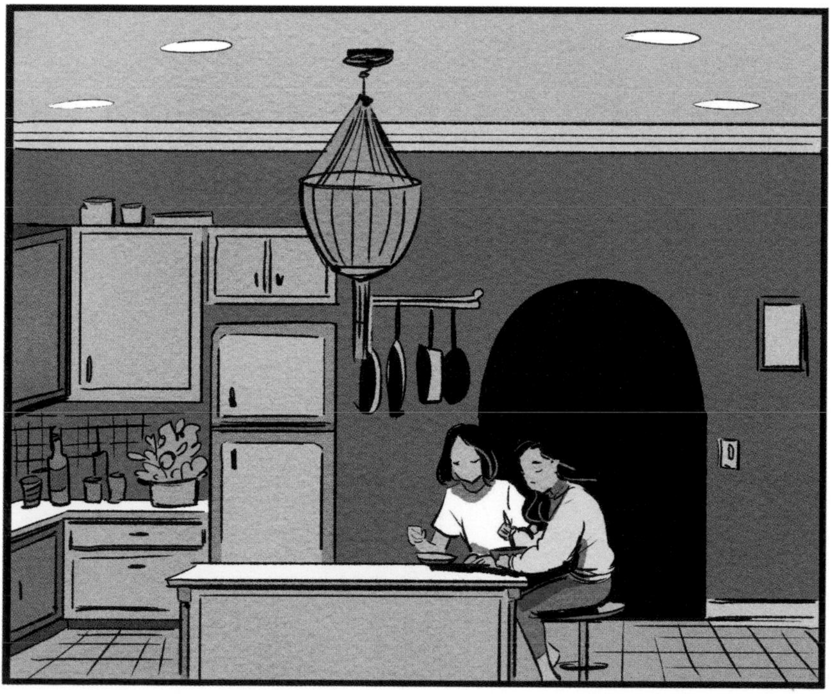

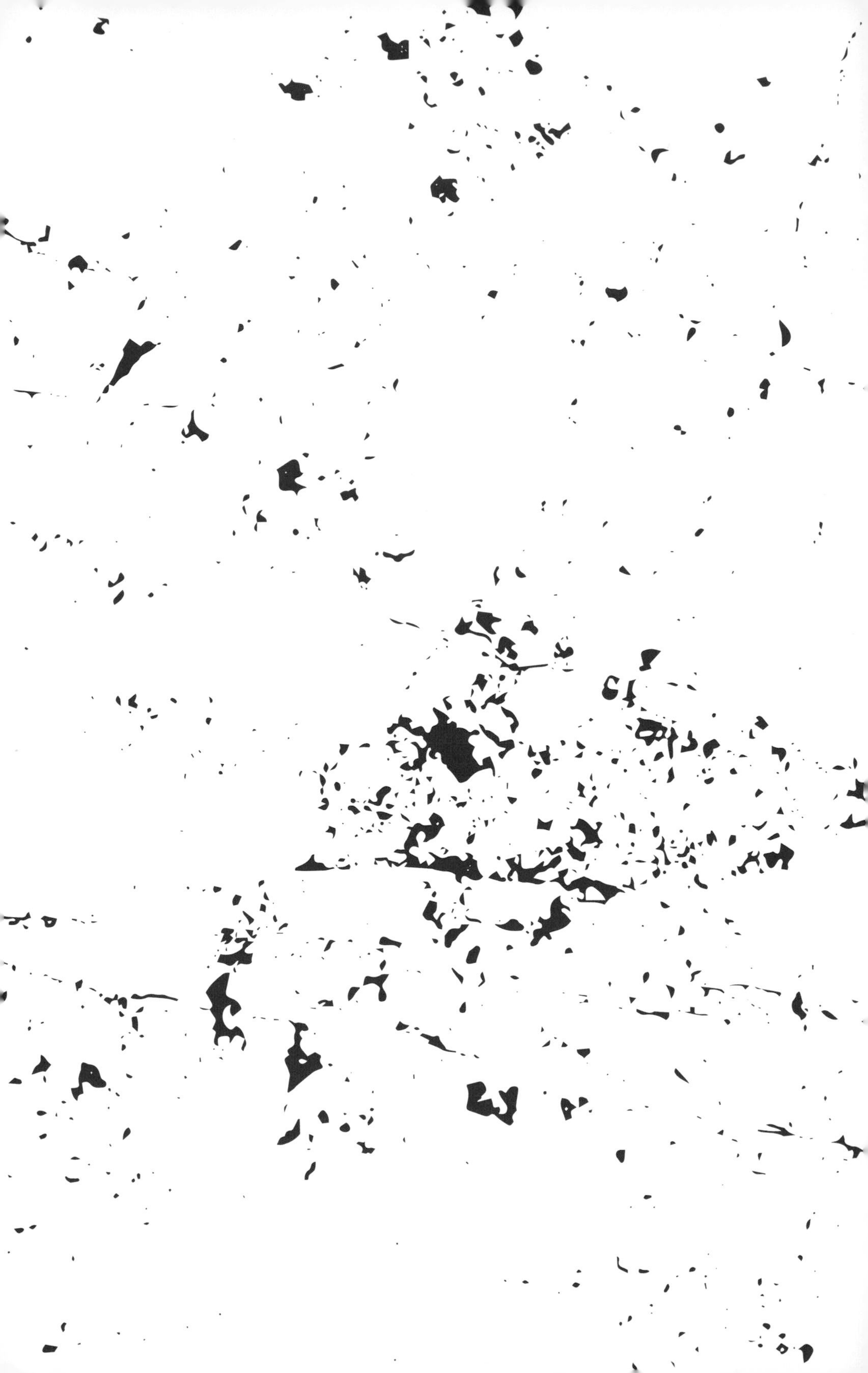

EPILOGUE

PROM

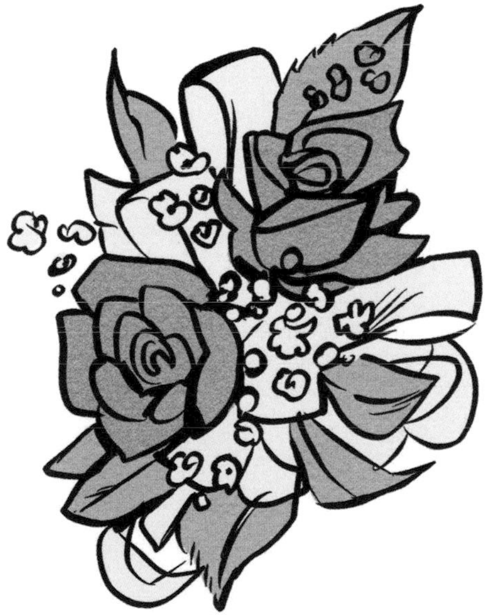

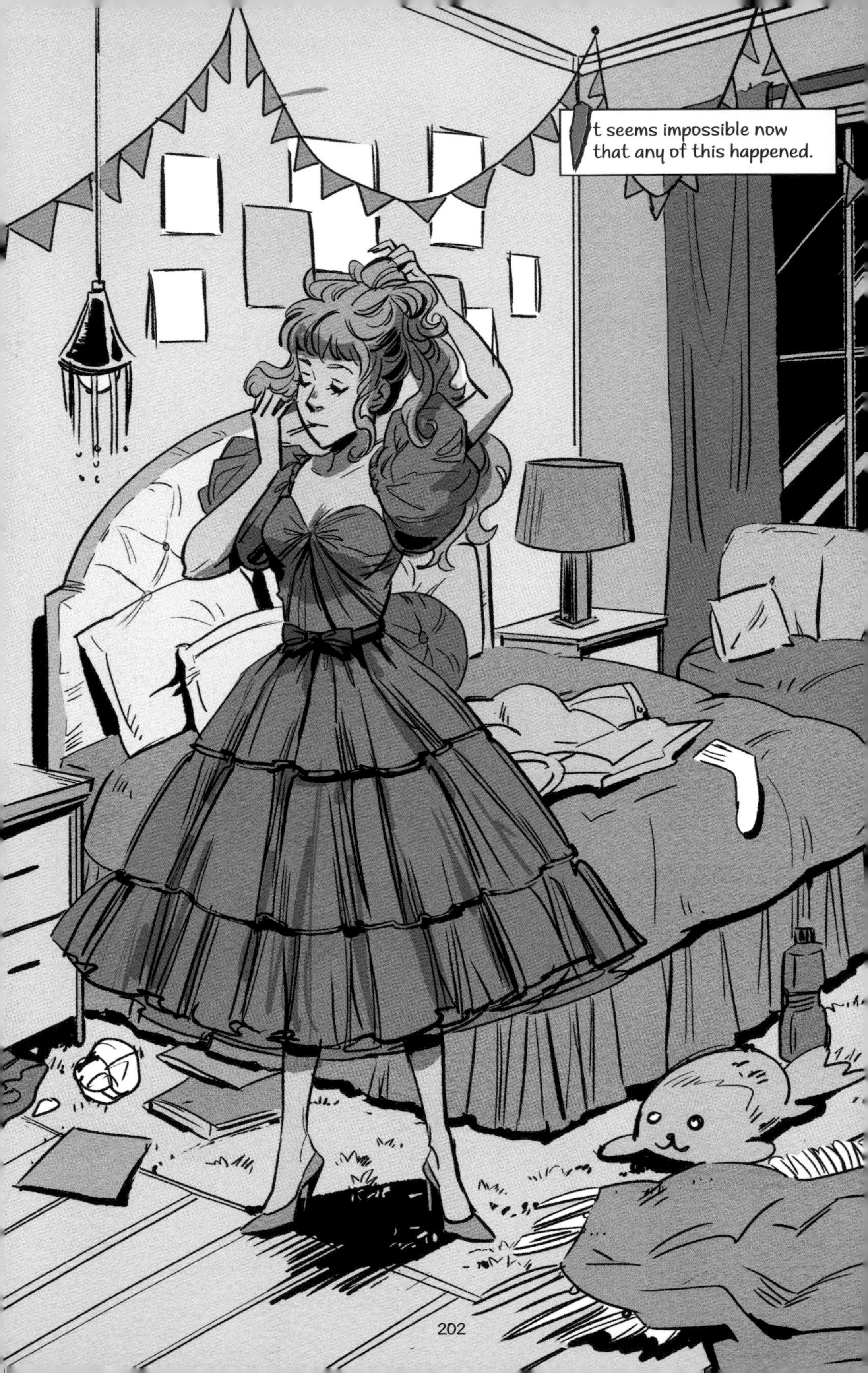
It seems impossible now that any of this happened.

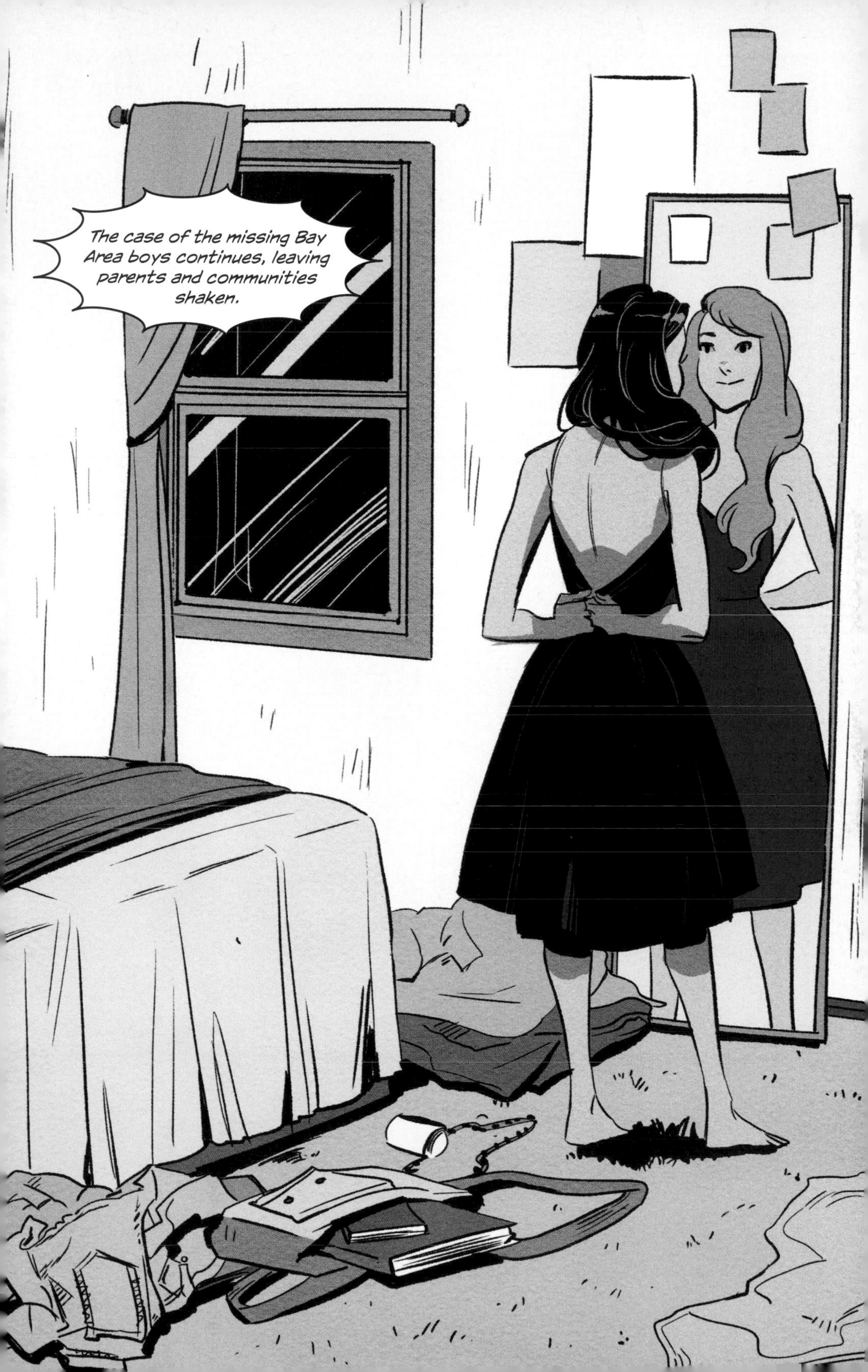
The case of the missing Bay Area boys continues, leaving parents and communities shaken.

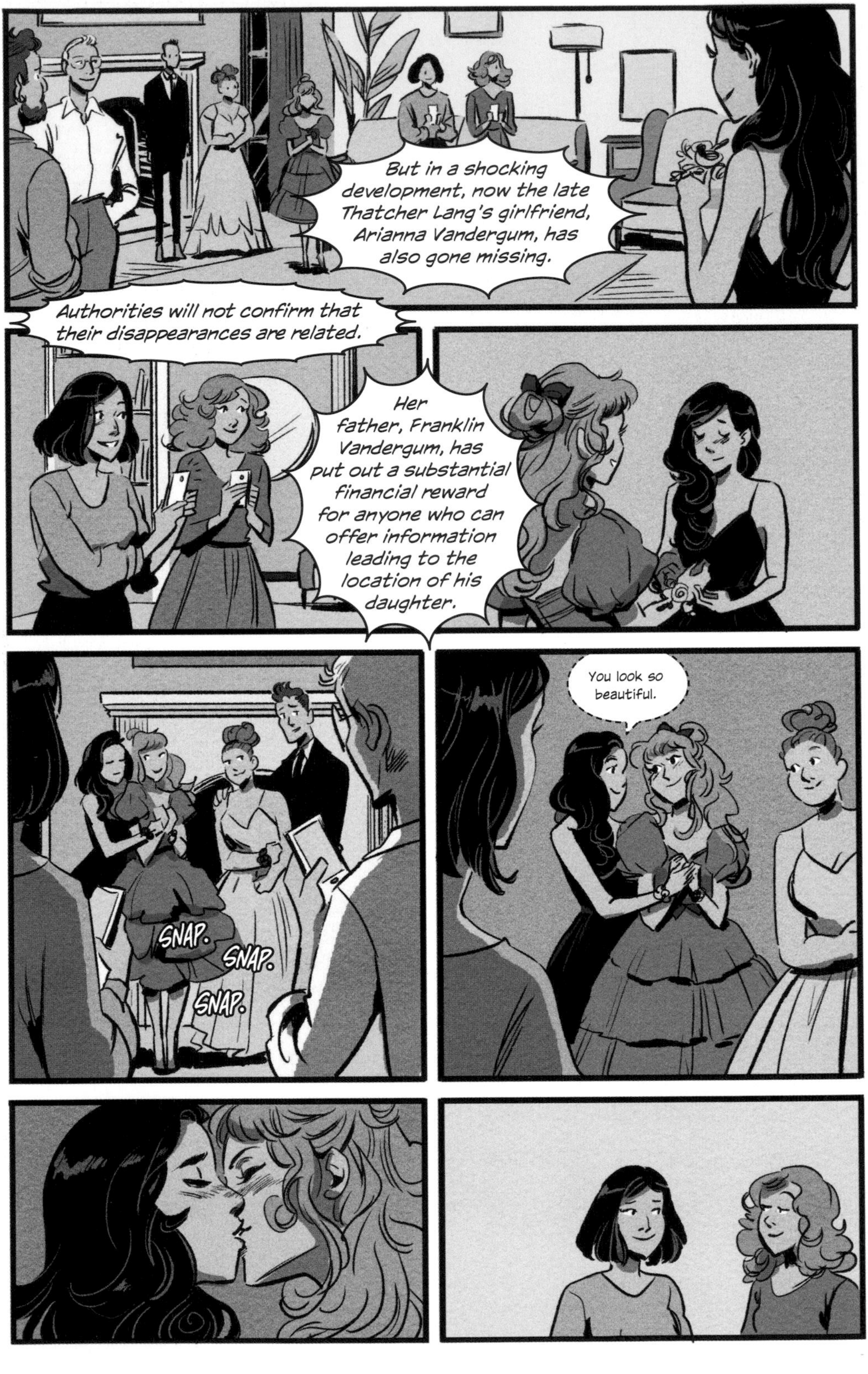
But in a shocking development, now the late Thatcher Lang's girlfriend, Arianna Vandergum, has also gone missing.
Authorities will not confirm that their disappearances are related.
Her father, Franklin Vandergum, has put out a substantial financial reward for anyone who can offer information leading to the location of his daughter.
SNAP.
SNAP.
SNAP.
You look so beautiful.

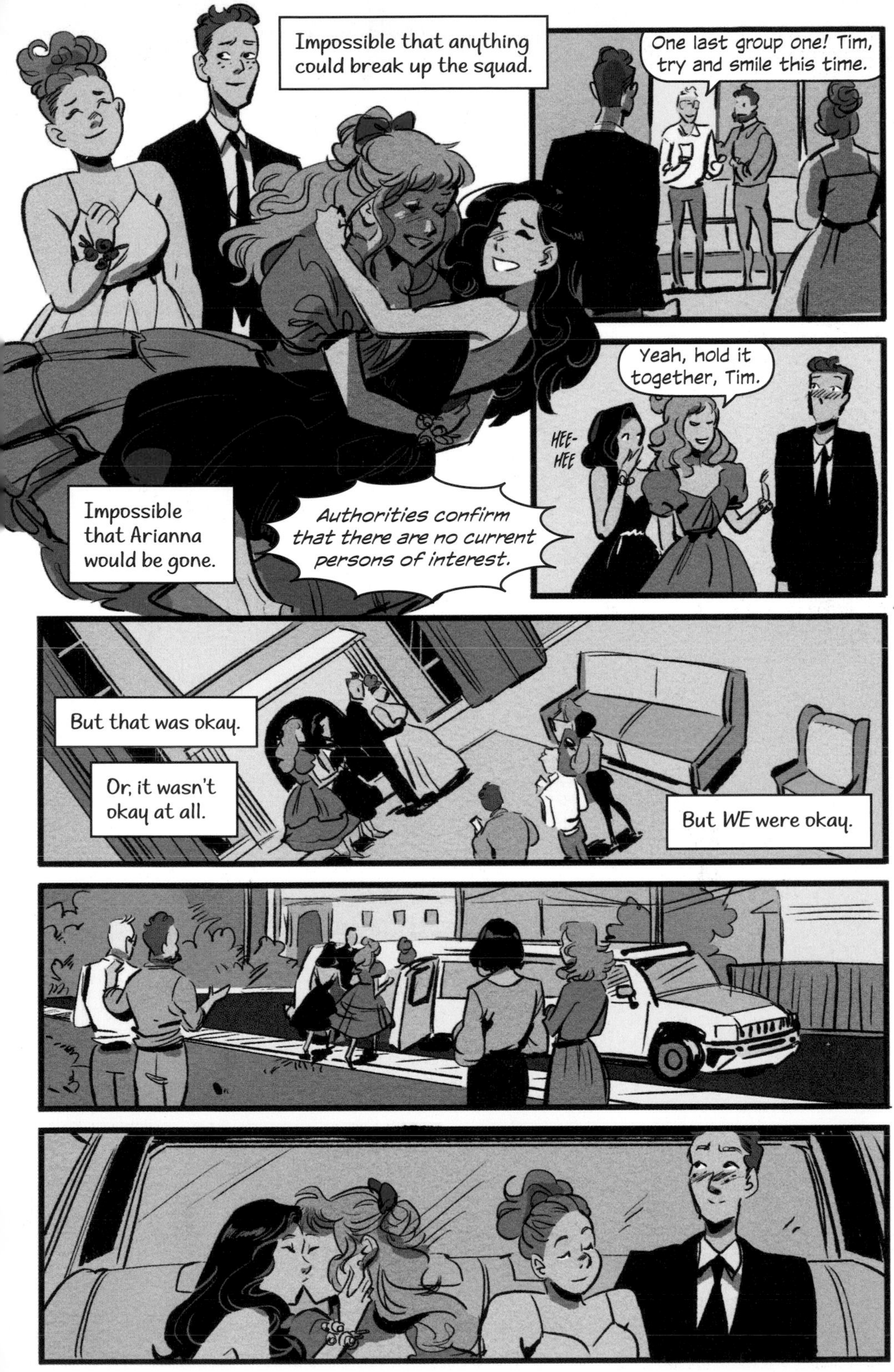
Impossible that anything could break up the squad.
One last group one! Tim, try and smile this time.
Yeah, hold it together, Tim.
HEE-HEE
Impossible that Arianna would be gone.
Authorities confirm that there are no current persons of interest.
But that was okay.
Or, it wasn't okay at all.
But WE were okay.

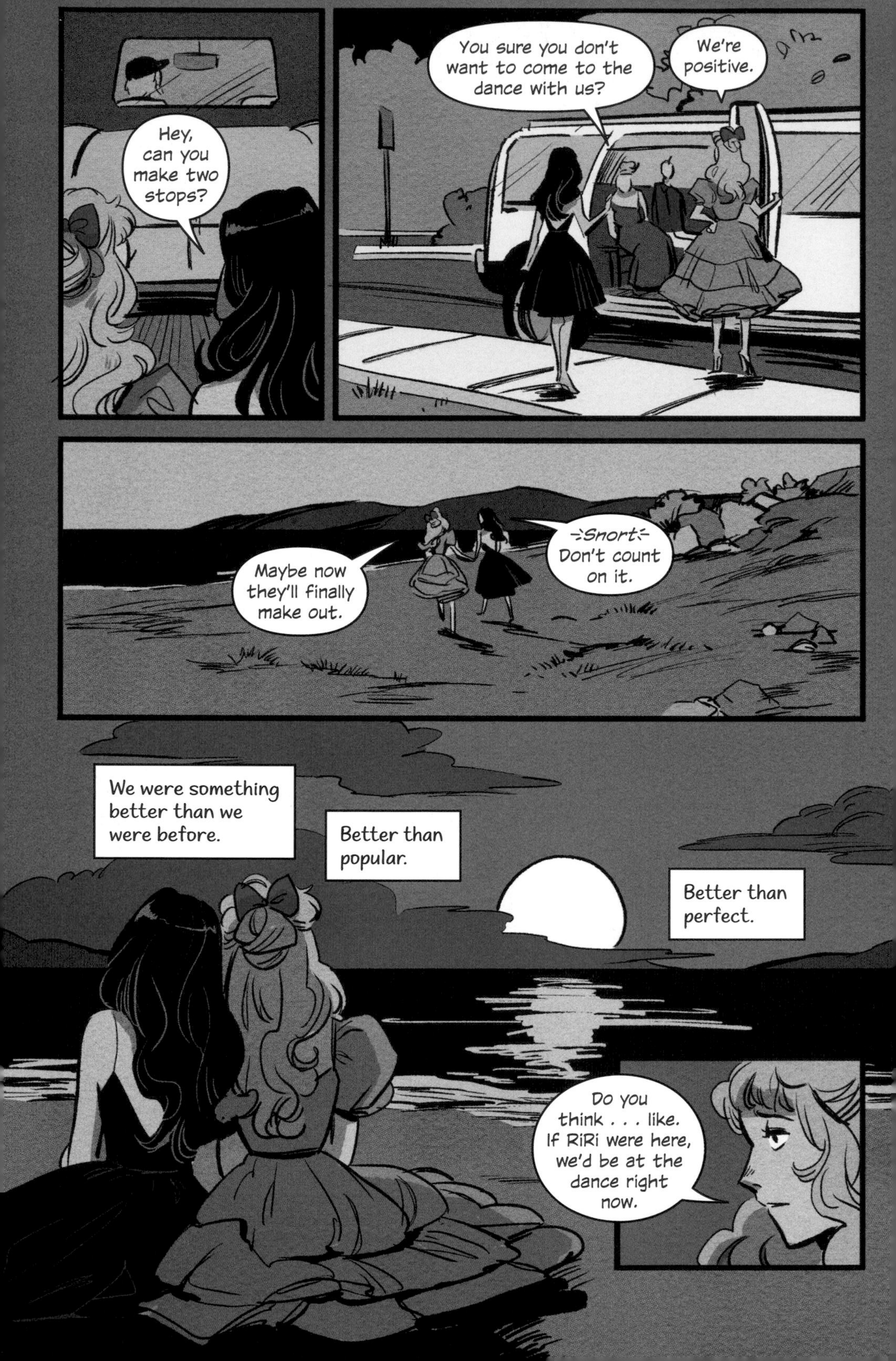
Hey, can you make two stops?
You sure you don't want to come to the dance with us?
We're positive.
Maybe now they'll finally make out.
Snort
Don't count on it.
We were something better than we were before.
Better than popular.
Better than perfect.
Do you think . . . like. If RiRi were here, we'd be at the dance right now.

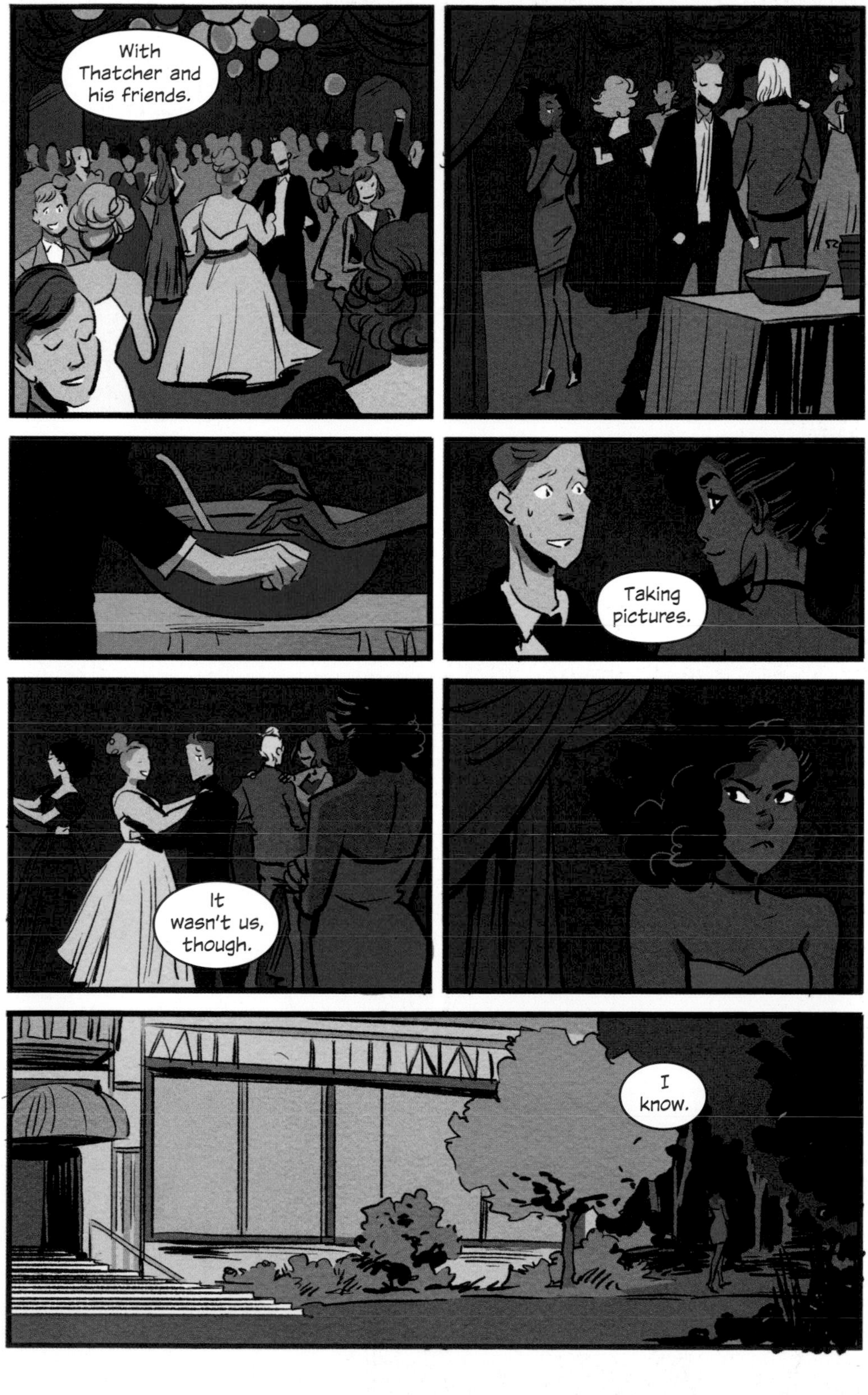
With Thatcher and his friends.
Taking pictures.
It wasn't us, though.
I know.

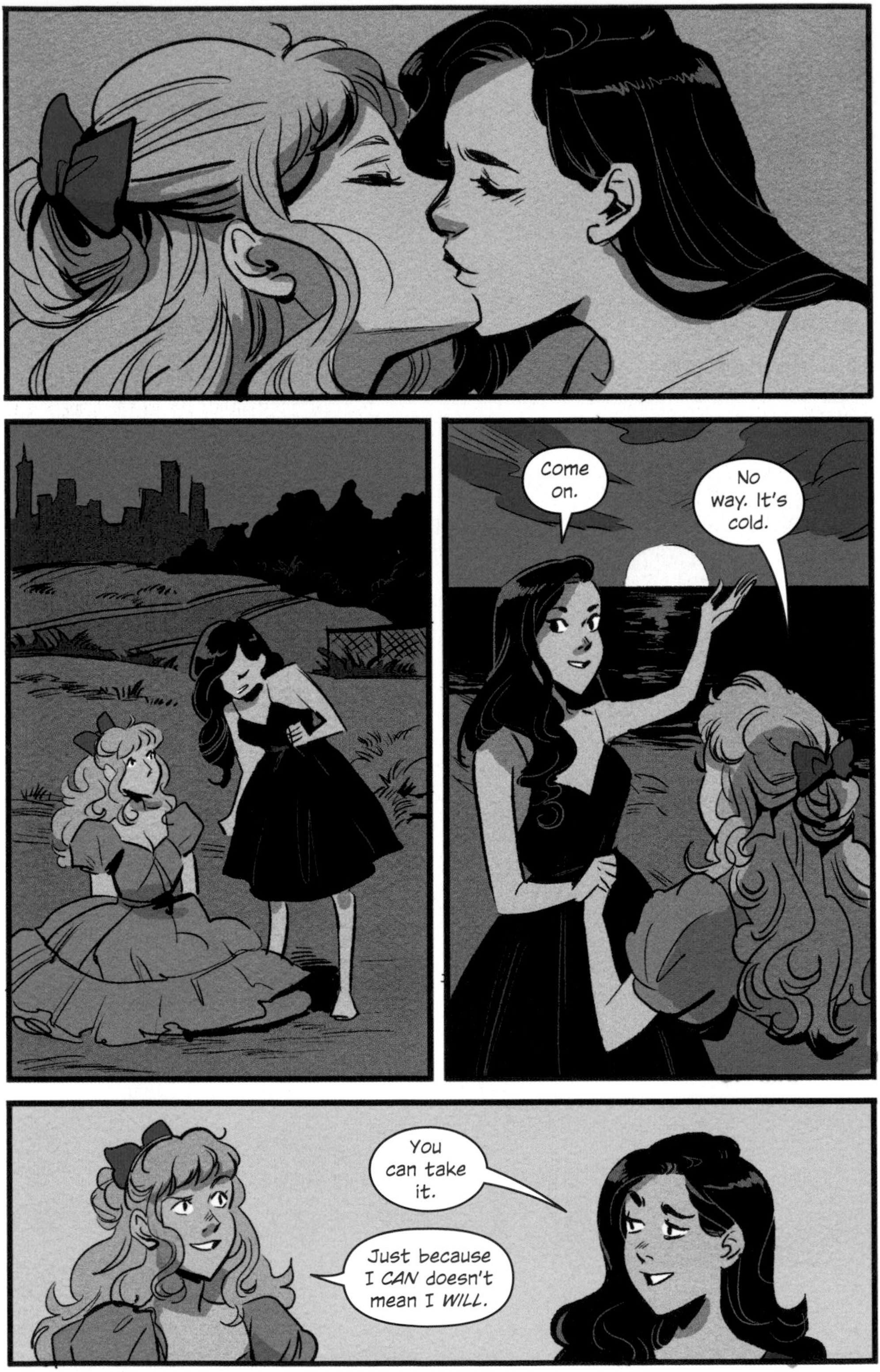
Come on.
No way. It's cold.
You can take it.
Just because I CAN doesn't mean I WILL.

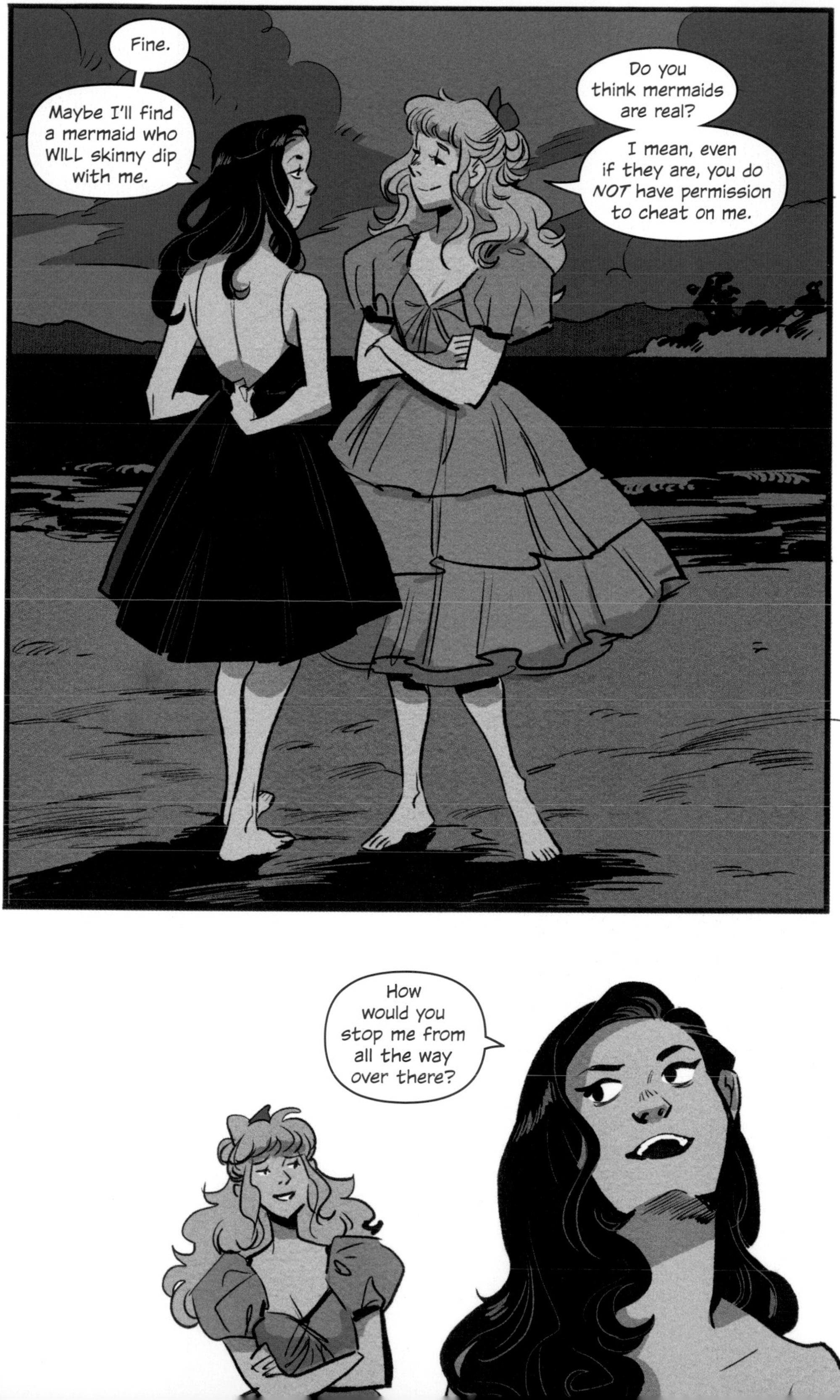
Fine.
Maybe I'll find a mermaid who WILL skinny dip with me.
Do you think mermaids are real?
I mean, even if they are, you do *NOT* have permission to cheat on me.
How would you stop me from all the way over there?

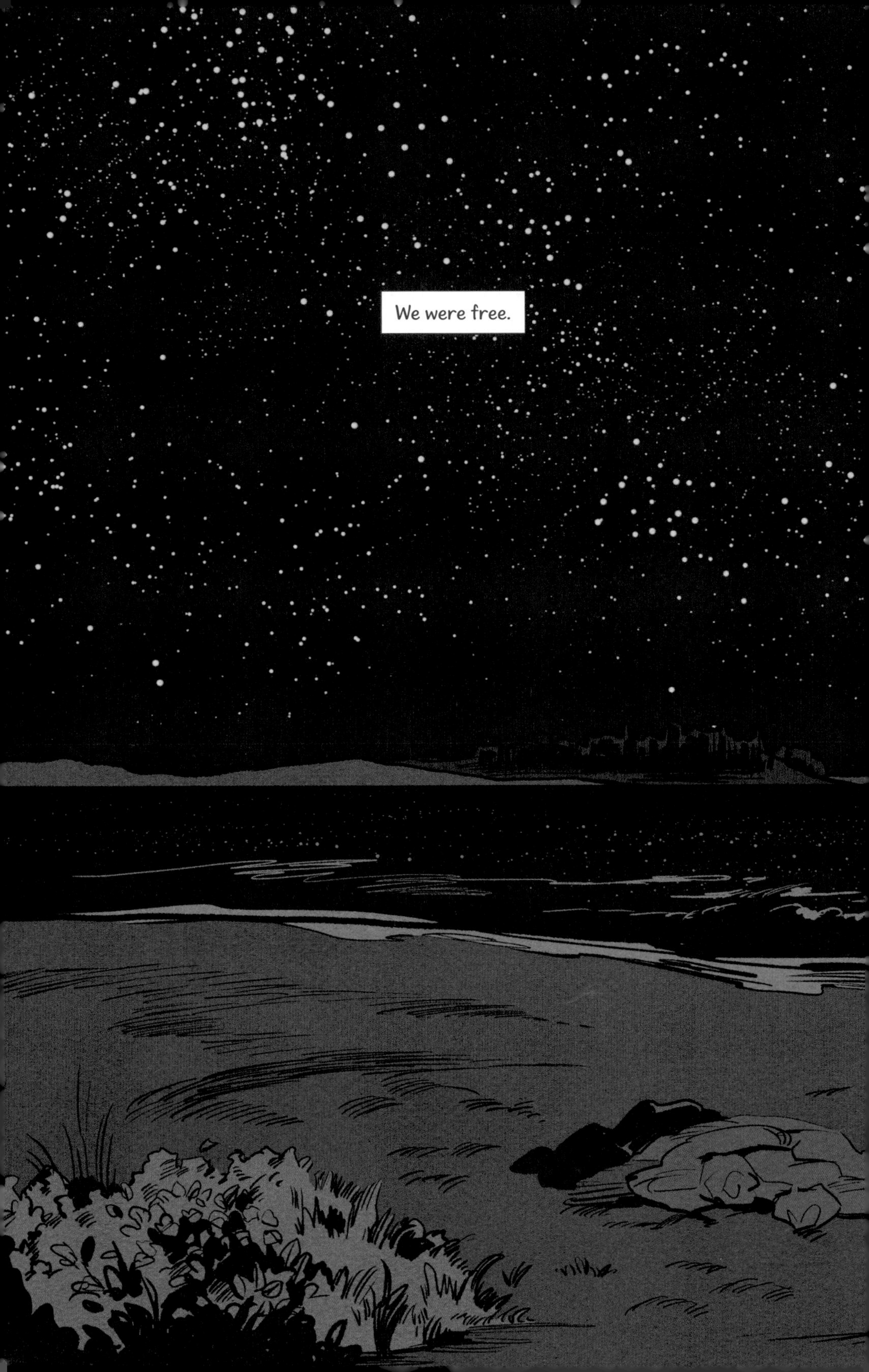
We were free.

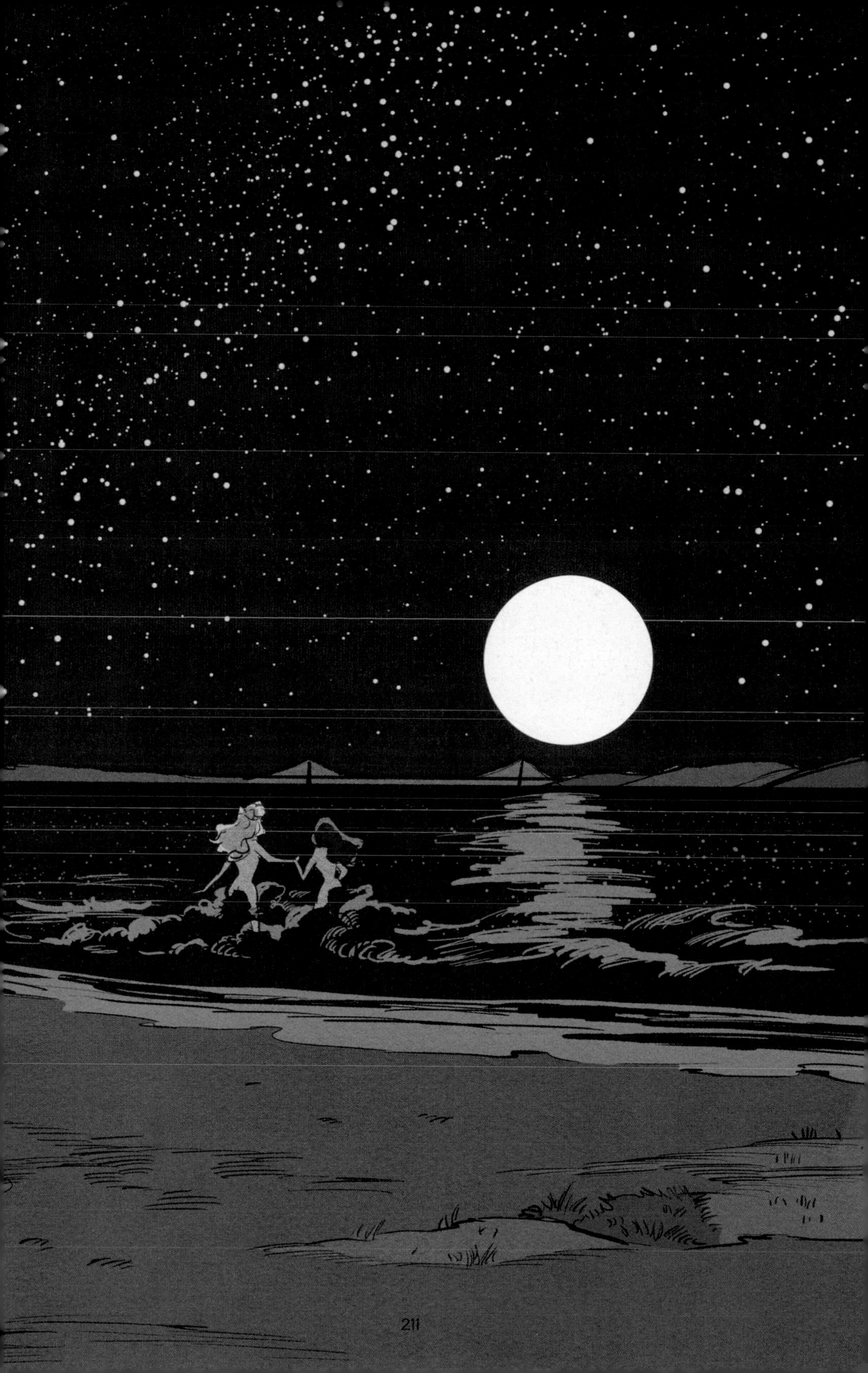

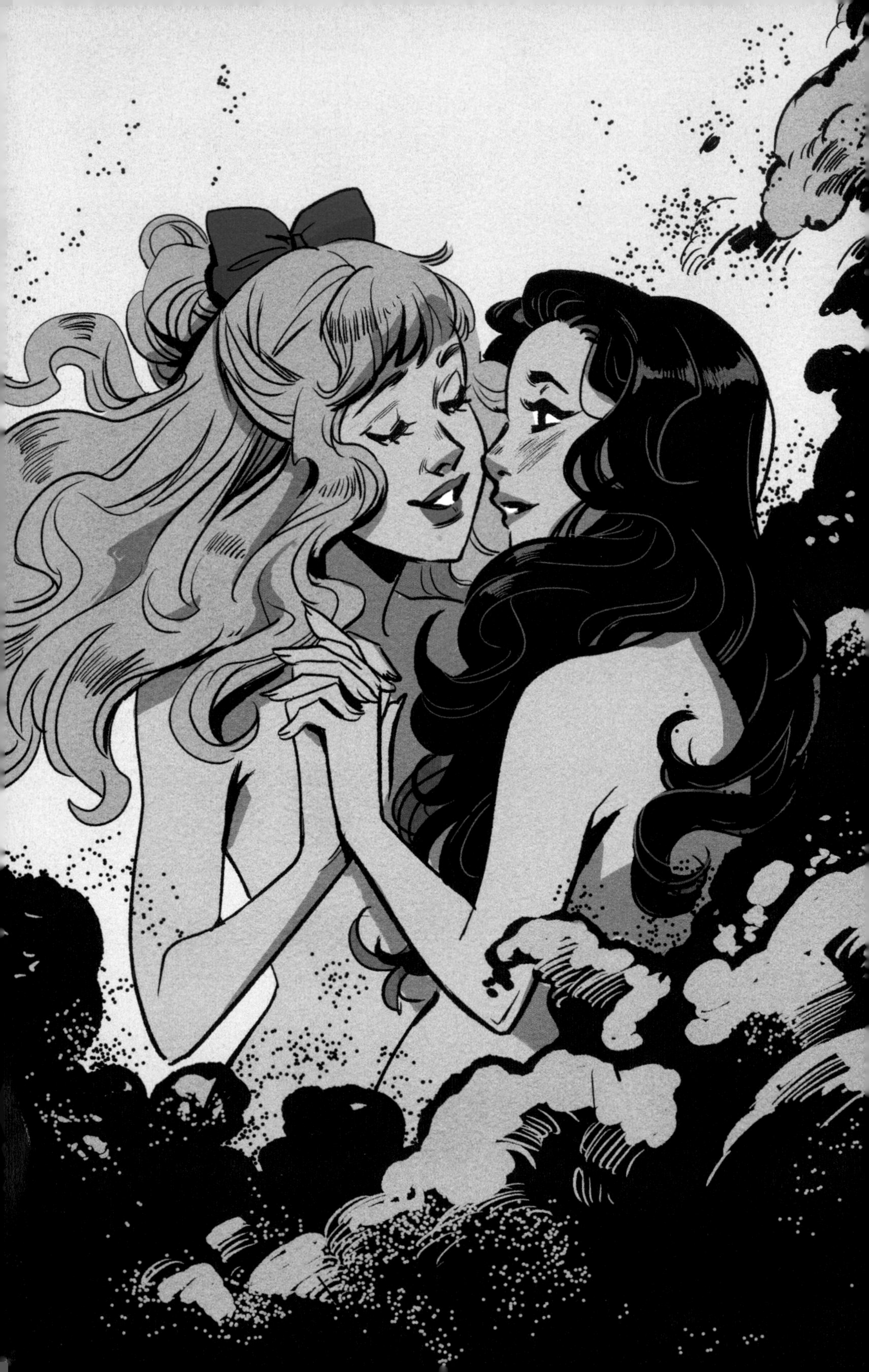

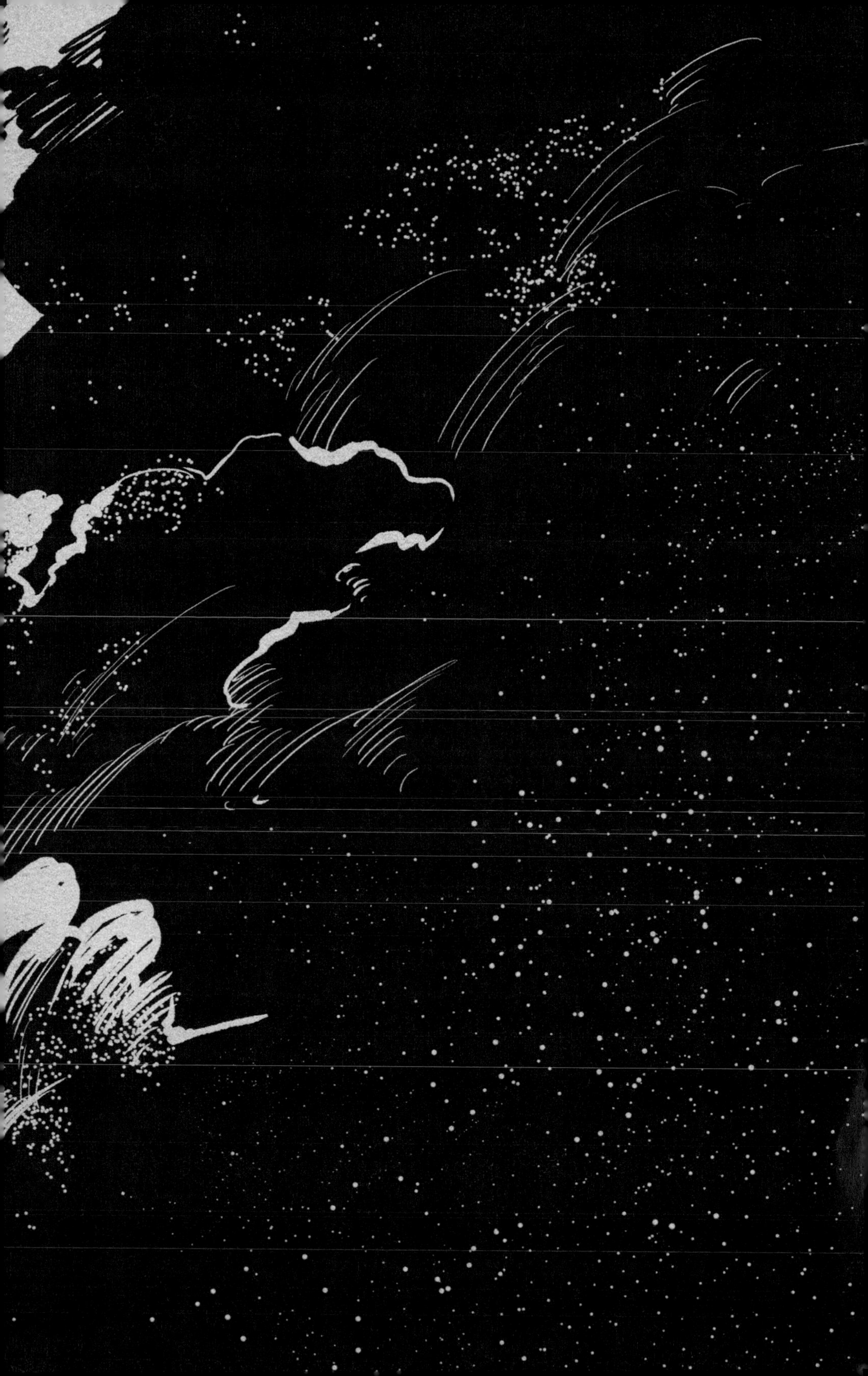

MAGGIE TOKUDA-HALL

is the author of the acclaimed young adult novel *The Mermaid, the Witch, and the Sea*, which was named to several best book of the year lists, including NPR, *Kirkus*, and *School Library Journal*. She is also the author of the 2017 Parents' Choice Gold Award–winning picture book, *Also an Octopus*, illustrated by Benji Davies. She received her BA in studio art from Scripps College and an MFA in writing from the University of San Francisco, and she has worked as a bookseller. She lives with her husband, son, and objectively perfect dog in Oakland, California.

www.prettyokmaggie.com

FIND MAGGIE TOKUDA-HALL ON

LISA STERLE

is a Columbus artist with work spanning from comic books to concept design to pop-culture-fueled illustration. Her work is often bright, expressive, and occasionally tinged with horror—marrying her two favorite themes. the beautiful and the grotesque. She is the co-creator of the monthly comics *Witchblood, Long Lost,* and *Submerged*, as well as the creator of the Modern Witch Tarot Deck. She received her BFA from Columbus College of Art & Design and currently resides in Columbus, Ohio.

www.lisasterle.com

FIND LISA STERLE ON